SUPERGIRL
BEING
SUPER

Written by
MARIKO TAMAKI

Illustrated by
JOËLLE JONES

with **SANDU FLOREA**

Colored by
JEREMY LAWSON
Lettered by
SAIDA TEMOFONTE

Supergirl based on characters created
by Jerry Siegel and Joe Shuster.
Superman created by
Jerry Siegel and Joe Shuster.
By special arrangement
with the Jerry Siegel family.

SUPERGIRL
BEING SUPER

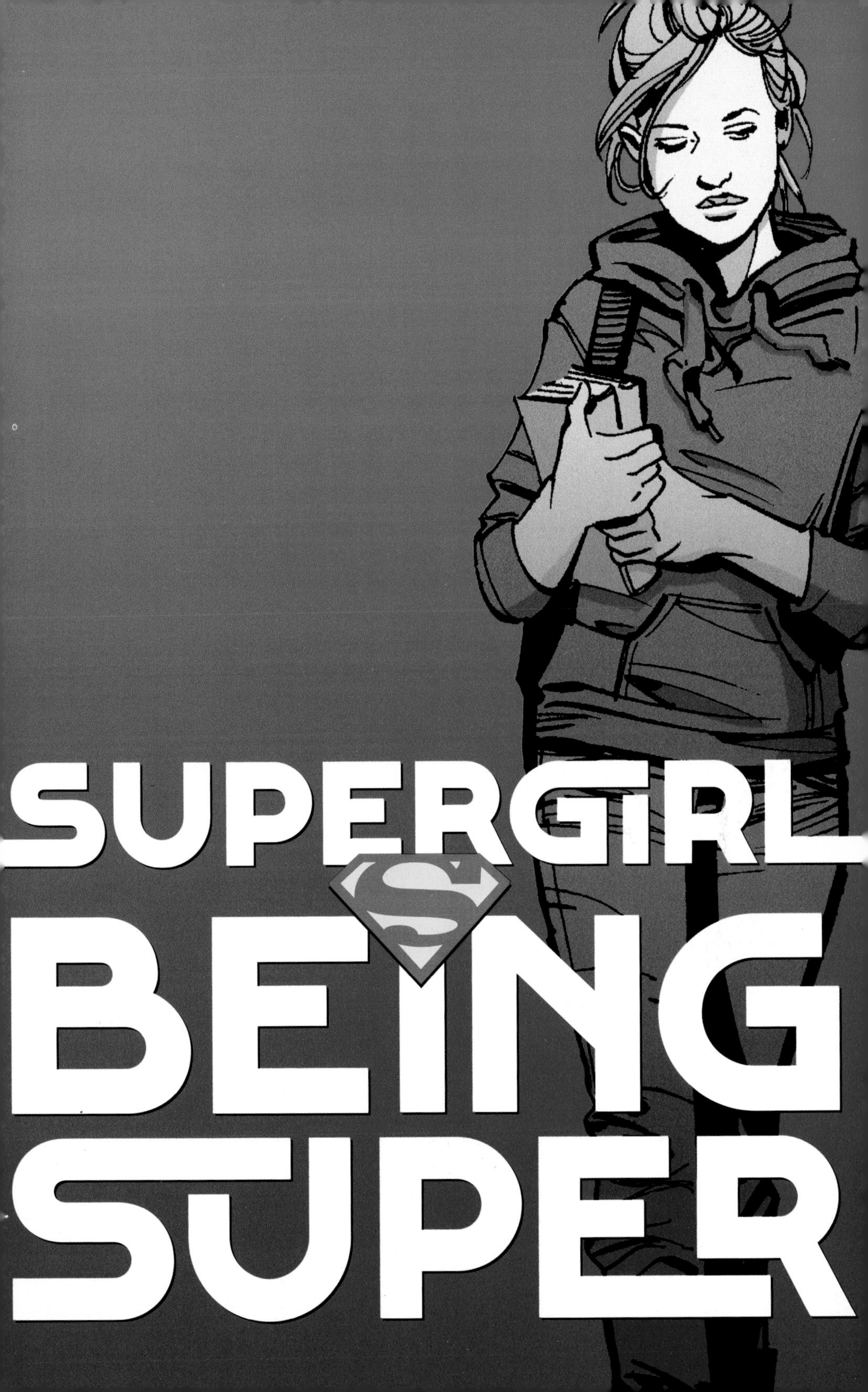

PAUL KAMINSKI & ANDREW MARINO Editors – Original Series

DIEGO LOPEZ Editor – Young Readers Collected Edition

STEVE COOK Design Director – Books

AMIE BROCKWAY-METCALF Publication Design

BOB HARRAS Senior VP – Editor-in-Chief, DC Comics

MICHELE R. WELLS VP & Executive Editor, Young Reader

DAN DiDIO Publisher

JIM LEE Publisher & Chief Creative Officer

BOBBIE CHASE VP – New Publishing Initiatives

DON FALLETTI VP – Manufacturing Operations & Workflow Management

LAWRENCE GANEM VP – Talent Services

ALISON GILL Senior VP – Manufacturing & Operations

HANK KANALZ Senior VP – Publishing Strategy & Support Services

DAN MIRON VP – Publishing Operations

NICK J. NAPOLITANO VP – Manufacturing Administration & Design

NANCY SPEARS VP – Sales

JONAH WEILAND VP - Marketing & Creative Services

SUPERGIRL: BEING SUPER

Published by DC Comics. Compilation and all
new material copyright © 2020 DC Comics. All
Rights Reserved. Originally published in single
magazine form in *Supergirl: Being Super* 1-4.

DC Comics, 2900 West Alameda Ave.,
Burbank, CA 91505
Printed by LSC Communications,
Crawfordsville, IN, USA.
5/29/20.
First Printing.
ISBN: 978-1-77950-319-0

Library of Congress Cataloging-in-Publication Data

Names: Tamaki, Mariko, writer. | Jones, Joëlle, artist. | Florea, Sandu,
    artist. | Lawson, Jeremy, colourist. | Temofonte, Saida, letterer.
Title: Supergirl : being super / written by Mariko Tamaki ; illustrated by
    Joëlle Jones with Sandu Floria ; colored by Jeremy Lawson ; lettered by
    Saida Temofonte.
Description: DC Young Readers collected edition. | Burbanks, CA : DC
    Comics, [2020] | "Supergirl based on characters created by Jerry Siegel
    and Joe Shuster. Superman created by Jerry Siegel and Joe Shuster. By
    special arrangement with the Jerry Siegel family." | Audience: Ages 13+.
    | Audience: Grades 10-12. | Summary: When an earthquake shatters
    Midvale, uncovering secrets sixteen-year-old Kara Danvers thought would
    stay buried forever, she must choose between blending in and embracing
    her differences to save her hometown.
Identifiers: LCCN 2020015554 (print) | LCCN 2020015555 (ebook) | ISBN
    9781779503190 (paperback) | ISBN 9781779503206 (ebook)
Subjects: LCSH: Graphic novels. | CYAC: Graphic novels. | Coming of
    age--Fiction. | Superheroes--Fiction.
Classification: LCC PZ7.7.T355 Su 2020 (print) | LCC PZ7.7.T355 (ebook)

    DDC 741.5/973--dc23

LC record available at https://lccn.loc.gov/2020015554
LC ebook record available at https://lccn.loc.gov/2020015555

CHAPTER ONE: WHERE DO I BEGIN?

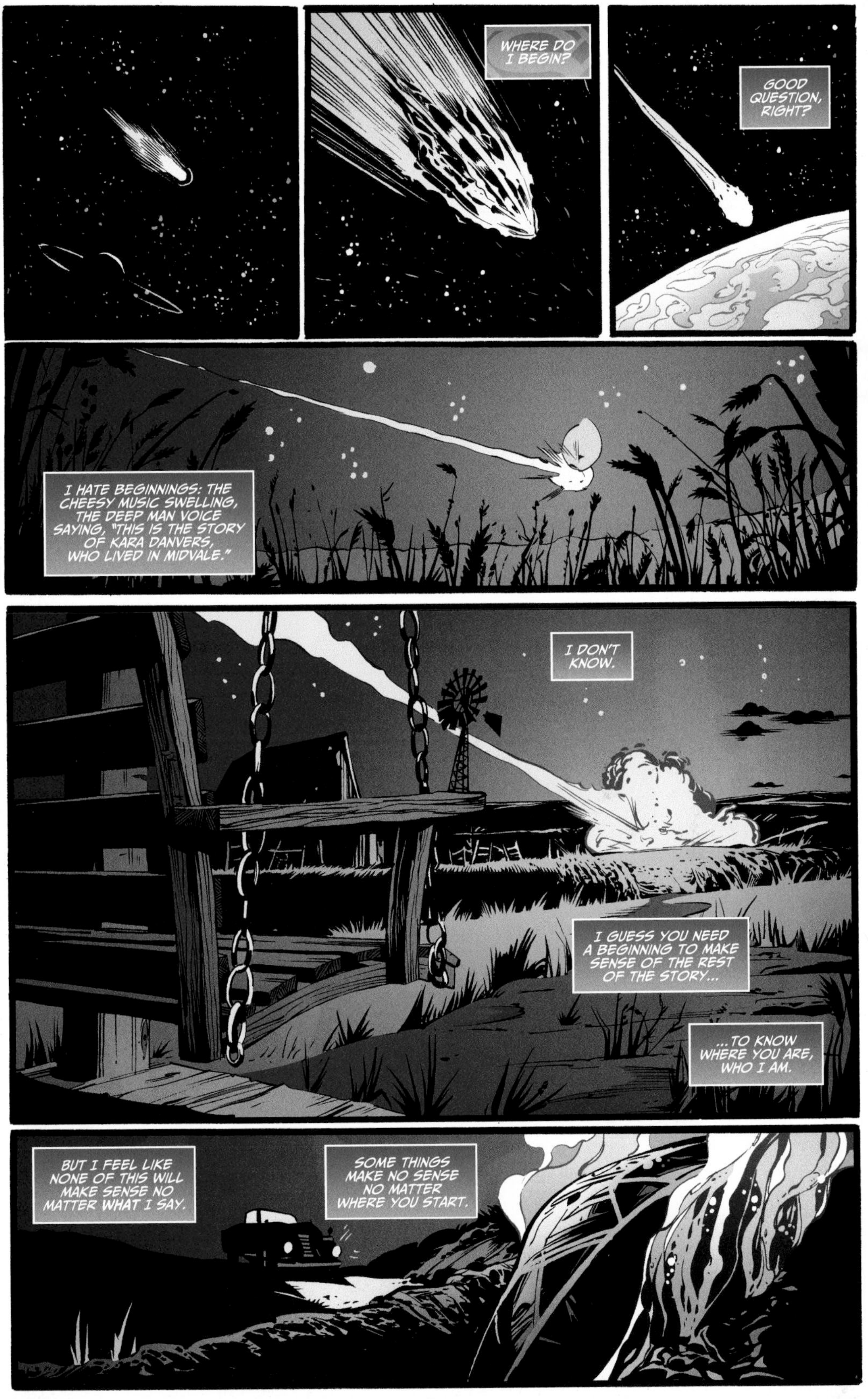
WHERE DO I BEGIN?
GOOD QUESTION, RIGHT?
I HATE BEGINNINGS: THE CHEESY MUSIC SWELLING, THE DEEP MAN VOICE SAYING, "THIS IS THE STORY OF KARA DANVERS, WHO LIVED IN MIDVALE."
I DON'T KNOW.
I GUESS YOU NEED A BEGINNING TO MAKE SENSE OF THE REST OF THE STORY...
...TO KNOW WHERE YOU ARE, WHO I AM.
BUT I FEEL LIKE NONE OF THIS WILL MAKE SENSE NO MATTER WHAT I SAY.
SOME THINGS MAKE NO SENSE NO MATTER WHERE YOU START.

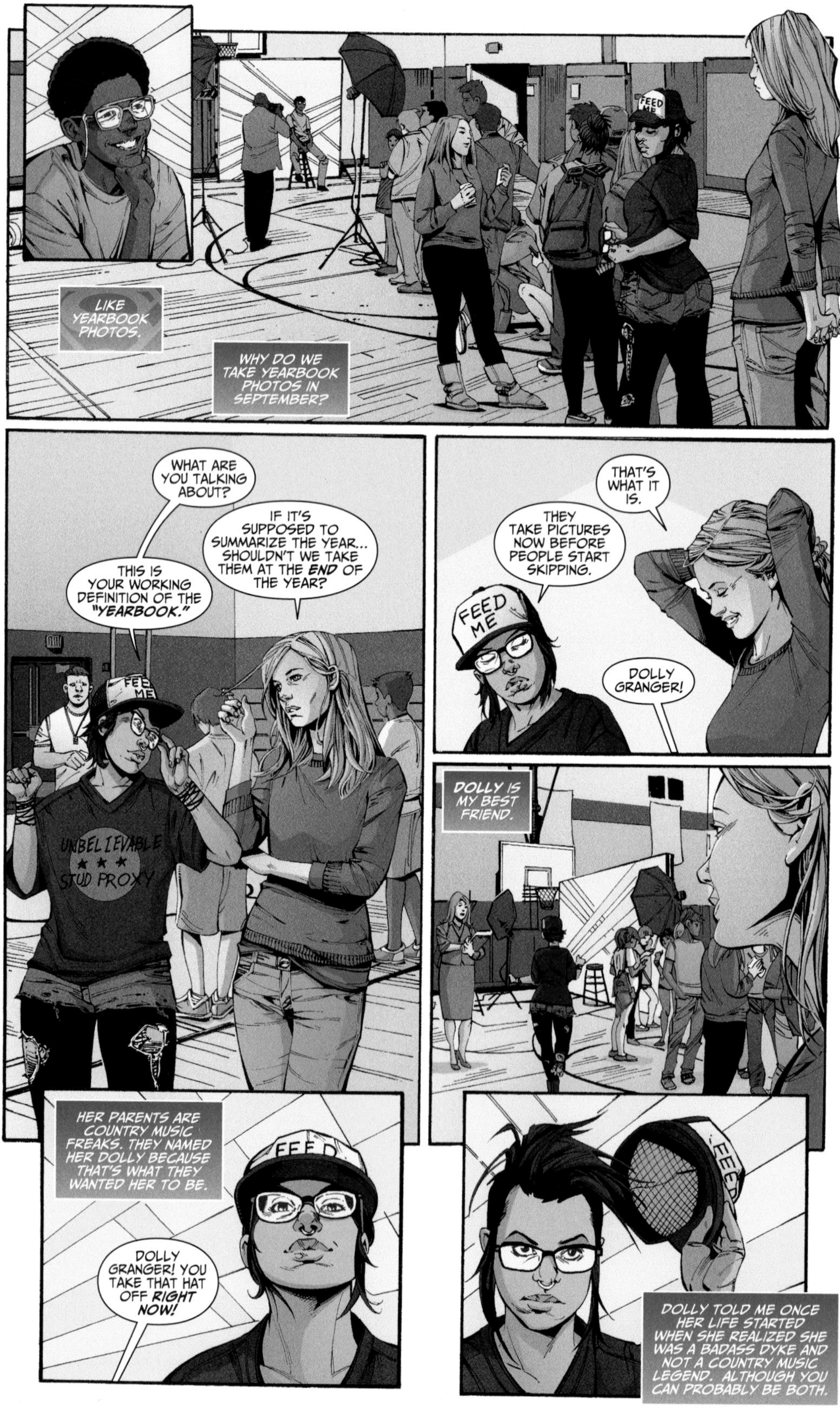
LIKE YEARBOOK PHOTOS.
WHY DO WE TAKE YEARBOOK PHOTOS IN SEPTEMBER?
FEED ME
WHAT ARE YOU TALKING ABOUT?
IF IT'S SUPPOSED TO SUMMARIZE THE YEAR... SHOULDN'T WE TAKE THEM AT THE END OF THE YEAR?
THIS IS YOUR WORKING DEFINITION OF THE "YEARBOOK."
UNBELIEVABLE ★★★ STUD PROXY
THAT'S WHAT IT IS.
THEY TAKE PICTURES NOW BEFORE PEOPLE START SKIPPING.
DOLLY GRANGER!
DOLLY IS MY BEST FRIEND.
HER PARENTS ARE COUNTRY MUSIC FREAKS. THEY NAMED HER DOLLY BECAUSE THAT'S WHAT THEY WANTED HER TO BE.
DOLLY GRANGER! YOU TAKE THAT HAT OFF RIGHT NOW!
DOLLY TOLD ME ONCE HER LIFE STARTED WHEN SHE REALIZED SHE WAS A BADASS DYKE AND NOT A COUNTRY MUSIC LEGEND. ALTHOUGH YOU CAN PROBABLY BE BOTH.

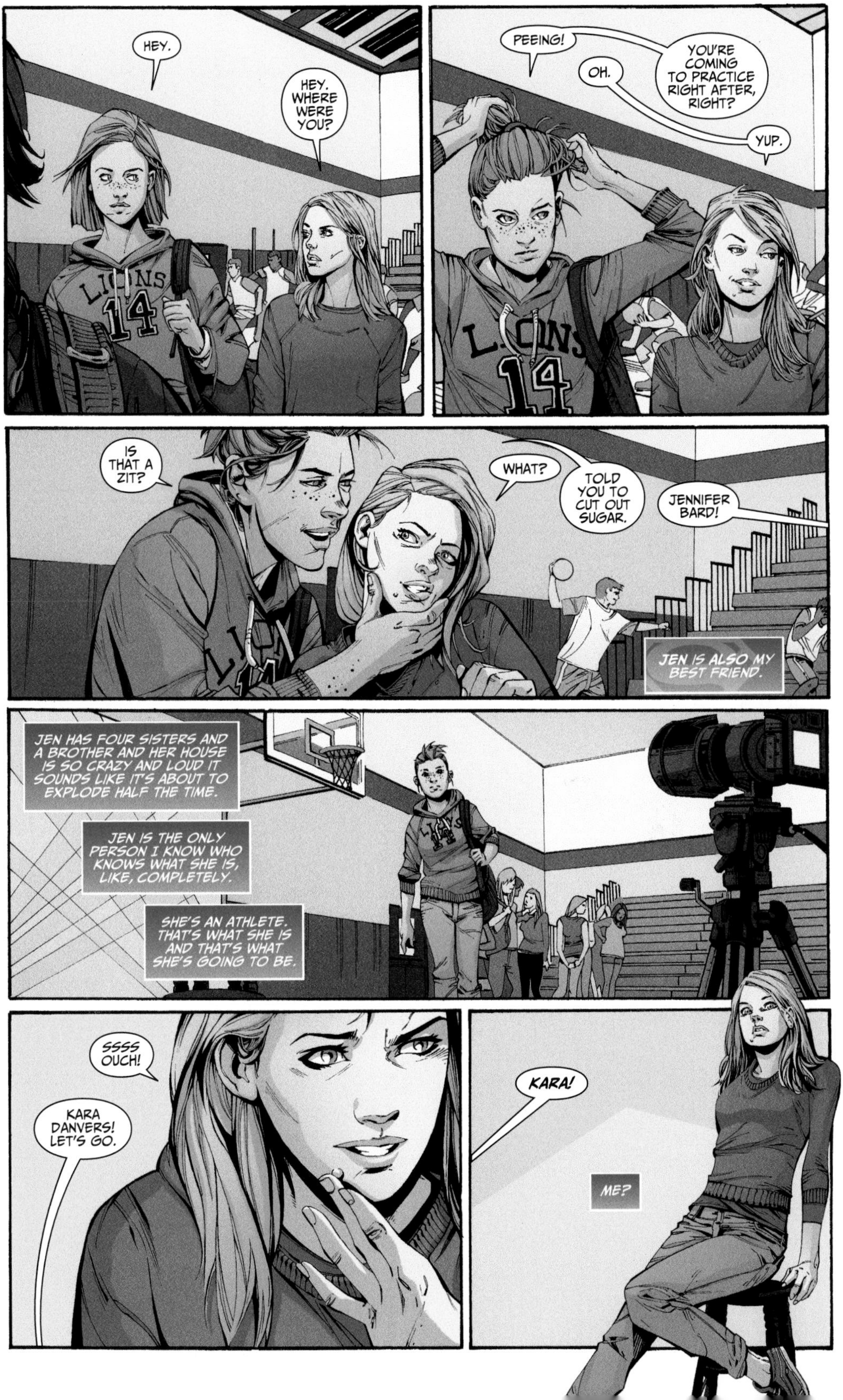
HEY.
HEY. WHERE WERE YOU?
PEEING!
YOU'RE COMING TO PRACTICE RIGHT AFTER, RIGHT?
OH.
YUP.
IS THAT A ZIT?
WHAT?
TOLD YOU TO CUT OUT SUGAR.
JENNIFER BARD!
JEN IS ALSO MY BEST FRIEND.
JEN HAS FOUR SISTERS AND A BROTHER AND HER HOUSE IS SO CRAZY AND LOUD IT SOUNDS LIKE IT'S ABOUT TO EXPLODE HALF THE TIME.
JEN IS THE ONLY PERSON I KNOW WHO KNOWS WHAT SHE IS, LIKE, COMPLETELY.
SHE'S AN ATHLETE. THAT'S WHAT SHE IS AND THAT'S WHAT SHE'S GOING TO BE.
SSSS OUCH!
KARA DANVERS! LET'S GO.
KARA!
ME?

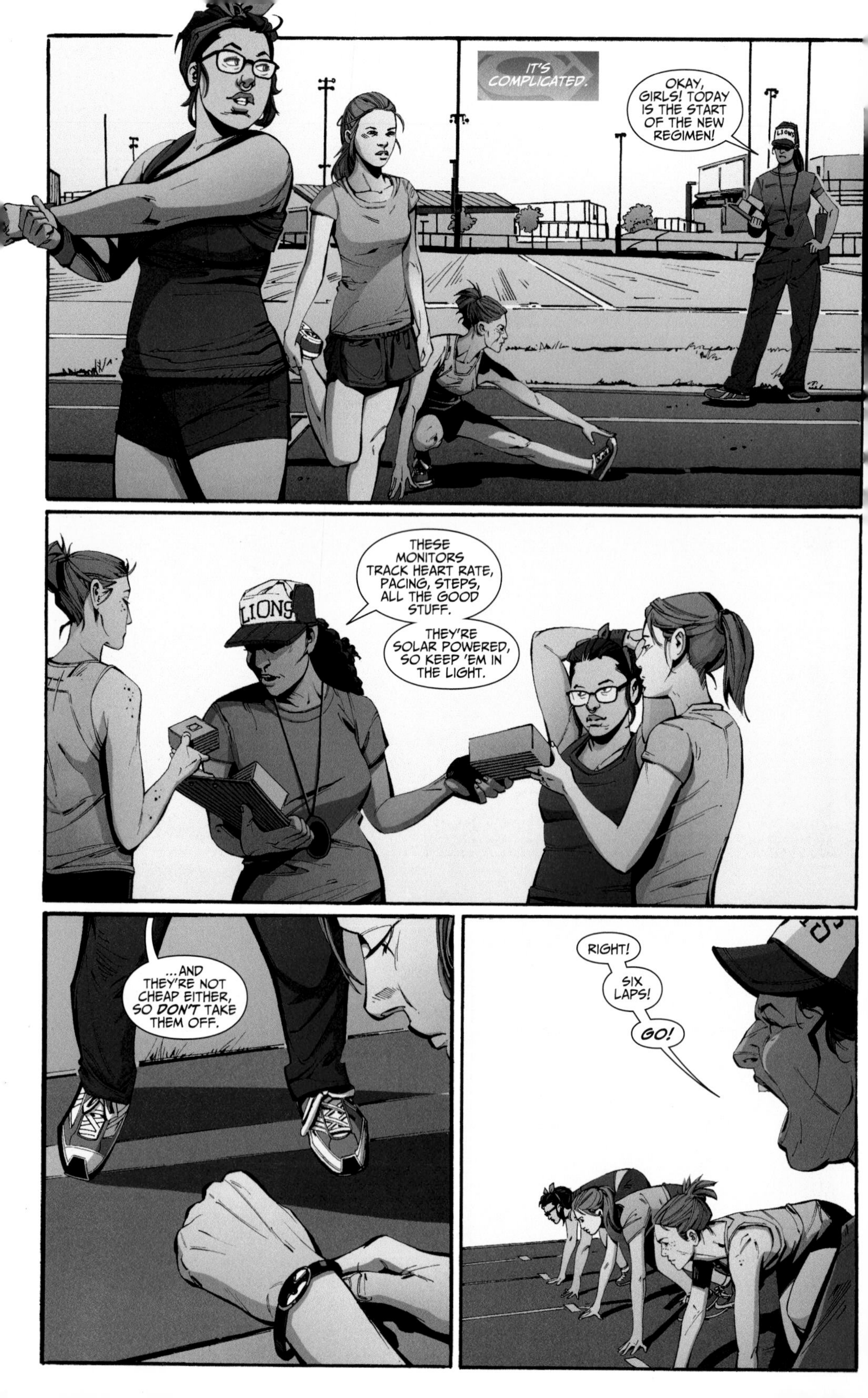
IT'S COMPLICATED.
OKAY, GIRLS! TODAY IS THE START OF THE NEW REGIMEN!
LIONS
THESE MONITORS TRACK HEART RATE, PACING, STEPS, ALL THE GOOD STUFF.
THEY'RE SOLAR POWERED, SO KEEP 'EM IN THE LIGHT.
LIONS
...AND THEY'RE NOT CHEAP EITHER, SO DON'T TAKE THEM OFF.
RIGHT!
SIX LAPS!
GO!

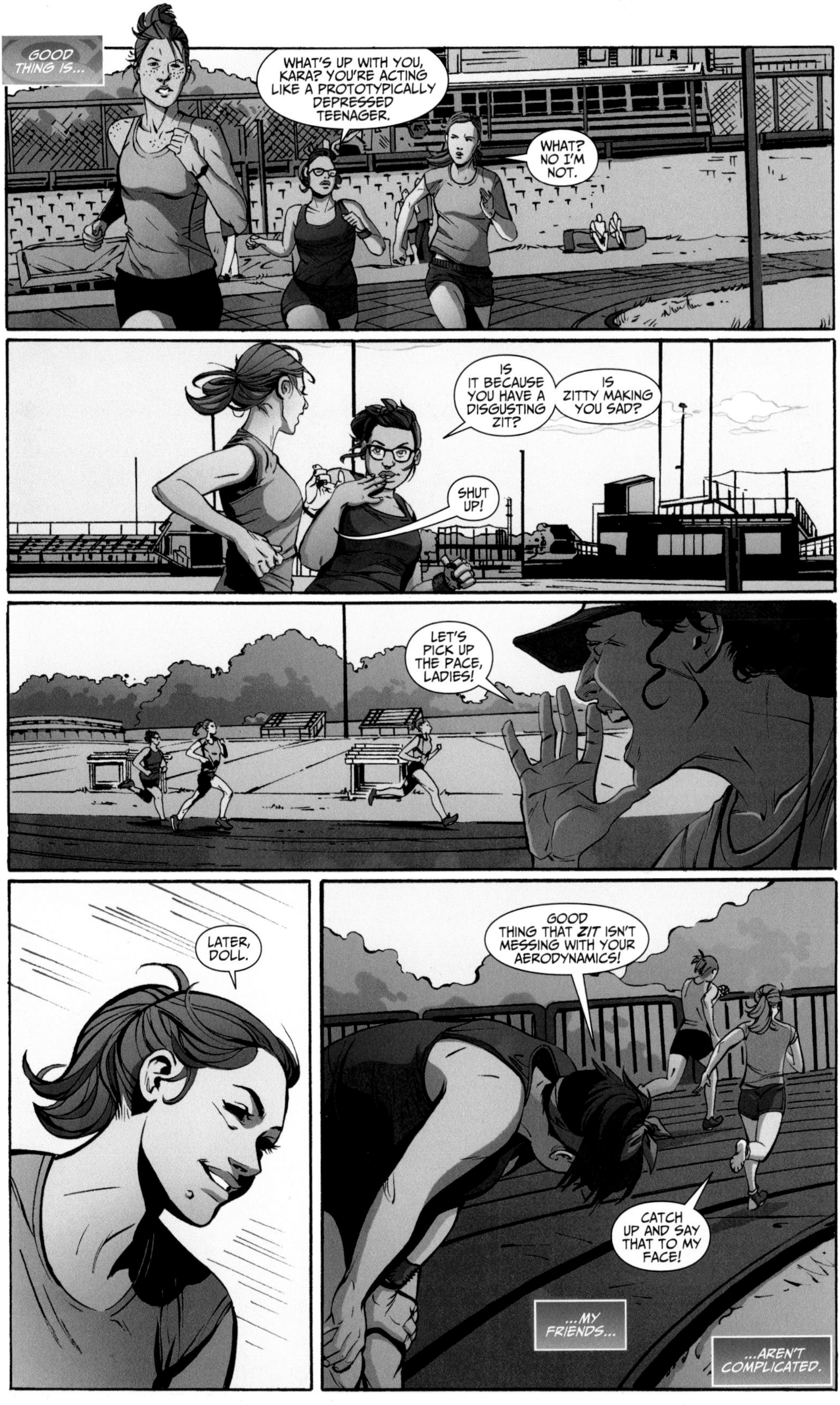
GOOD THING IS...
WHAT'S UP WITH YOU, KARA? YOU'RE ACTING LIKE A PROTOTYPICALLY DEPRESSED TEENAGER.
WHAT? NO I'M NOT.
IS IT BECAUSE YOU HAVE A DISGUSTING ZIT?
IS ZITTY MAKING YOU SAD?
SHUT UP!
LET'S PICK UP THE PACE, LADIES!
LATER, DOLL.
GOOD THING THAT ZIT ISN'T MESSING WITH YOUR AERODYNAMICS!
CATCH UP AND SAY THAT TO MY FACE!
...MY FRIENDS...
...AREN'T COMPLICATED.

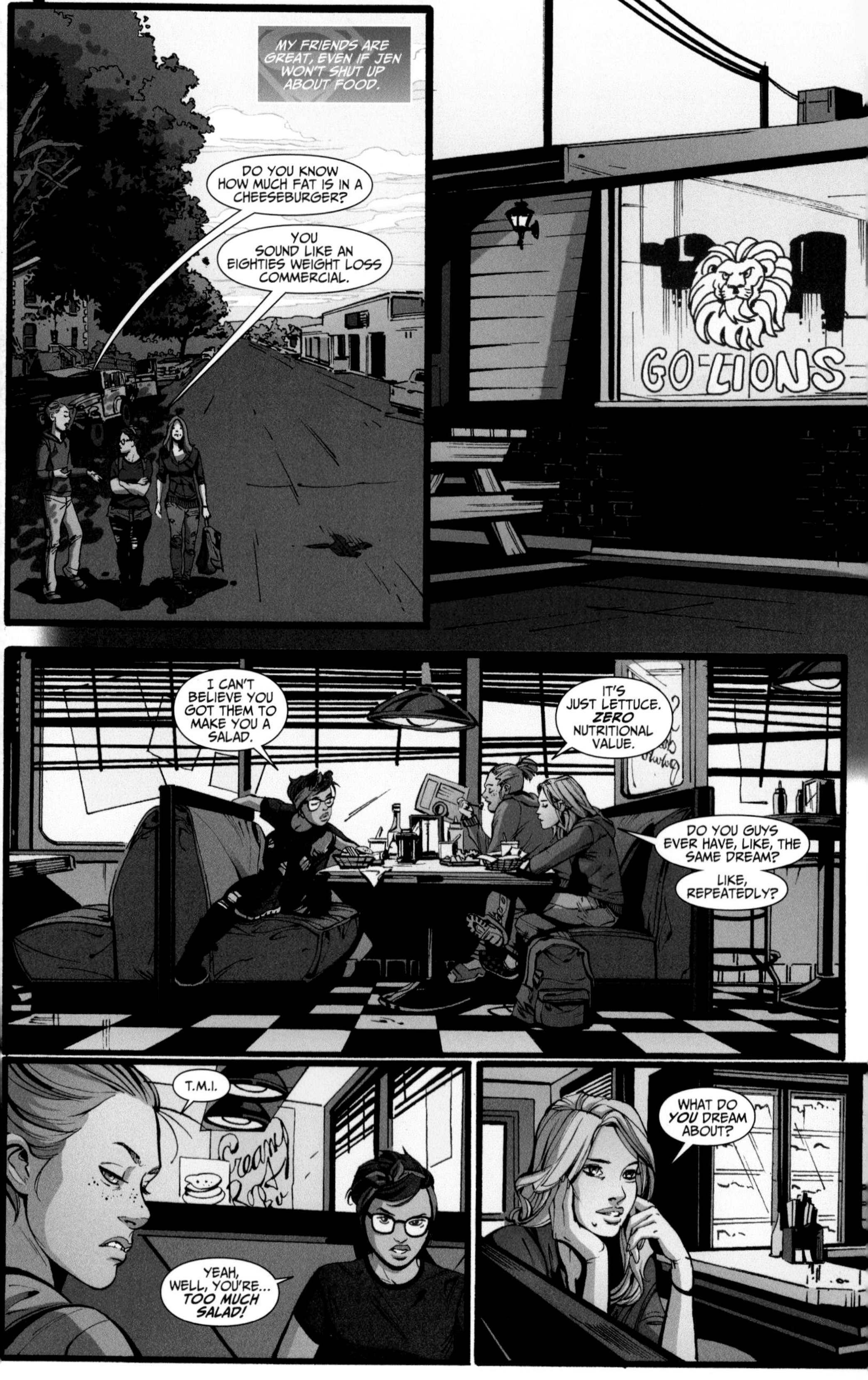
MY FRIENDS ARE GREAT, EVEN IF JEN WON'T SHUT UP ABOUT FOOD.
DO YOU KNOW HOW MUCH FAT IS IN A CHEESEBURGER?
YOU SOUND LIKE AN EIGHTIES WEIGHT LOSS COMMERCIAL.
GO LIONS
I CAN'T BELIEVE YOU GOT THEM TO MAKE YOU A SALAD.
IT'S JUST LETTUCE. ZERO NUTRITIONAL VALUE.
DO YOU GUYS EVER HAVE, LIKE, THE SAME DREAM?
LIKE, REPEATEDLY?
T.M.I.
YEAH, WELL, YOU'RE... TOO MUCH SALAD!
WHAT DO YOU DREAM ABOUT?

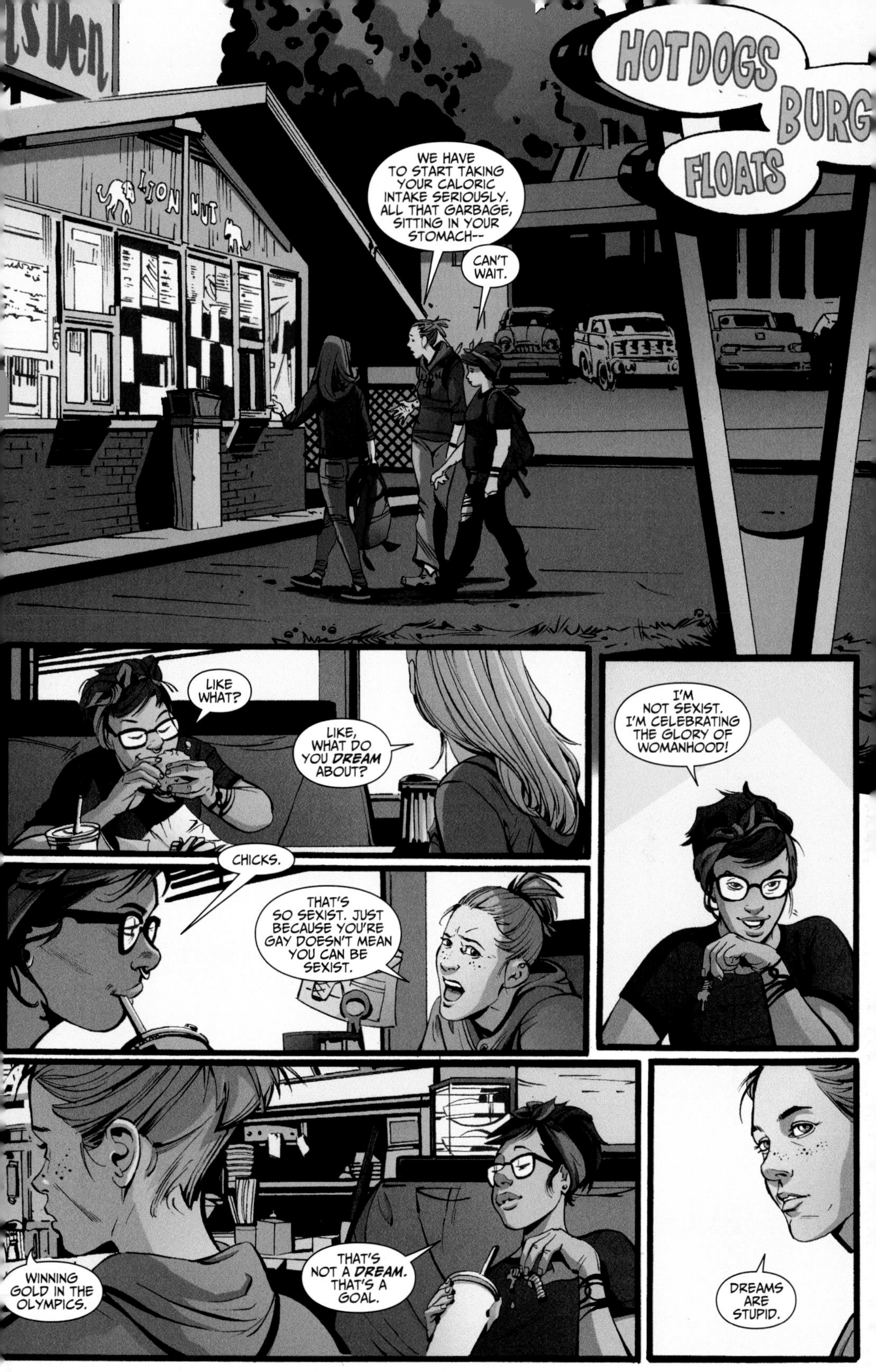
HOTDOGS
BURG
FLOATS
LION HUT
WE HAVE TO START TAKING YOUR CALORIC INTAKE SERIOUSLY. ALL THAT GARBAGE, SITTING IN YOUR STOMACH--
CAN'T WAIT.
LIKE WHAT?
LIKE, WHAT DO YOU *DREAM* ABOUT?
CHICKS.
THAT'S SO SEXIST. JUST BECAUSE YOU'RE GAY DOESN'T MEAN YOU CAN BE SEXIST.
I'M NOT SEXIST. I'M CELEBRATING THE GLORY OF WOMANHOOD!
WINNING GOLD IN THE OLYMPICS.
THAT'S NOT A *DREAM.* THAT'S A GOAL.
DREAMS ARE STUPID.

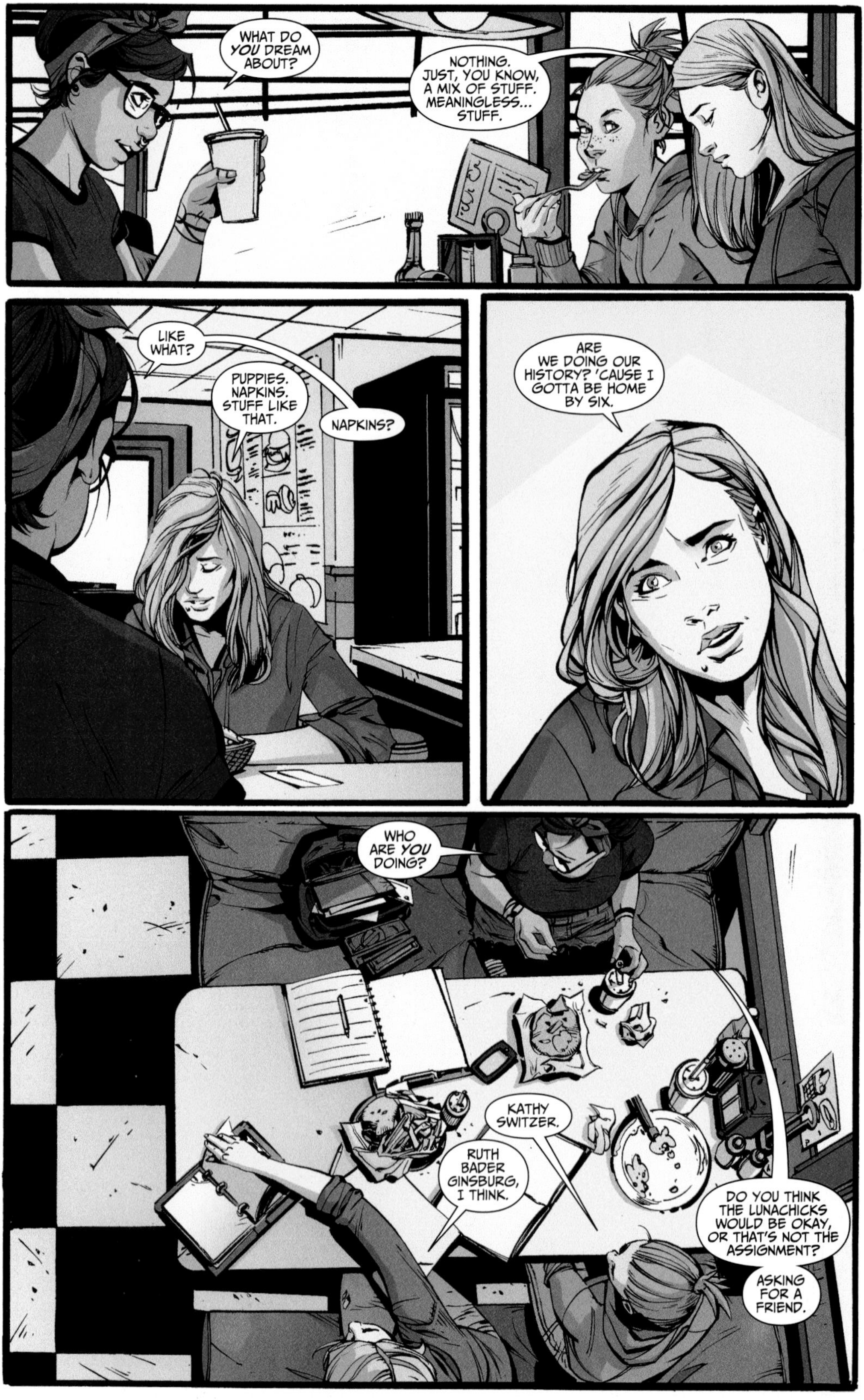
WHAT DO *YOU* DREAM ABOUT?
NOTHING. JUST, YOU KNOW, A MIX OF STUFF. MEANINGLESS... STUFF.
LIKE WHAT?
PUPPIES. NAPKINS. STUFF LIKE THAT.
NAPKINS?
ARE WE DOING OUR HISTORY? 'CAUSE I GOTTA BE HOME BY SIX.
WHO ARE *YOU* DOING?
KATHY SWITZER.
RUTH BADER GINSBURG, I THINK.
DO YOU THINK THE LUNACHICKS WOULD BE OKAY, OR THAT'S NOT THE ASSIGNMENT?
ASKING FOR A FRIEND.

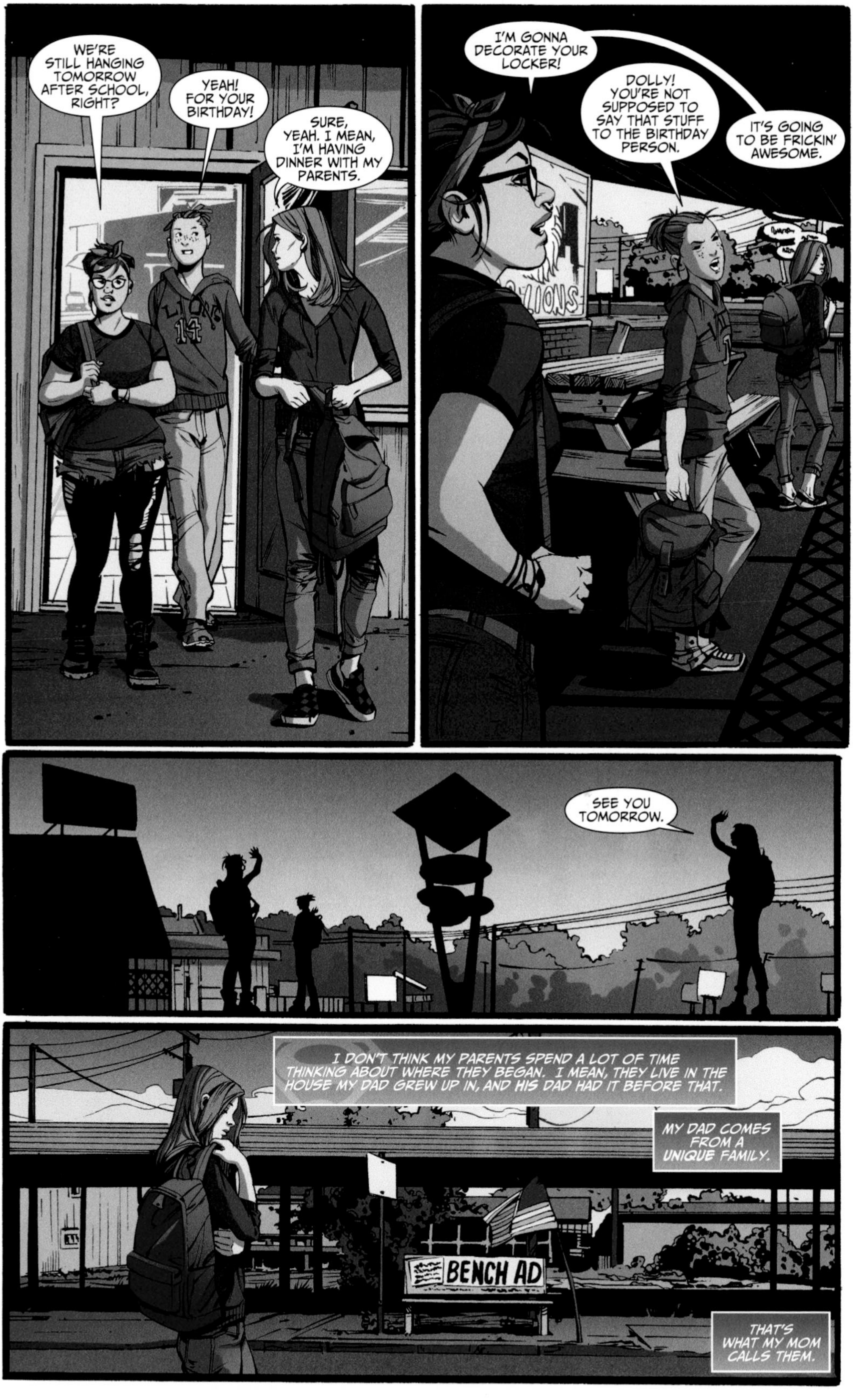
WE'RE STILL HANGING TOMORROW AFTER SCHOOL, RIGHT?
YEAH! FOR YOUR BIRTHDAY!
SURE, YEAH. I MEAN, I'M HAVING DINNER WITH MY PARENTS.
I'M GONNA DECORATE YOUR LOCKER!
DOLLY! YOU'RE NOT SUPPOSED TO SAY THAT STUFF TO THE BIRTHDAY PERSON.
IT'S GOING TO BE FRICKIN' AWESOME.
LIONS
SEE YOU TOMORROW.
I DON'T THINK MY PARENTS SPEND A LOT OF TIME THINKING ABOUT WHERE THEY BEGAN. I MEAN, THEY LIVE IN THE HOUSE MY DAD GREW UP IN, AND HIS DAD HAD IT BEFORE THAT.
MY DAD COMES FROM A UNIQUE FAMILY.
BENCH AD
THAT'S WHAT MY MOM CALLS THEM.

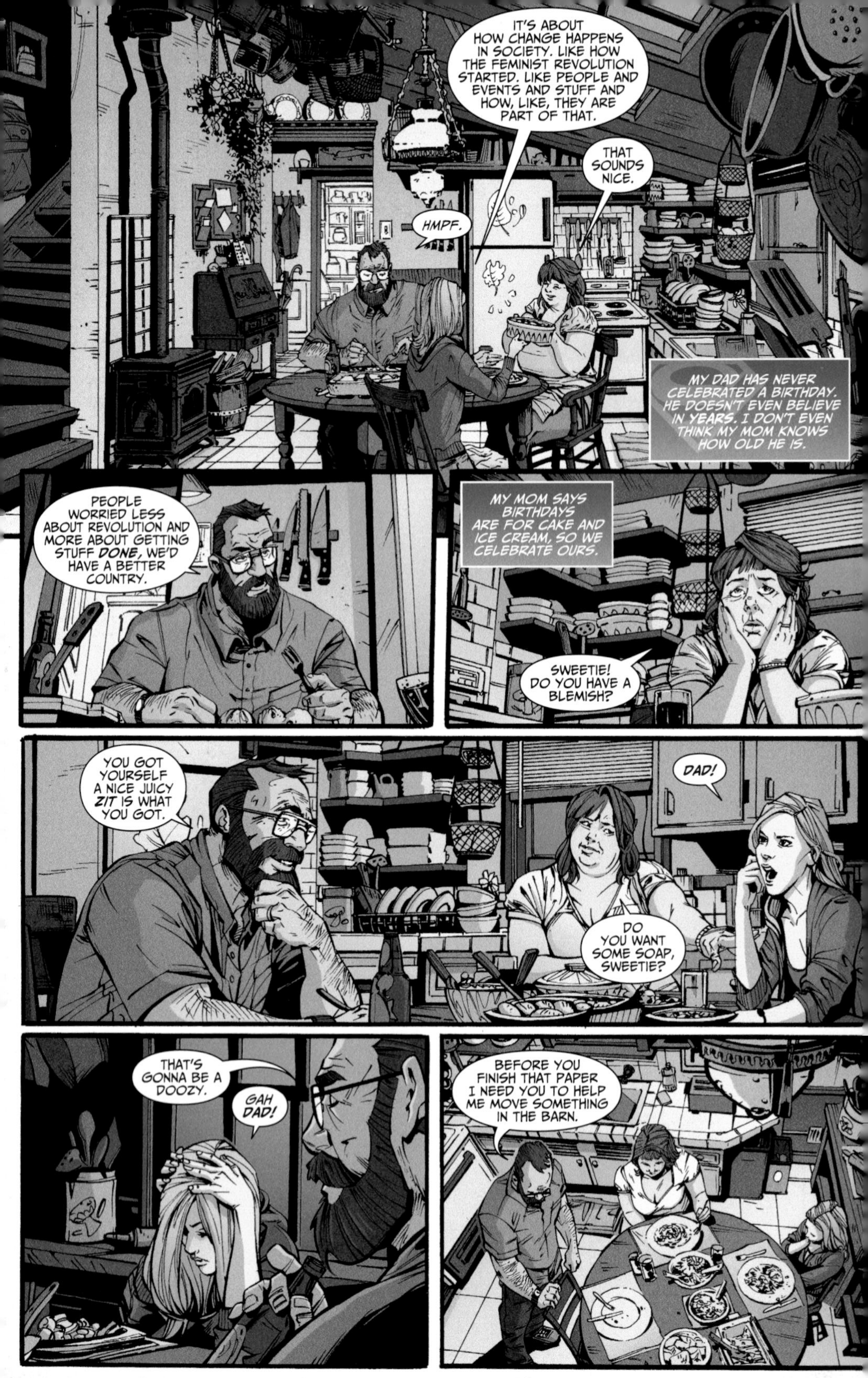
IT'S ABOUT HOW CHANGE HAPPENS IN SOCIETY. LIKE HOW THE FEMINIST REVOLUTION STARTED. LIKE PEOPLE AND EVENTS AND STUFF AND HOW, LIKE, THEY ARE PART OF THAT.
HMPF.
THAT SOUNDS NICE.
MY DAD HAS NEVER CELEBRATED A BIRTHDAY. HE DOESN'T EVEN BELIEVE IN YEARS. I DON'T EVEN THINK MY MOM KNOWS HOW OLD HE IS.
PEOPLE WORRIED LESS ABOUT REVOLUTION AND MORE ABOUT GETTING STUFF DONE, WE'D HAVE A BETTER COUNTRY.
MY MOM SAYS BIRTHDAYS ARE FOR CAKE AND ICE CREAM, SO WE CELEBRATE OURS.
SWEETIE! DO YOU HAVE A BLEMISH?
YOU GOT YOURSELF A NICE JUICY ZIT IS WHAT YOU GOT.
DAD!
DO YOU WANT SOME SOAP, SWEETIE?
THAT'S GONNA BE A DOOZY.
GAH DAD!
BEFORE YOU FINISH THAT PAPER I NEED YOU TO HELP ME MOVE SOMETHING IN THE BARN.

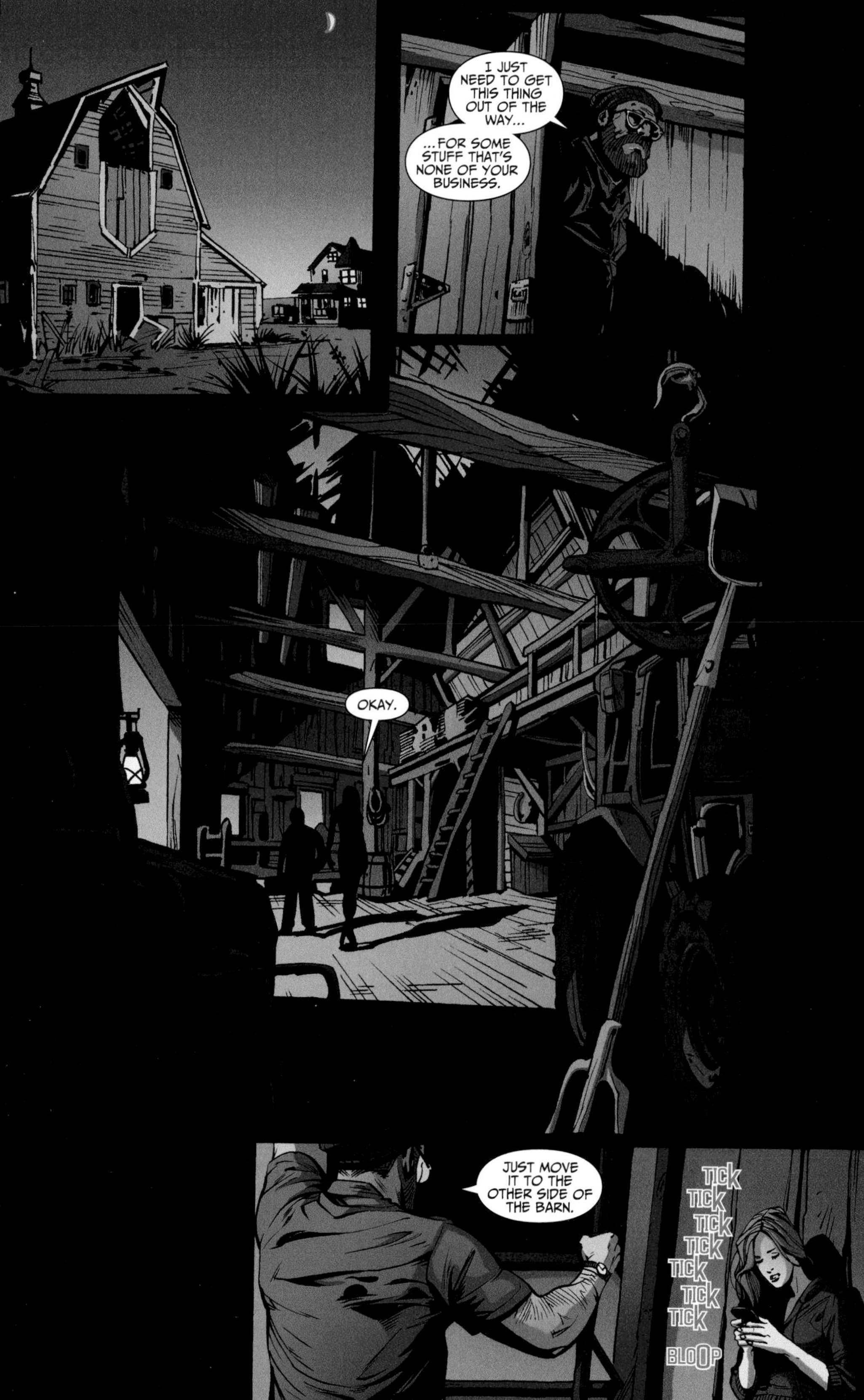
I JUST NEED TO GET THIS THING OUT OF THE WAY...
...FOR SOME STUFF THAT'S NONE OF YOUR BUSINESS.
OKAY.
JUST MOVE IT TO THE OTHER SIDE OF THE BARN.
TICK
TICK
TICK
TICK
TICK
TICK
TICK
BLOOP

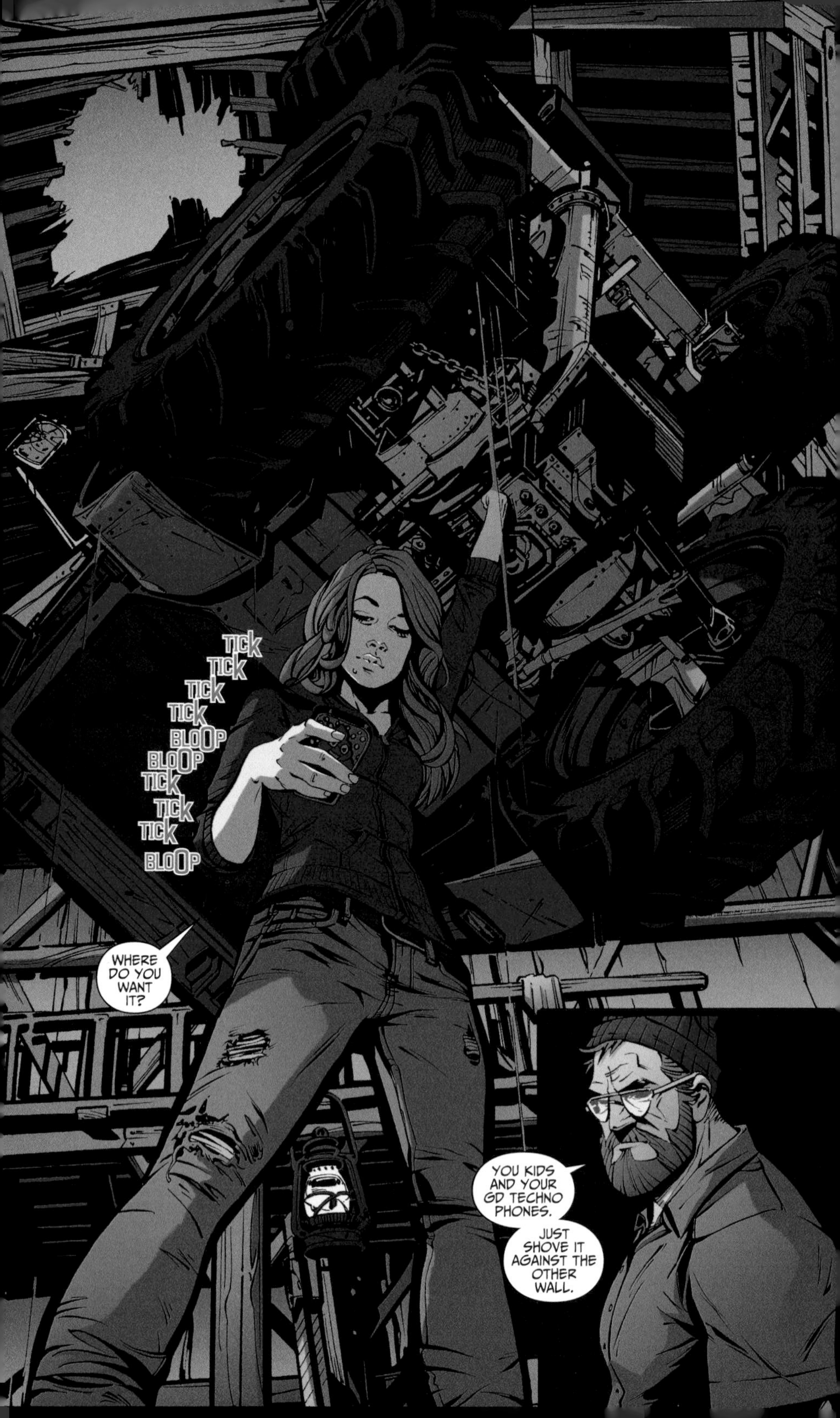
TICK
TICK
TICK
TICK
BLOOP
BLOOP
TICK
TICK
TICK
BLOOP
WHERE DO YOU WANT IT?
YOU KIDS AND YOUR GD TECHNO PHONES.
JUST SHOVE IT AGAINST THE OTHER WALL.

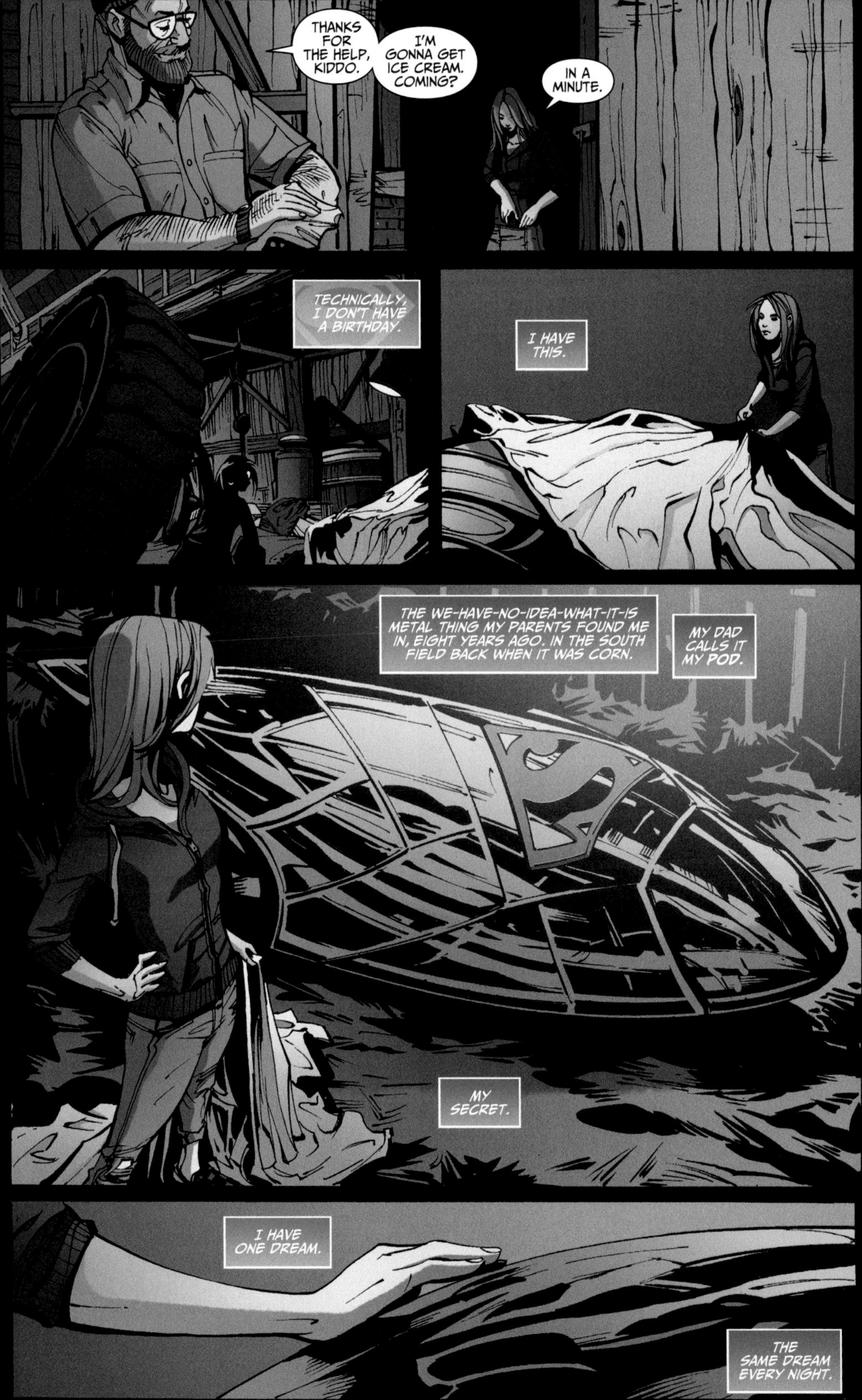
THANKS FOR THE HELP, KIDDO.
I'M GONNA GET ICE CREAM. COMING?
IN A MINUTE.
TECHNICALLY, I DON'T HAVE A BIRTHDAY.
I HAVE THIS.
THE WE-HAVE-NO-IDEA-WHAT-IT-IS METAL THING MY PARENTS FOUND ME IN, EIGHT YEARS AGO. IN THE SOUTH FIELD BACK WHEN IT WAS CORN.
MY DAD CALLS IT MY POD.
MY SECRET.
I HAVE ONE DREAM.
THE SAME DREAM EVERY NIGHT.

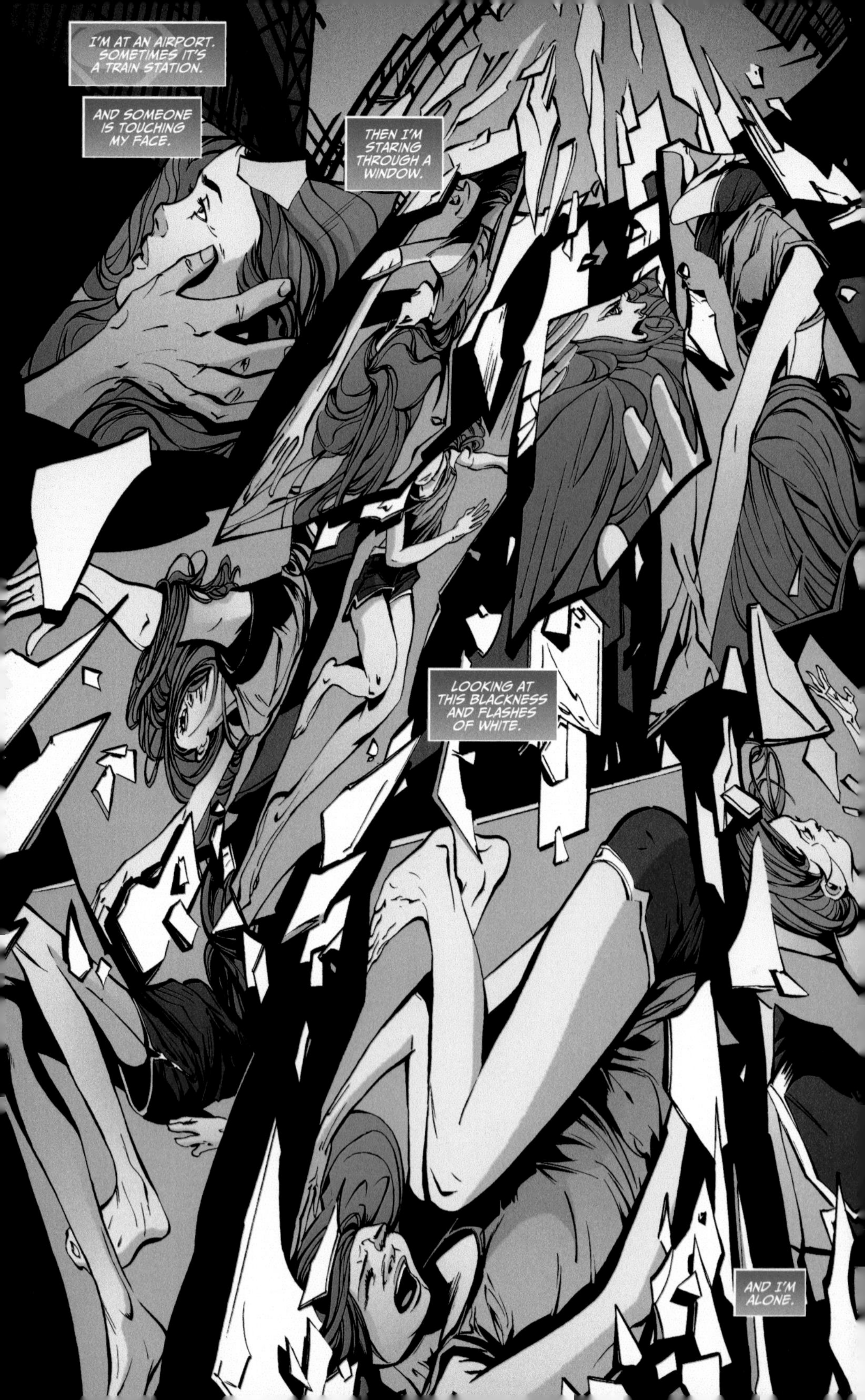
I'M AT AN AIRPORT. SOMETIMES IT'S A TRAIN STATION.
AND SOMEONE IS TOUCHING MY FACE.
THEN I'M STARING THROUGH A WINDOW.
LOOKING AT THIS BLACKNESS AND FLASHES OF WHITE.
AND I'M ALONE.

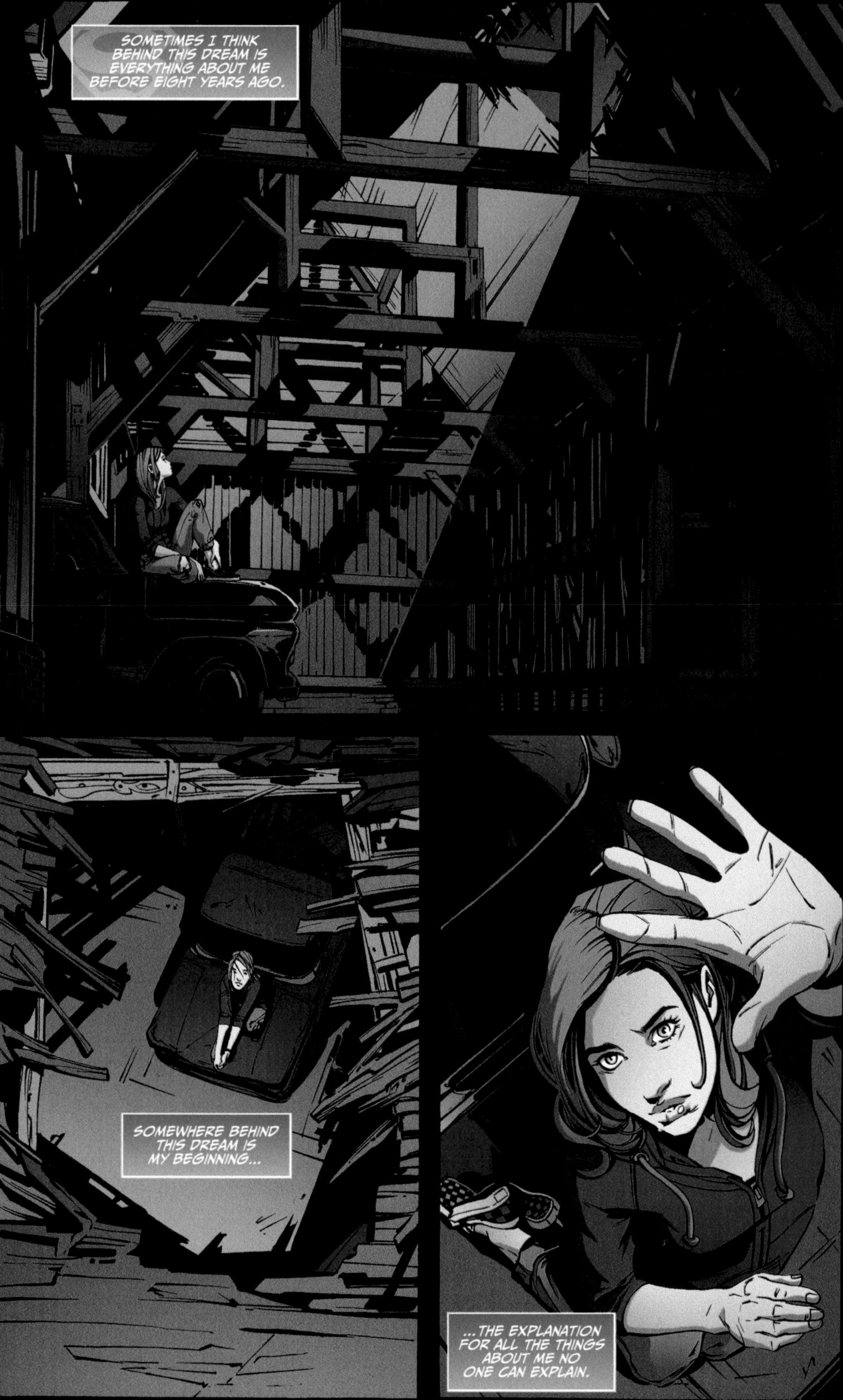
SOMETIMES I THINK BEHIND THIS DREAM IS EVERYTHING ABOUT ME BEFORE EIGHT YEARS AGO.
SOMEWHERE BEHIND THIS DREAM IS MY BEGINNING...
...THE EXPLANATION FOR ALL THE THINGS ABOUT ME NO ONE CAN EXPLAIN.

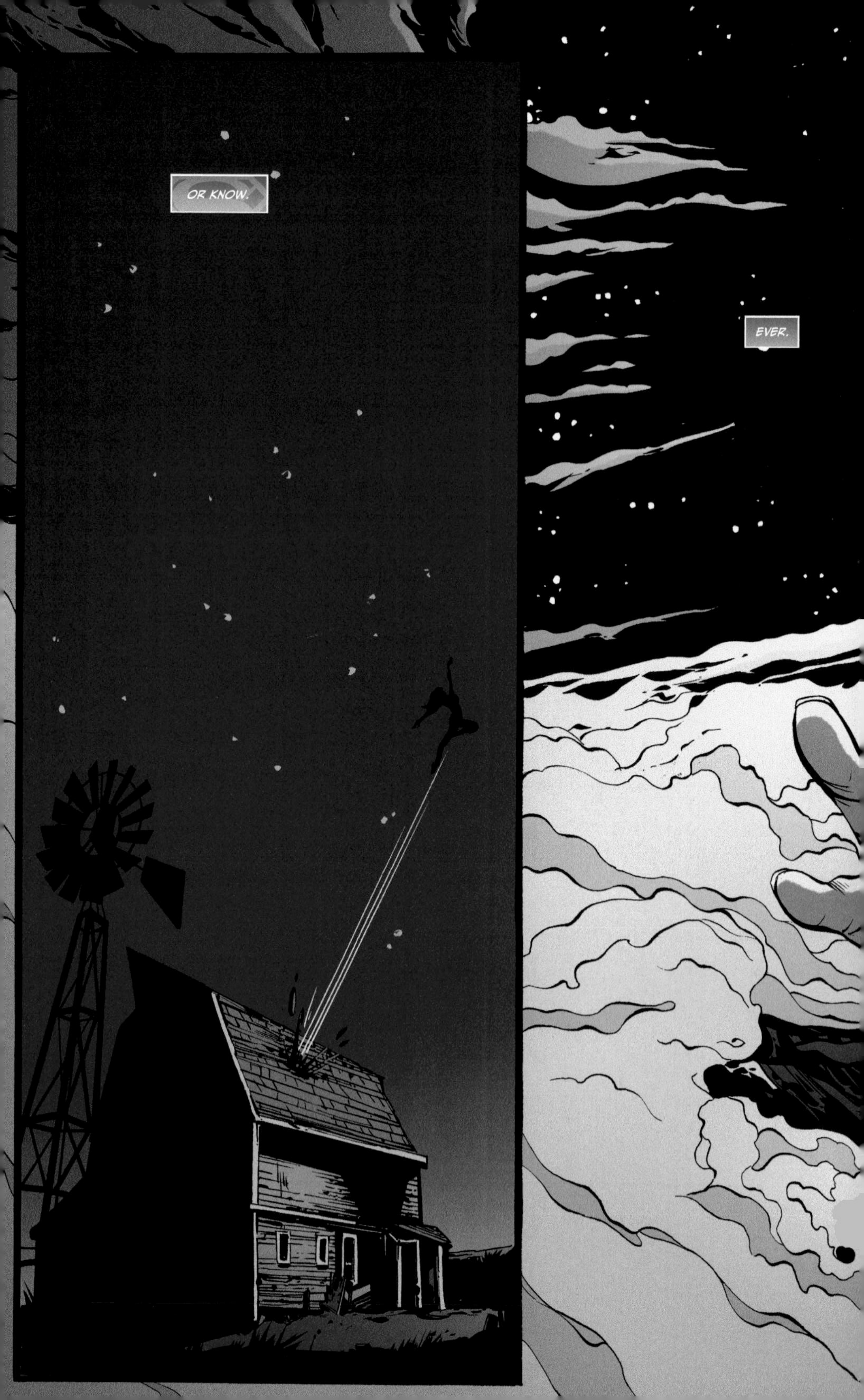
OR KNOW.
EVER.

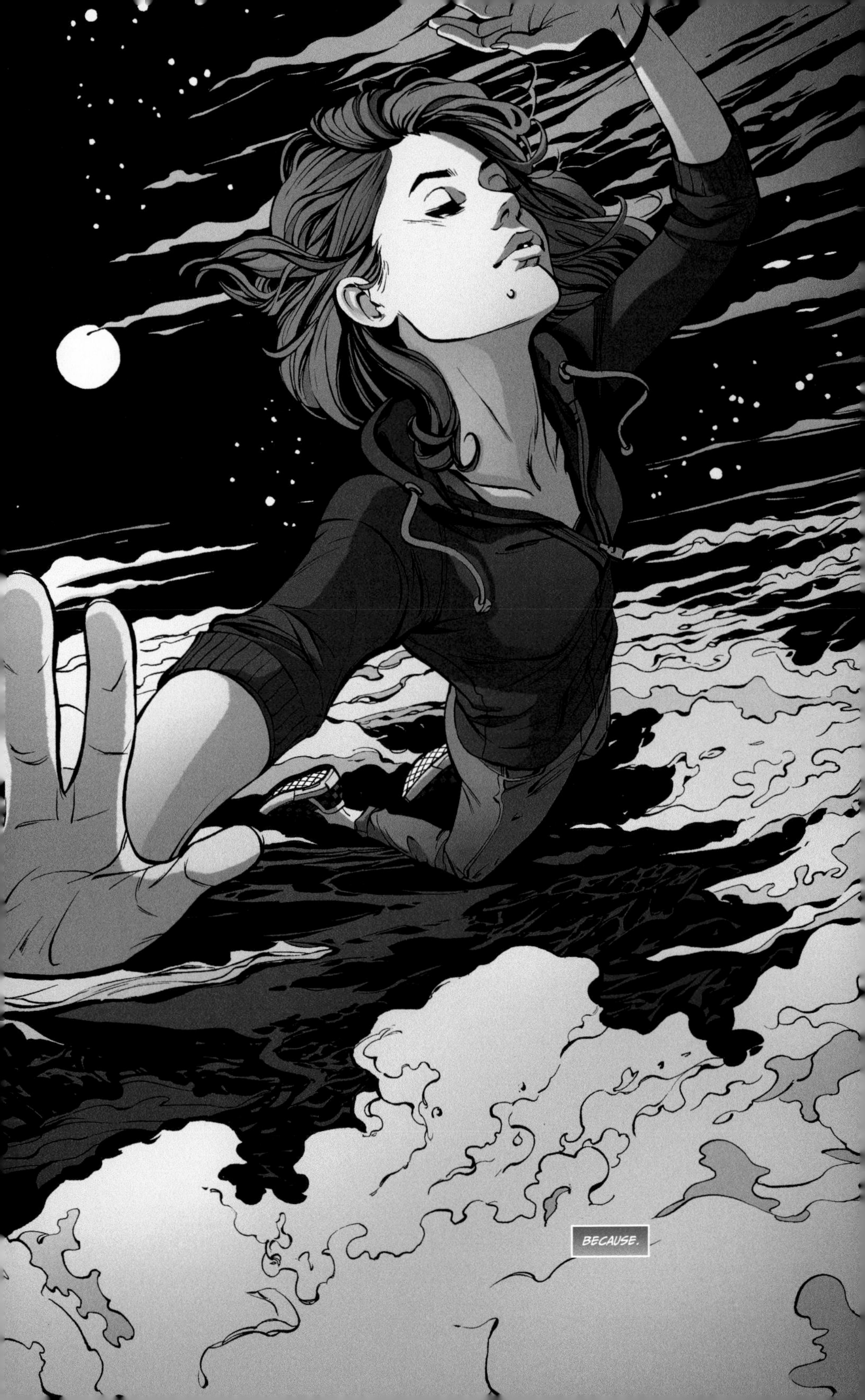
BECAUSE.

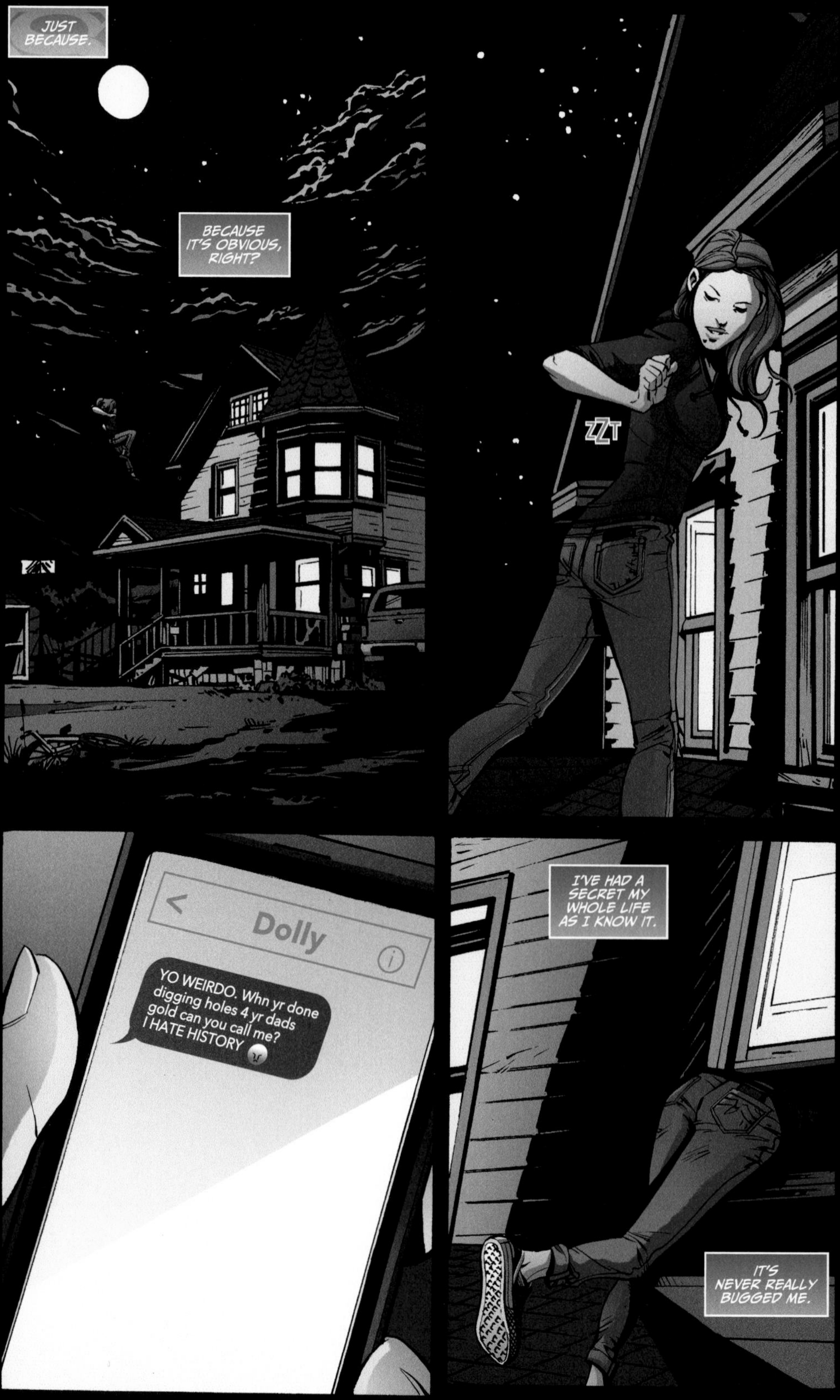
JUST BECAUSE.
BECAUSE IT'S OBVIOUS, RIGHT?
ZZZT
Dolly
YO WEIRDO. Whn yr done digging holes 4 yr dads gold can you call me? I HATE HISTORY
I'VE HAD A SECRET MY WHOLE LIFE AS I KNOW IT.
IT'S NEVER REALLY BUGGED ME.

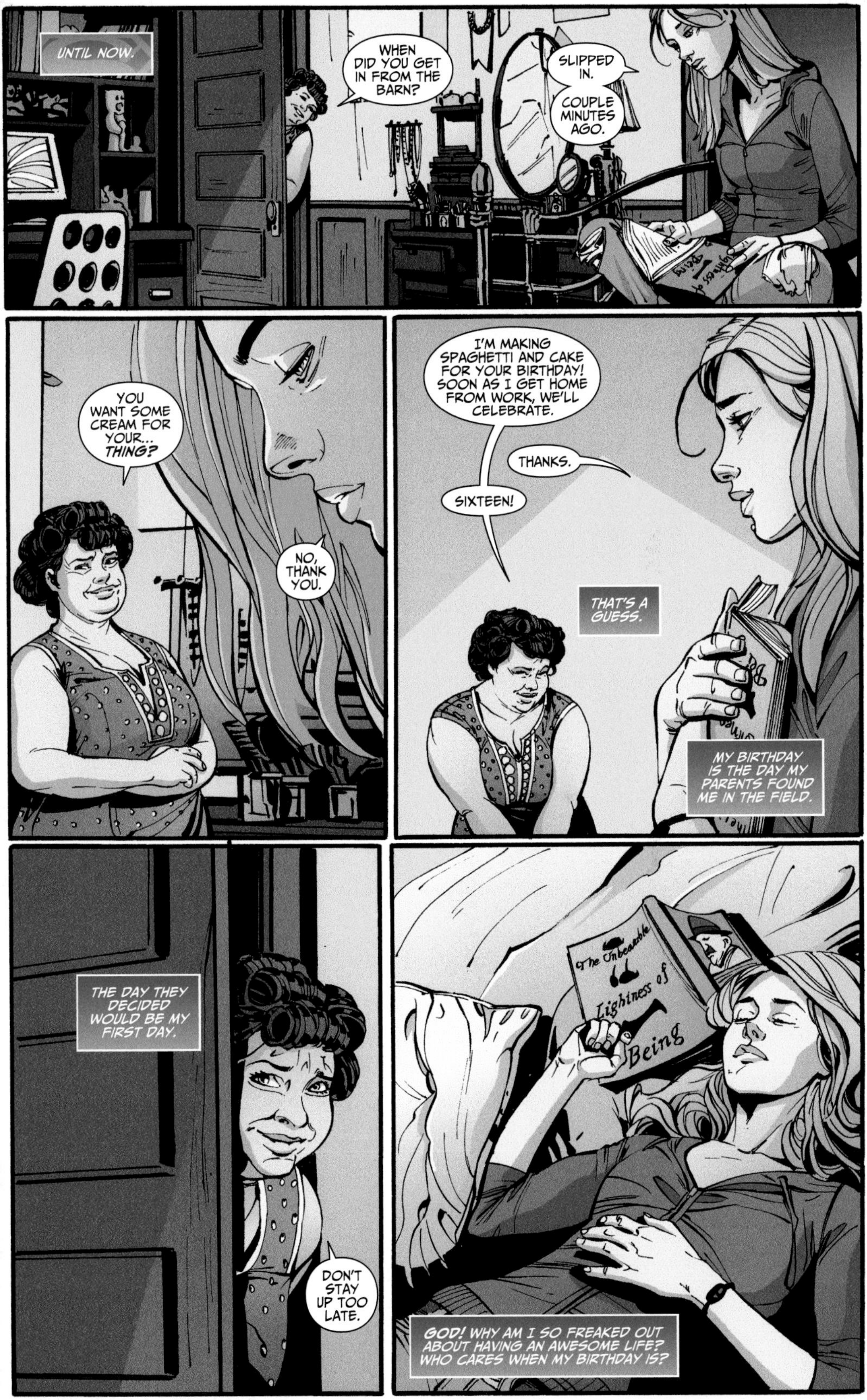
UNTIL NOW.
WHEN DID YOU GET IN FROM THE BARN?
SLIPPED IN.
COUPLE MINUTES AGO.
YOU WANT SOME CREAM FOR YOUR... THING?
NO, THANK YOU.
I'M MAKING SPAGHETTI AND CAKE FOR YOUR BIRTHDAY! SOON AS I GET HOME FROM WORK, WE'LL CELEBRATE.
THANKS.
SIXTEEN!
THAT'S A GUESS.
MY BIRTHDAY IS THE DAY MY PARENTS FOUND ME IN THE FIELD.
THE DAY THEY DECIDED WOULD BE MY FIRST DAY.
DON'T STAY UP TOO LATE.
The Unbearable Lightness of Being
GOD! WHY AM I SO FREAKED OUT ABOUT HAVING AN AWESOME LIFE? WHO CARES WHEN MY BIRTHDAY IS?

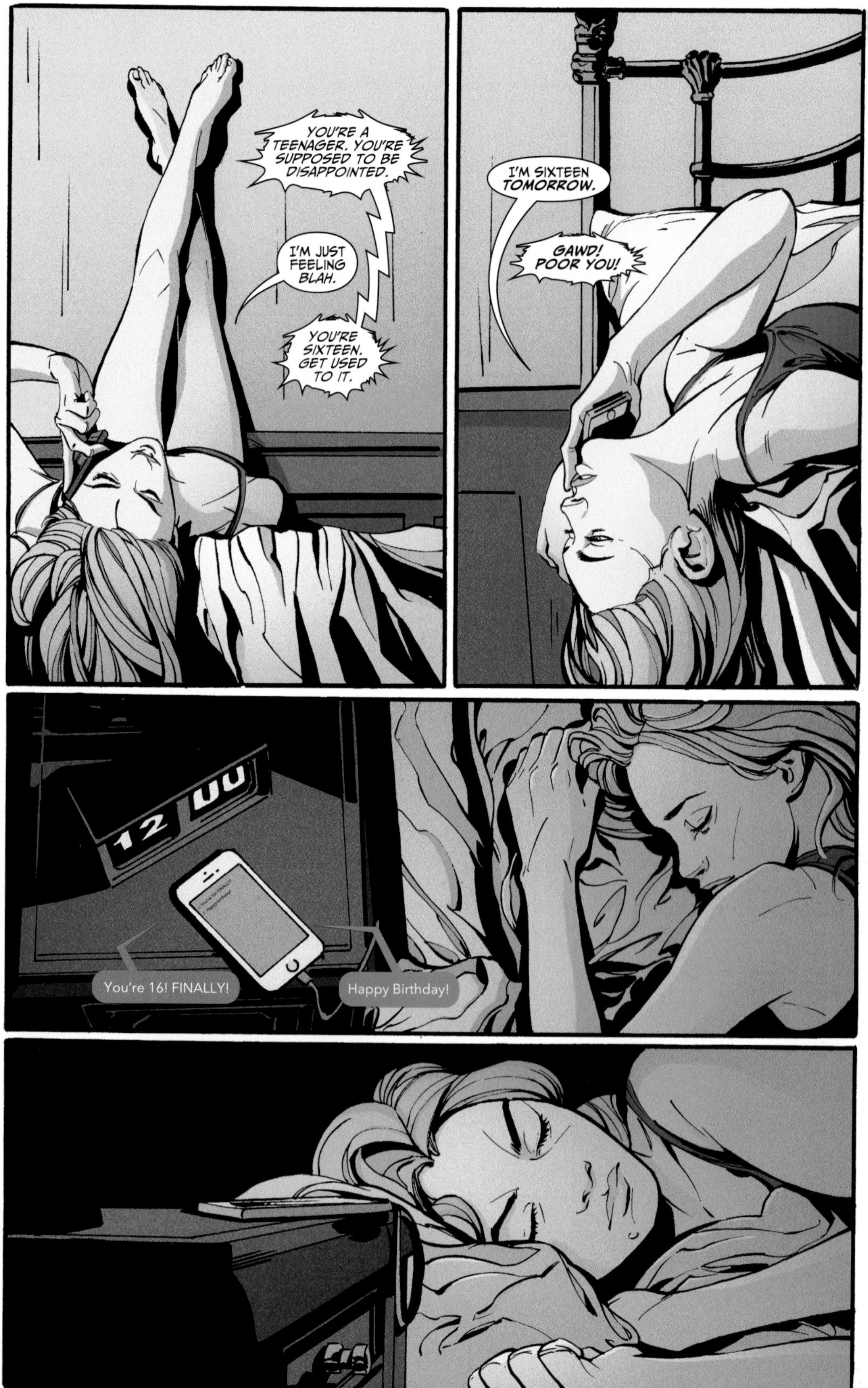
I'M JUST FEELING BLAH.
YOU'RE A TEENAGER. YOU'RE SUPPOSED TO BE DISAPPOINTED.
YOU'RE SIXTEEN. GET USED TO IT.
I'M SIXTEEN TOMORROW.
GAWD! POOR YOU!
12 00
You're 16! FINALLY!
Happy Birthday!

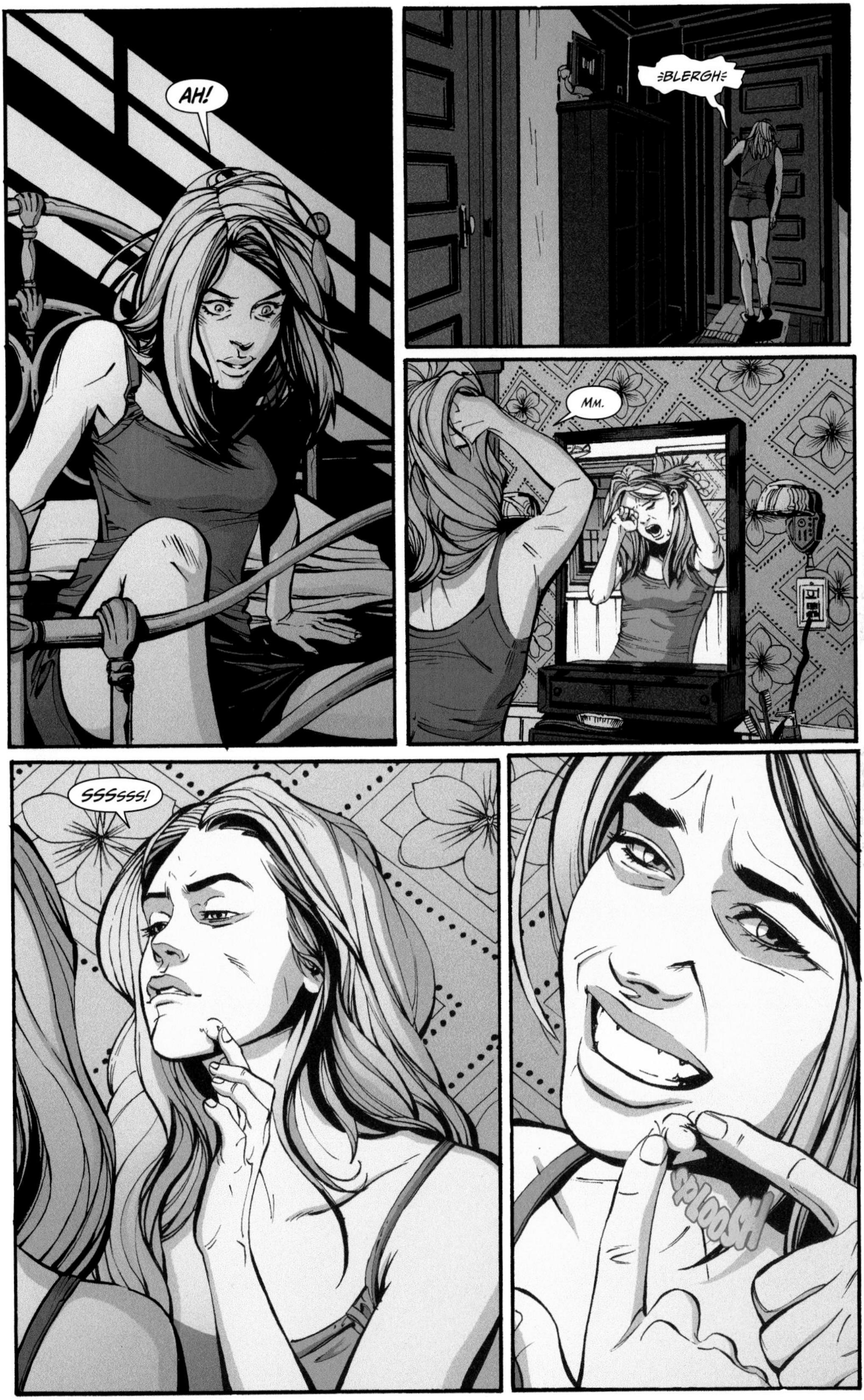
AH!
BLERGH
MM.
SSSSSS!
SPLOOSH

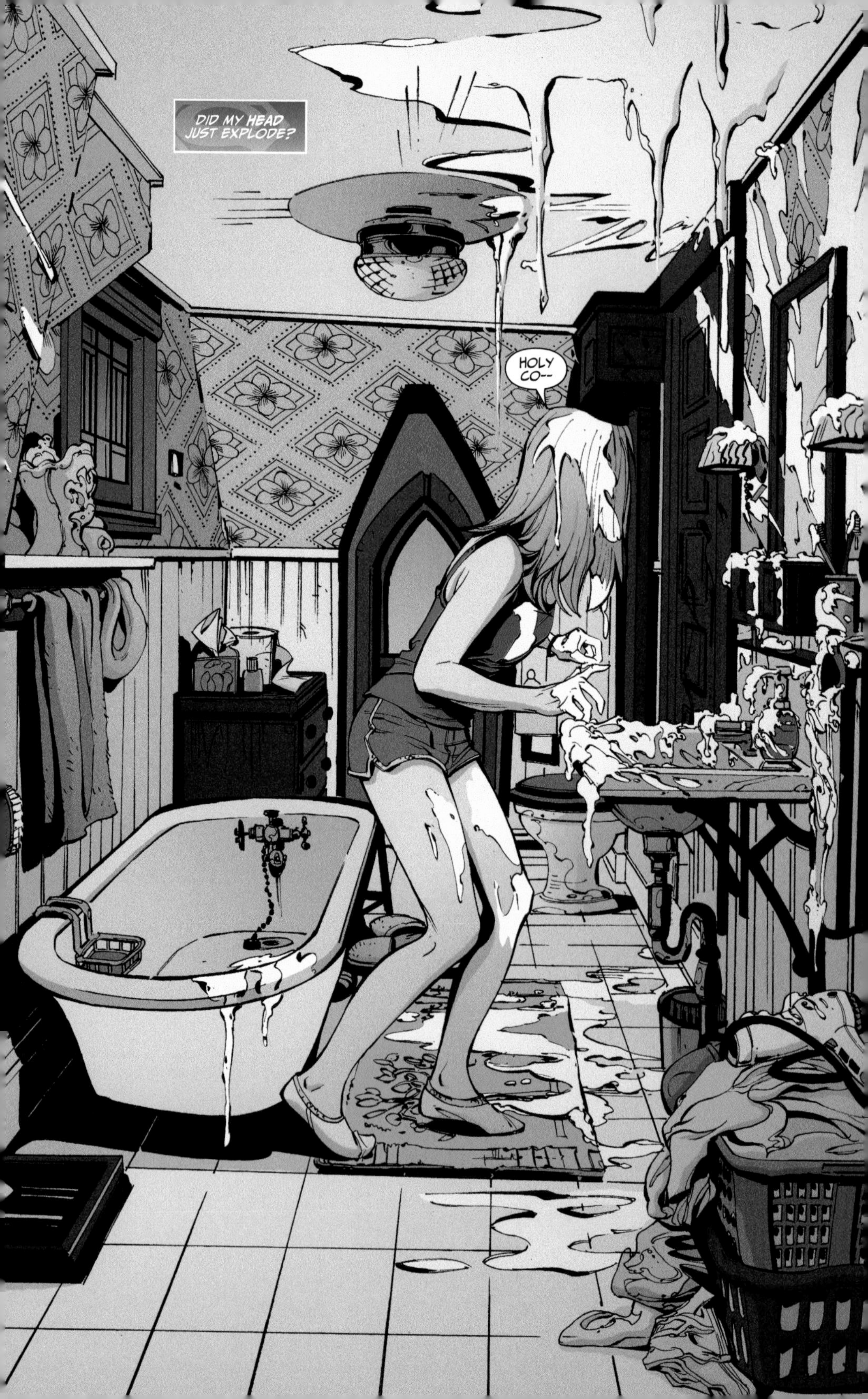
DID MY HEAD
JUST EXPLODE?
HOLY
CO--

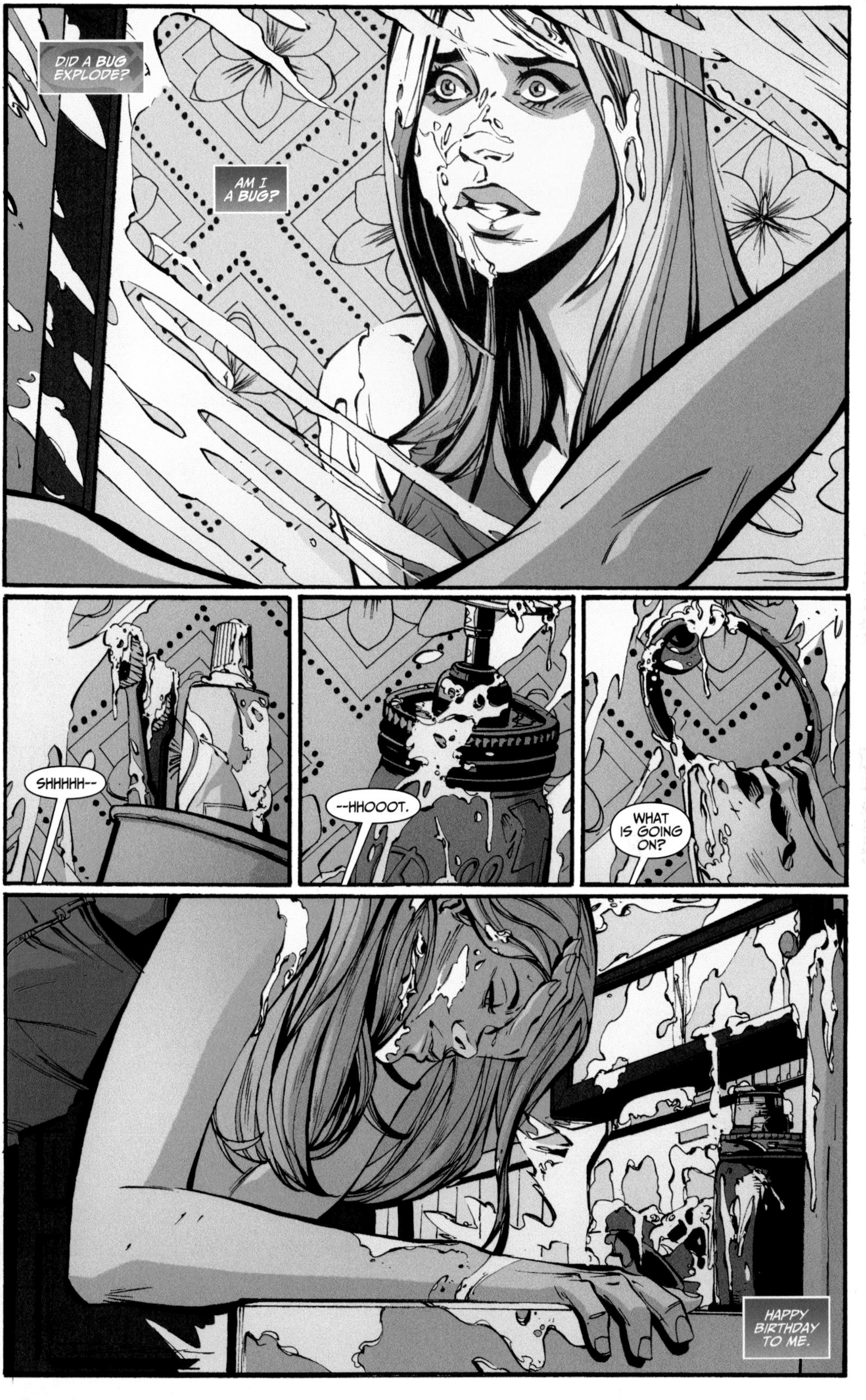
DID A BUG EXPLODE?
AM I A BUG?
SHHHHH--
--HHOOOT.
WHAT IS GOING ON?
HAPPY BIRTHDAY TO ME.

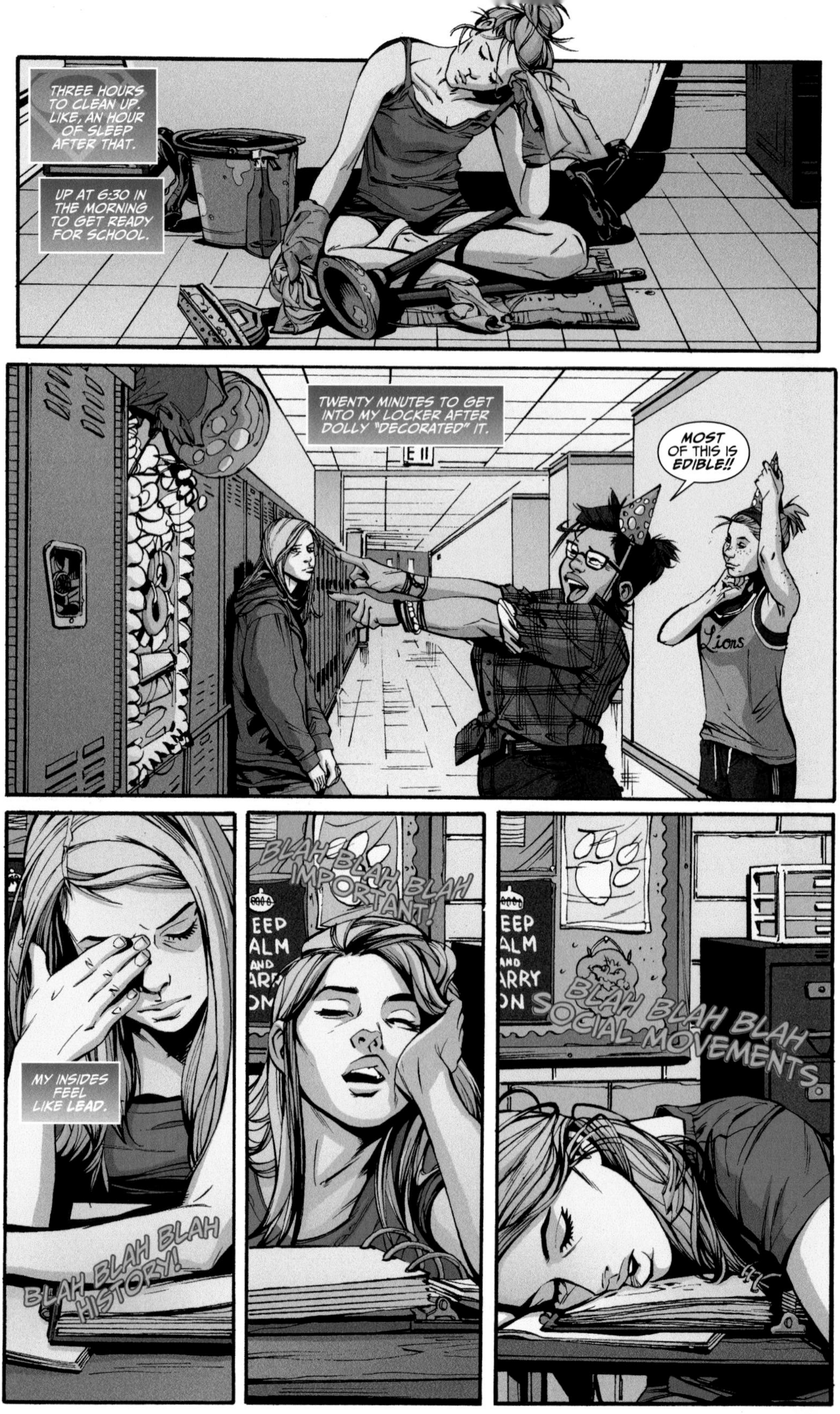
THREE HOURS TO CLEAN UP. LIKE, AN HOUR OF SLEEP AFTER THAT.
UP AT 6:30 IN THE MORNING TO GET READY FOR SCHOOL.
TWENTY MINUTES TO GET INTO MY LOCKER AFTER DOLLY "DECORATED" IT.
MOST OF THIS IS EDIBLE!!
Lions
MY INSIDES FEEL LIKE LEAD.
BLAH BLAH BLAH HISTORY!
BLAH BLAH BLAH IMPORTANT!
BLAH BLAH BLAH SOCIAL MOVEMENTS

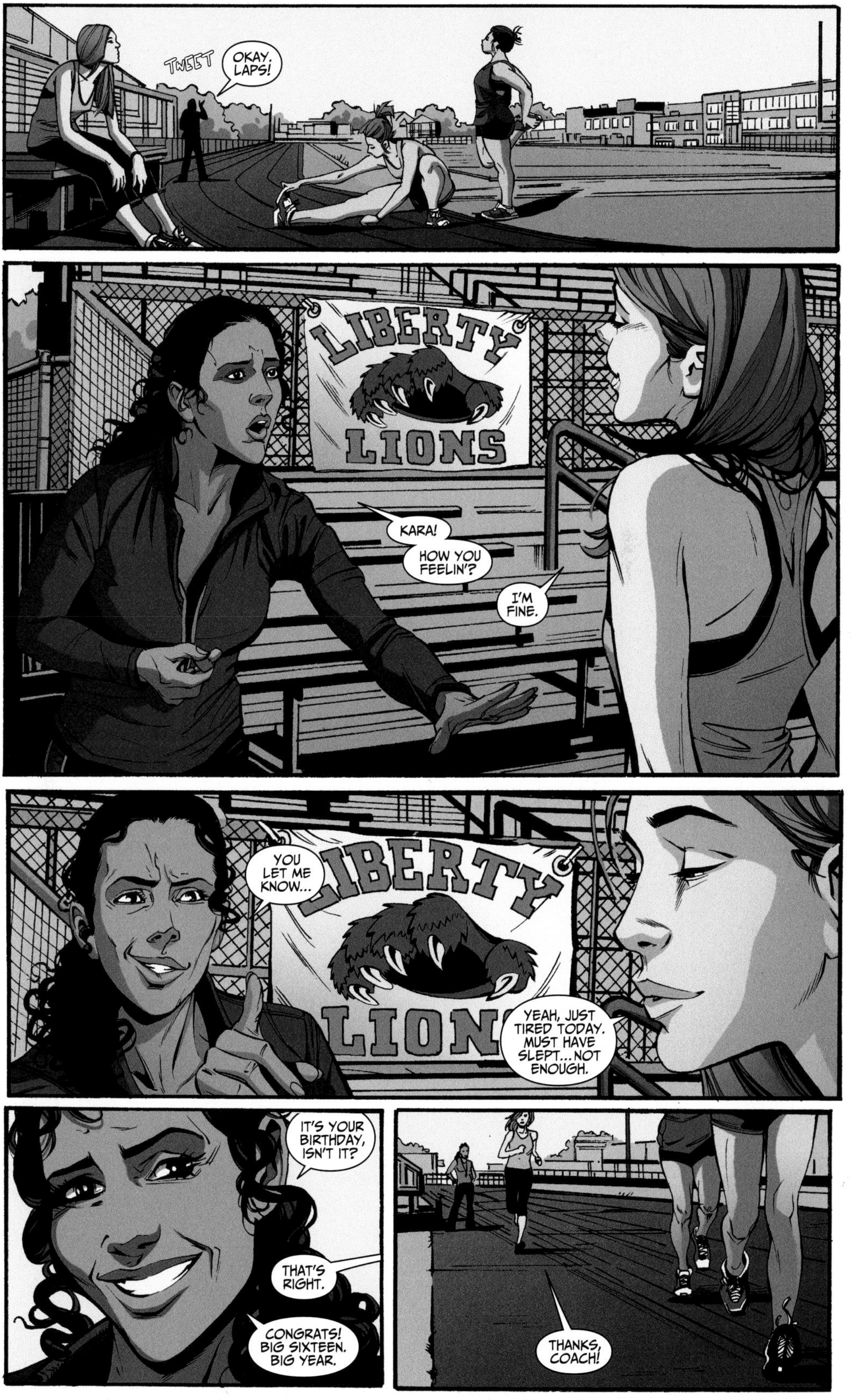
TWEET
OKAY. LAPS!
LIBERTY LIONS
KARA!
HOW YOU FEELIN'?
I'M FINE.
YOU LET ME KNOW...
LIBERTY
YEAH, JUST TIRED TODAY. MUST HAVE SLEPT...NOT ENOUGH.
IT'S YOUR BIRTHDAY, ISN'T IT?
THAT'S RIGHT.
CONGRATS! BIG SIXTEEN. BIG YEAR.
THANKS, COACH!

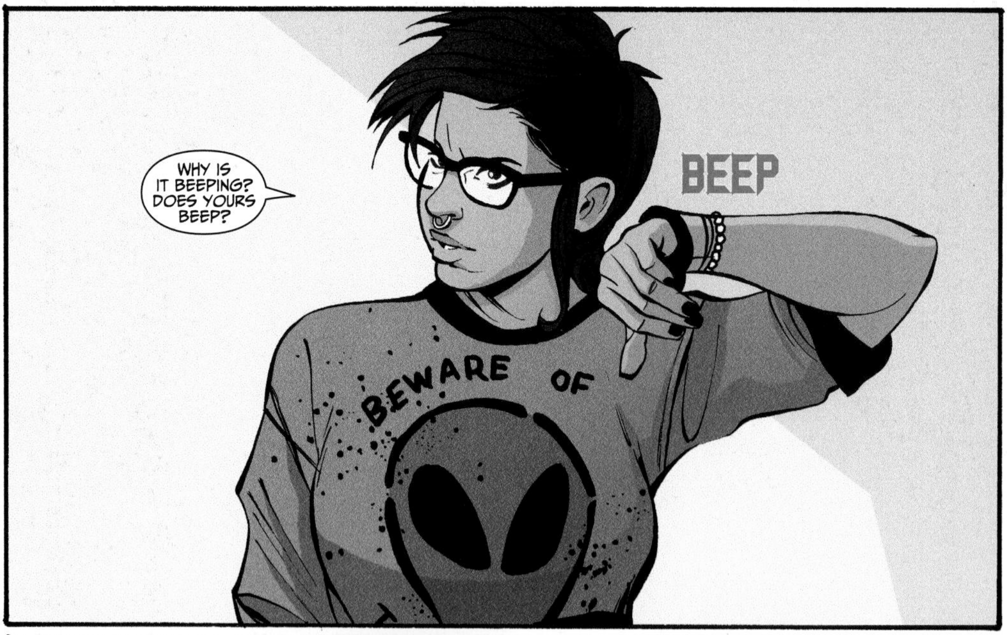
WHY IS IT BEEPING? DOES YOURS BEEP?
BEEP
BEWARE OF

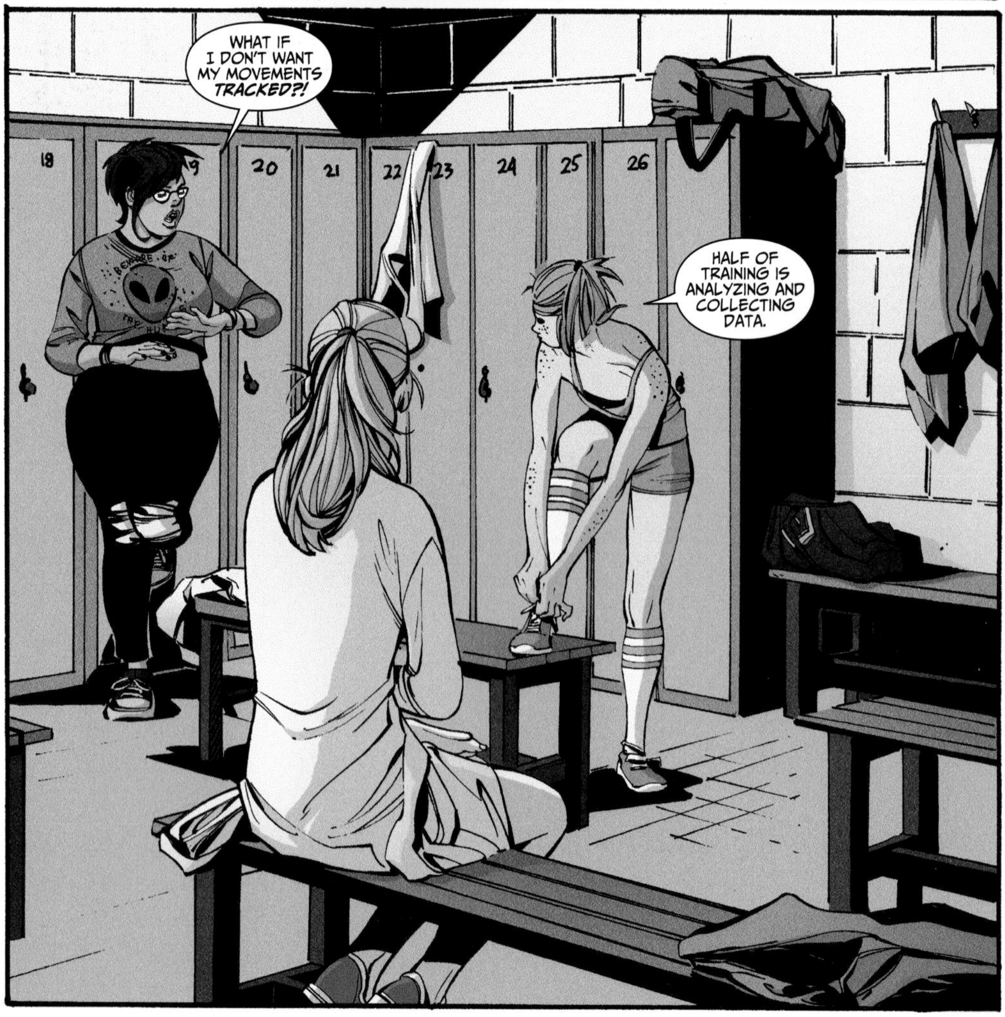
WHAT IF I DON'T WANT MY MOVEMENTS *TRACKED?!*
18
20
21
22
23
24
25
26
HALF OF TRAINING IS ANALYZING AND COLLECTING DATA.

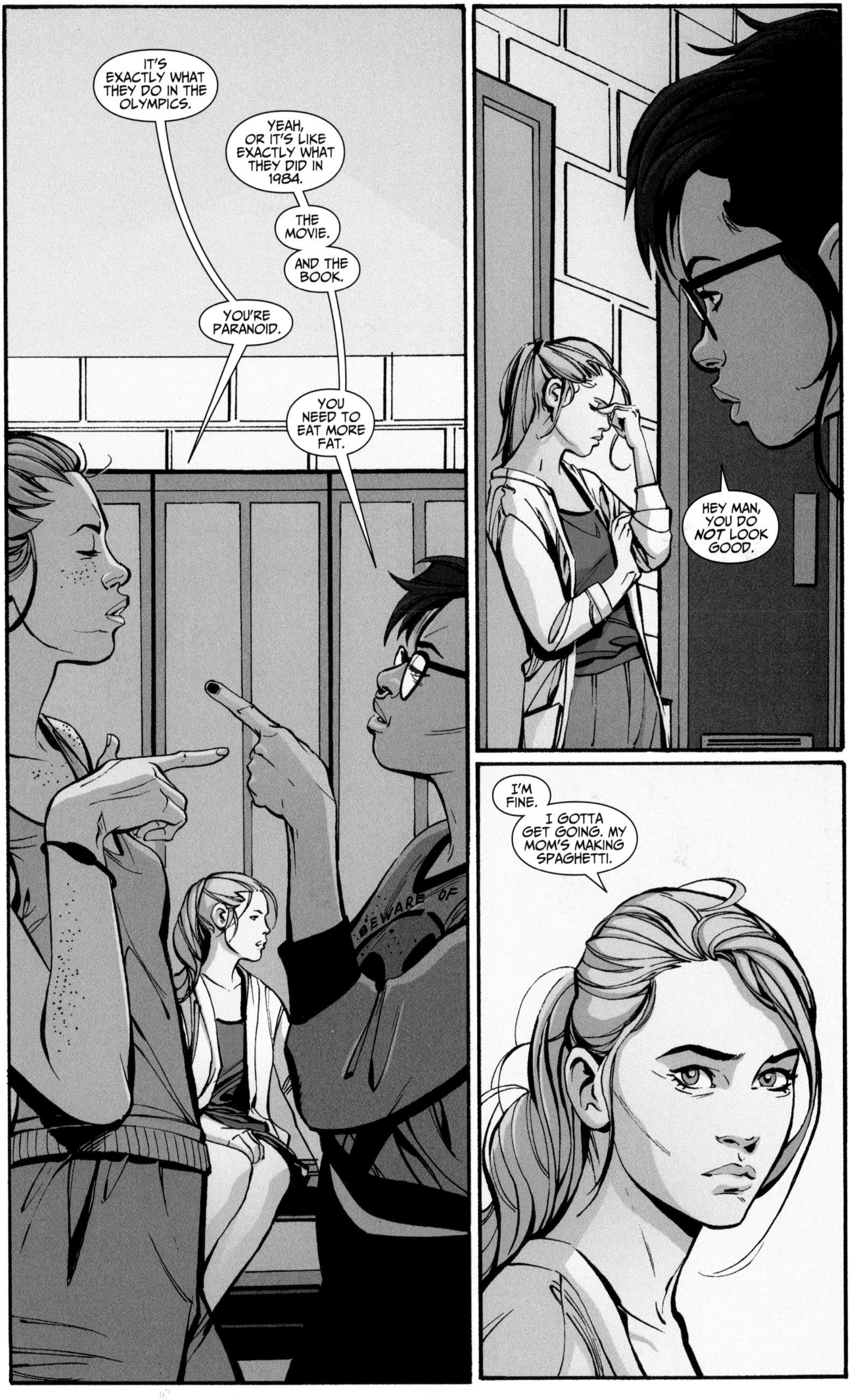
IT'S EXACTLY WHAT THEY DO IN THE OLYMPICS.
YEAH, OR IT'S LIKE EXACTLY WHAT THEY DID IN 1984.
THE MOVIE.
AND THE BOOK.
YOU'RE PARANOID.
YOU NEED TO EAT MORE FAT.
BEWARE OF
HEY MAN, YOU DO *NOT* LOOK GOOD.
I'M FINE.
I GOTTA GET GOING. MY MOM'S MAKING SPAGHETTI.

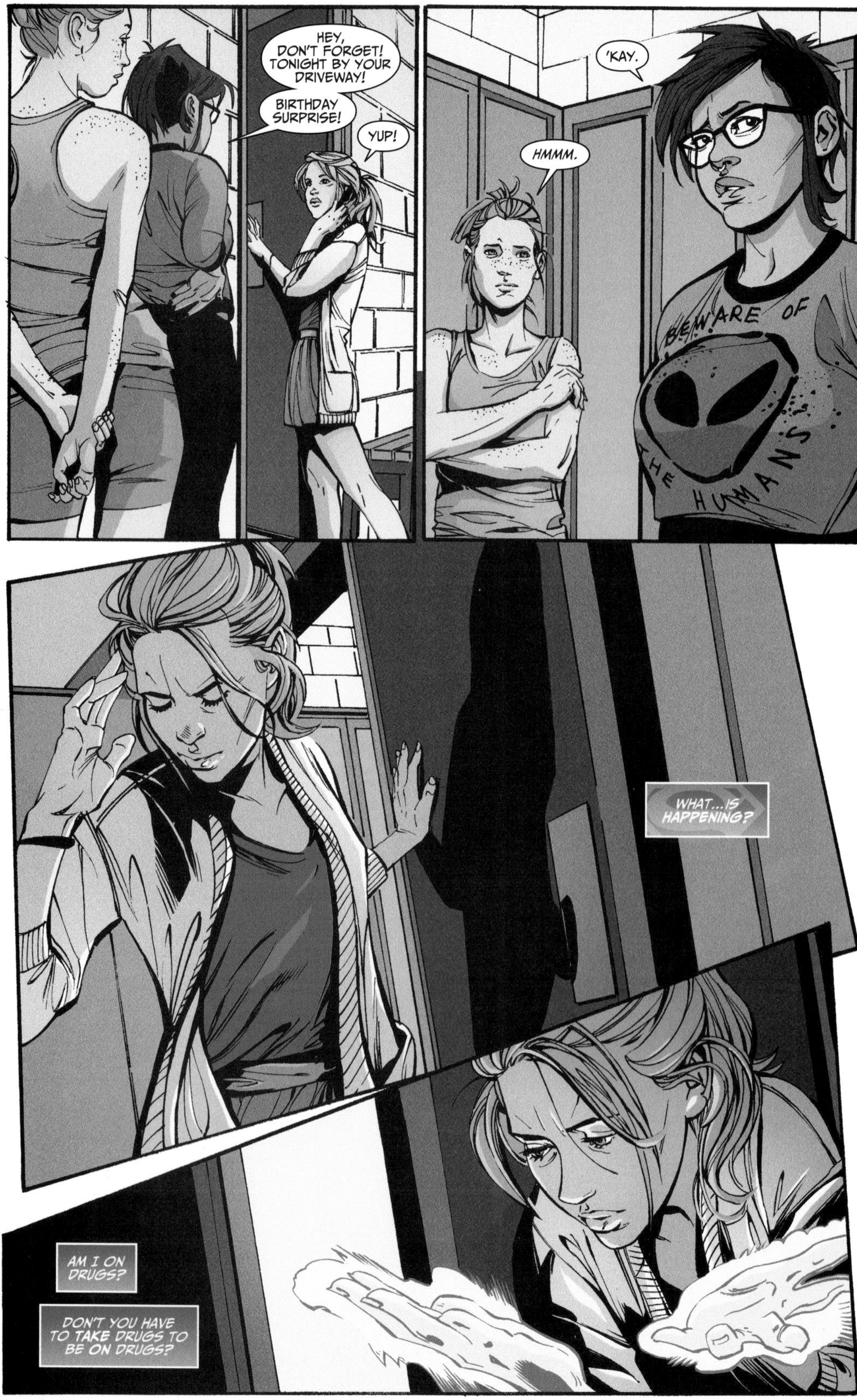
HEY, DON'T FORGET! TONIGHT BY YOUR DRIVEWAY!
BIRTHDAY SURPRISE!
YUP!
'KAY.
HMMM.
BEWARE OF THE HUMANS
WHAT...IS HAPPENING?
AM I ON DRUGS?
DON'T YOU HAVE TO *TAKE* DRUGS TO BE ON DRUGS?

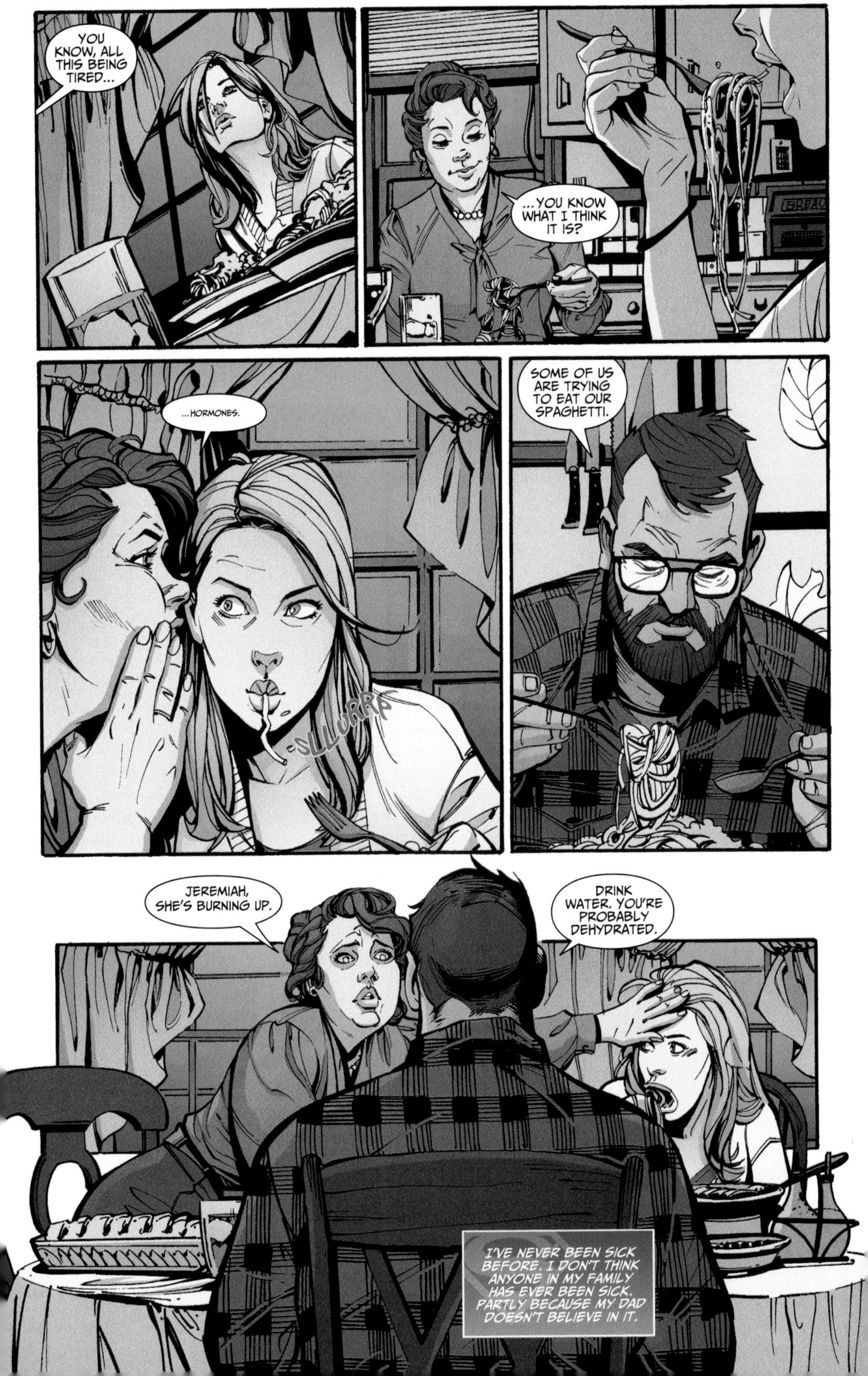
YOU KNOW, ALL THIS BEING TIRED...
...YOU KNOW WHAT I THINK IT IS?
...HORMONES.
SLLURRP
SOME OF US ARE TRYING TO EAT OUR SPAGHETTI.
JEREMIAH, SHE'S BURNING UP.
DRINK WATER. YOU'RE PROBABLY DEHYDRATED.
I'VE NEVER BEEN SICK BEFORE. I DON'T THINK ANYONE IN MY FAMILY HAS EVER BEEN SICK. PARTLY BECAUSE MY DAD DOESN'T BELIEVE IN IT.

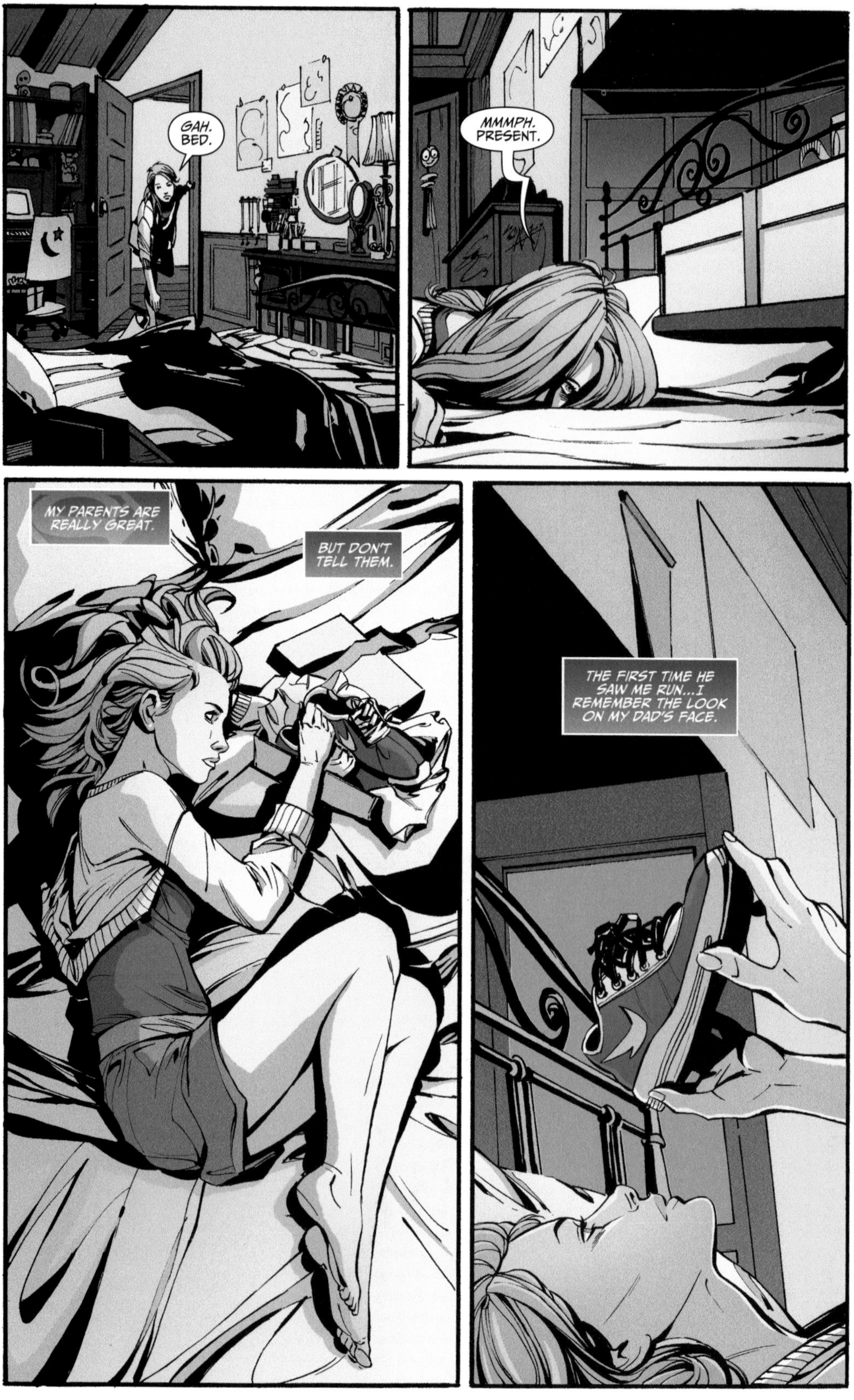
GAH. BED.
MMMPH. PRESENT.
MY PARENTS ARE REALLY GREAT.
BUT DON'T TELL THEM.
THE FIRST TIME HE SAW ME RUN...I REMEMBER THE LOOK ON MY DAD'S FACE.

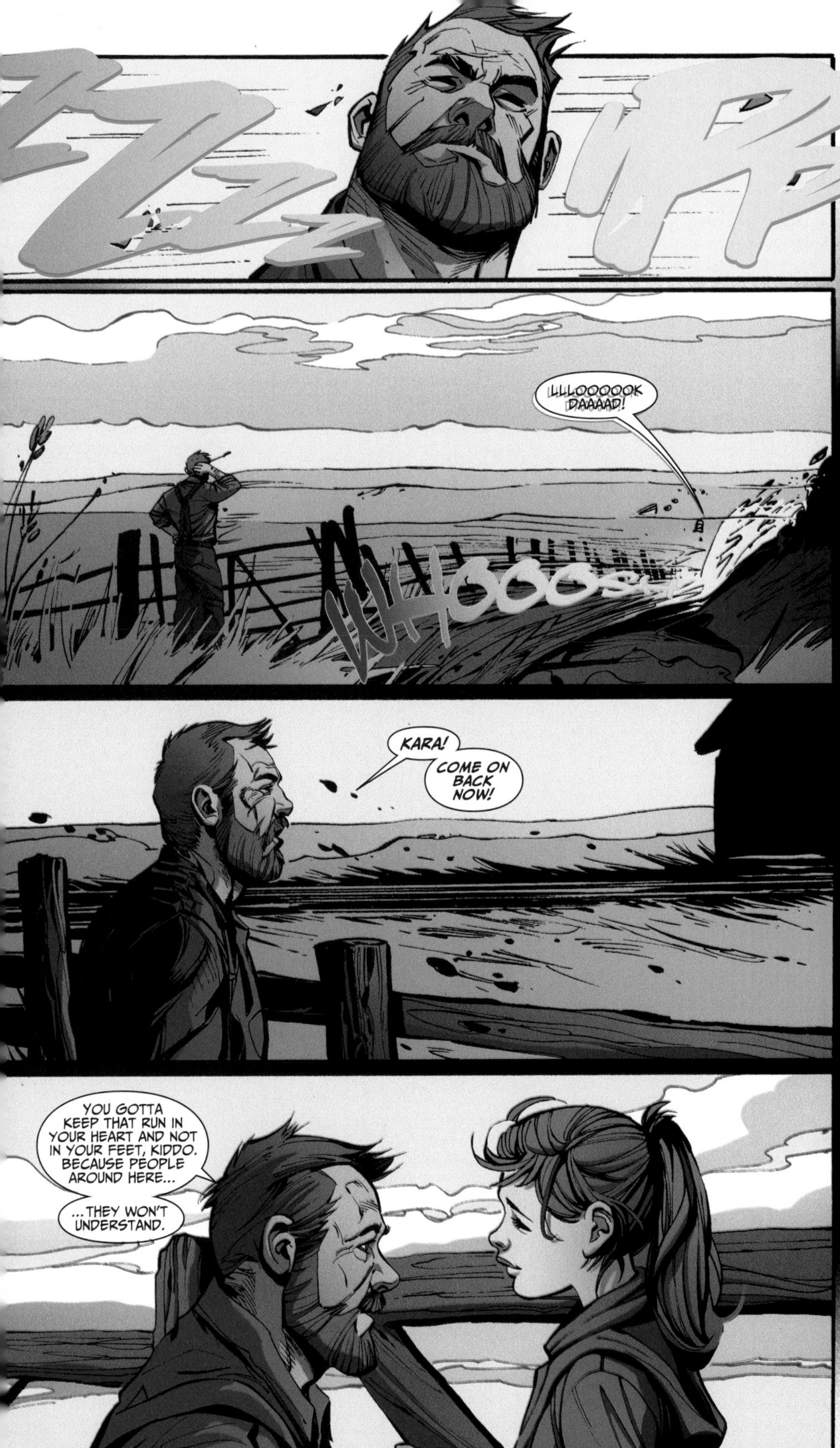
LLLOOOOOK DAAAAD!
KARA!
COME ON BACK NOW!
YOU GOTTA KEEP THAT RUN IN YOUR HEART AND NOT IN YOUR FEET, KIDDO. BECAUSE PEOPLE AROUND HERE...
...THEY WON'T UNDERSTAND.

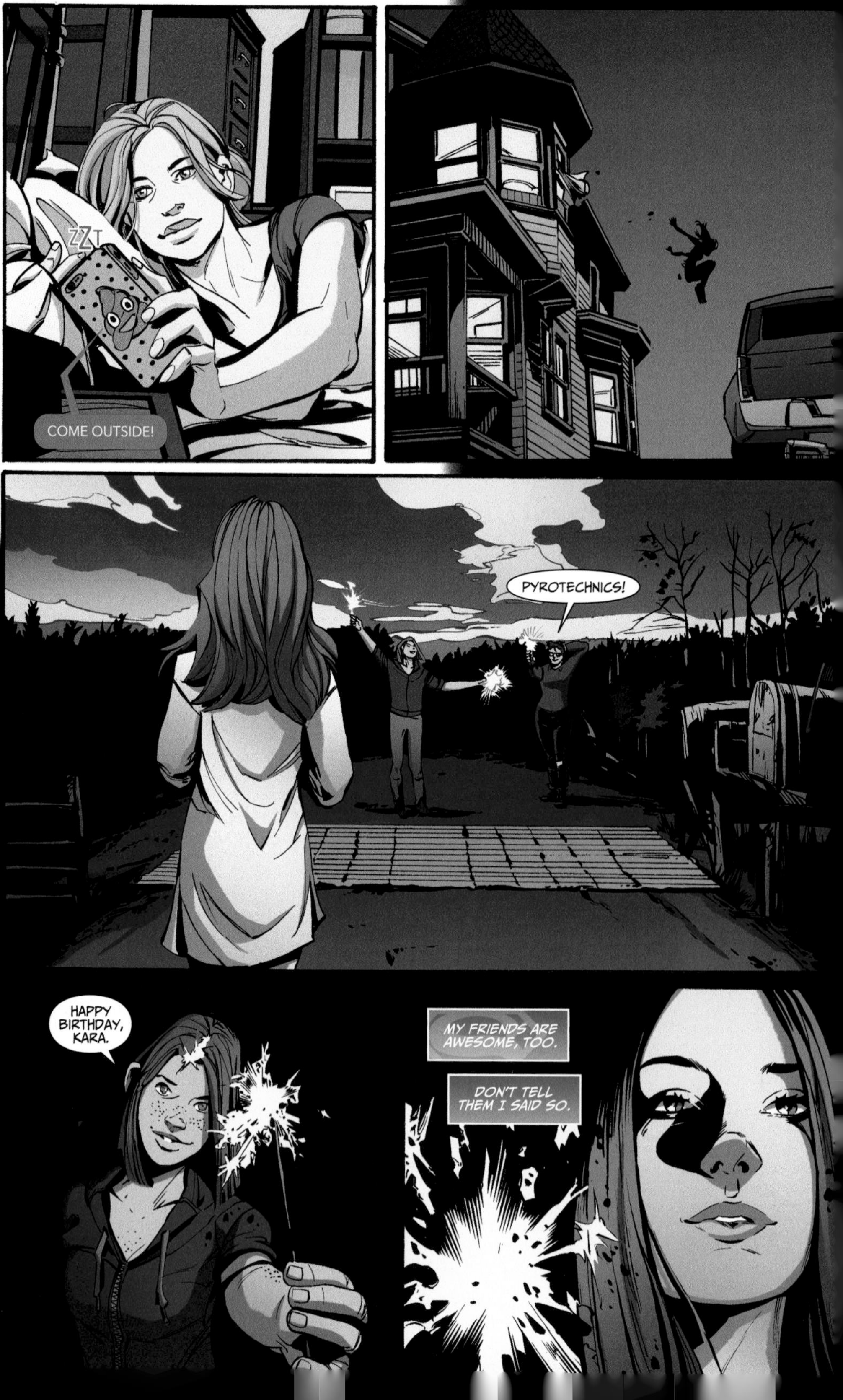
ZZT
COME OUTSIDE!
PYROTECHNICS!
HAPPY BIRTHDAY, KARA.
MY FRIENDS ARE AWESOME, TOO.
DON'T TELL THEM I SAID SO.

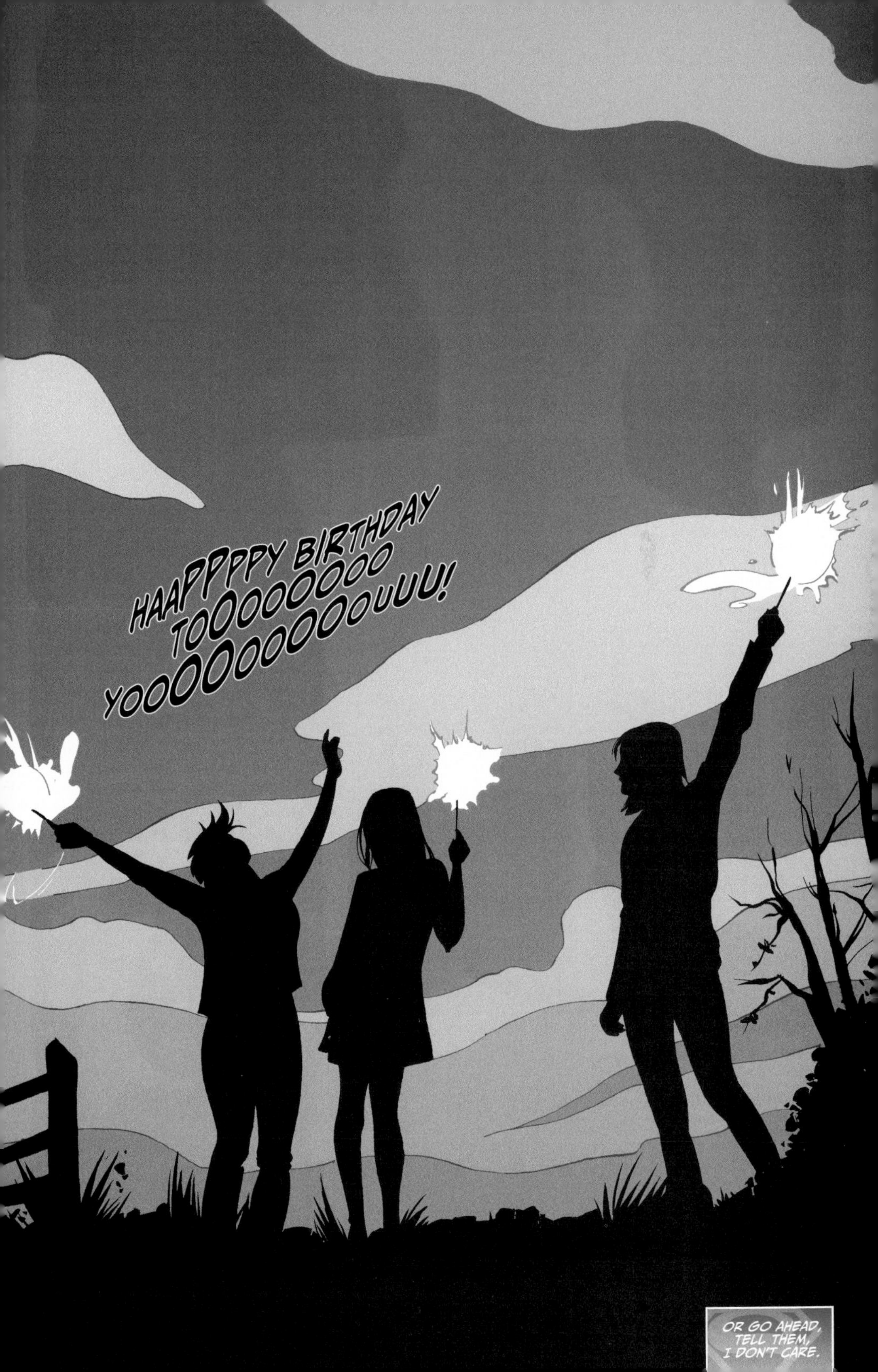
HAAPPPPPY BIRTHDAY TOOOOOOOOO YOOOOOOOOOOOuuu!
OR GO AHEAD, TELL THEM, I DON'T CARE.

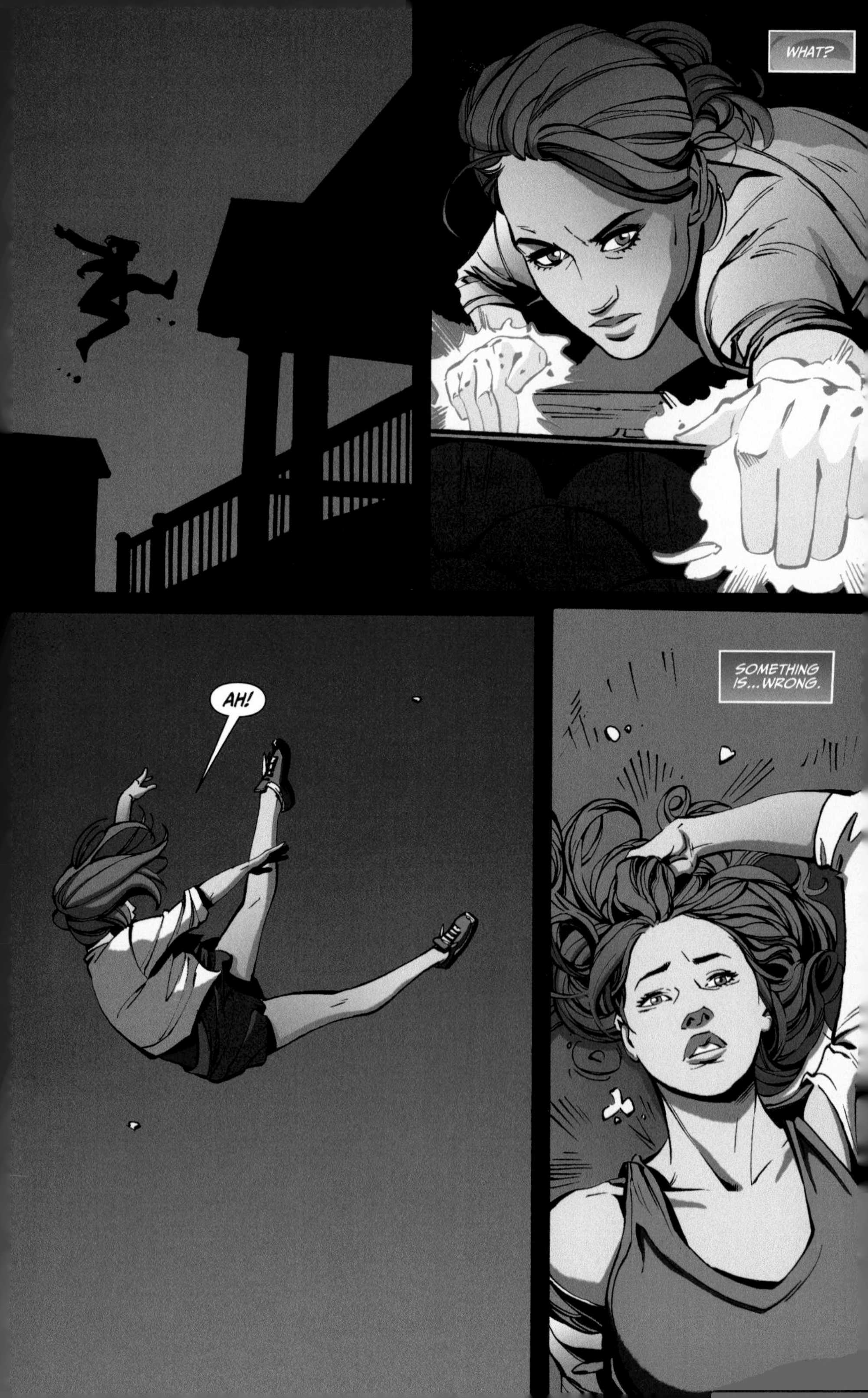
WHAT?
AH!
SOMETHING IS...WRONG.

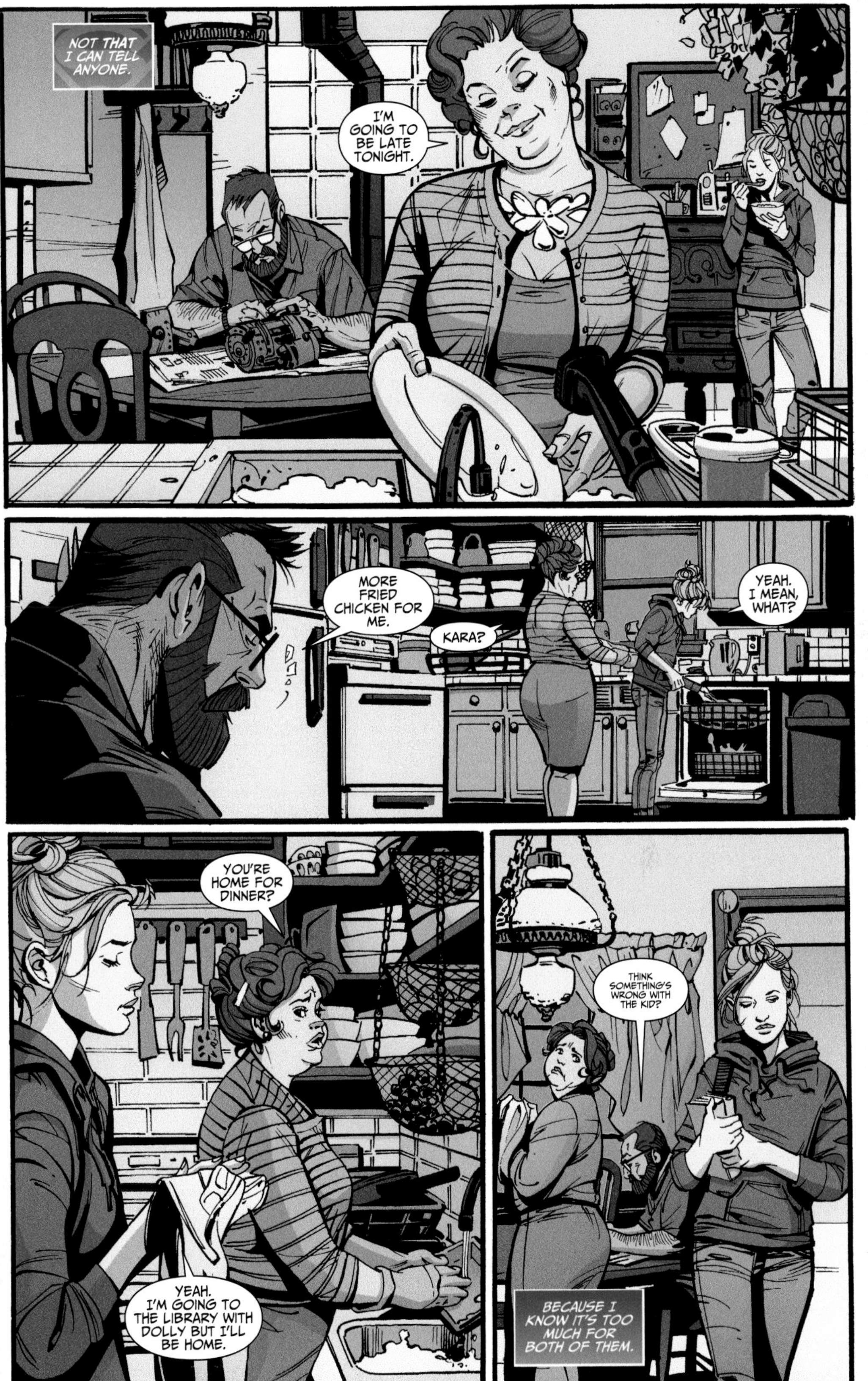
NOT THAT I CAN TELL ANYONE.
I'M GOING TO BE LATE TONIGHT.
MORE FRIED CHICKEN FOR ME.
KARA?
YEAH. I MEAN, WHAT?
YOU'RE HOME FOR DINNER?
YEAH. I'M GOING TO THE LIBRARY WITH DOLLY BUT I'LL BE HOME.
THINK SOMETHING'S WRONG WITH THE KID?
BECAUSE I KNOW IT'S TOO MUCH FOR BOTH OF THEM.

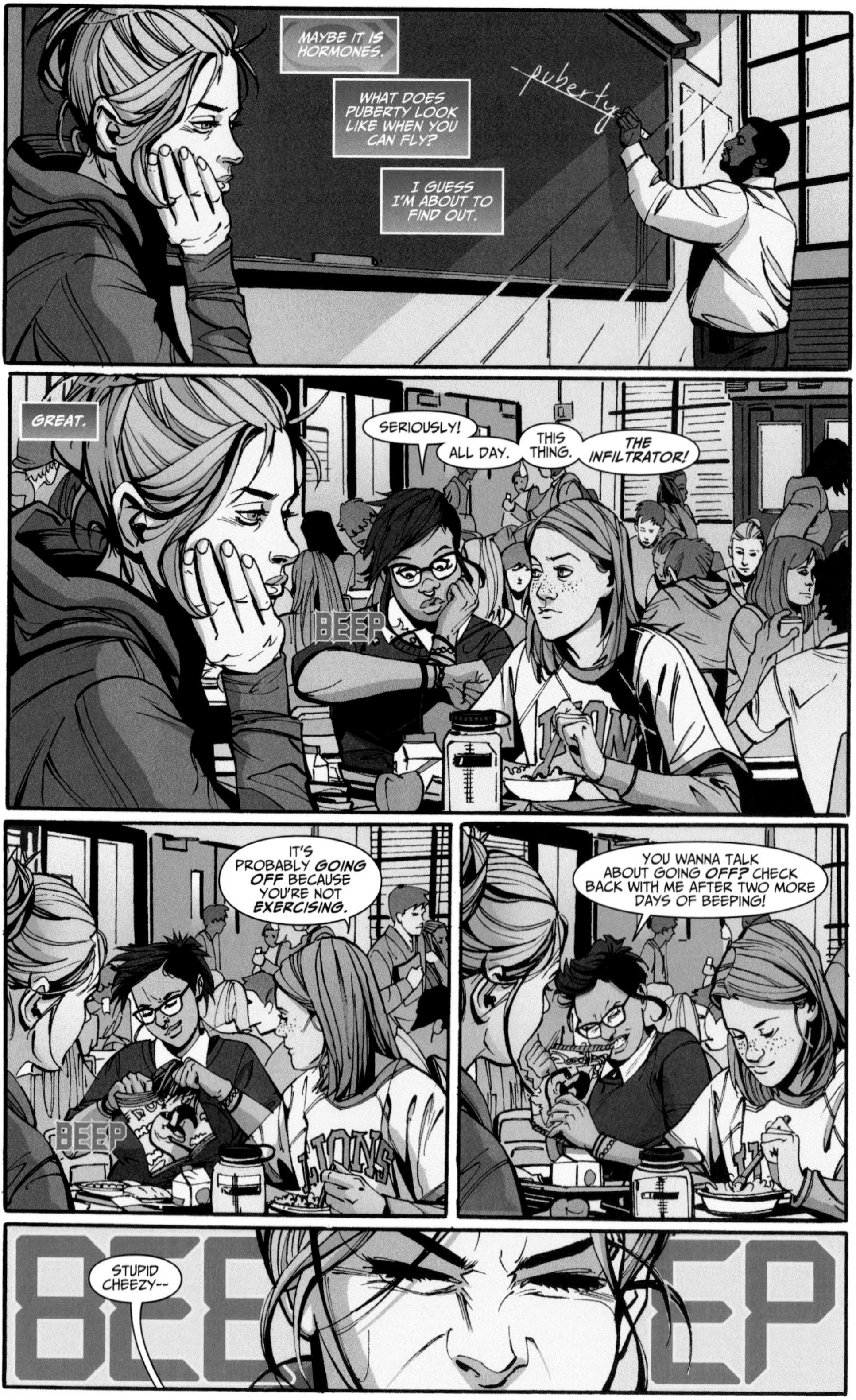
MAYBE IT IS HORMONES.
WHAT DOES PUBERTY LOOK LIKE WHEN YOU CAN FLY?
I GUESS I'M ABOUT TO FIND OUT.
puberty
GREAT.
SERIOUSLY!
ALL DAY.
THIS THING.
THE INFILTRATOR!
BEEP
IT'S PROBABLY GOING OFF BECAUSE YOU'RE NOT EXERCISING.
BEEP
YOU WANNA TALK ABOUT GOING OFF? CHECK BACK WITH ME AFTER TWO MORE DAYS OF BEEPING!
STUPID CHEEZY--
BEEEP

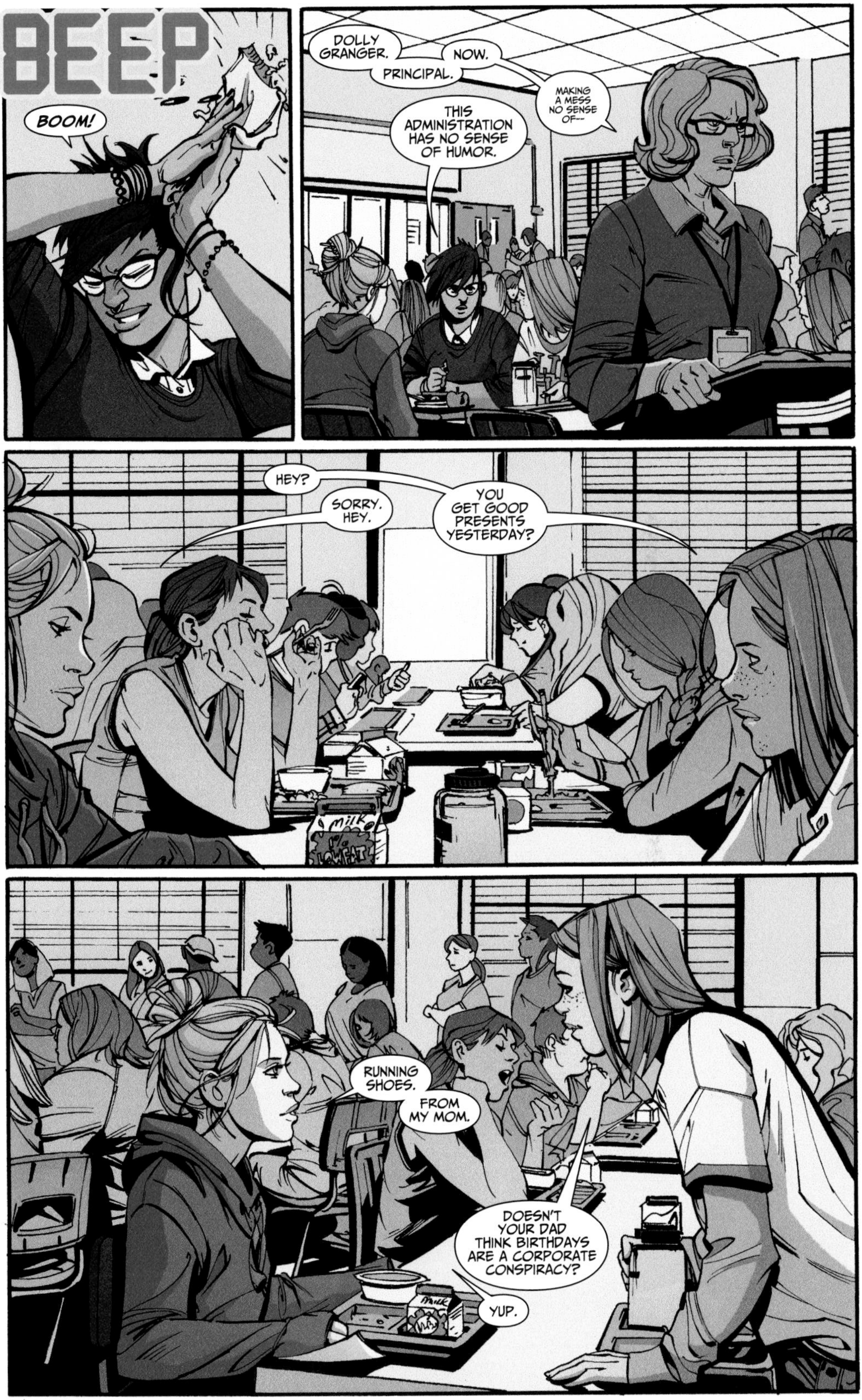
BEEP
BOOM!
DOLLY GRANGER.
PRINCIPAL.
NOW.
MAKING A MESS NO SENSE OF--
THIS ADMINISTRATION HAS NO SENSE OF HUMOR.
HEY?
SORRY. HEY.
YOU GET GOOD PRESENTS YESTERDAY?
MILK 1% LOWFAT
RUNNING SHOES.
FROM MY MOM.
DOESN'T YOUR DAD THINK BIRTHDAYS ARE A CORPORATE CONSPIRACY?
YUP.

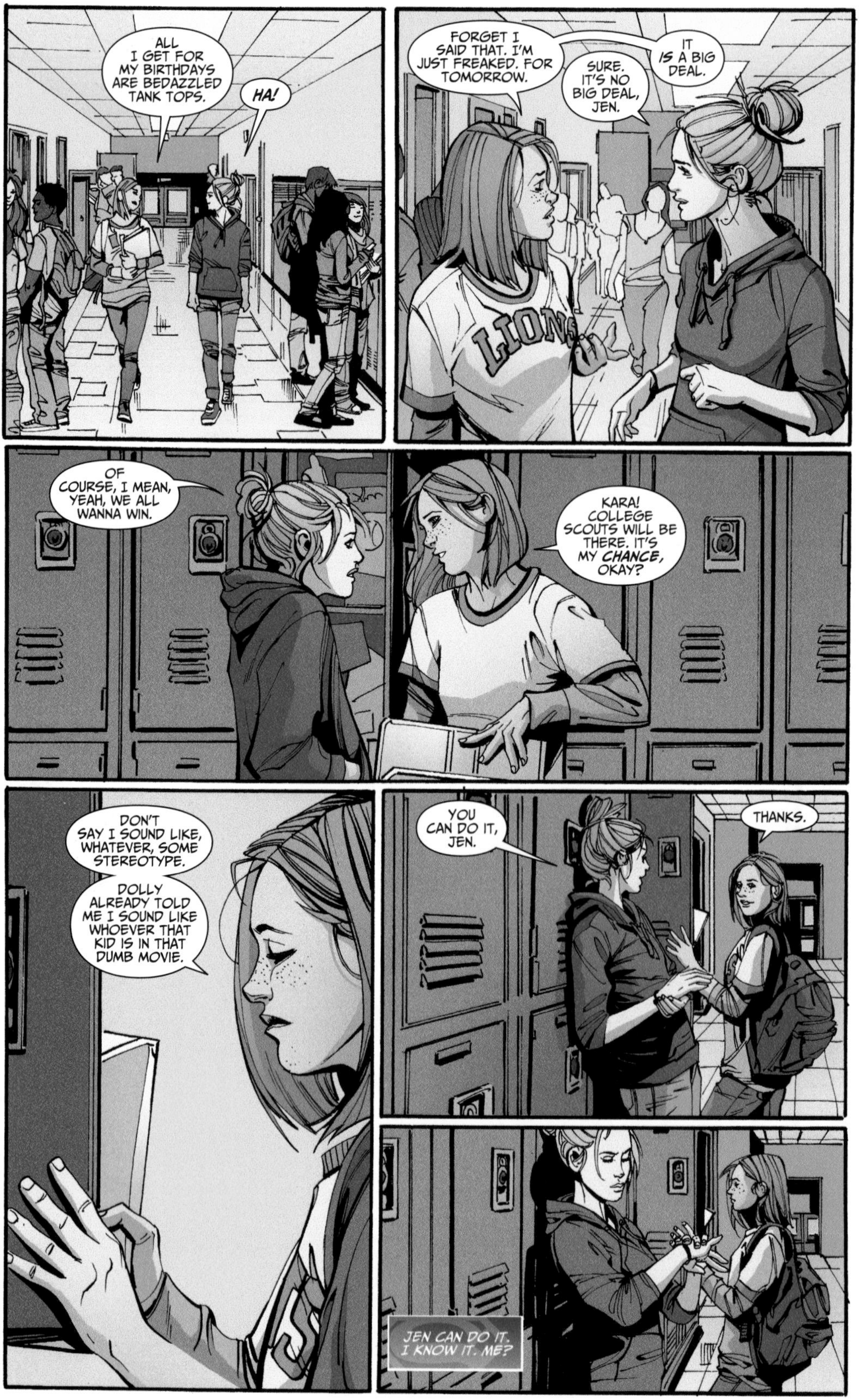
ALL I GET FOR MY BIRTHDAYS ARE BEDAZZLED TANK TOPS.
HA!
FORGET I SAID THAT. I'M JUST FREAKED. FOR TOMORROW.
SURE. IT'S NO BIG DEAL, JEN.
IT IS A BIG DEAL.
LIONS
OF COURSE, I MEAN, YEAH, WE ALL WANNA WIN.
KARA! COLLEGE SCOUTS WILL BE THERE. IT'S MY CHANCE, OKAY?
DON'T SAY I SOUND LIKE, WHATEVER, SOME STEREOTYPE.
DOLLY ALREADY TOLD ME I SOUND LIKE WHOEVER THAT KID IS IN THAT DUMB MOVIE.
YOU CAN DO IT, JEN.
THANKS.
JEN CAN DO IT. I KNOW IT. ME?

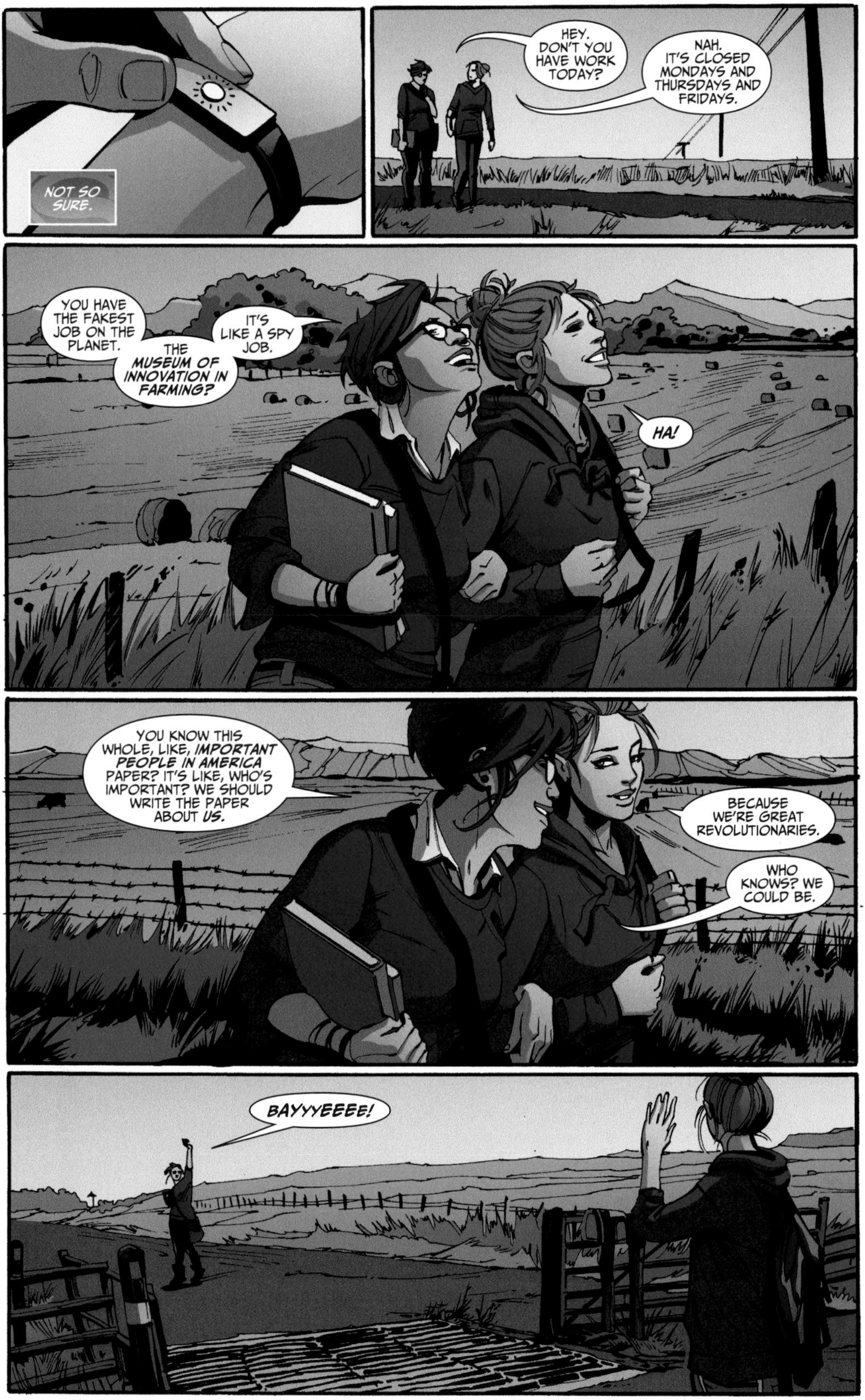
NOT SO SURE.
HEY. DON'T YOU HAVE WORK TODAY?
NAH. IT'S CLOSED MONDAYS AND THURSDAYS AND FRIDAYS.
YOU HAVE THE FAKEST JOB ON THE PLANET.
THE *MUSEUM OF INNOVATION IN FARMING?*
IT'S LIKE A SPY JOB.
HA!
YOU KNOW THIS WHOLE, LIKE, *IMPORTANT PEOPLE IN AMERICA* PAPER? IT'S LIKE, WHO'S IMPORTANT? WE SHOULD WRITE THE PAPER ABOUT *US.*
BECAUSE WE'RE GREAT REVOLUTIONARIES.
WHO KNOWS? WE COULD BE.
BAYYYEEEE!

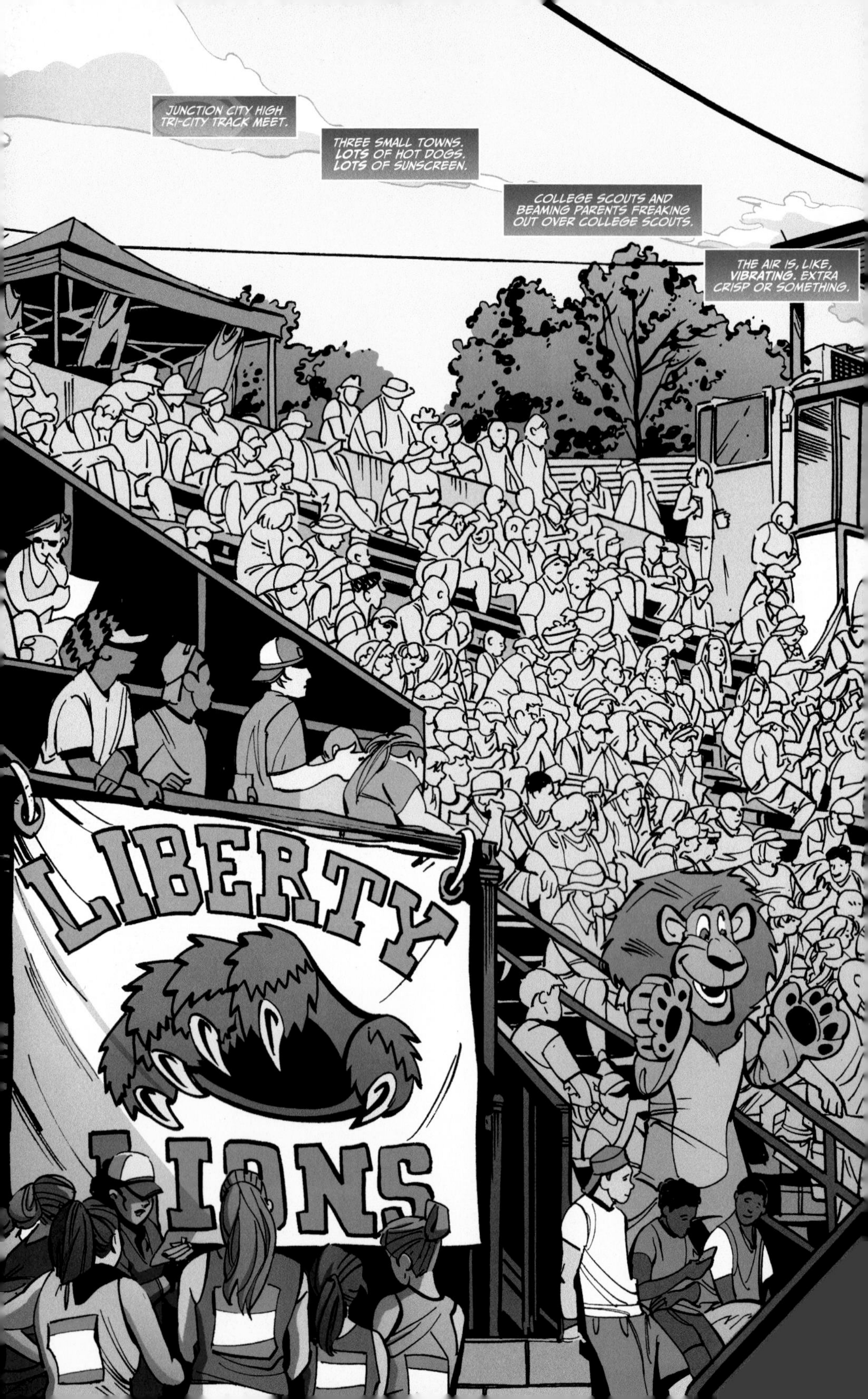
JUNCTION CITY HIGH
TRI-CITY TRACK MEET.
THREE SMALL TOWNS.
LOTS OF HOT DOGS.
LOTS OF SUNSCREEN.
COLLEGE SCOUTS AND
BEAMING PARENTS FREAKING
OUT OVER COLLEGE SCOUTS.
THE AIR IS, LIKE,
VIBRATING. EXTRA
CRISP OR SOMETHING.
LIBERTY
LIONS

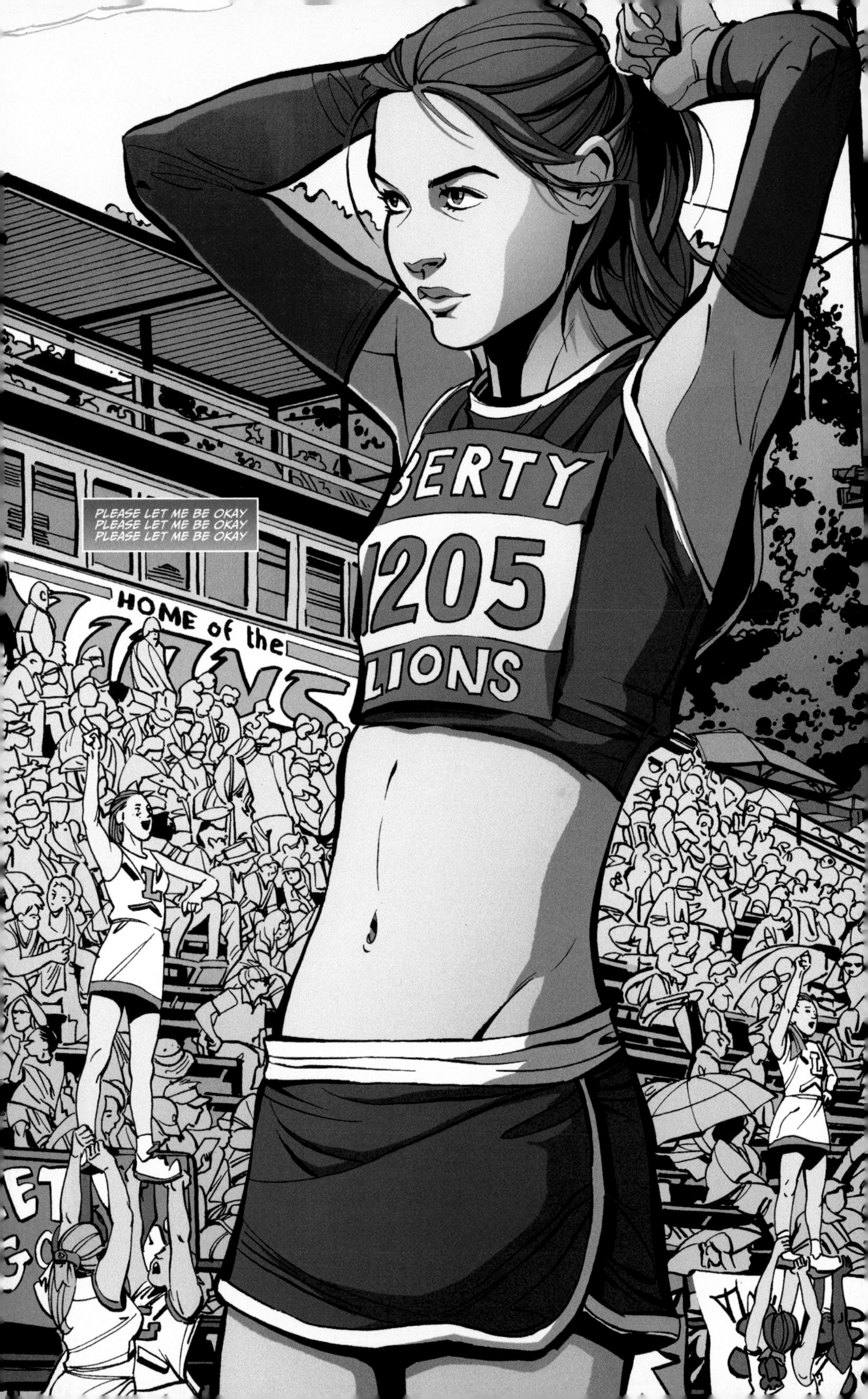
PLEASE LET ME BE OKAY
PLEASE LET ME BE OKAY
PLEASE LET ME BE OKAY
HOME of the
BERTY
1205
LIONS

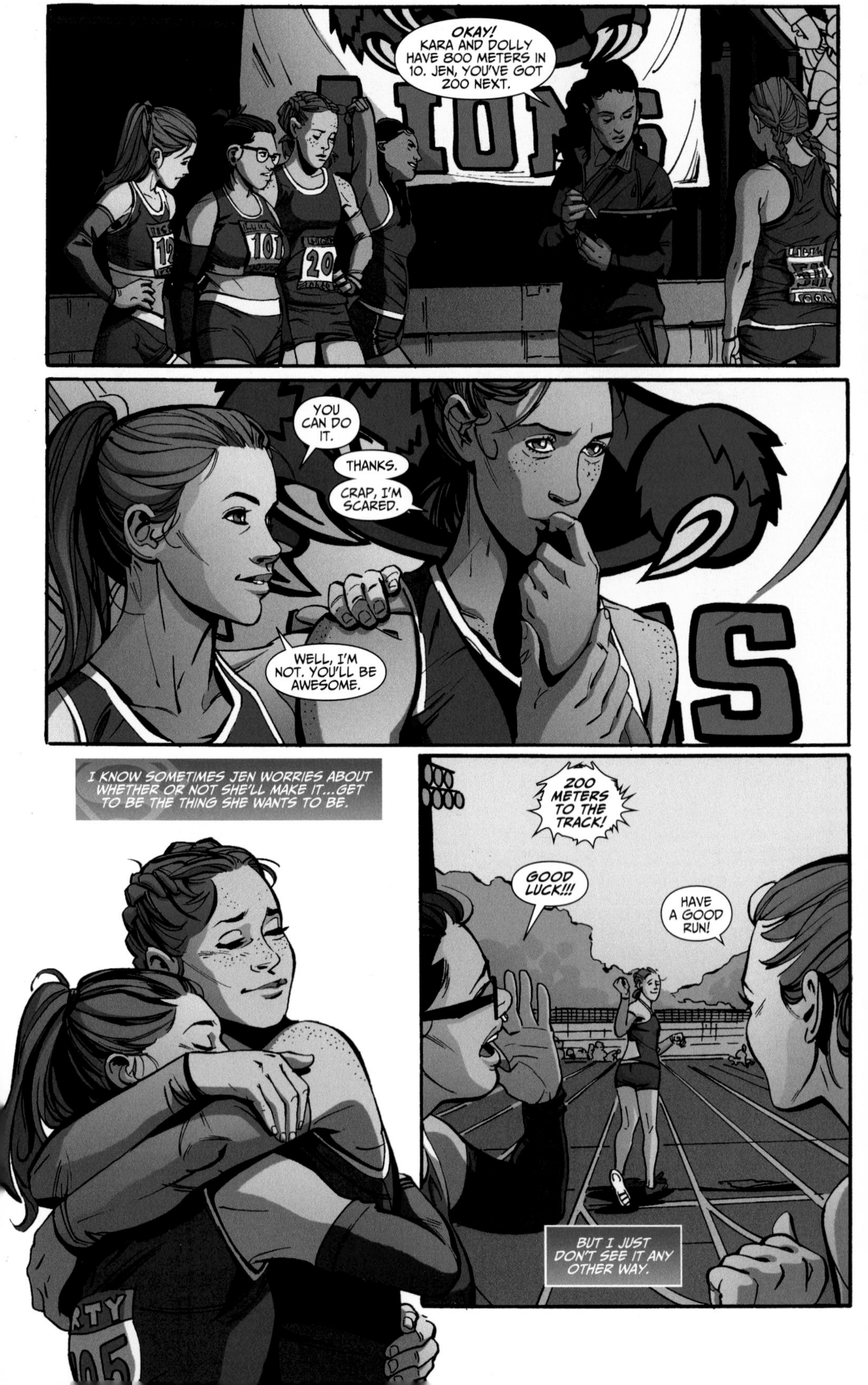
OKAY!
KARA AND DOLLY HAVE 800 METERS IN 10. JEN, YOU'VE GOT 200 NEXT.
YOU CAN DO IT.
THANKS.
CRAP, I'M SCARED.
WELL, I'M NOT. YOU'LL BE AWESOME.
I KNOW SOMETIMES JEN WORRIES ABOUT WHETHER OR NOT SHE'LL MAKE IT...GET TO BE THE THING SHE WANTS TO BE.
200 METERS TO THE TRACK!
GOOD LUCK!!!
HAVE A GOOD RUN!
BUT I JUST DON'T SEE IT ANY OTHER WAY.

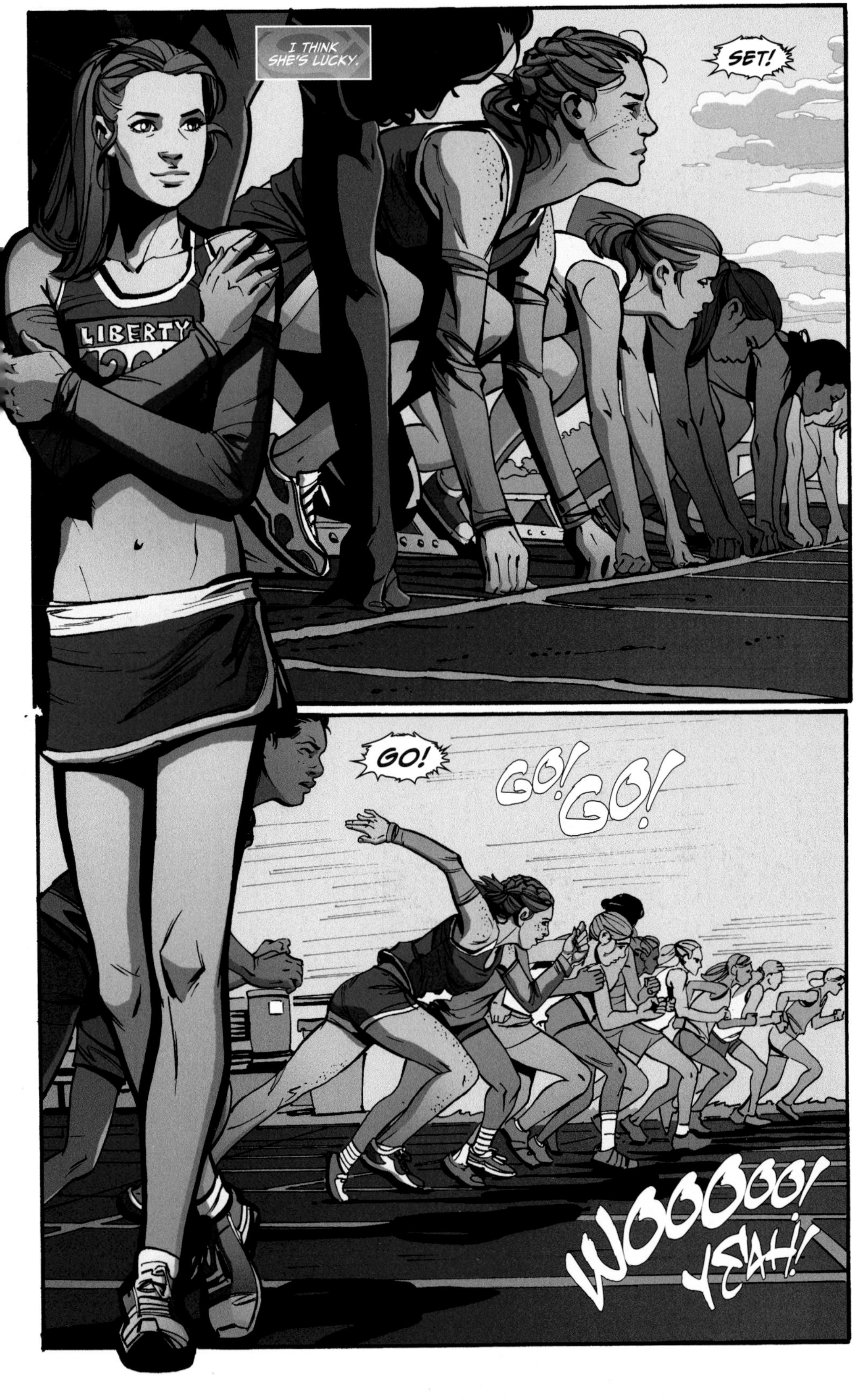
I THINK SHE'S LUCKY.
SET!
LIBERTY
GO!
GO! GO!
WOOOOO! YEAH!

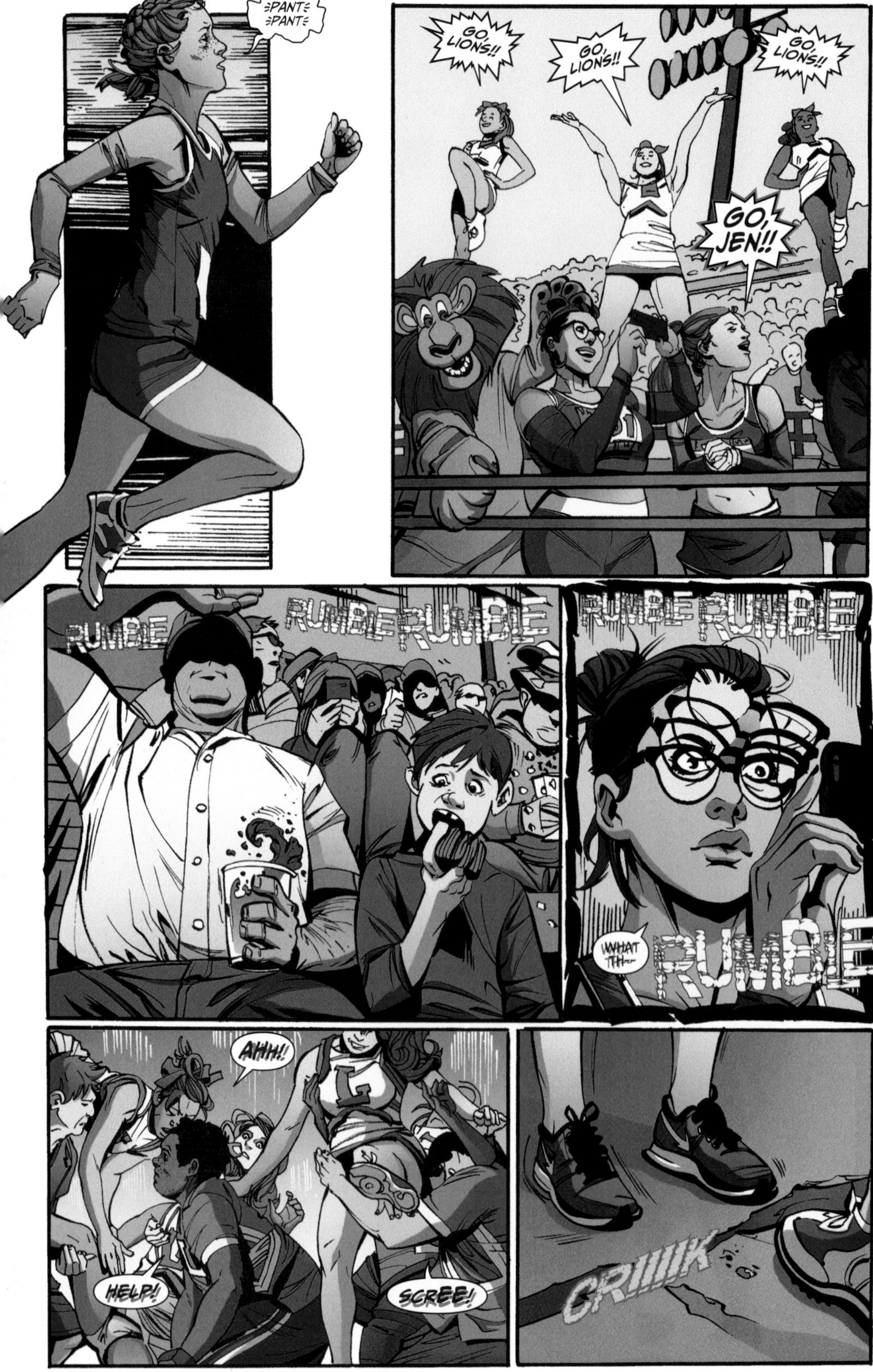
PANT PANT
GO, LIONS!!
GO, LIONS!!
GO, LIONS!!
GO, JEN!!
RUMBLE RUMBLE RUMBLE
RUMBLE RUMBLE
WHAT TH--
RUMBLE
AHH!!
HELP!
SCREE!
CRIIIIK

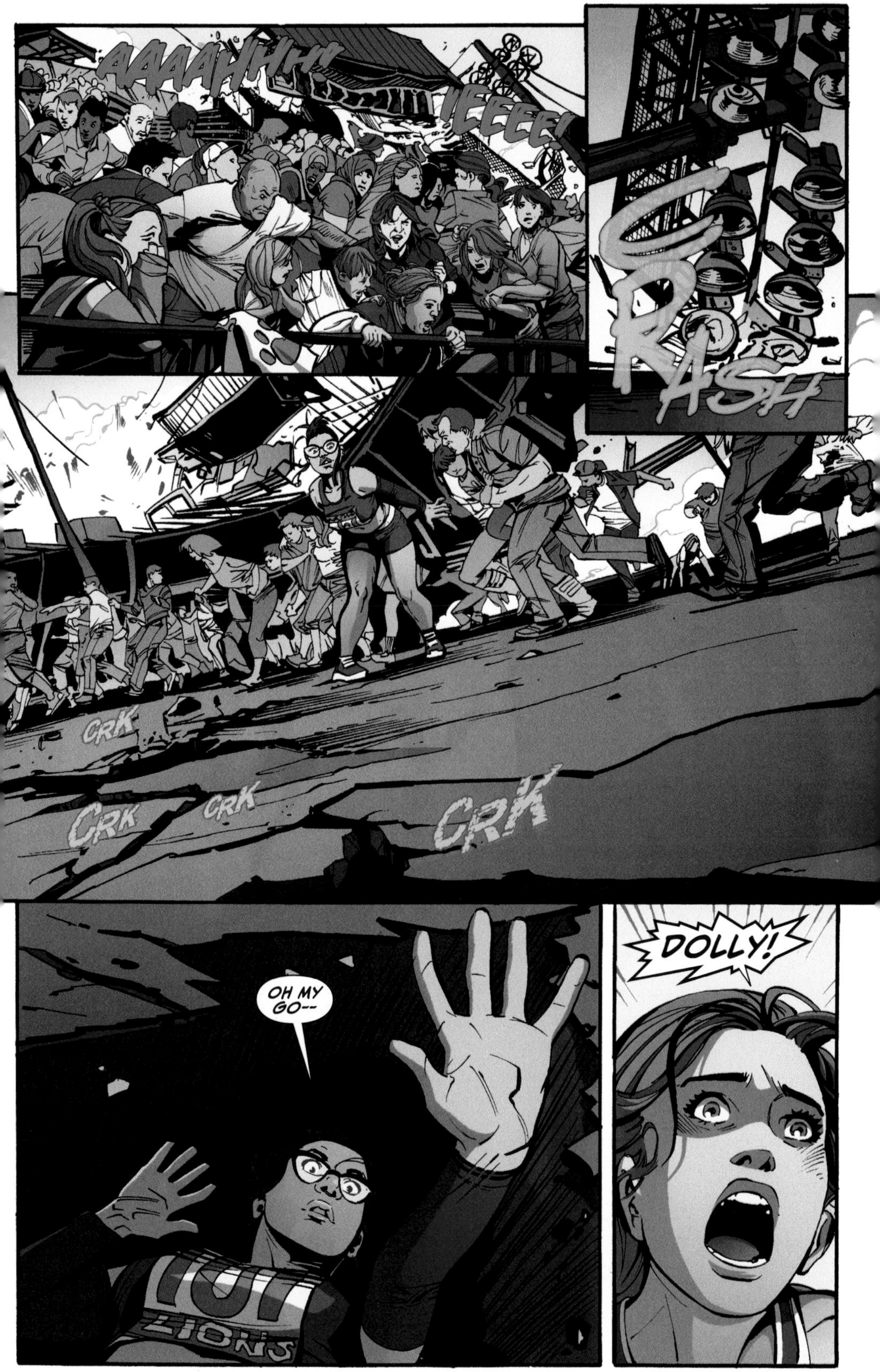
AAAAHHH!!
IEEEEE!
CRASH
CRK
CRK
CRK
CRK
OH MY GO--
DOLLY!

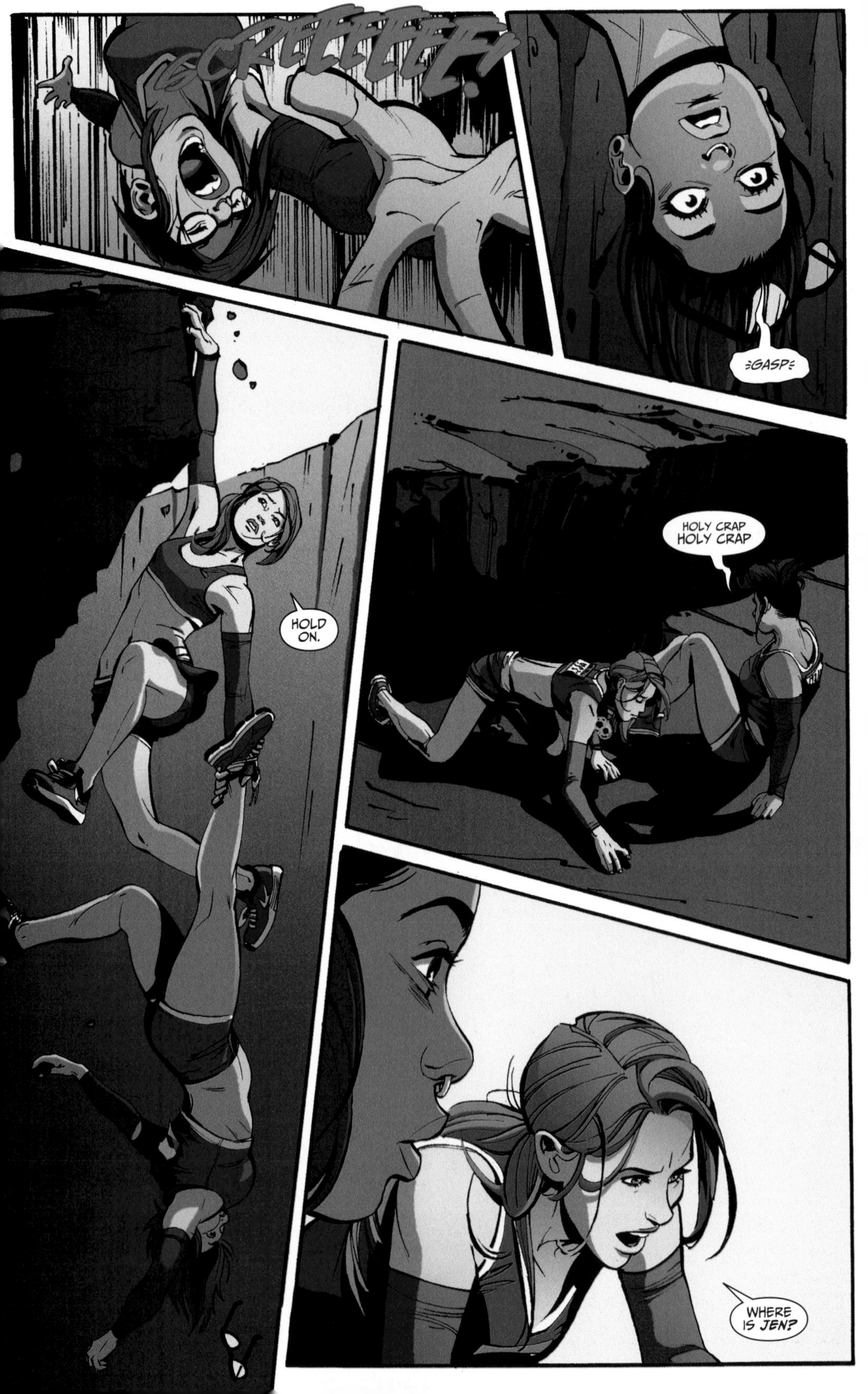
GASP
HOLD ON.
HOLY CRAP
HOLY CRAP
WHERE IS JEN?

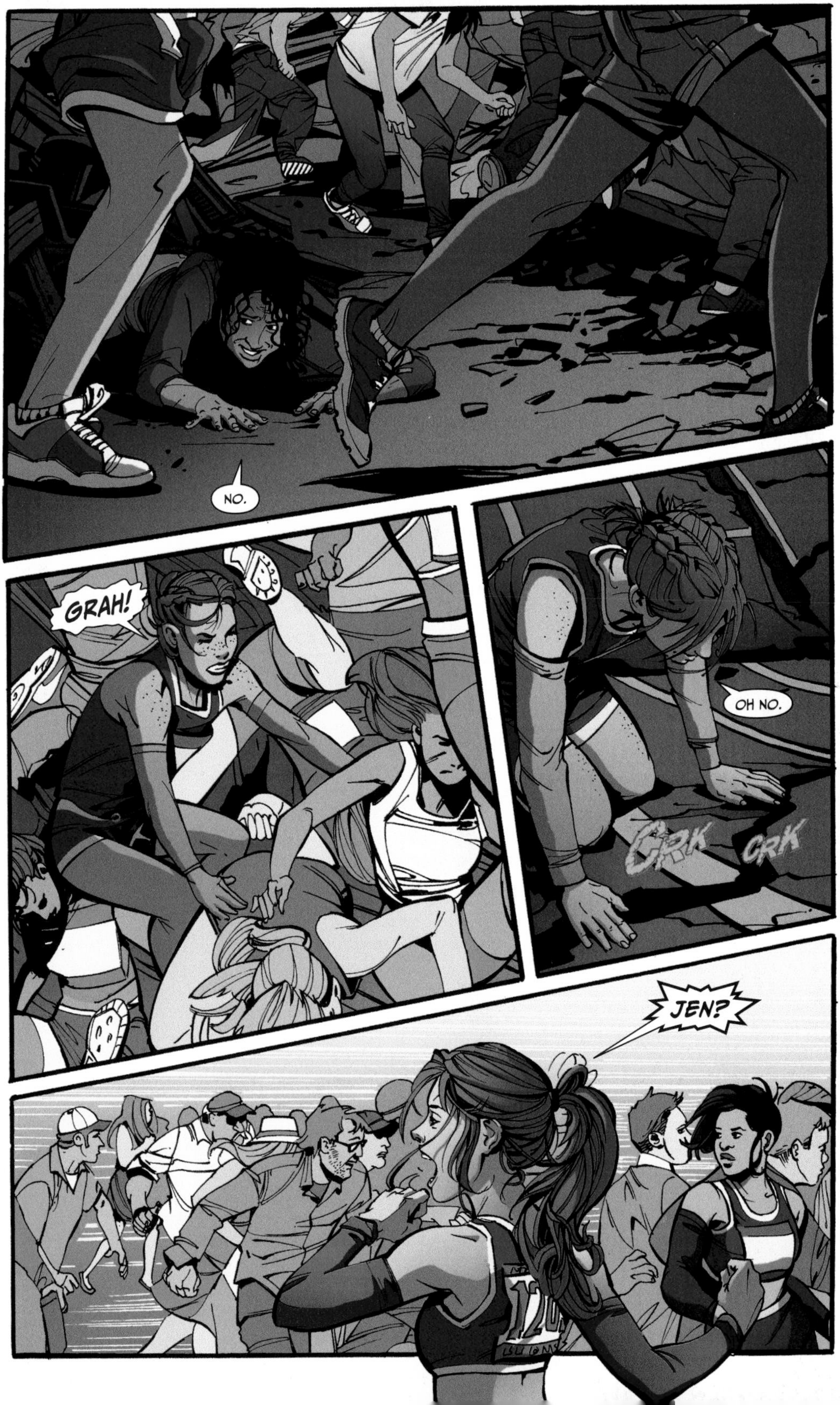
NO.
GRAH!
OH NO.
CRK
CRK
JEN?

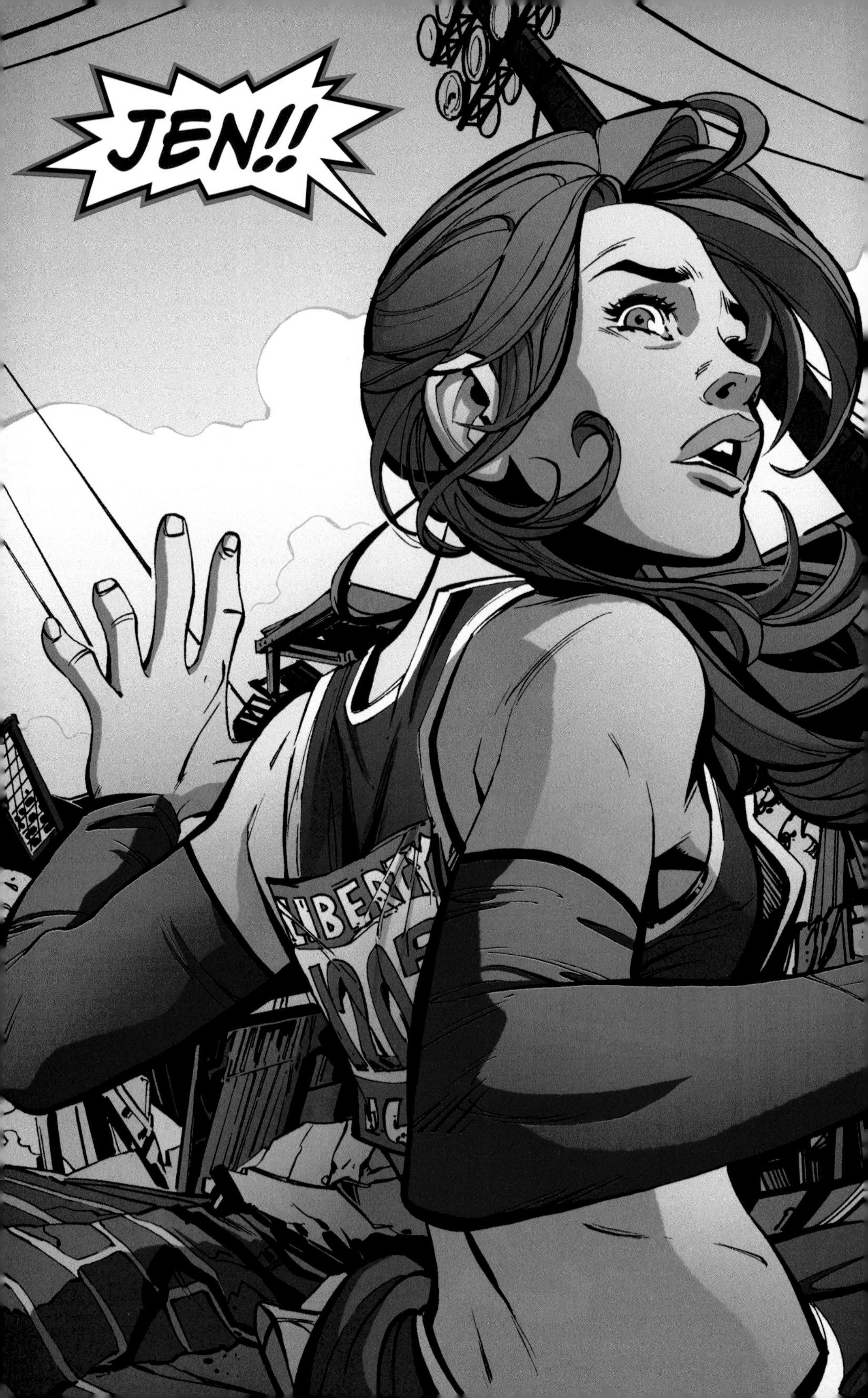
JEN!!

CHAPTER Two:
HOLD ON!

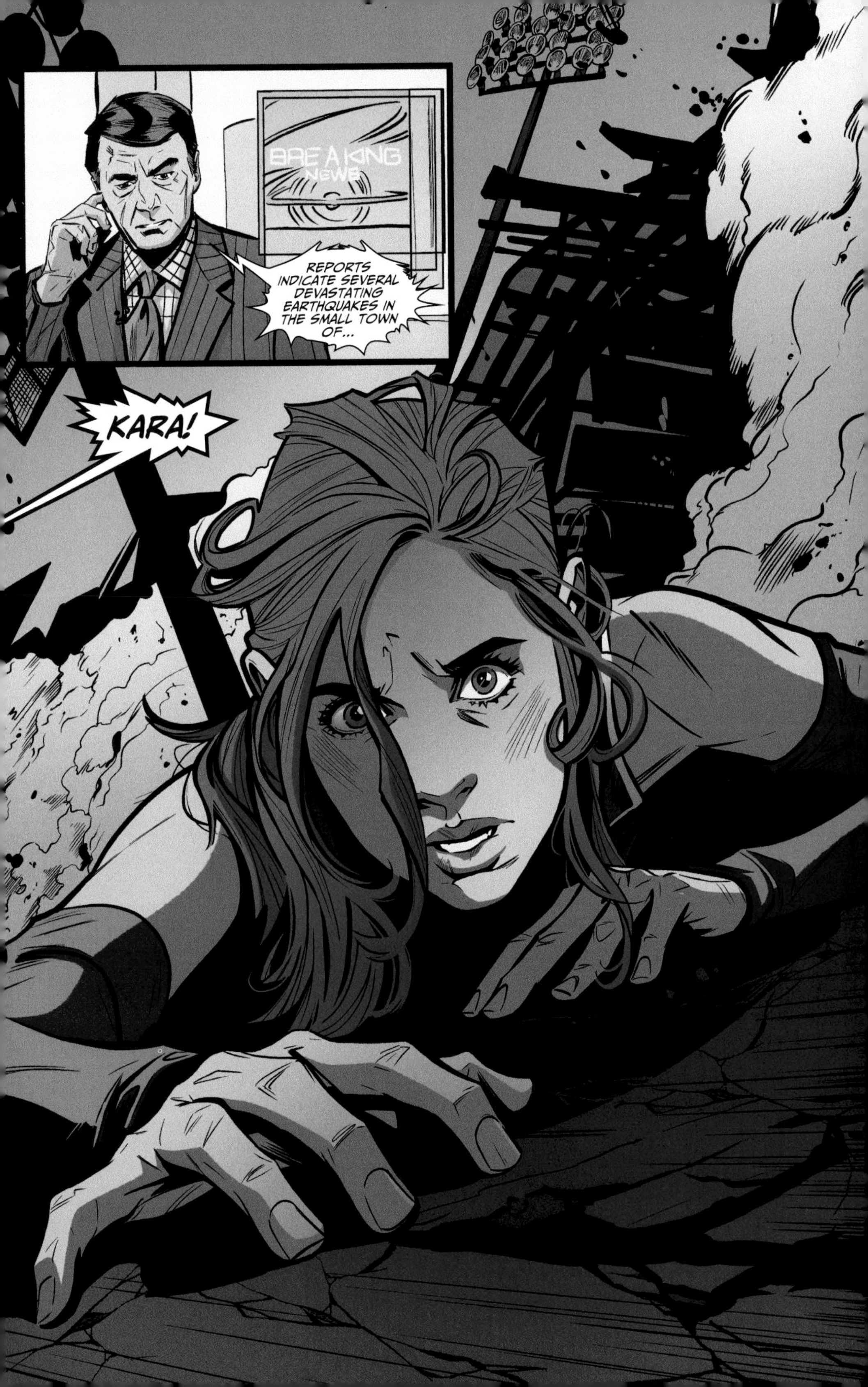
BREAKING NEWS
REPORTS INDICATE SEVERAL DEVASTATING EARTHQUAKES IN THE SMALL TOWN OF...
KARA!

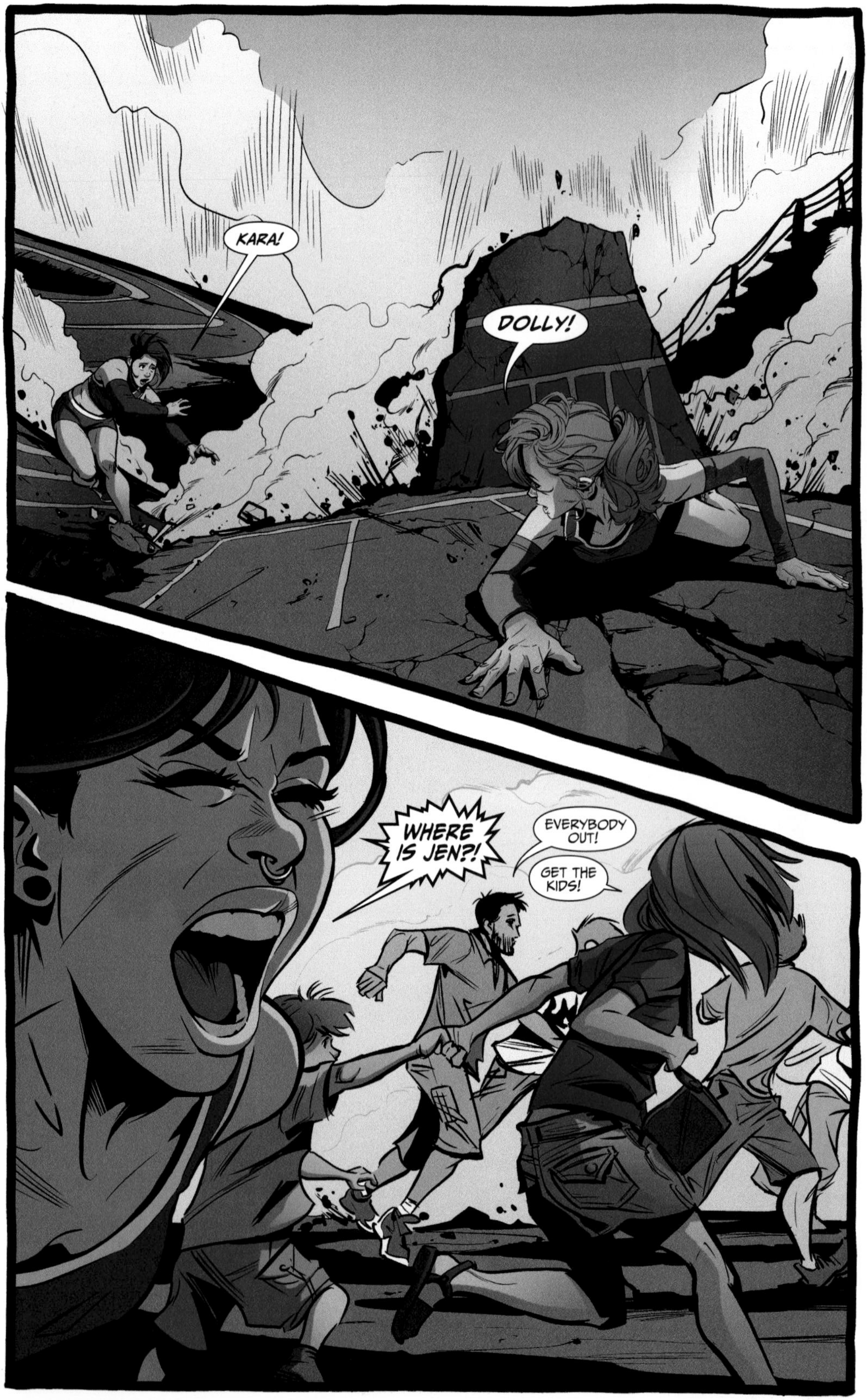
KARA!
DOLLY!
WHERE IS JEN?!
EVERYBODY OUT!
GET THE KIDS!

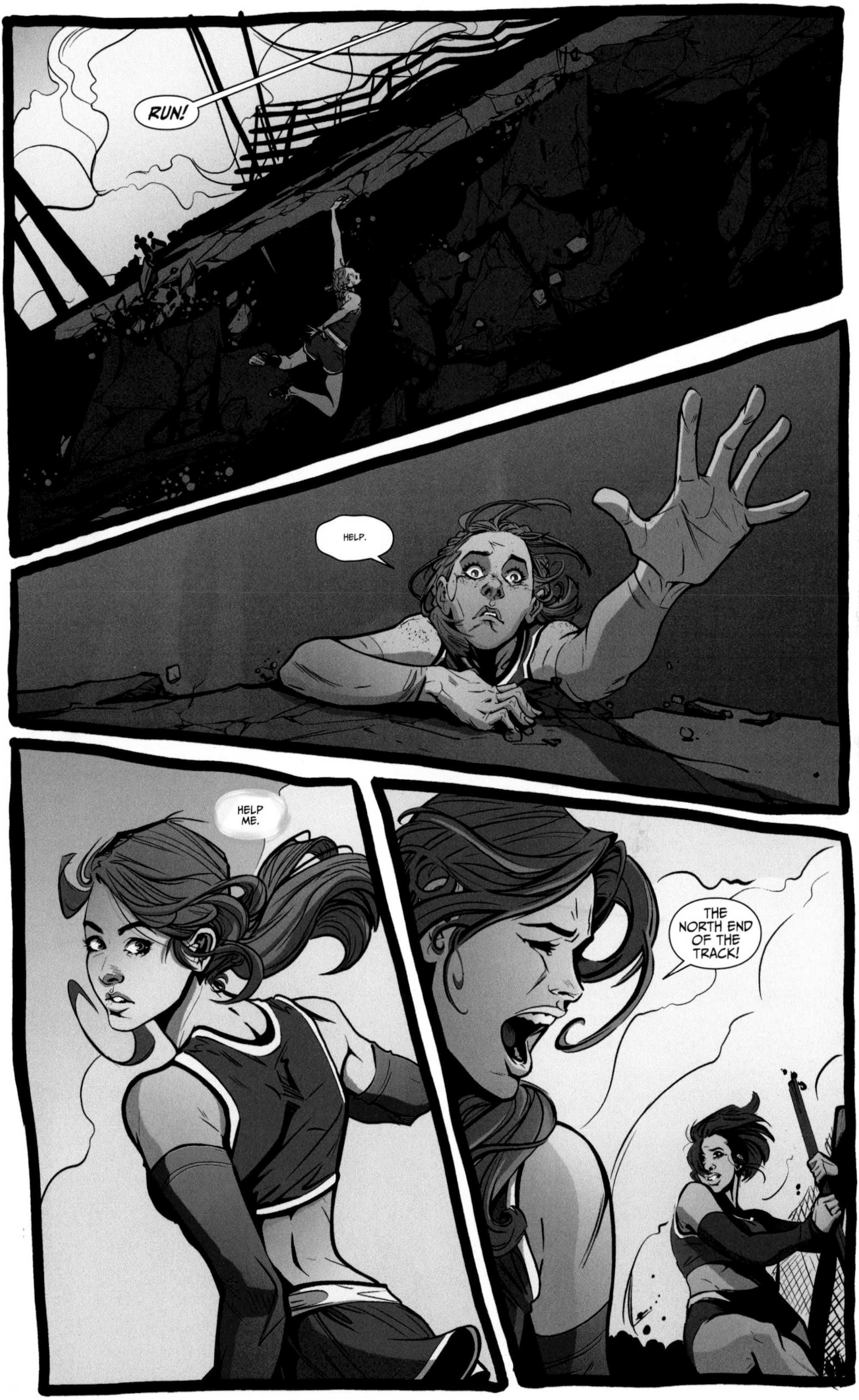
RUN!
HELP.
HELP ME.
THE NORTH END OF THE TRACK!

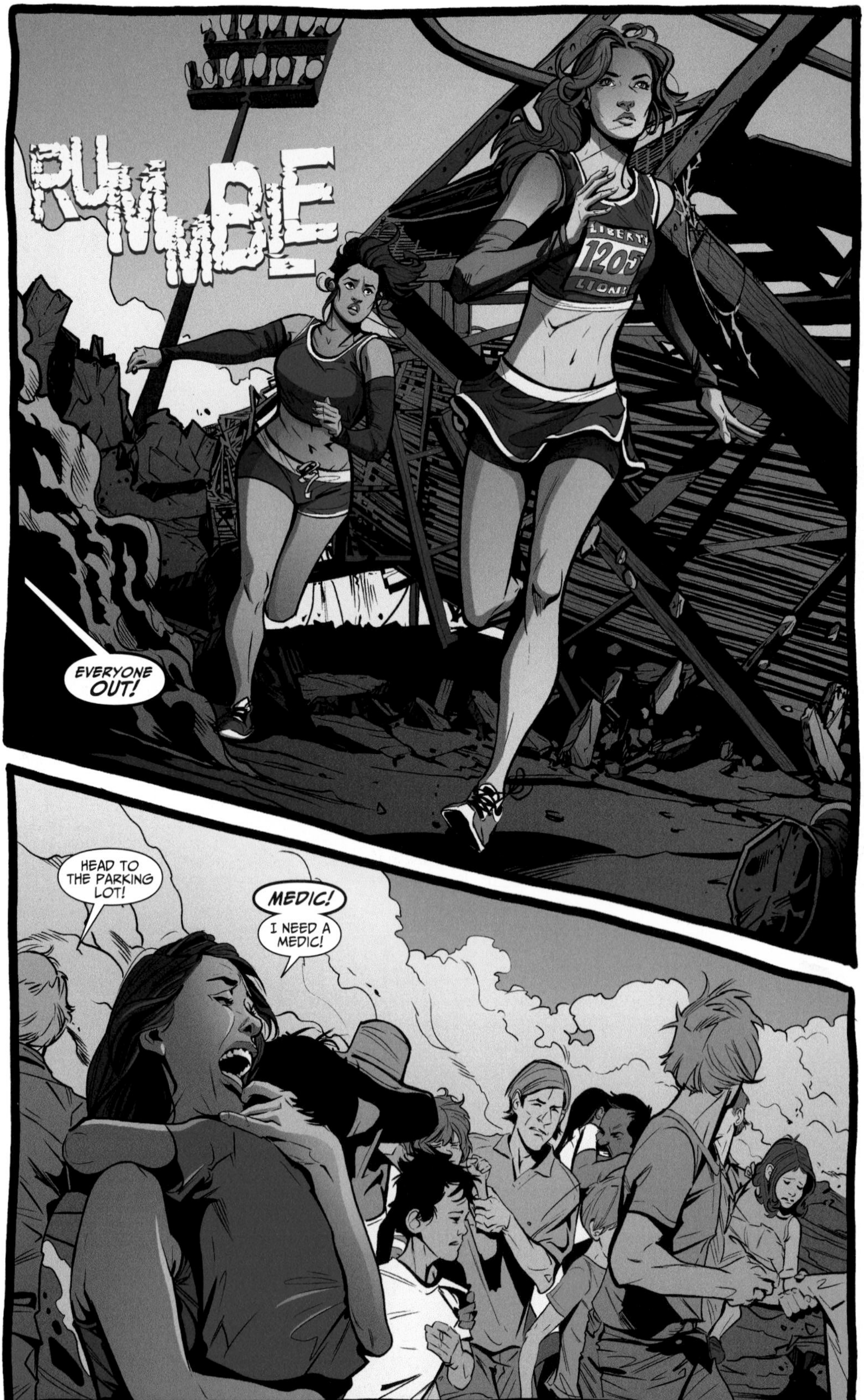
RUMBLE
LIBERTY 1205 LIONS
EVERYONE OUT!
HEAD TO THE PARKING LOT!
MEDIC!
I NEED A MEDIC!

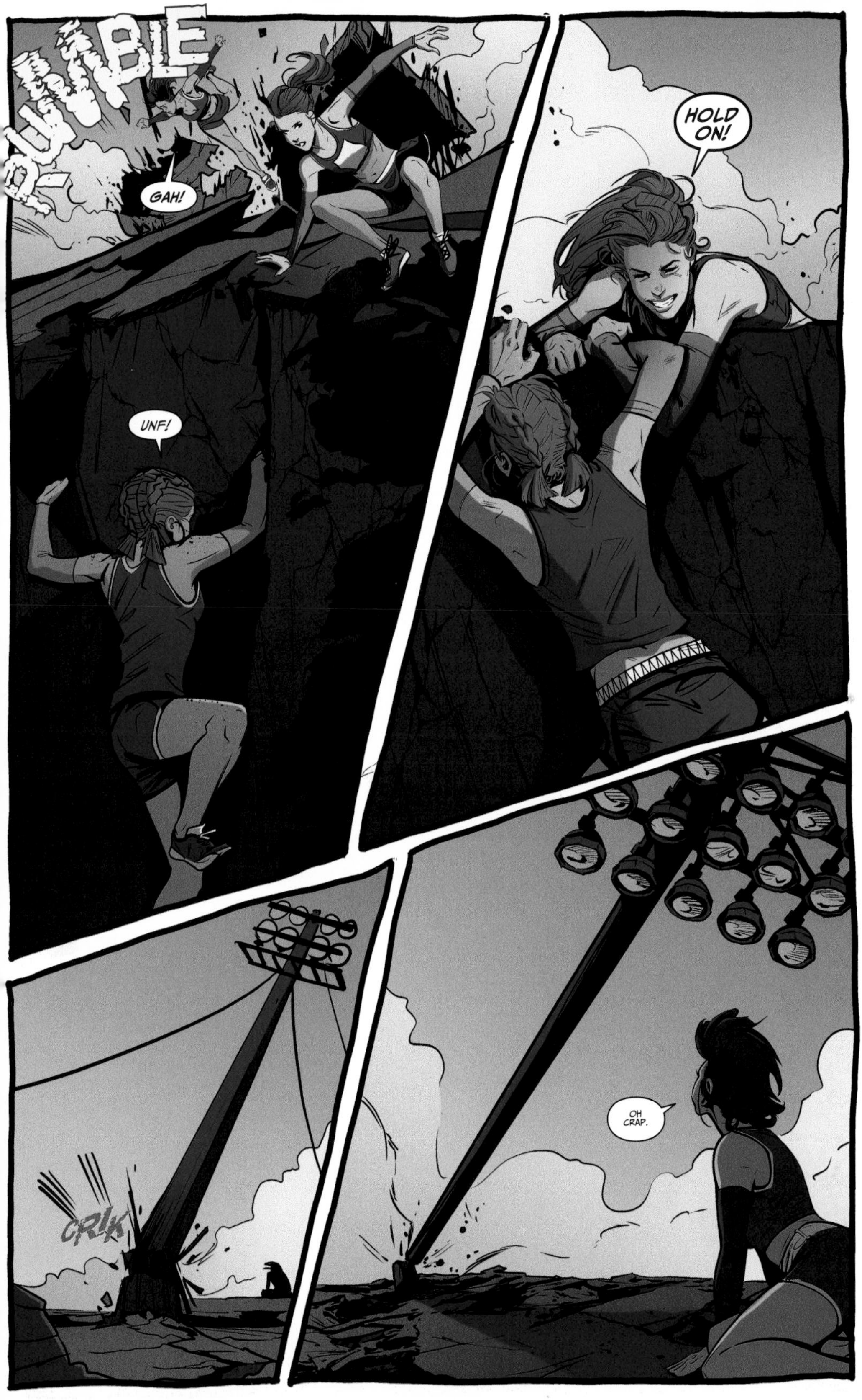
RUMBLE
GAH!
UNF!
HOLD ON!
CRIK
OH CRAP.

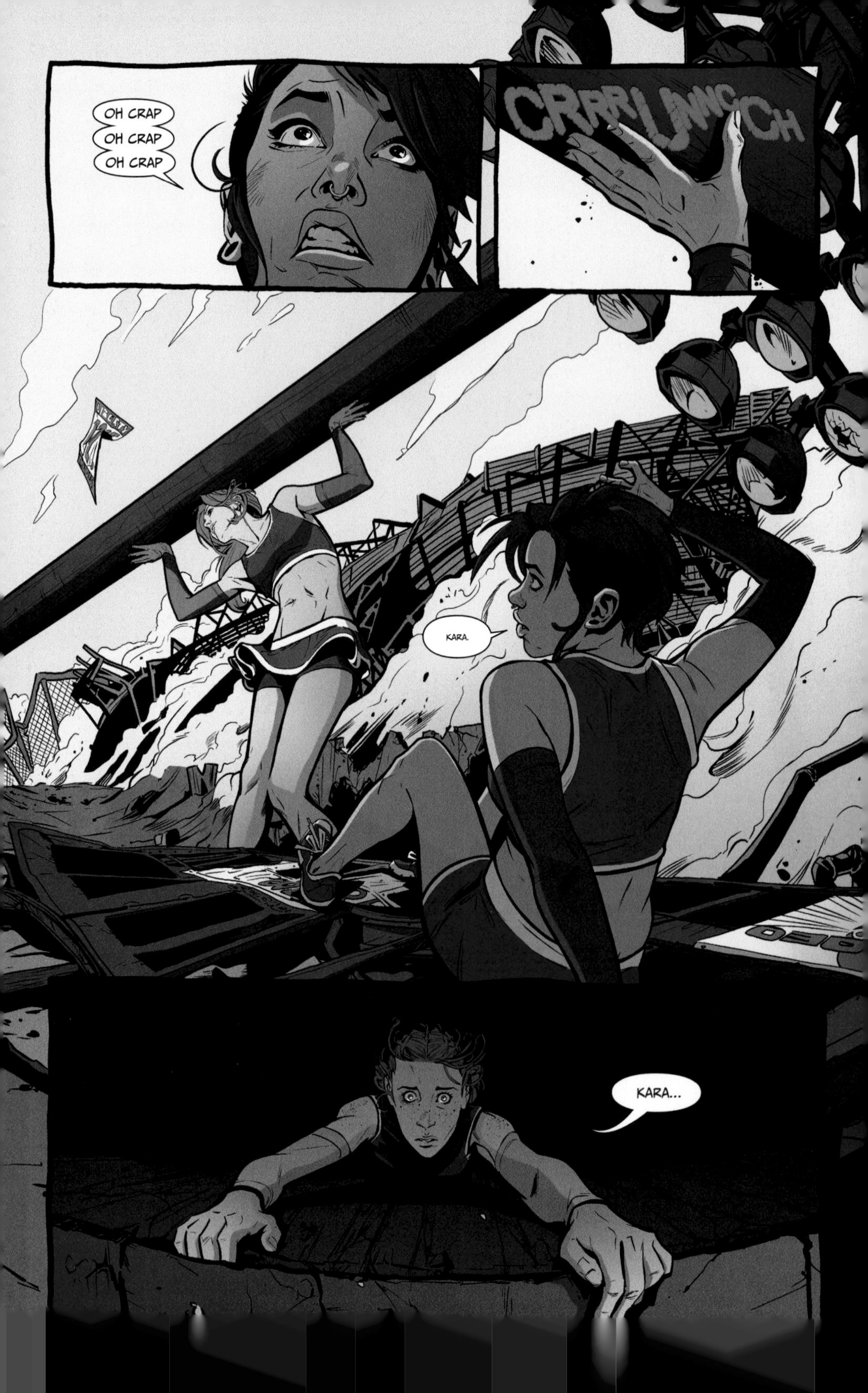
OH CRAP
OH CRAP
OH CRAP
CRRRUNNCCH
KARA.
KARA...

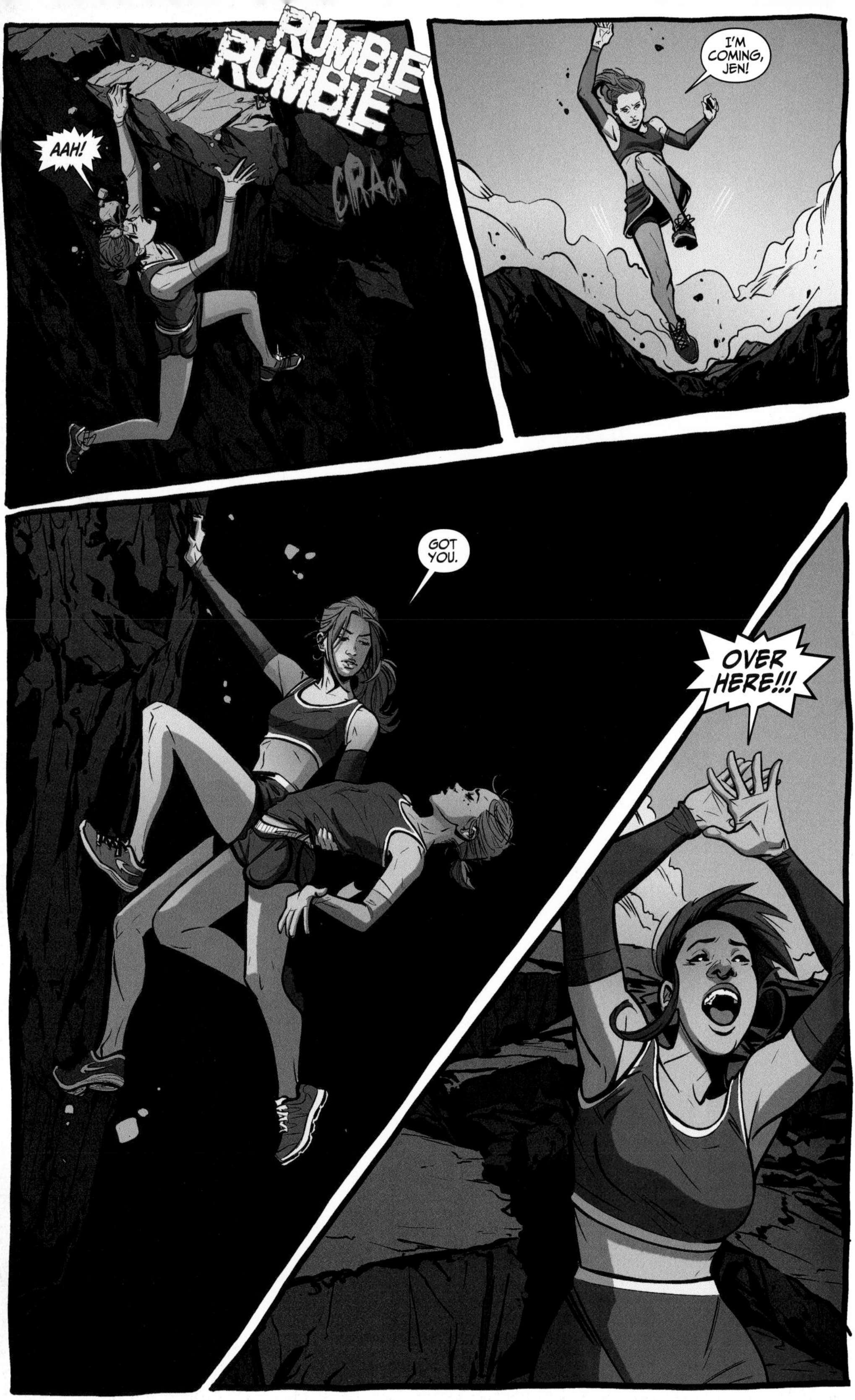
RUMBLE
RUMBLE
AAH!
CRACK
I'M COMING, JEN!
GOT YOU.
OVER HERE!!!

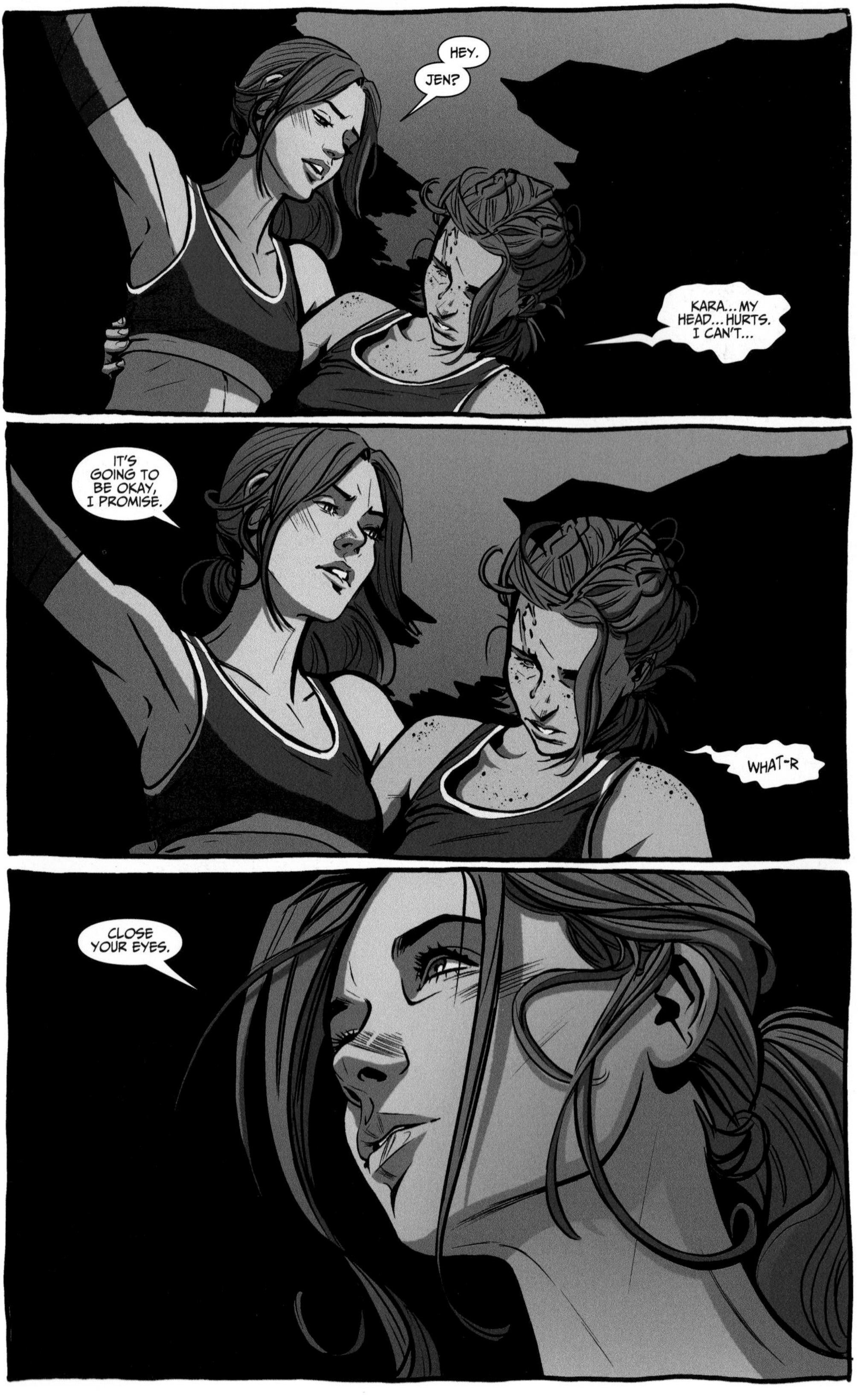
HEY.
JEN?
KARA... MY HEAD... HURTS. I CAN'T...
IT'S GOING TO BE OKAY, I PROMISE.
WHAT-R
CLOSE YOUR EYES.

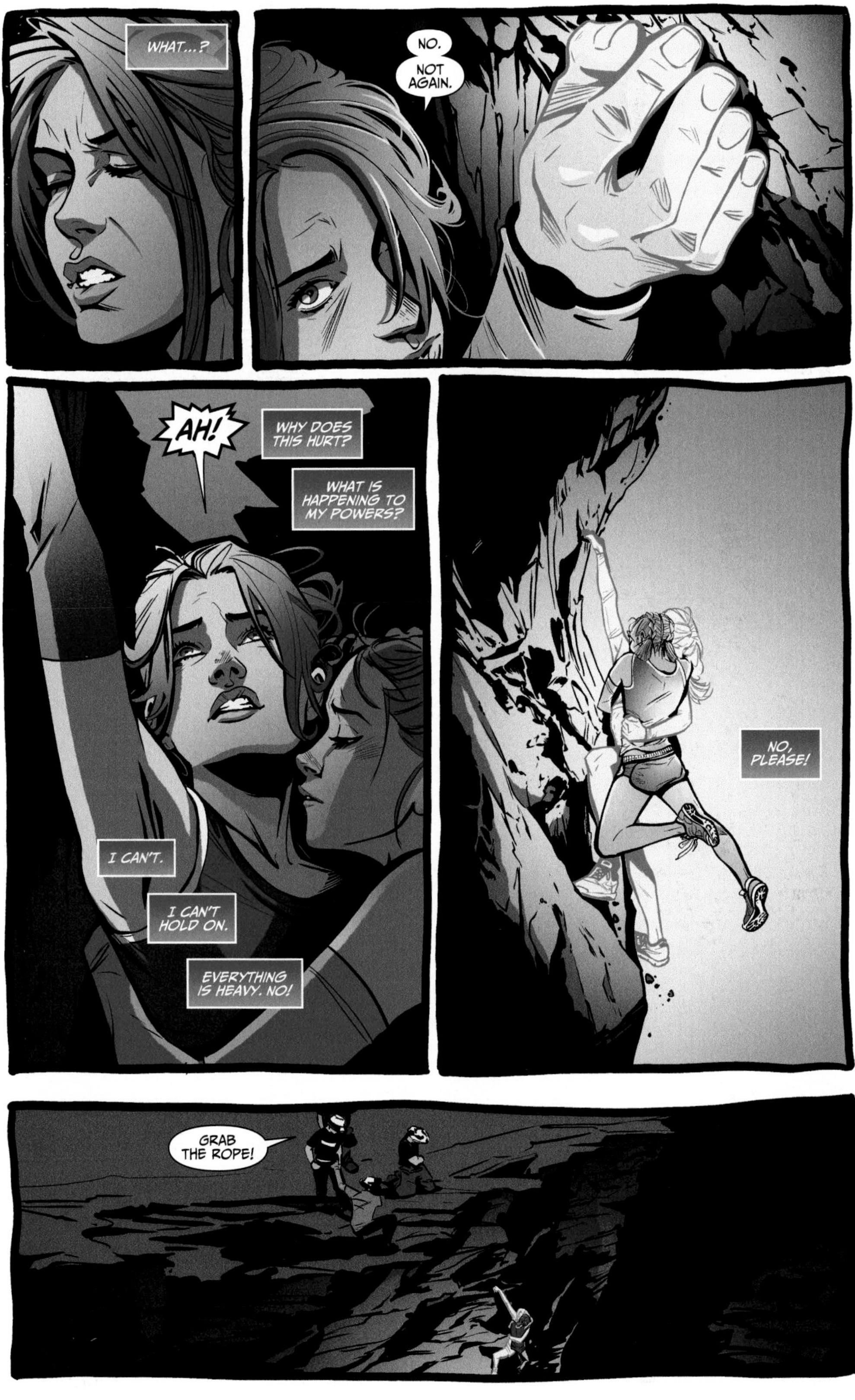
WHAT...?
NO.
NOT AGAIN.
AH!
WHY DOES THIS HURT?
WHAT IS HAPPENING TO MY POWERS?
I CAN'T.
I CAN'T HOLD ON.
EVERYTHING IS HEAVY. NO!
NO, PLEASE!
GRAB THE ROPE!

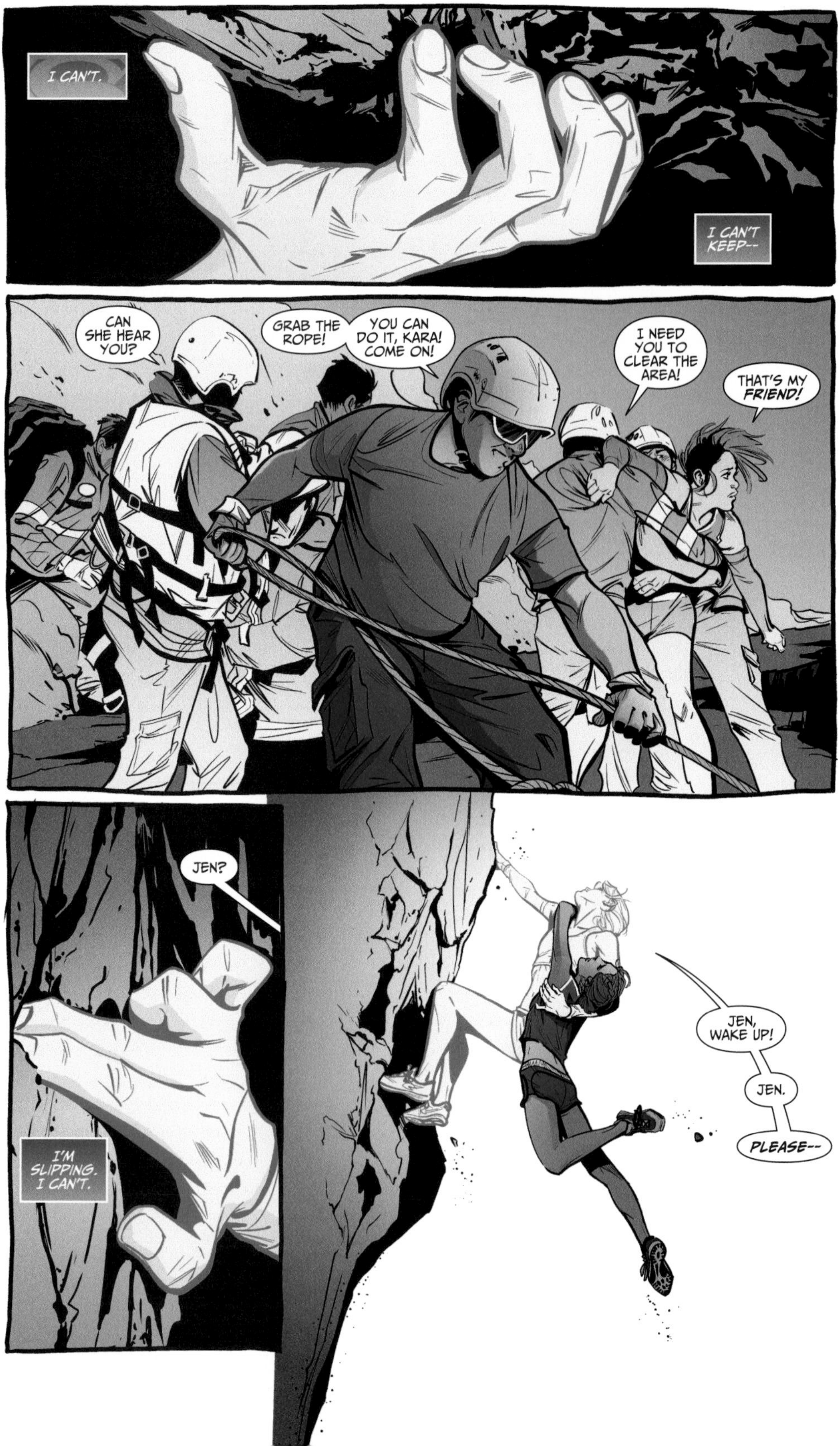
I CAN'T.
I CAN'T KEEP--
CAN SHE HEAR YOU?
GRAB THE ROPE!
YOU CAN DO IT, KARA! COME ON!
I NEED YOU TO CLEAR THE AREA!
THAT'S MY FRIEND!
JEN?
I'M SLIPPING. I CAN'T.
JEN, WAKE UP!
JEN.
PLEASE--

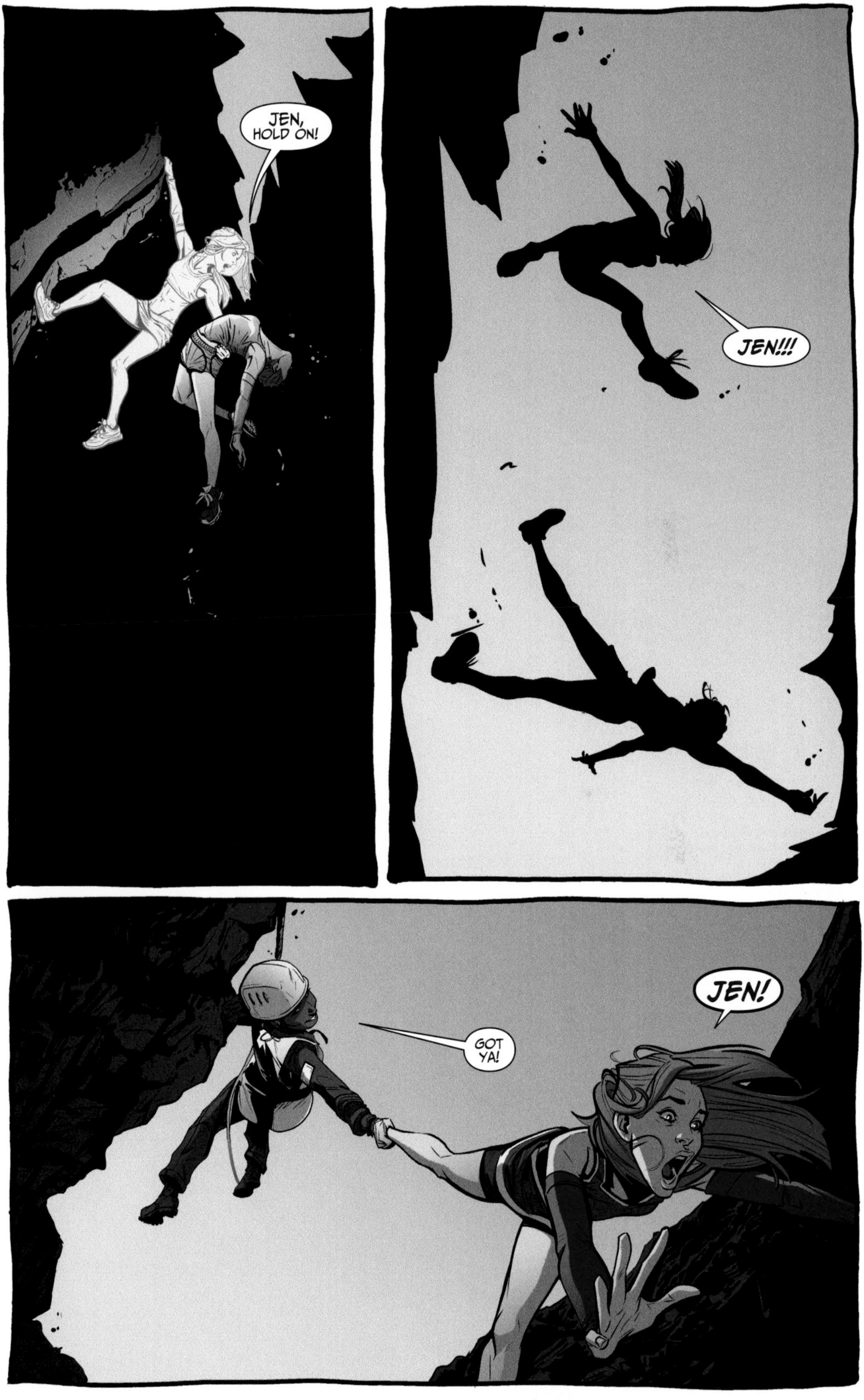
JEN, HOLD ON!
JEN!!!
JEN!
GOT YA!

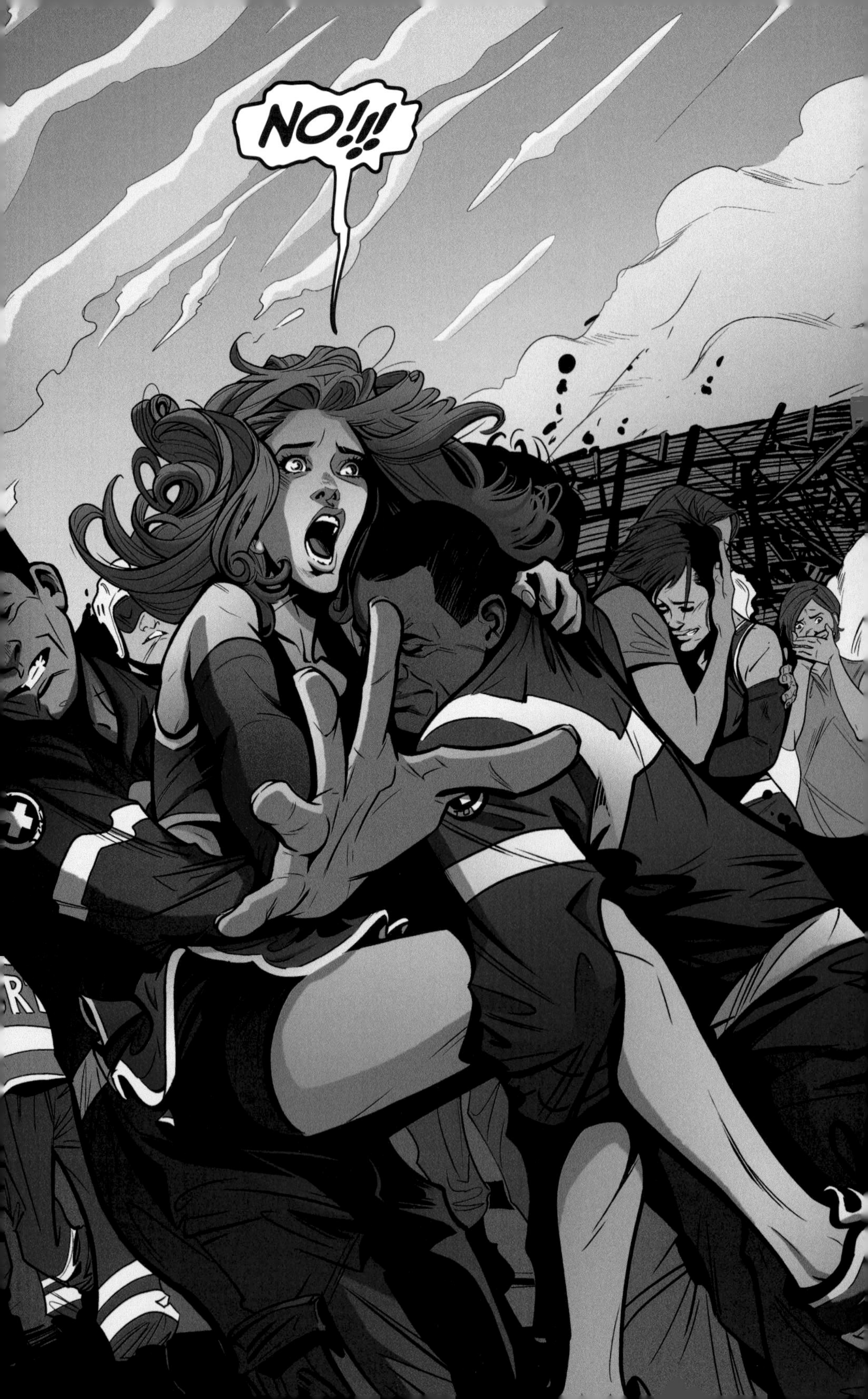
NO!!!

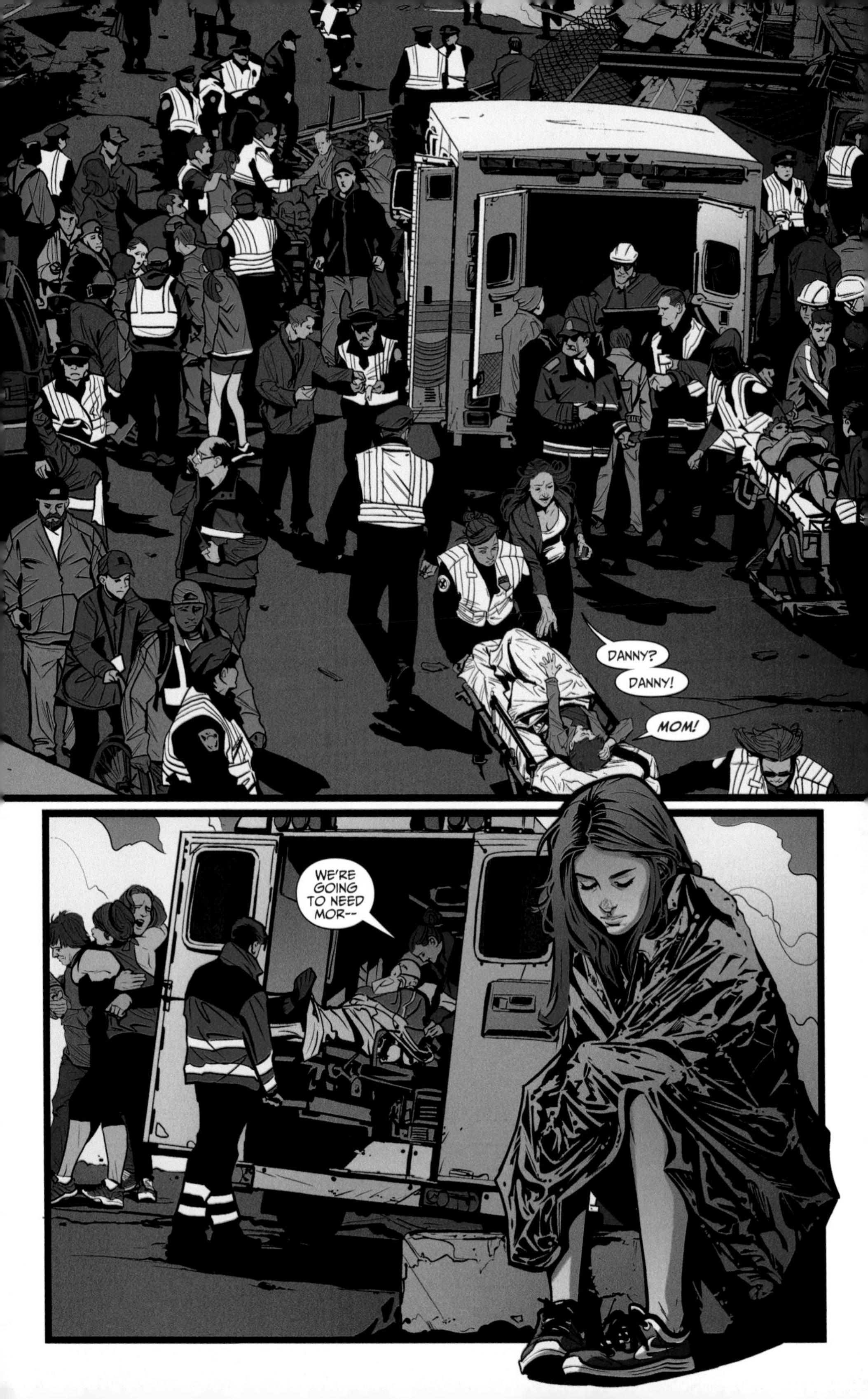
DANNY?
DANNY!
MOM!
WE'RE GOING TO NEED MOR--

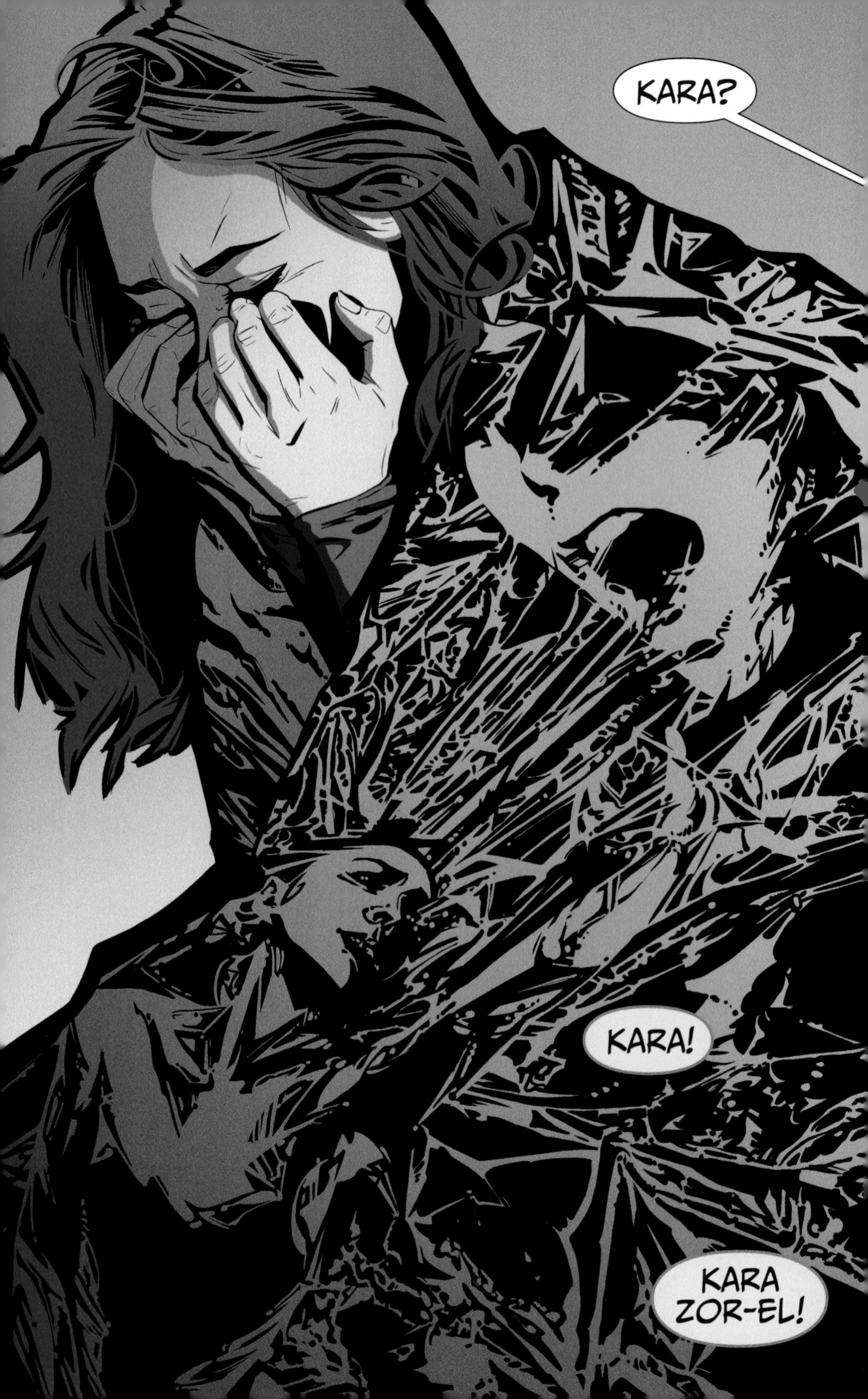
KARA?
KARA!
KARA ZOR-EL!

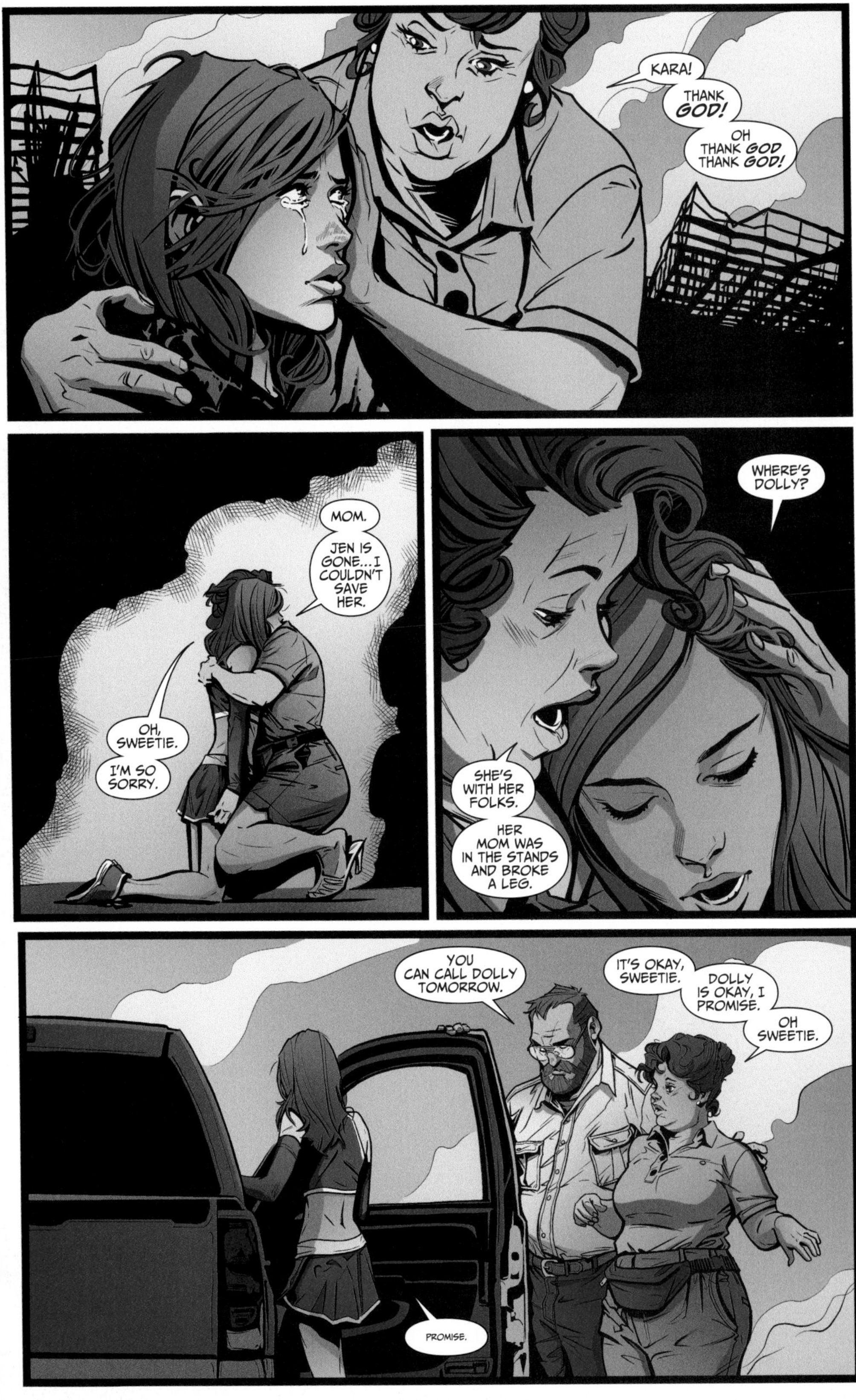
KARA!
THANK GOD!
OH THANK GOD THANK GOD!
MOM.
JEN IS GONE... I COULDN'T SAVE HER.
OH, SWEETIE.
I'M SO SORRY.
WHERE'S DOLLY?
SHE'S WITH HER FOLKS.
HER MOM WAS IN THE STANDS AND BROKE A LEG.
YOU CAN CALL DOLLY TOMORROW.
IT'S OKAY, SWEETIE.
DOLLY IS OKAY, I PROMISE.
OH SWEETIE.
PROMISE.

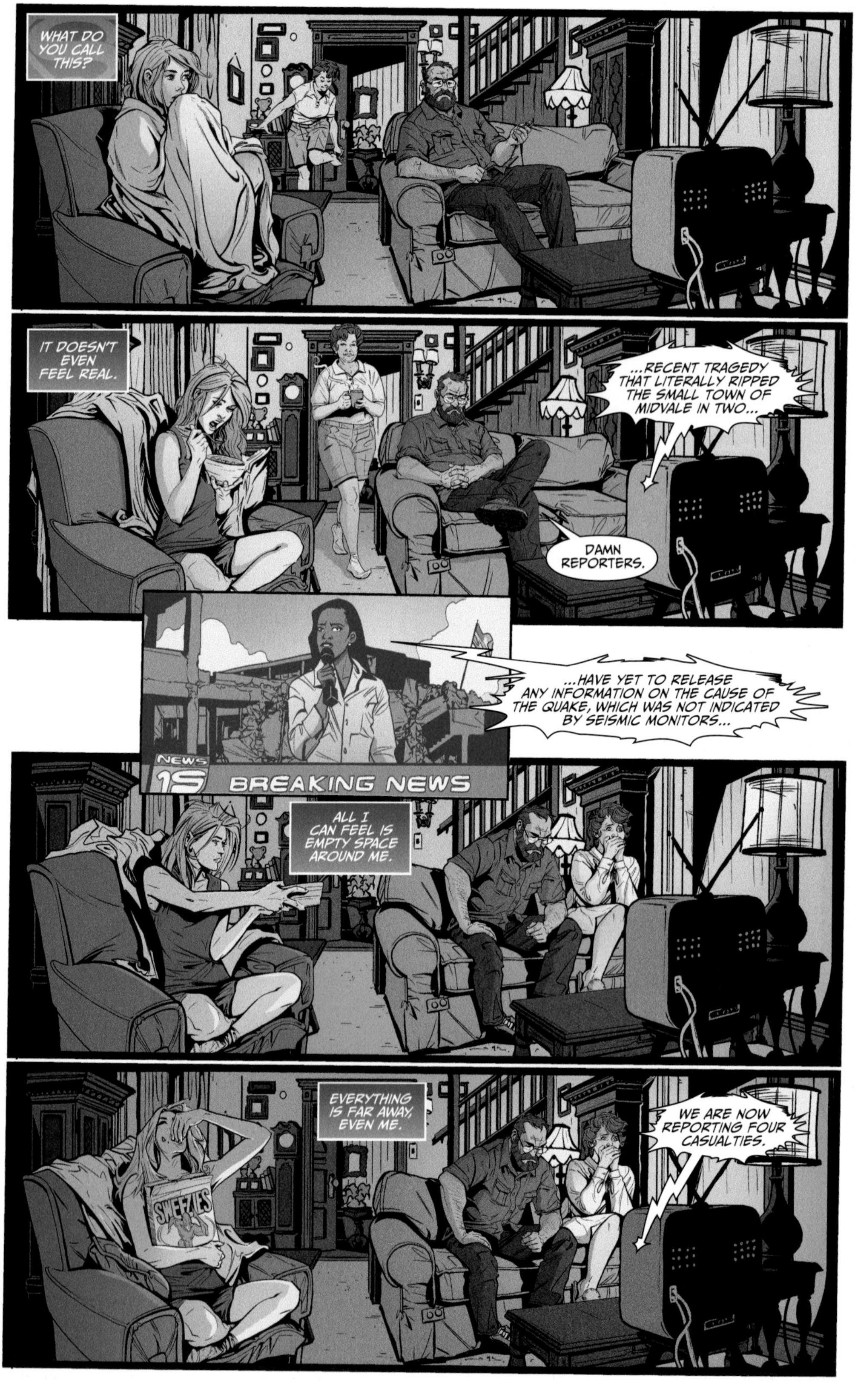
WHAT DO YOU CALL THIS?
IT DOESN'T EVEN FEEL REAL.
...RECENT TRAGEDY THAT LITERALLY RIPPED THE SMALL TOWN OF MIDVALE IN TWO...
DAMN REPORTERS.
...HAVE YET TO RELEASE ANY INFORMATION ON THE CAUSE OF THE QUAKE, WHICH WAS NOT INDICATED BY SEISMIC MONITORS...
NEWS 15 BREAKING NEWS
ALL I CAN FEEL IS EMPTY SPACE AROUND ME.
EVERYTHING IS FAR AWAY, EVEN ME.
WE ARE NOW REPORTING FOUR CASUALTIES.
SHEEZIES

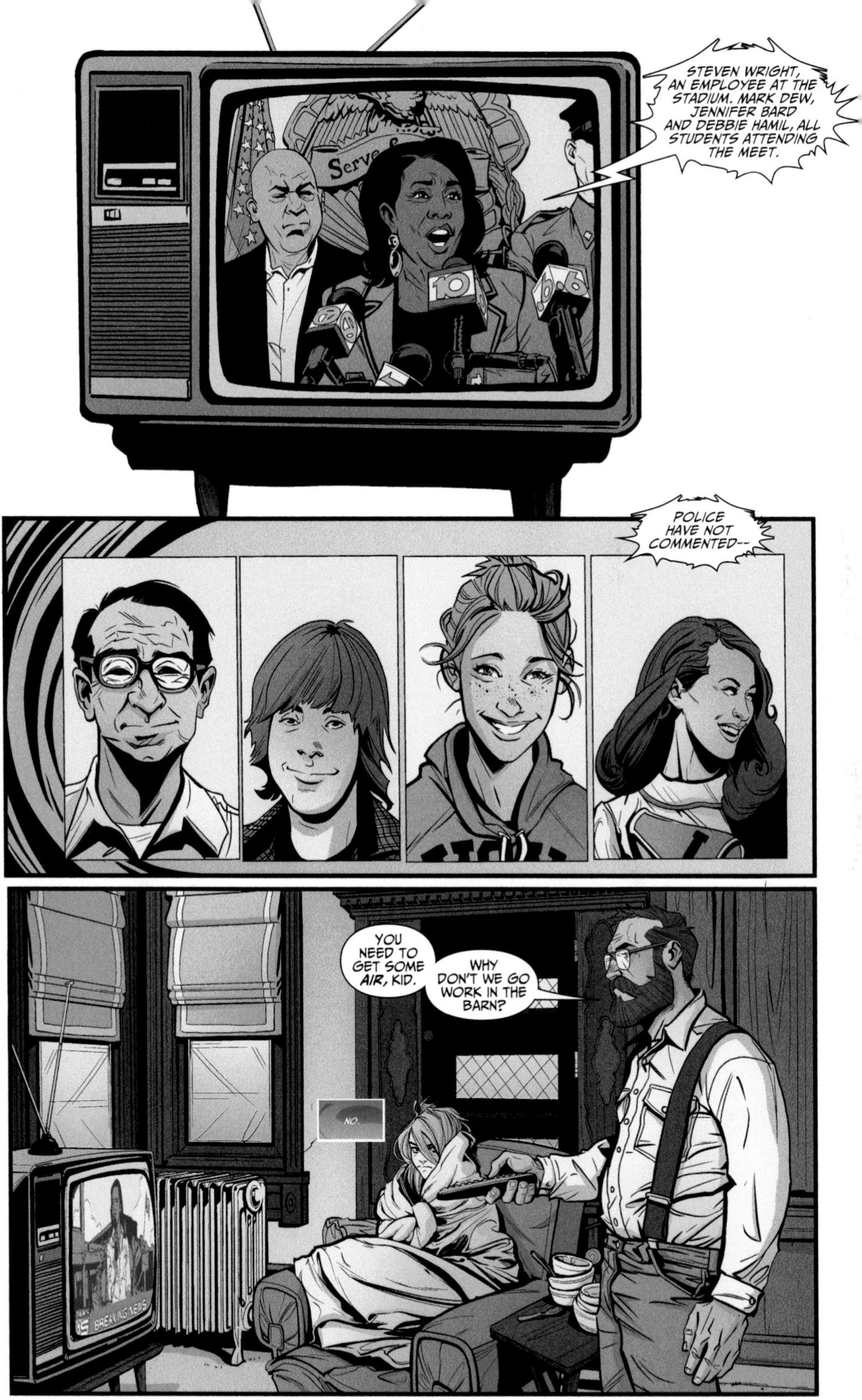
STEVEN WRIGHT, AN EMPLOYEE AT THE STADIUM. MARK DEW, JENNIFER BARD AND DEBBIE HAMIL, ALL STUDENTS ATTENDING THE MEET.
POLICE HAVE NOT COMMENTED--
YOU NEED TO GET SOME AIR, KID.
WHY DON'T WE GO WORK IN THE BARN?
NO.
BREAKING NEWS

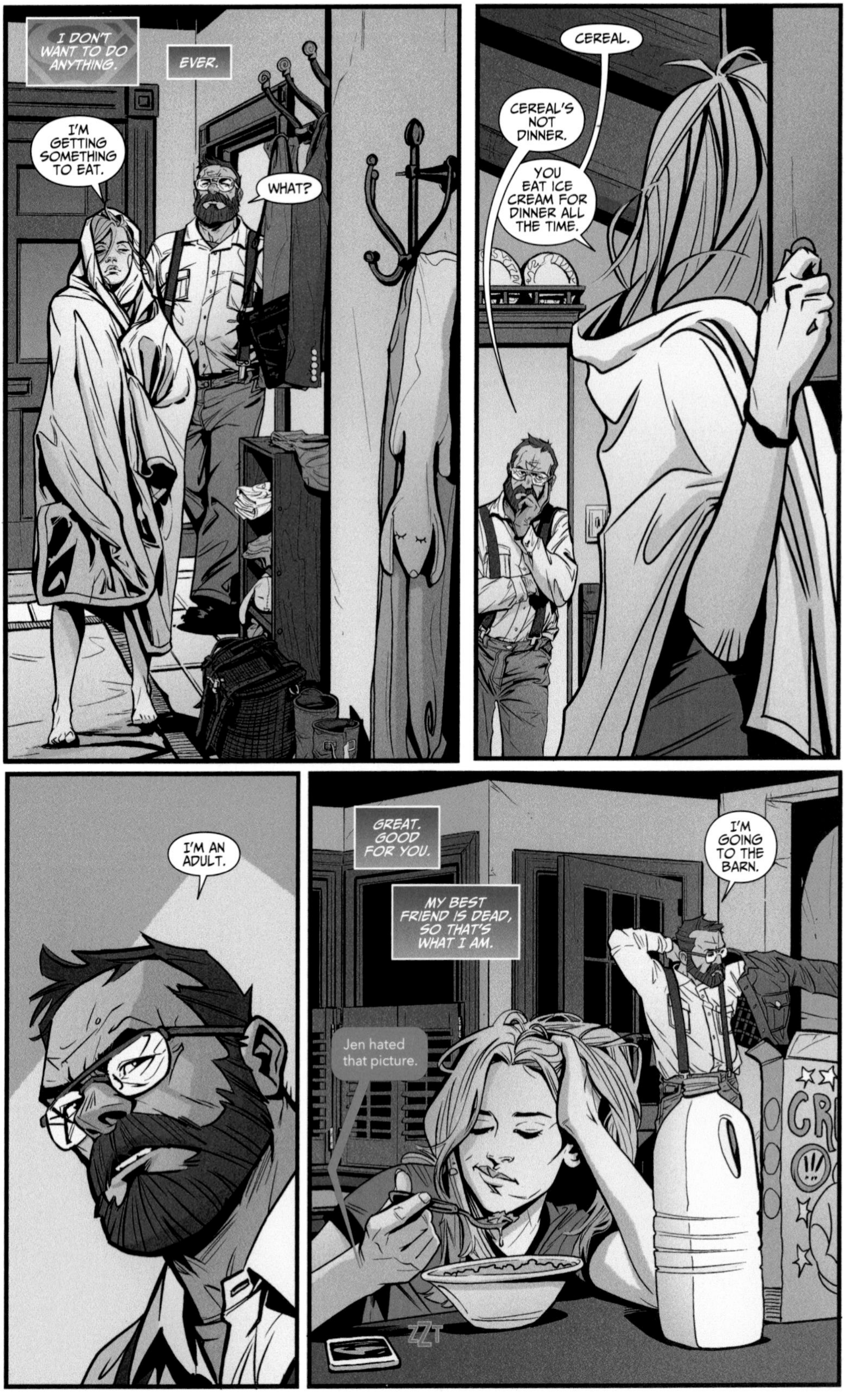
I DON'T WANT TO DO ANYTHING.
EVER.
I'M GETTING SOMETHING TO EAT.
WHAT?
CEREAL.
CEREAL'S NOT DINNER.
YOU EAT ICE CREAM FOR DINNER ALL THE TIME.
I'M AN ADULT.
GREAT. GOOD FOR YOU.
MY BEST FRIEND IS DEAD, SO THAT'S WHAT I AM.
I'M GOING TO THE BARN.
Jen hated that picture.
ZZT

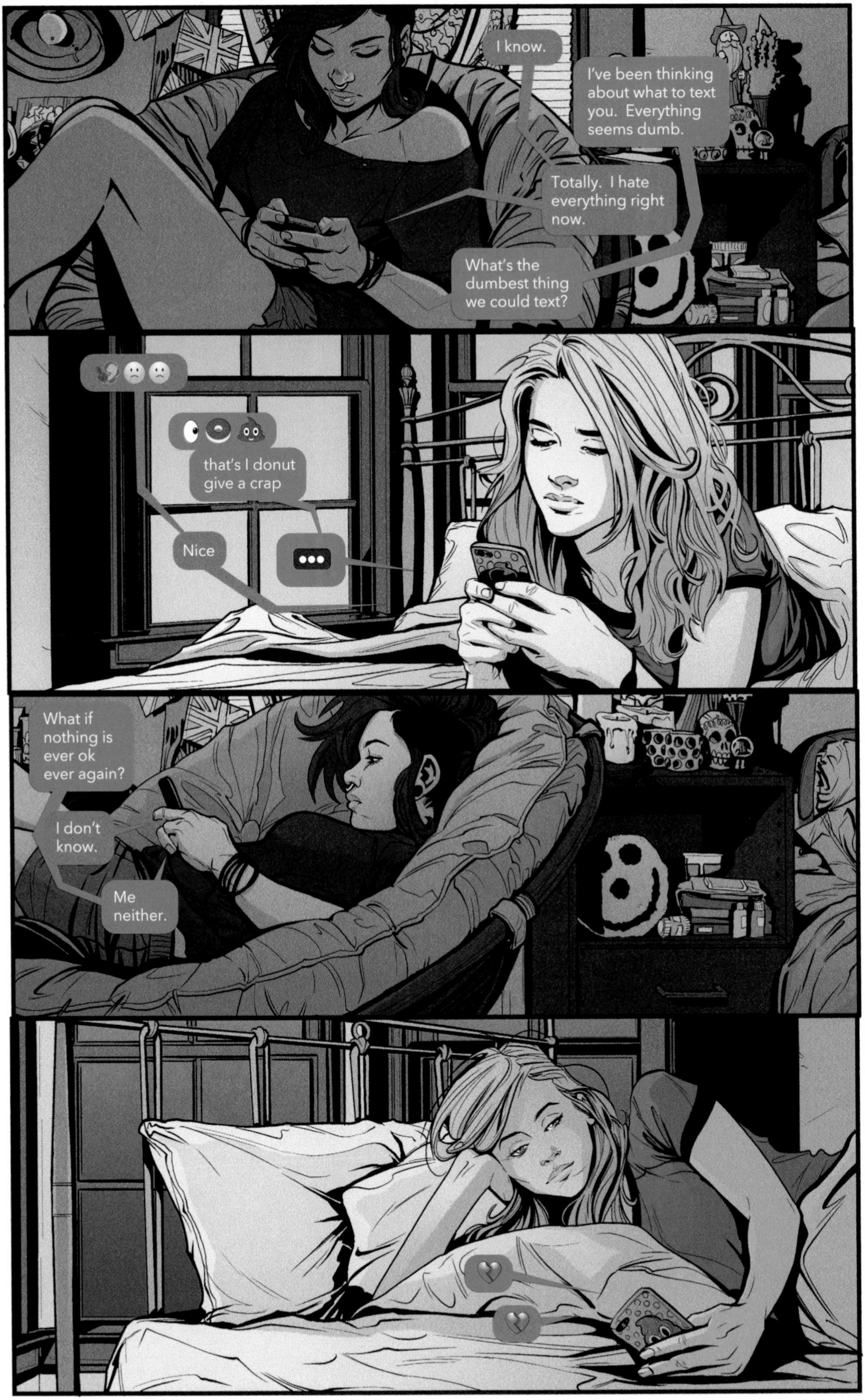
I know.
I've been thinking about what to text you. Everything seems dumb.
Totally. I hate everything right now.
What's the dumbest thing we could text?
that's I donut give a crap
Nice
What if nothing is ever ok ever again?
I don't know.
Me neither.

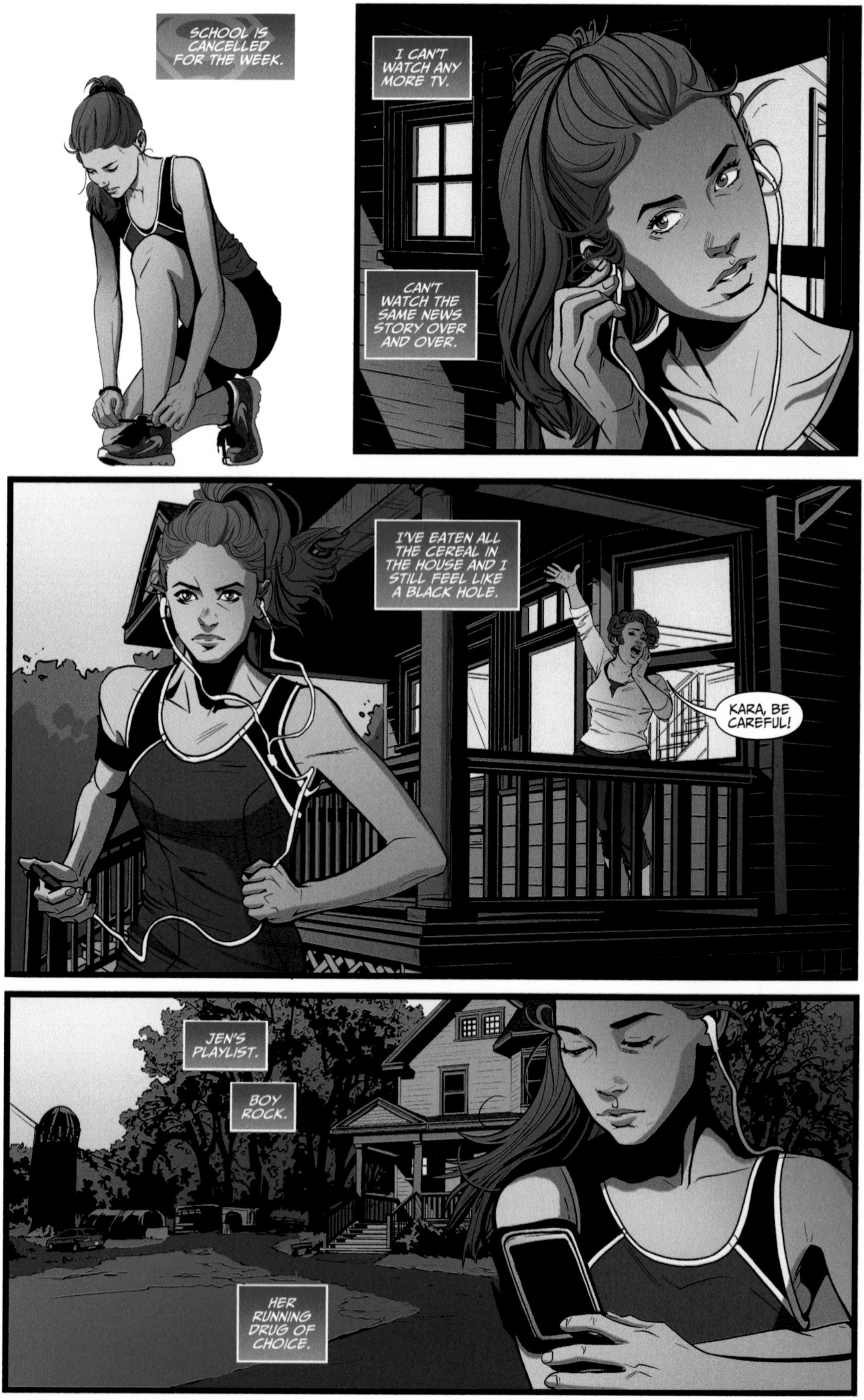
SCHOOL IS CANCELLED FOR THE WEEK.
I CAN'T WATCH ANY MORE TV.
CAN'T WATCH THE SAME NEWS STORY OVER AND OVER.
I'VE EATEN ALL THE CEREAL IN THE HOUSE AND I STILL FEEL LIKE A BLACK HOLE.
KARA, BE CAREFUL!
JEN'S PLAYLIST.
BOY ROCK.
HER RUNNING DRUG OF CHOICE.

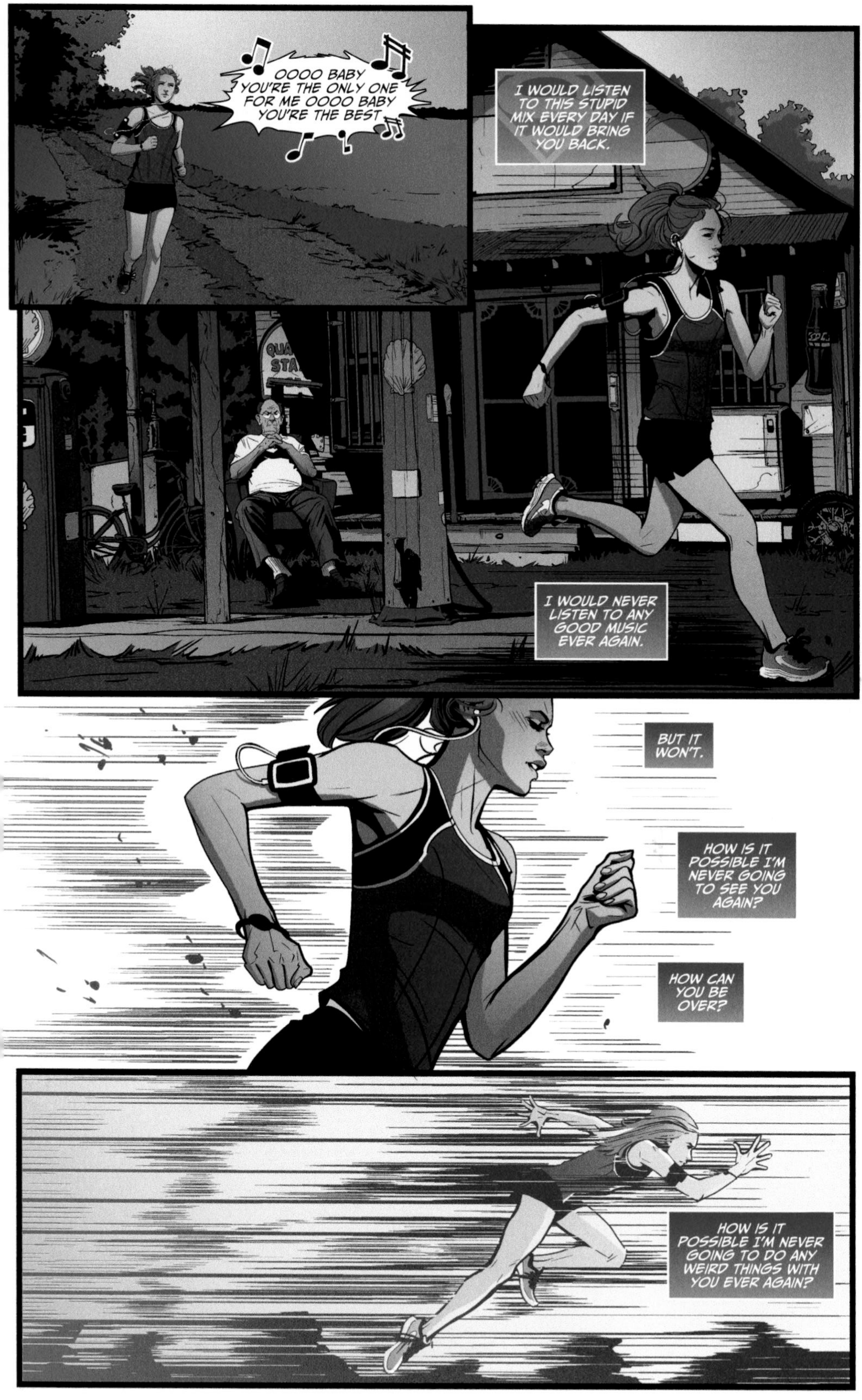
OOOO BABY YOU'RE THE ONLY ONE FOR ME OOOO BABY YOU'RE THE BEST
I WOULD LISTEN TO THIS STUPID MIX EVERY DAY IF IT WOULD BRING YOU BACK.
I WOULD NEVER LISTEN TO ANY GOOD MUSIC EVER AGAIN.
BUT IT WON'T.
HOW IS IT POSSIBLE I'M NEVER GOING TO SEE YOU AGAIN?
HOW CAN YOU BE OVER?
HOW IS IT POSSIBLE I'M NEVER GOING TO DO ANY WEIRD THINGS WITH YOU EVER AGAIN?

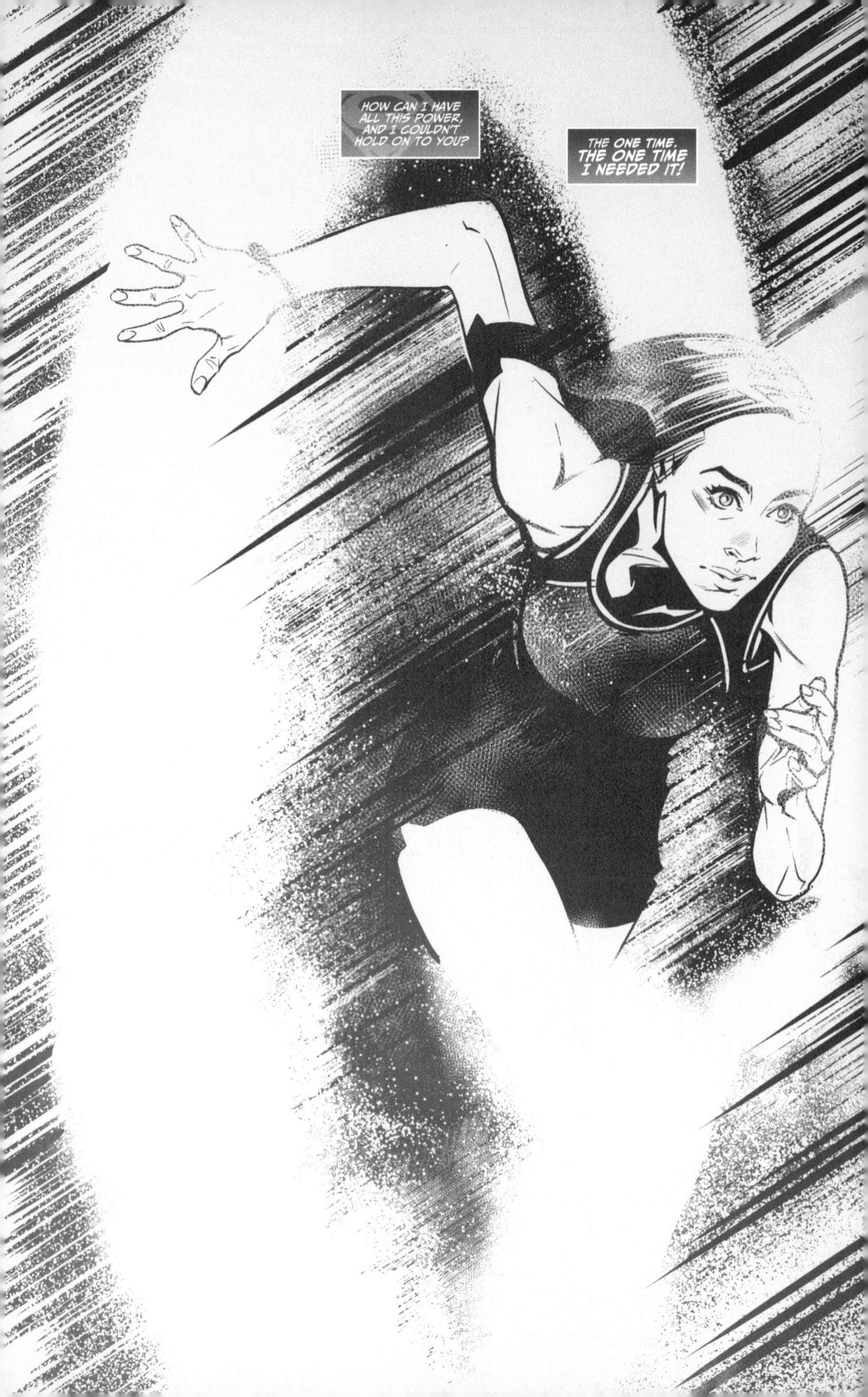
HOW CAN I HAVE ALL THIS POWER, AND I COULDN'T HOLD ON TO YOU?
THE ONE TIME, THE ONE TIME I NEEDED IT!

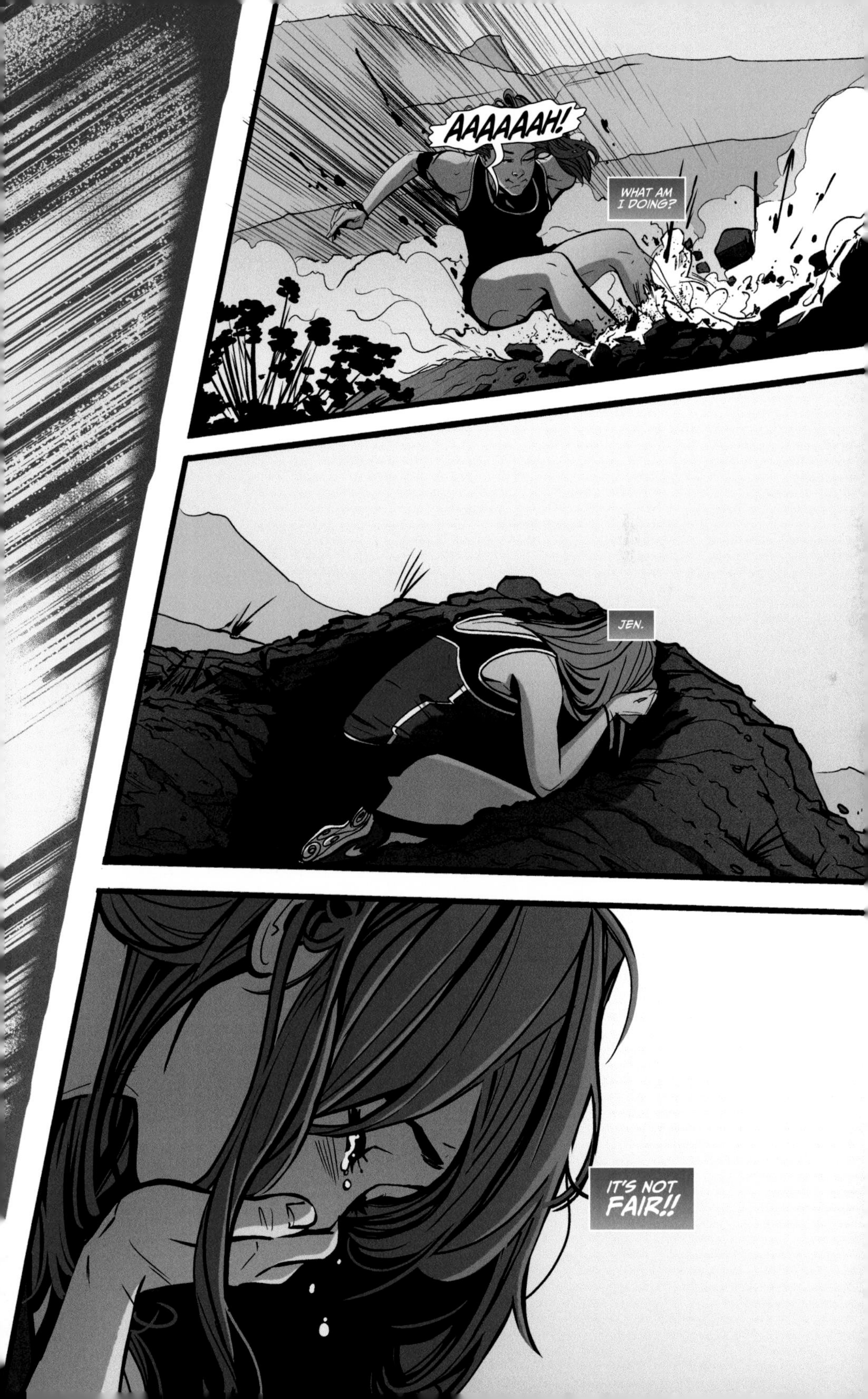
AAAAAAH!
WHAT AM I DOING?
JEN.
IT'S NOT FAIR!!

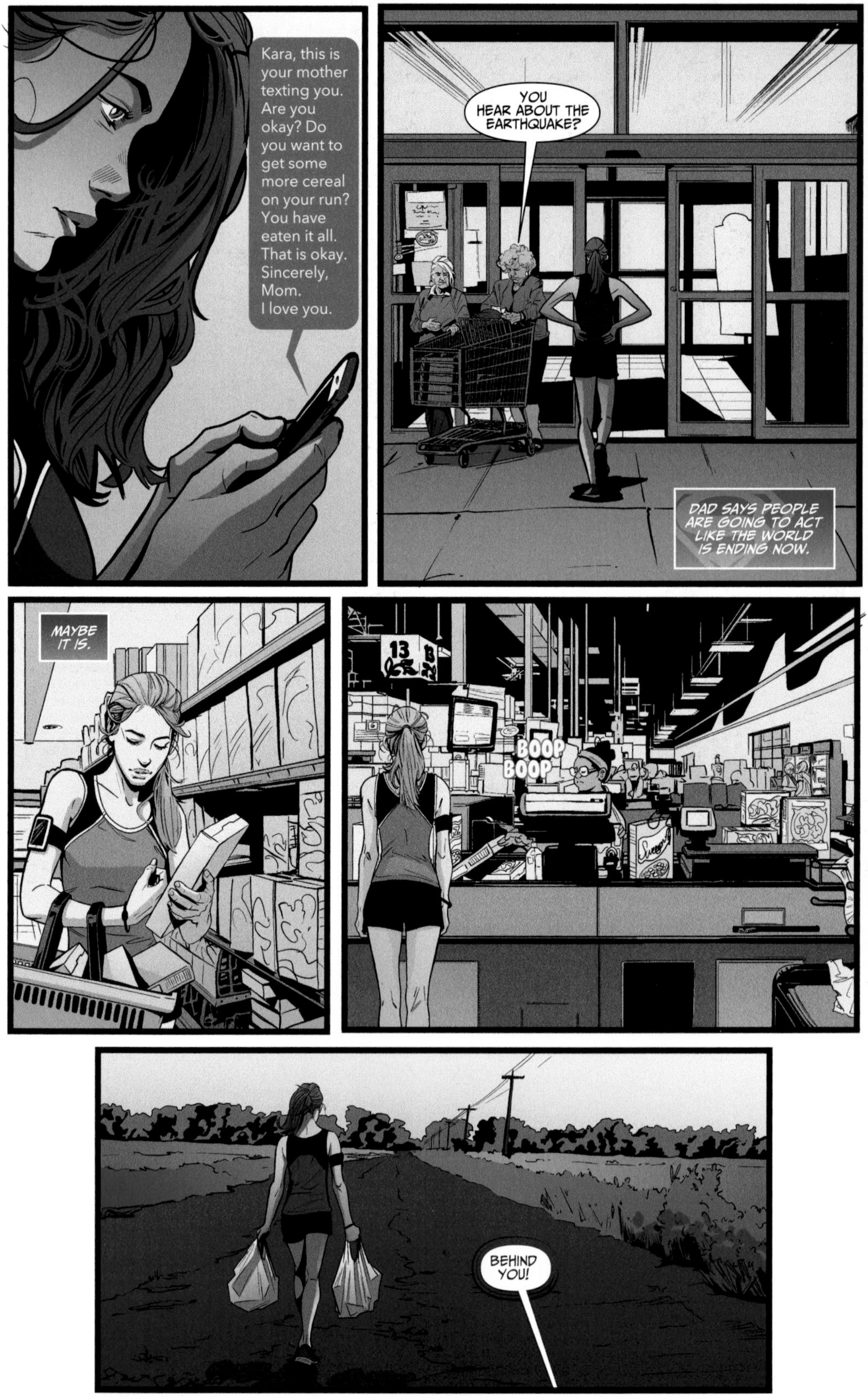
Kara, this is your mother texting you. Are you okay? Do you want to get some more cereal on your run? You have eaten it all. That is okay. Sincerely, Mom. I love you.
YOU HEAR ABOUT THE EARTHQUAKE?
DAD SAYS PEOPLE ARE GOING TO ACT LIKE THE WORLD IS ENDING NOW.
MAYBE IT IS.
BOOP BOOP
BEHIND YOU!

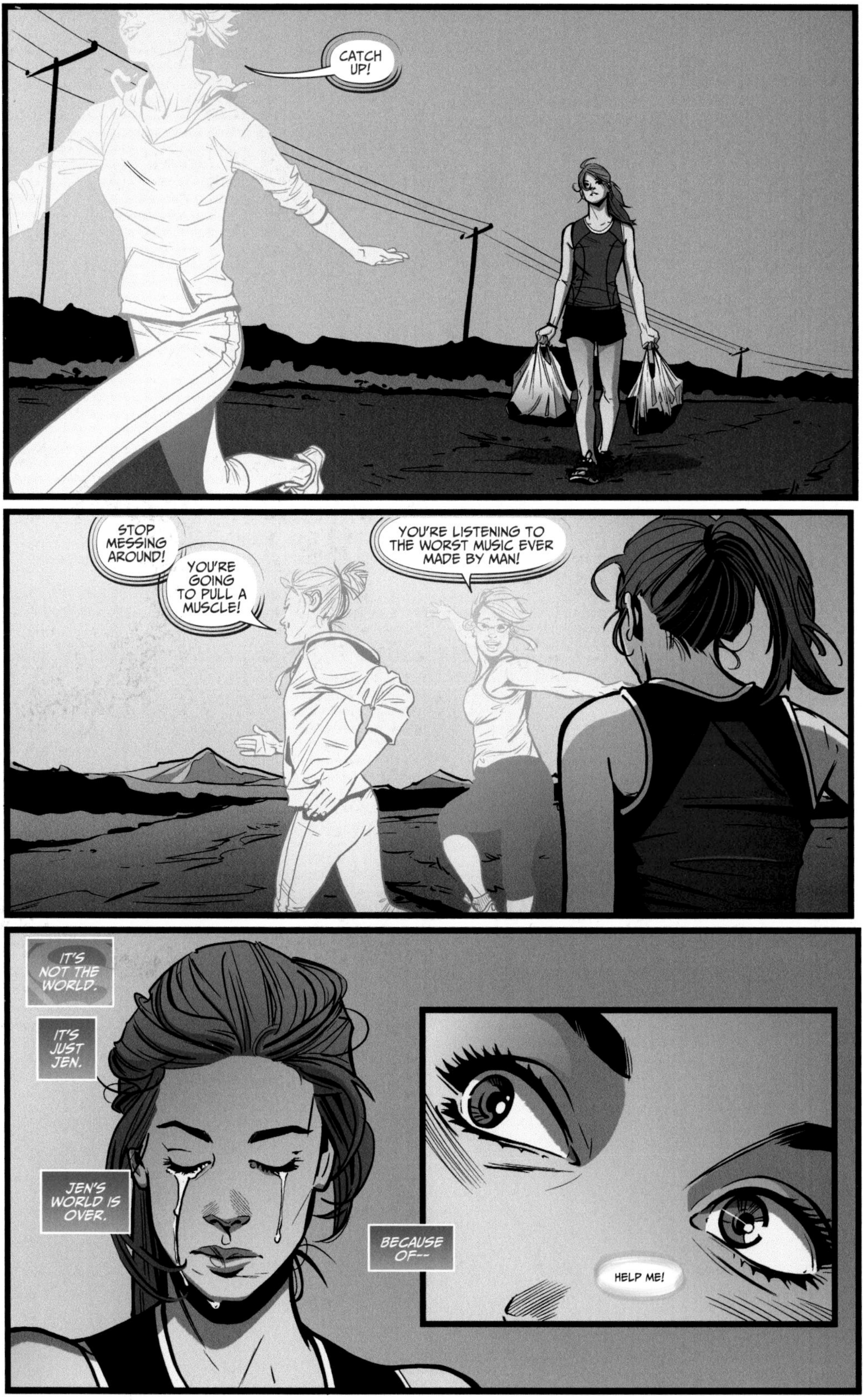
CATCH UP!
STOP MESSING AROUND!
YOU'RE GOING TO PULL A MUSCLE!
YOU'RE LISTENING TO THE WORST MUSIC EVER MADE BY MAN!
IT'S NOT THE WORLD.
IT'S JUST JEN.
JEN'S WORLD IS OVER.
BECAUSE OF--
HELP ME!

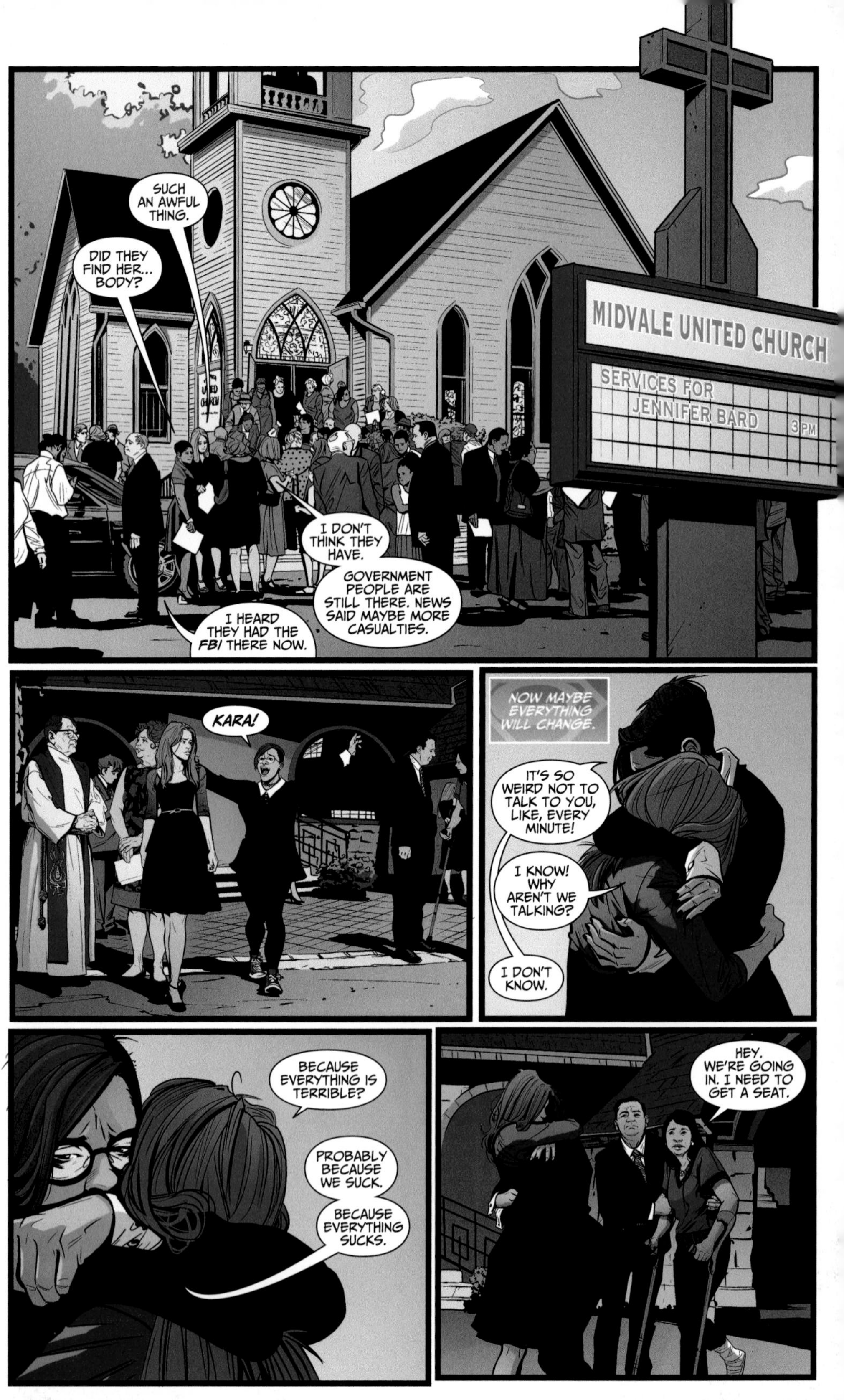
SUCH AN AWFUL THING.
DID THEY FIND HER... BODY?
I DON'T THINK THEY HAVE.
GOVERNMENT PEOPLE ARE STILL THERE. NEWS SAID MAYBE MORE CASUALTIES.
I HEARD THEY HAD THE FBI THERE NOW.
MIDVALE UNITED CHURCH
SERVICES FOR JENNIFER BARD 3PM
KARA!
NOW MAYBE EVERYTHING WILL CHANGE.
IT'S SO WEIRD NOT TO TALK TO YOU, LIKE, EVERY MINUTE!
I KNOW! WHY AREN'T WE TALKING?
I DON'T KNOW.
BECAUSE EVERYTHING IS TERRIBLE?
PROBABLY BECAUSE WE SUCK.
BECAUSE EVERYTHING SUCKS.
HEY. WE'RE GOING IN. I NEED TO GET A SEAT.

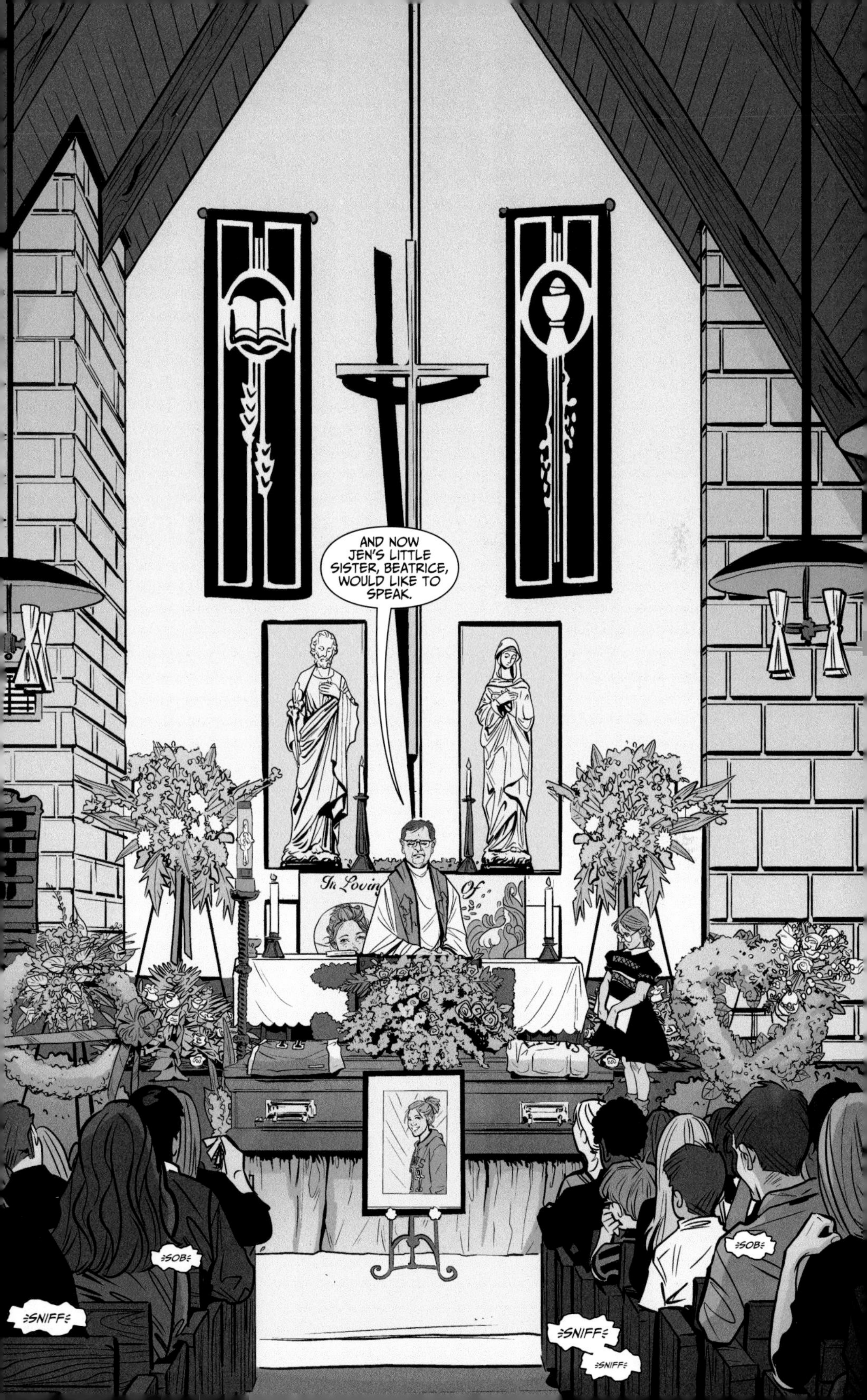
AND NOW JEN'S LITTLE SISTER, BEATRICE, WOULD LIKE TO SPEAK.
In Loving ... Of
SOB
SNIFF
SOB
SNIFF
SNIFF

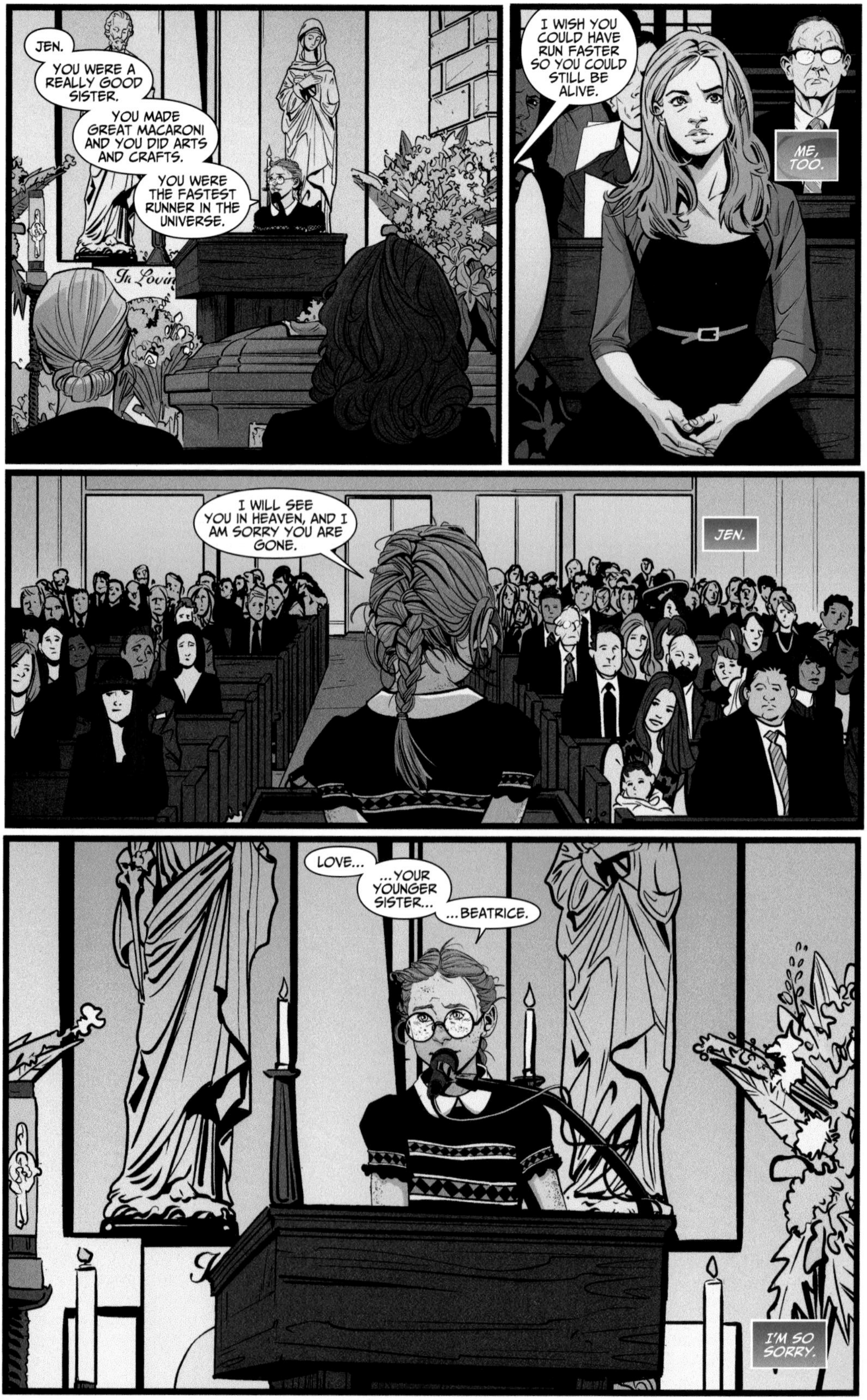
JEN.
YOU WERE A REALLY GOOD SISTER.
YOU MADE GREAT MACARONI AND YOU DID ARTS AND CRAFTS.
YOU WERE THE FASTEST RUNNER IN THE UNIVERSE.
In Lovin
I WISH YOU COULD HAVE RUN FASTER SO YOU COULD STILL BE ALIVE.
ME, TOO.
I WILL SEE YOU IN HEAVEN, AND I AM SORRY YOU ARE GONE.
JEN.
LOVE...
...YOUR YOUNGER SISTER...
...BEATRICE.
I'M SO SORRY.

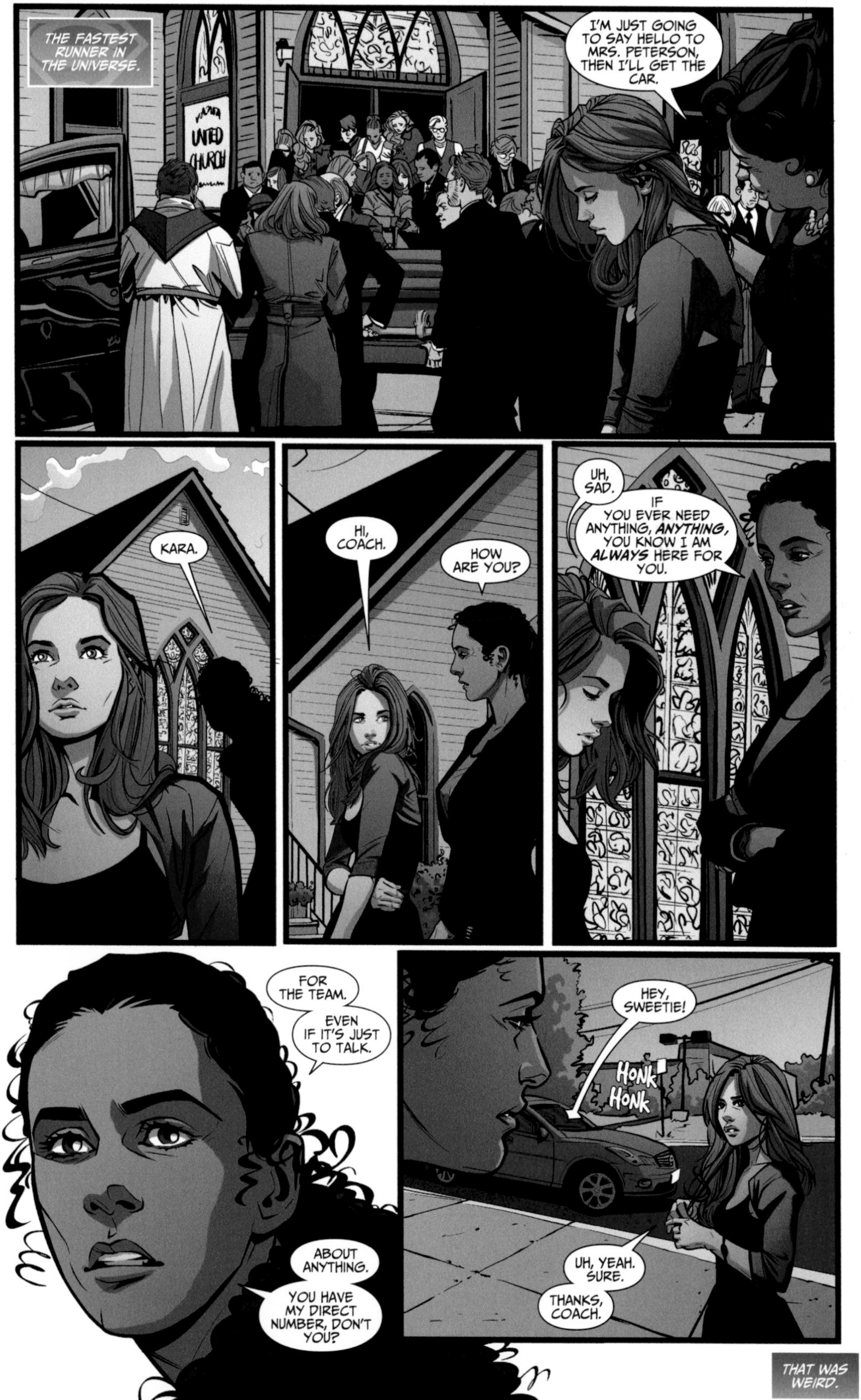
THE FASTEST RUNNER IN THE UNIVERSE.
UNITED CHURCH
I'M JUST GOING TO SAY HELLO TO MRS. PETERSON, THEN I'LL GET THE CAR.
KARA.
HI, COACH.
HOW ARE YOU?
UH, SAD.
IF YOU EVER NEED ANYTHING, ANYTHING, YOU KNOW I AM ALWAYS HERE FOR YOU.
FOR THE TEAM.
EVEN IF IT'S JUST TO TALK.
ABOUT ANYTHING.
YOU HAVE MY DIRECT NUMBER, DON'T YOU?
HEY, SWEETIE!
HONK HONK
UH, YEAH. SURE.
THANKS, COACH.
THAT WAS WEIRD.

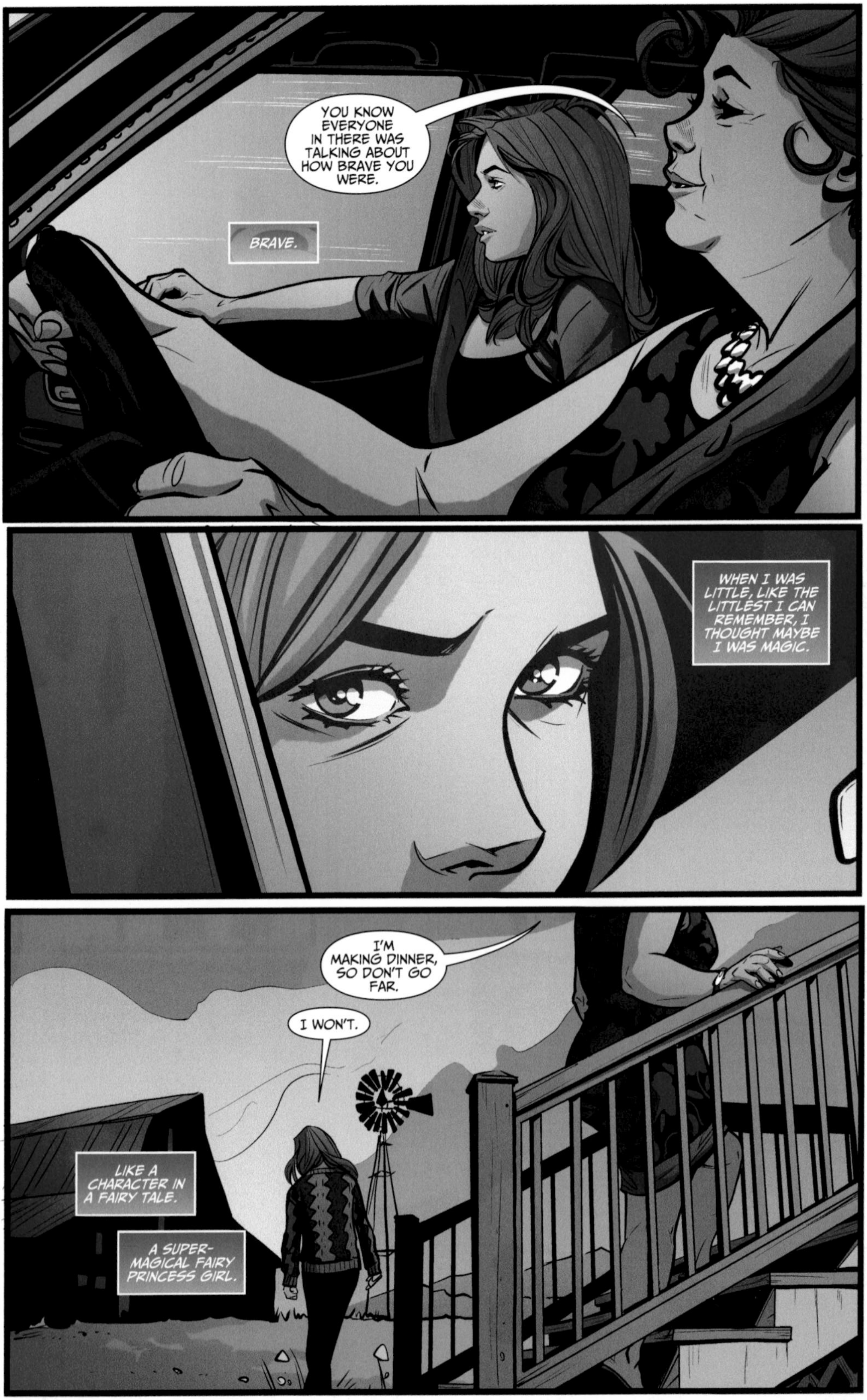
YOU KNOW EVERYONE IN THERE WAS TALKING ABOUT HOW BRAVE YOU WERE.
BRAVE.
WHEN I WAS LITTLE, LIKE THE LITTLEST I CAN REMEMBER, I THOUGHT MAYBE I WAS MAGIC.
I'M MAKING DINNER, SO DON'T GO FAR.
I WON'T.
LIKE A CHARACTER IN A FAIRY TALE.
A SUPER-MAGICAL FAIRY PRINCESS GIRL.

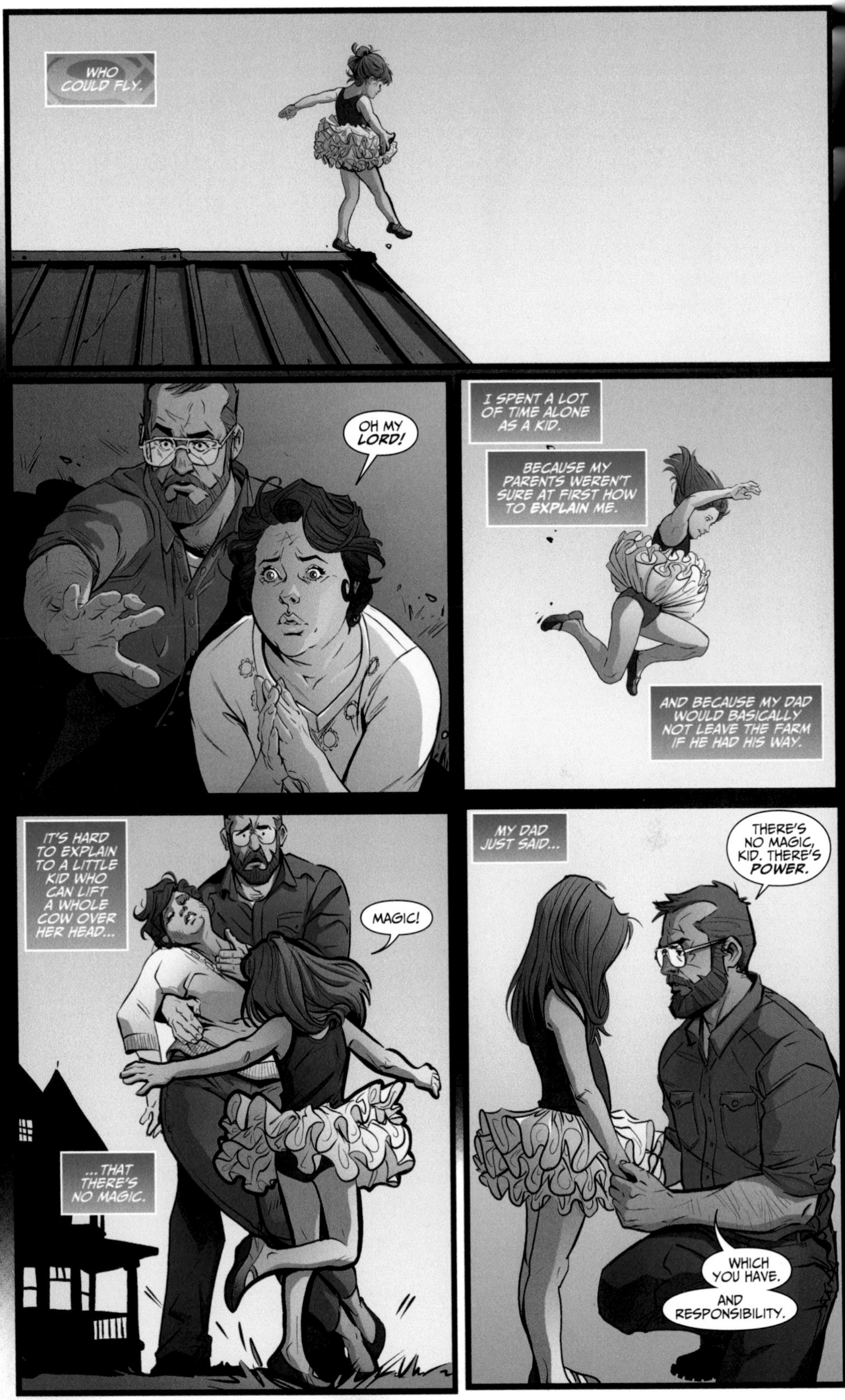
WHO COULD FLY.
OH MY LORD!
I SPENT A LOT OF TIME ALONE AS A KID.
BECAUSE MY PARENTS WEREN'T SURE AT FIRST HOW TO EXPLAIN ME.
AND BECAUSE MY DAD WOULD BASICALLY NOT LEAVE THE FARM IF HE HAD HIS WAY.
IT'S HARD TO EXPLAIN TO A LITTLE KID WHO CAN LIFT A WHOLE COW OVER HER HEAD...
MAGIC!
...THAT THERE'S NO MAGIC.
MY DAD JUST SAID...
THERE'S NO MAGIC, KID. THERE'S POWER.
WHICH YOU HAVE.
AND RESPONSIBILITY.

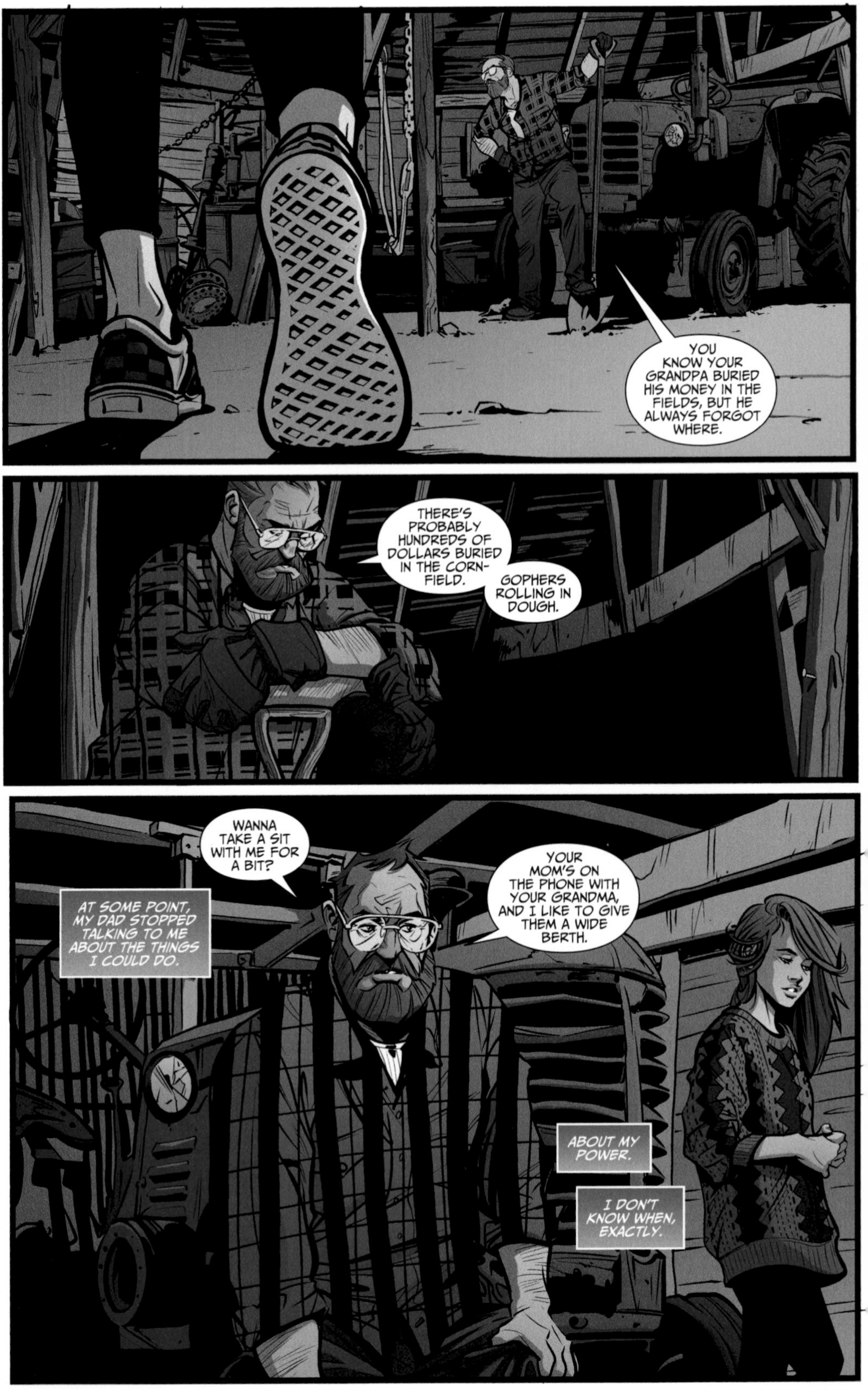
YOU KNOW YOUR GRANDPA BURIED HIS MONEY IN THE FIELDS, BUT HE ALWAYS FORGOT WHERE.
THERE'S PROBABLY HUNDREDS OF DOLLARS BURIED IN THE CORN-FIELD.
GOPHERS ROLLING IN DOUGH.
AT SOME POINT, MY DAD STOPPED TALKING TO ME ABOUT THE THINGS I COULD DO.
WANNA TAKE A SIT WITH ME FOR A BIT?
YOUR MOM'S ON THE PHONE WITH YOUR GRANDMA, AND I LIKE TO GIVE THEM A WIDE BERTH.
ABOUT MY POWER.
I DON'T KNOW WHEN, EXACTLY.

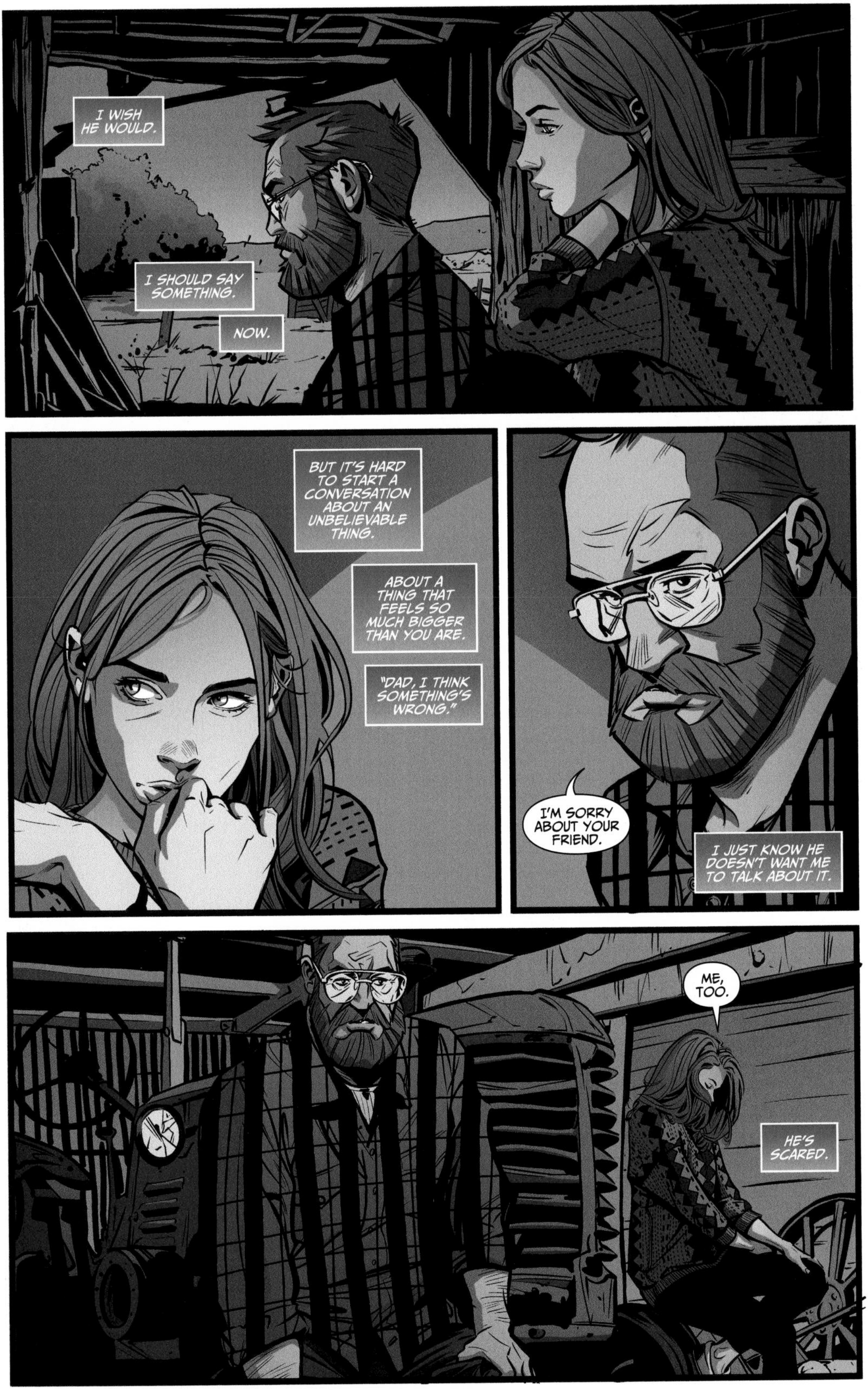
I WISH HE WOULD.
I SHOULD SAY SOMETHING.
NOW.
BUT IT'S HARD TO START A CONVERSATION ABOUT AN UNBELIEVABLE THING.
ABOUT A THING THAT FEELS SO MUCH BIGGER THAN YOU ARE.
"DAD, I THINK SOMETHING'S WRONG."
I'M SORRY ABOUT YOUR FRIEND.
I JUST KNOW HE DOESN'T WANT ME TO TALK ABOUT IT.
ME, TOO.
HE'S SCARED.

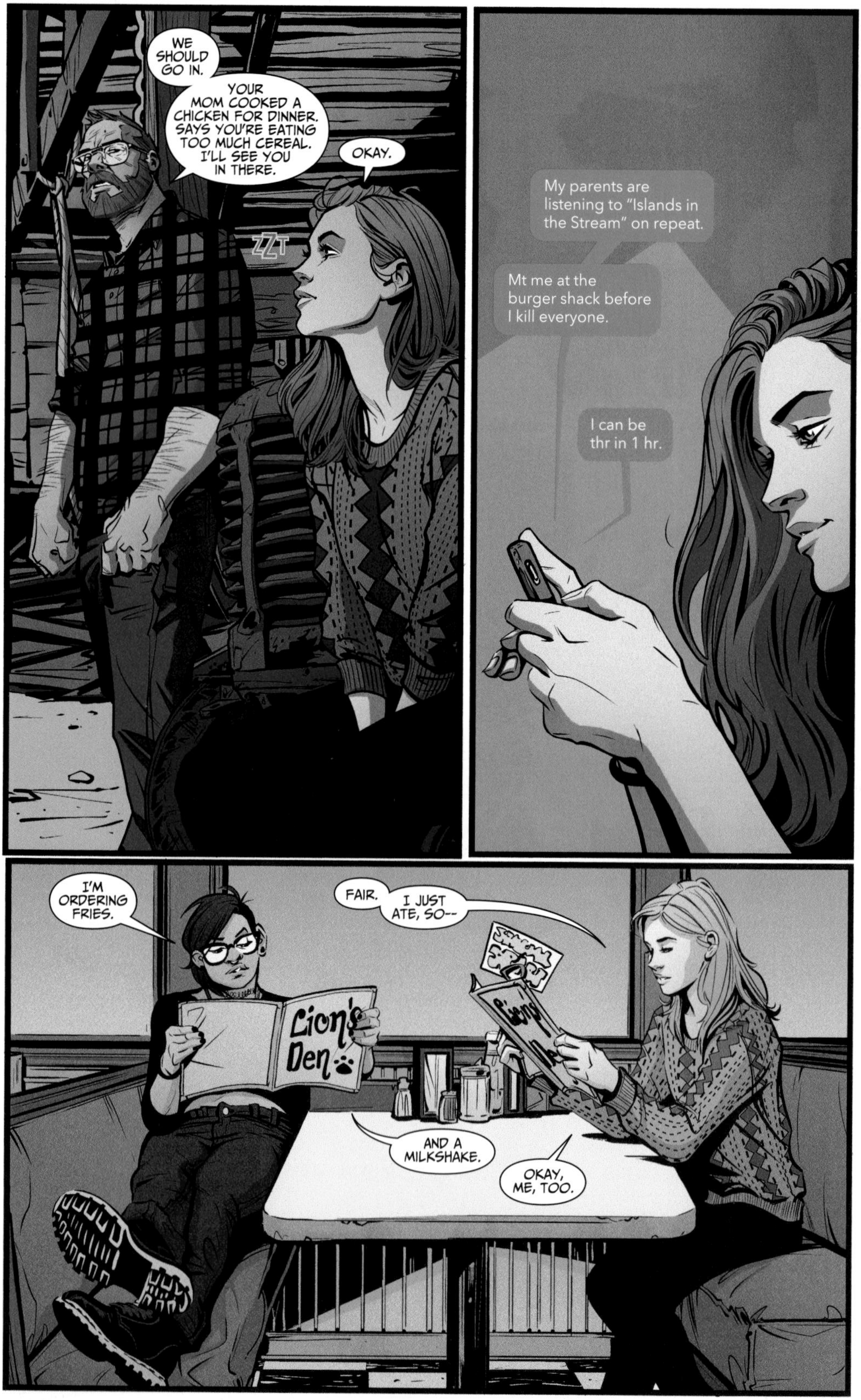
WE SHOULD GO IN.
YOUR MOM COOKED A CHICKEN FOR DINNER. SAYS YOU'RE EATING TOO MUCH CEREAL. I'LL SEE YOU IN THERE.
OKAY.
ZZT
My parents are listening to "Islands in the Stream" on repeat.
Mt me at the burger shack before I kill everyone.
I can be thr in 1 hr.
I'M ORDERING FRIES.
FAIR.
I JUST ATE, SO--
Lion's Den
AND A MILKSHAKE.
OKAY, ME, TOO.

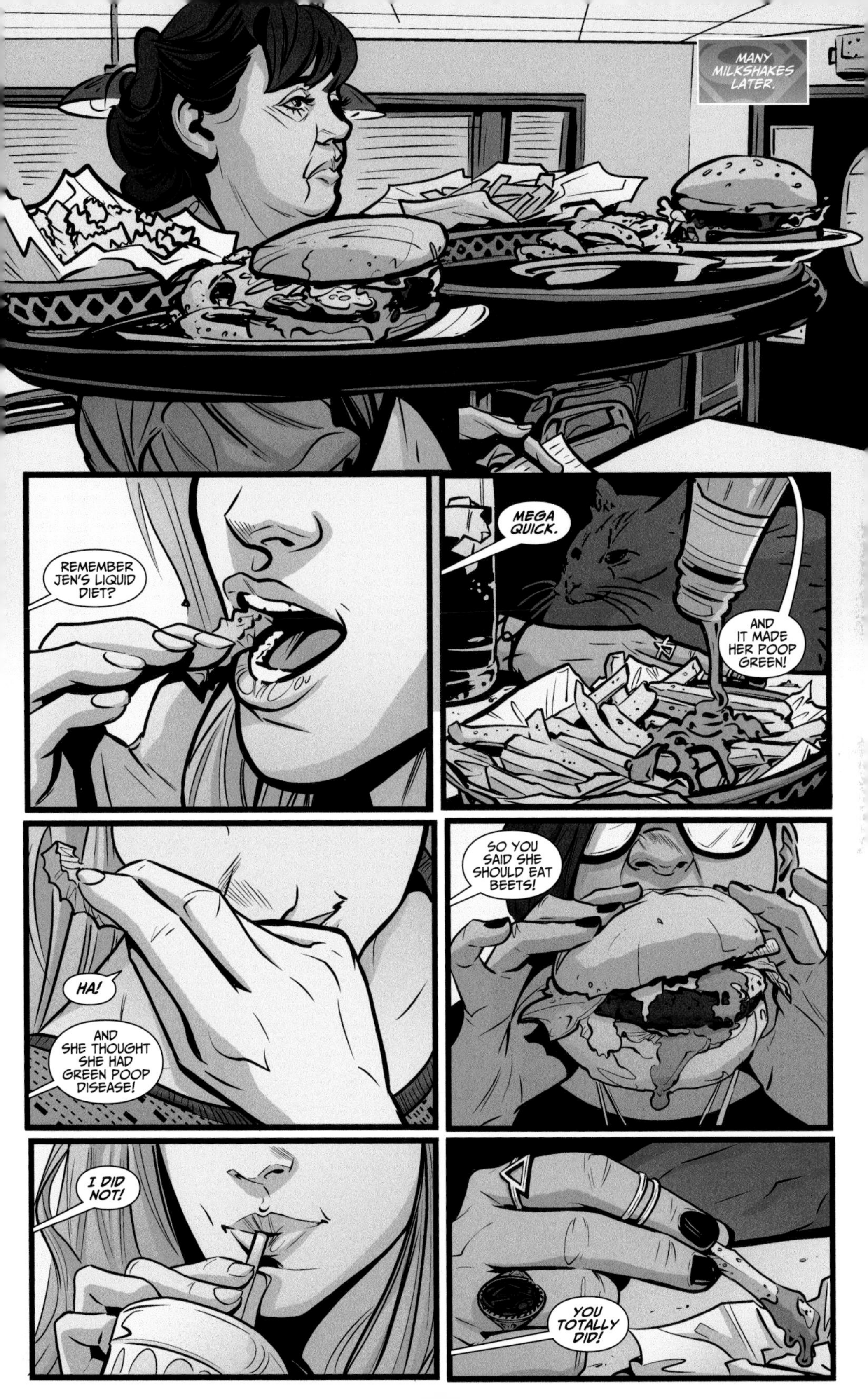
MANY MILKSHAKES LATER.
REMEMBER JEN'S LIQUID DIET?
MEGA QUICK.
AND IT MADE HER POOP GREEN!
HA!
AND SHE THOUGHT SHE HAD GREEN POOP DISEASE!
SO YOU SAID SHE SHOULD EAT BEETS!
I DID NOT!
YOU TOTALLY DID!

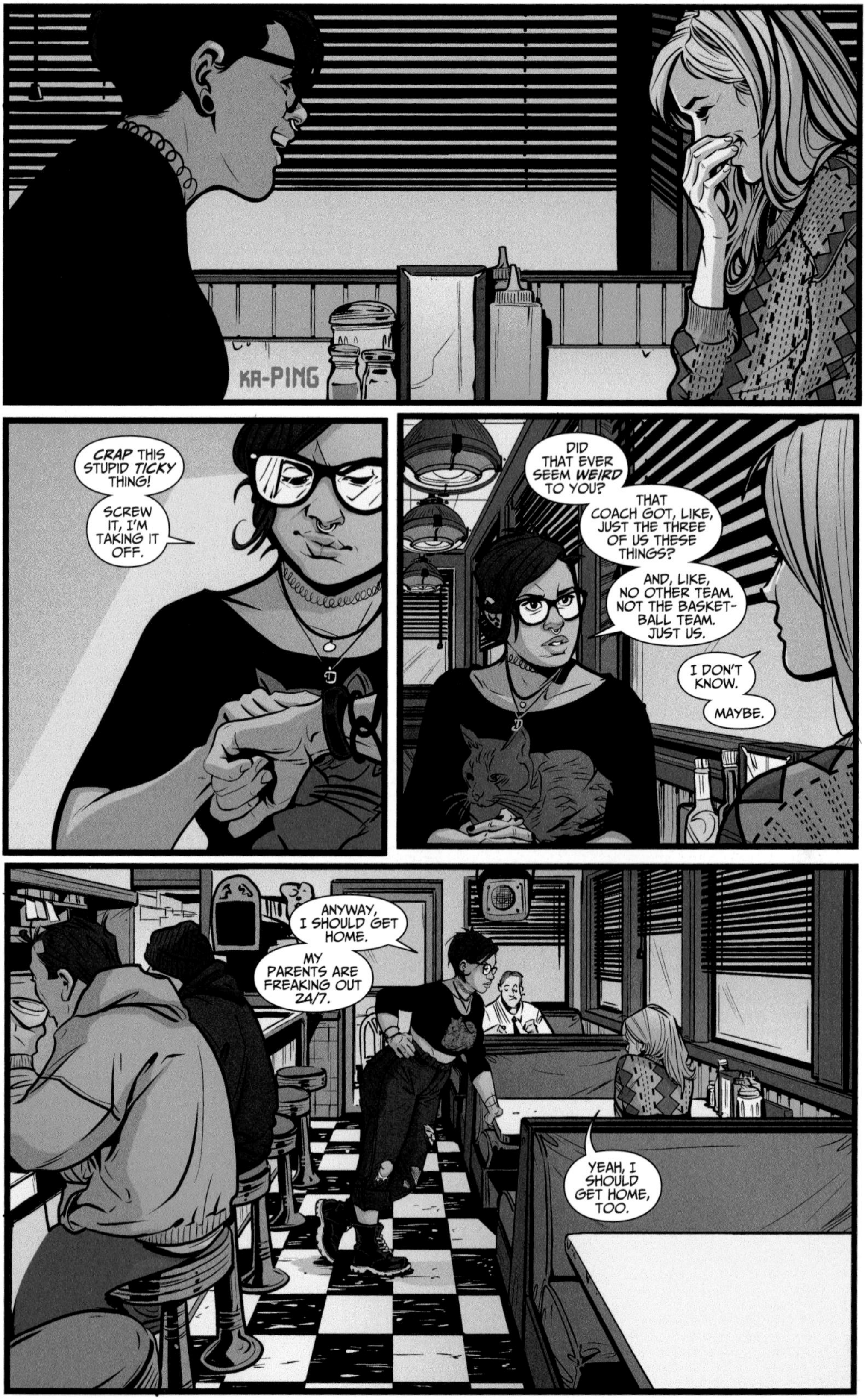
KA-PING
CRAP THIS STUPID TICKY THING!
SCREW IT, I'M TAKING IT OFF.
DID THAT EVER SEEM WEIRD TO YOU?
THAT COACH GOT, LIKE, JUST THE THREE OF US THESE THINGS?
AND, LIKE, NO OTHER TEAM. NOT THE BASKET-BALL TEAM. JUST US.
I DON'T KNOW.
MAYBE.
ANYWAY, I SHOULD GET HOME.
MY PARENTS ARE FREAKING OUT 24/7.
YEAH, I SHOULD GET HOME, TOO.

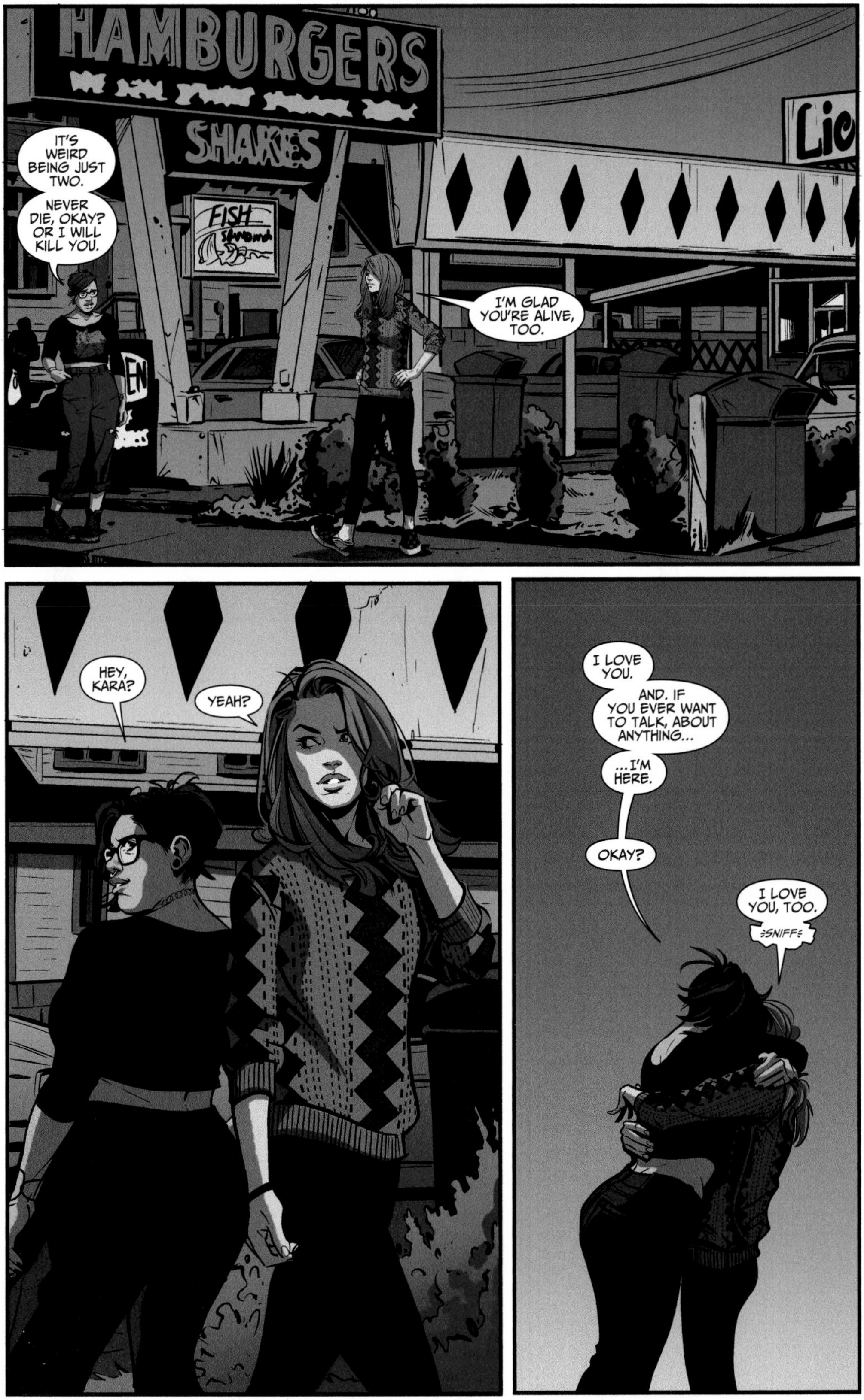
HAMBURGERS
SHAKES
FISH
IT'S WEIRD BEING JUST TWO.
NEVER DIE, OKAY? OR I WILL KILL YOU.
I'M GLAD YOU'RE ALIVE, TOO.
HEY, KARA?
YEAH?
I LOVE YOU.
AND. IF YOU EVER WANT TO TALK, ABOUT ANYTHING...
...I'M HERE.
OKAY?
I LOVE YOU, TOO.
SNIFF

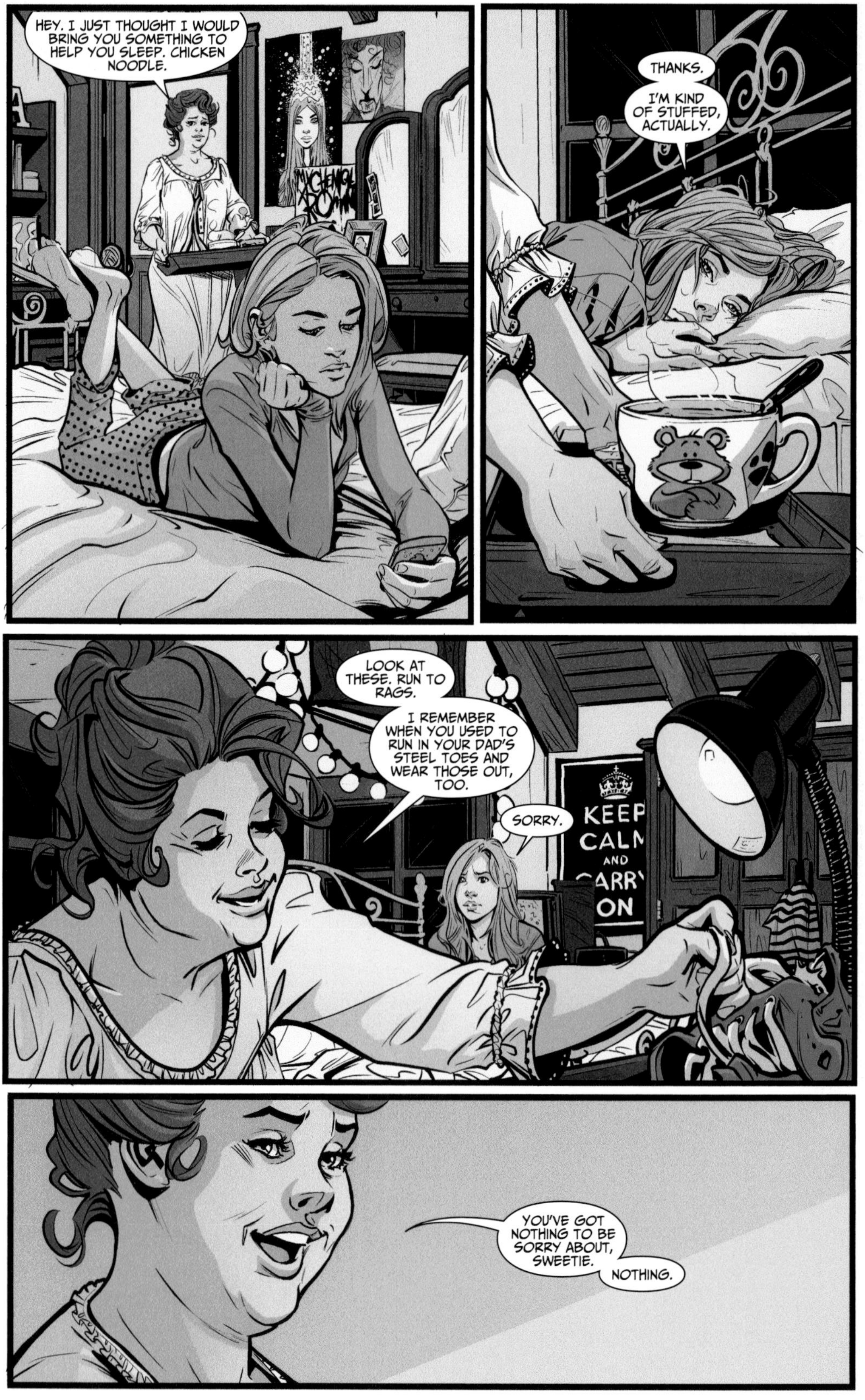
HEY. I JUST THOUGHT I WOULD BRING YOU SOMETHING TO HELP YOU SLEEP. CHICKEN NOODLE.
THANKS.
I'M KIND OF STUFFED, ACTUALLY.
LOOK AT THESE. RUN TO RAGS.
I REMEMBER WHEN YOU USED TO RUN IN YOUR DAD'S STEEL TOES AND WEAR THOSE OUT, TOO.
SORRY.
KEEP CALM AND CARRY ON
YOU'VE GOT NOTHING TO BE SORRY ABOUT, SWEETIE.
NOTHING.

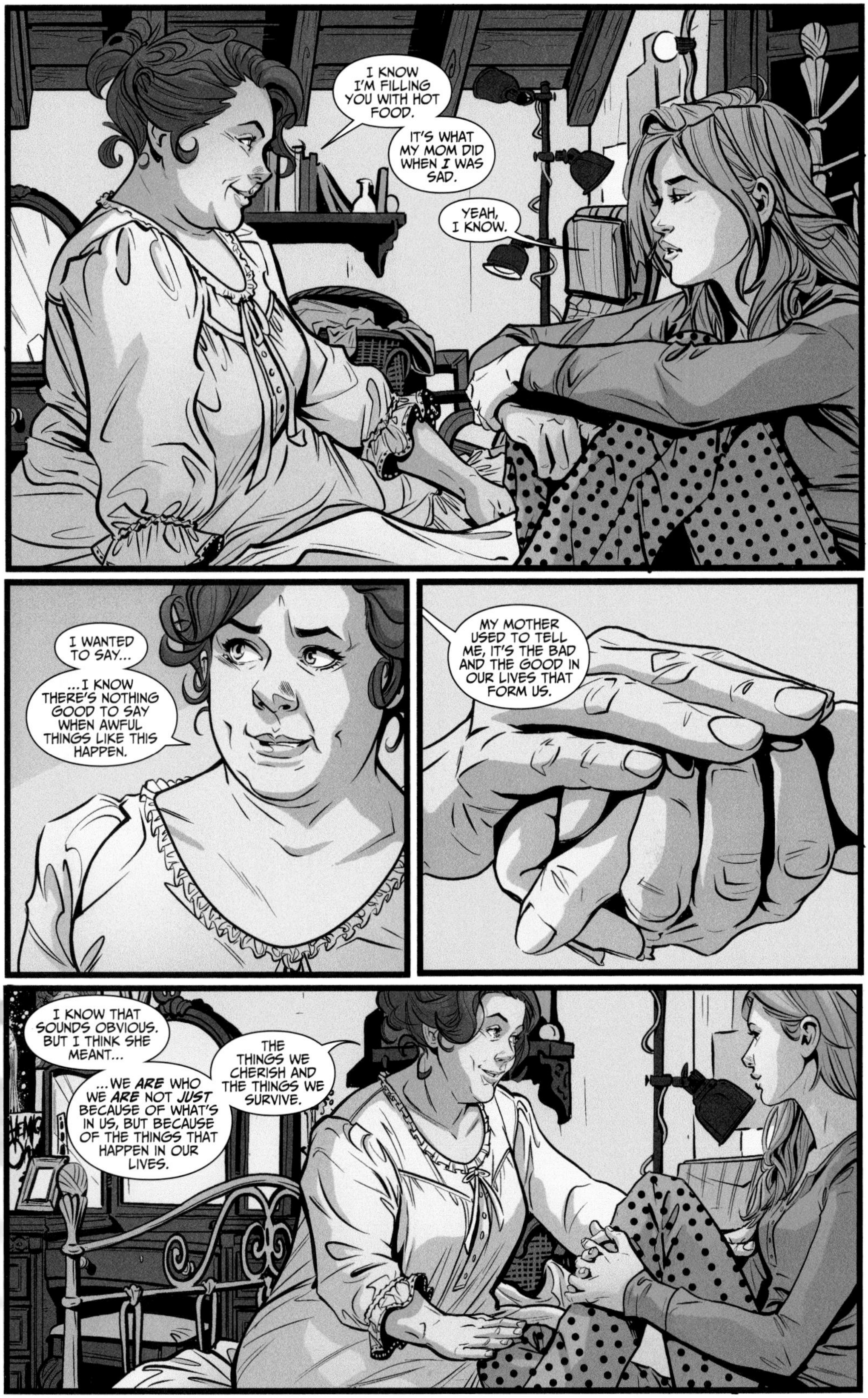
I KNOW I'M FILLING YOU WITH HOT FOOD.
IT'S WHAT MY MOM DID WHEN I WAS SAD.
YEAH, I KNOW.
I WANTED TO SAY...
...I KNOW THERE'S NOTHING GOOD TO SAY WHEN AWFUL THINGS LIKE THIS HAPPEN.
MY MOTHER USED TO TELL ME, IT'S THE BAD AND THE GOOD IN OUR LIVES THAT FORM US.
I KNOW THAT SOUNDS OBVIOUS. BUT I THINK SHE MEANT...
...WE ARE WHO WE ARE NOT JUST BECAUSE OF WHAT'S IN US, BUT BECAUSE OF THE THINGS THAT HAPPEN IN OUR LIVES.
THE THINGS WE CHERISH AND THE THINGS WE SURVIVE.

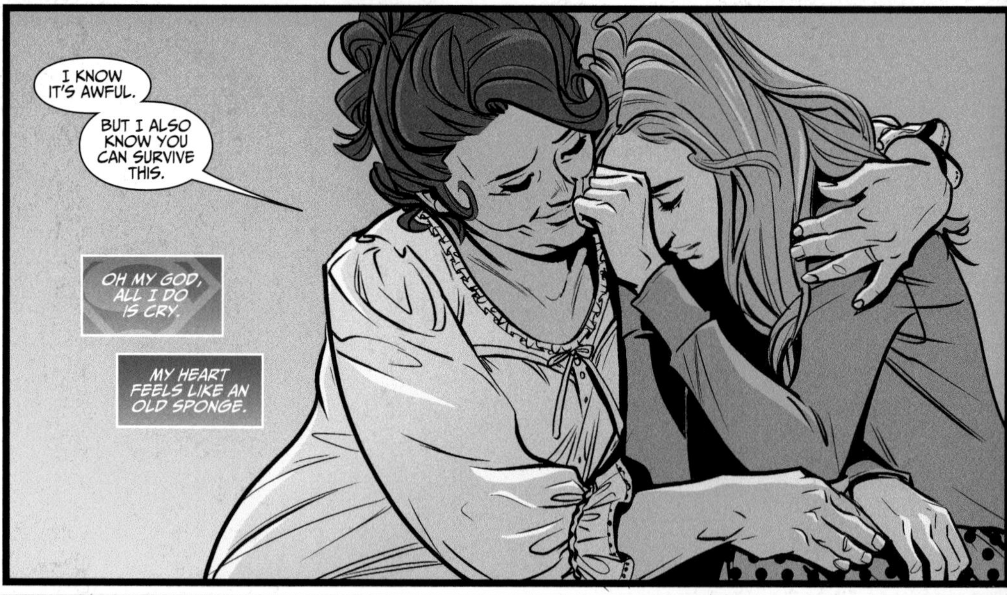
I KNOW IT'S AWFUL.
BUT I ALSO KNOW YOU CAN SURVIVE THIS.
OH MY GOD, ALL I DO IS CRY.
MY HEART FEELS LIKE AN OLD SPONGE.

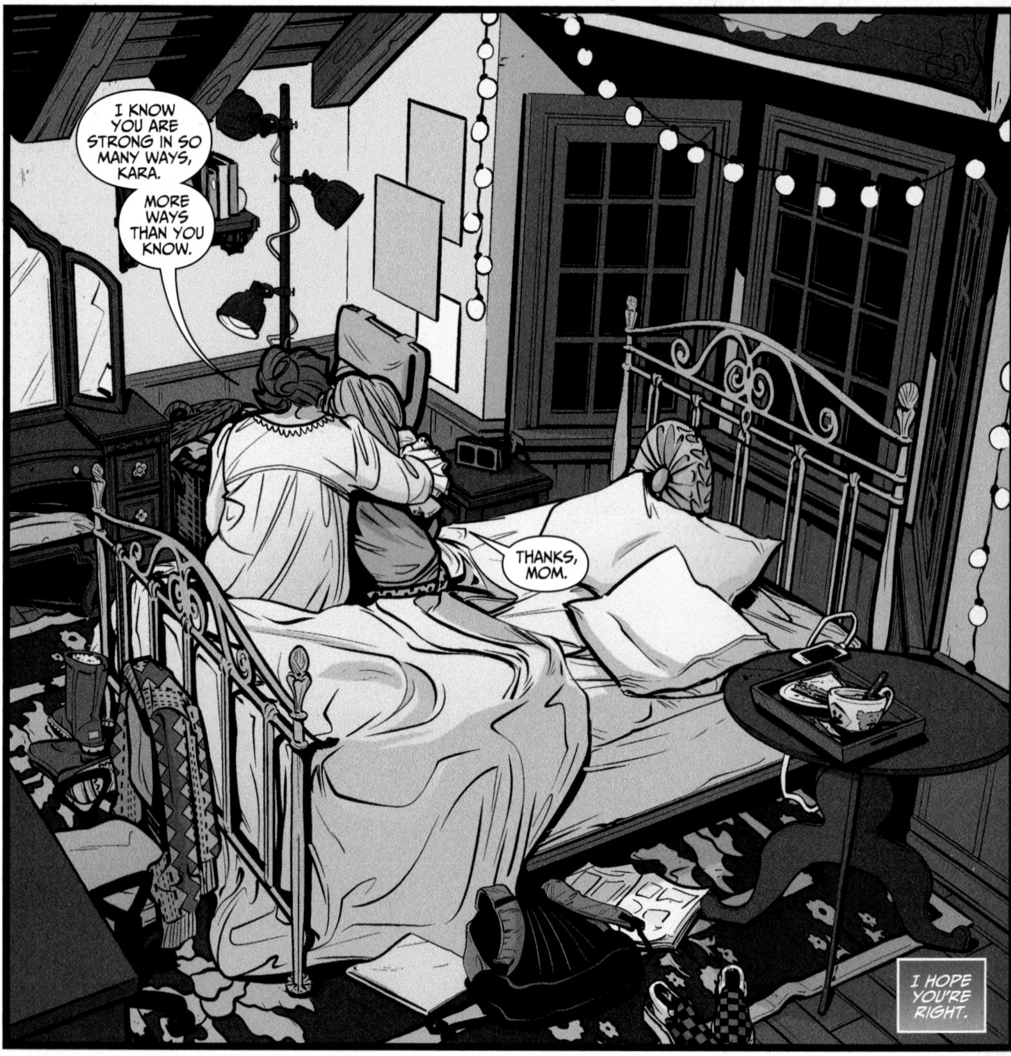
I KNOW YOU ARE STRONG IN SO MANY WAYS, KARA.
MORE WAYS THAN YOU KNOW.
THANKS, MOM.
I HOPE YOU'RE RIGHT.

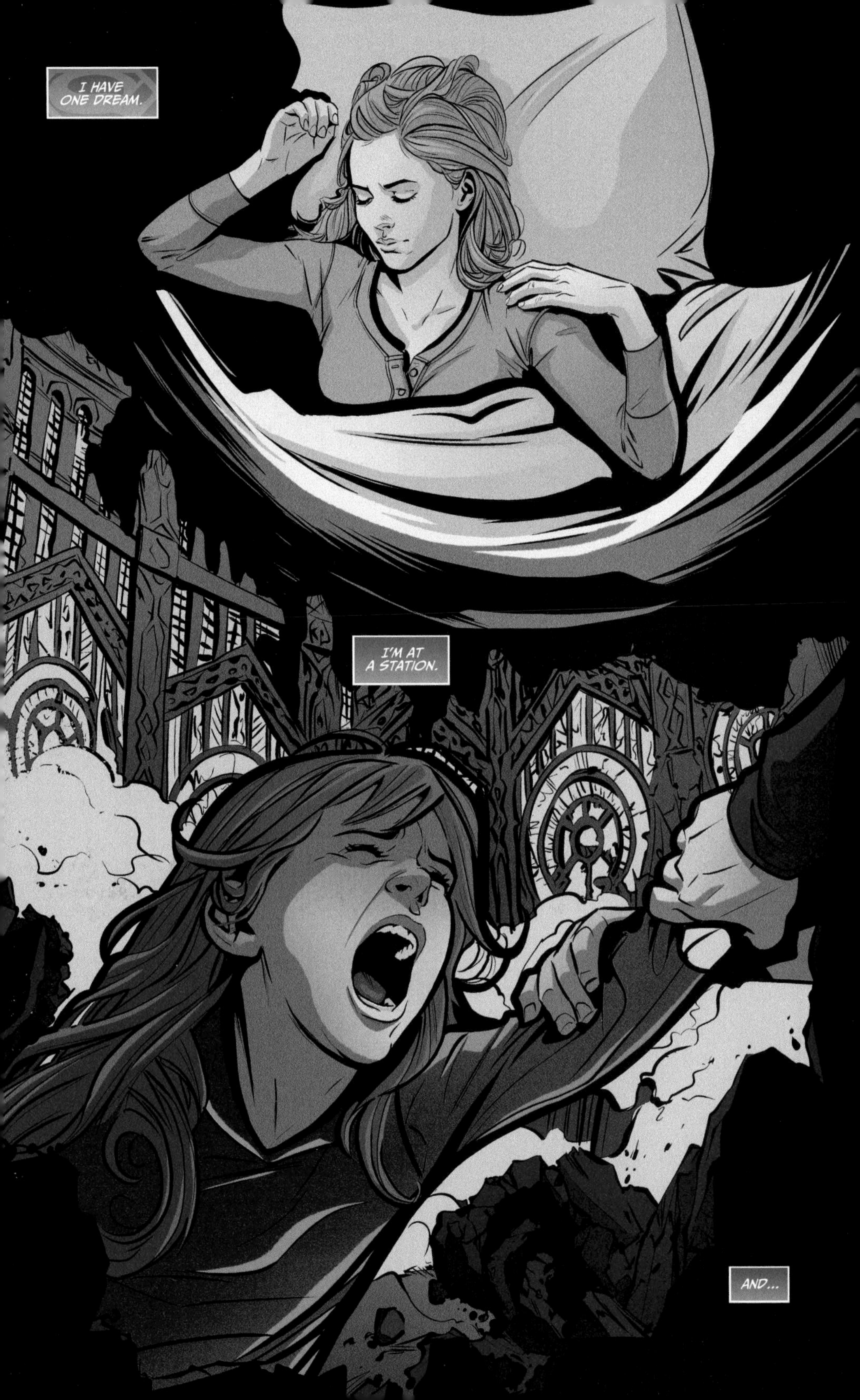
I HAVE ONE DREAM.
I'M AT A STATION.
AND...

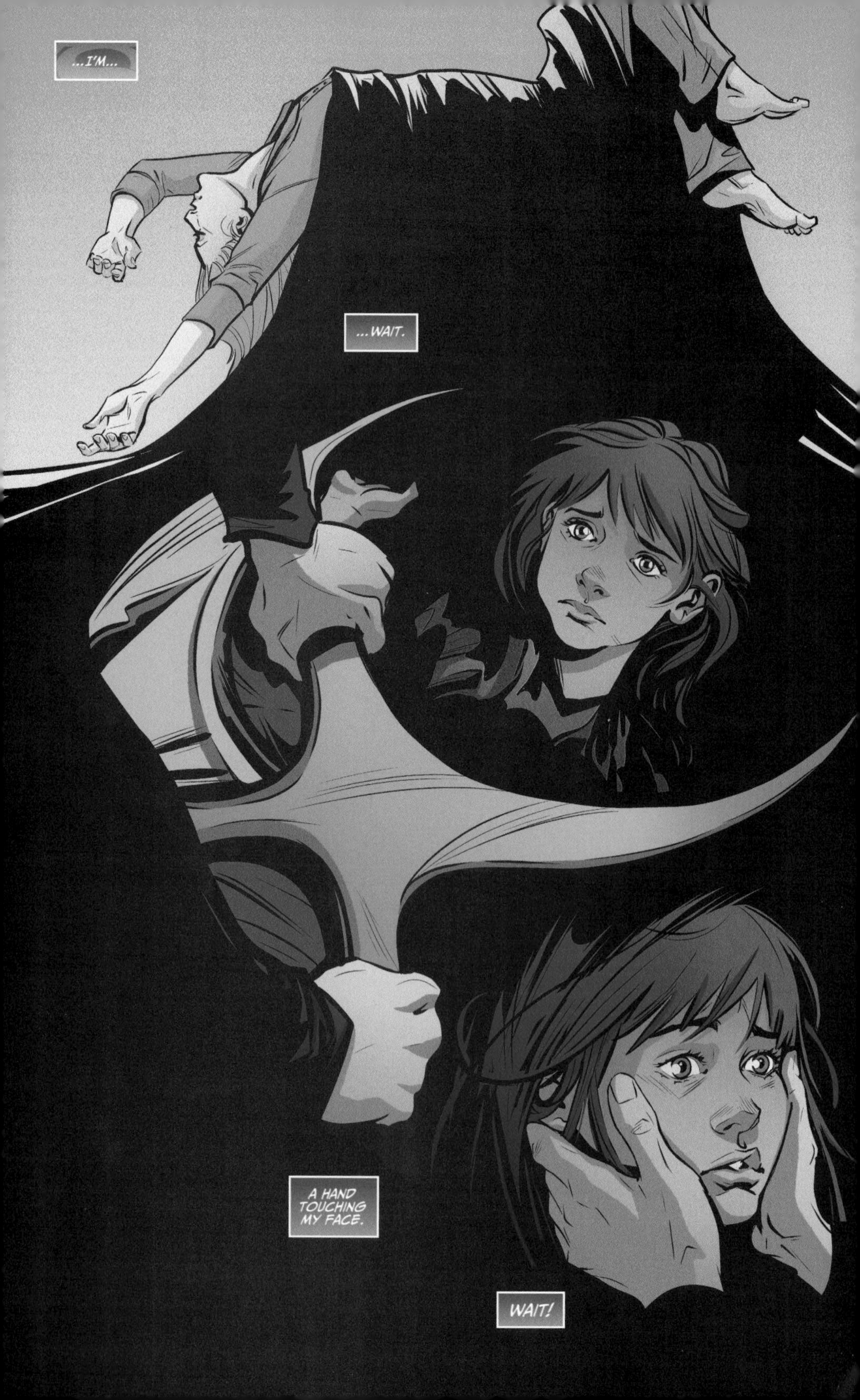
...I'M...
...WAIT.
A HAND TOUCHING MY FACE.
WAIT!

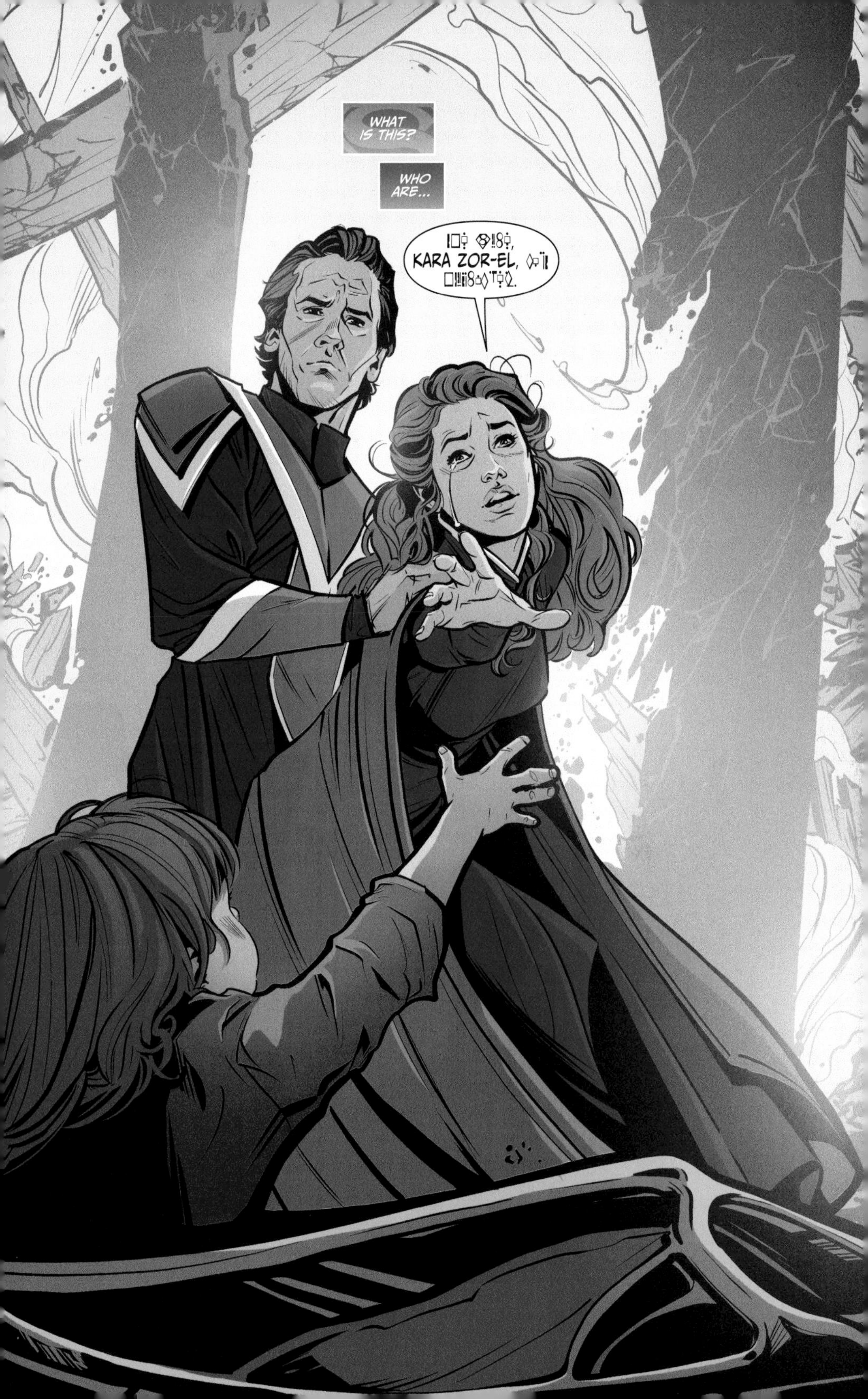
WHAT IS THIS?
WHO ARE...
KARA ZOR-EL,

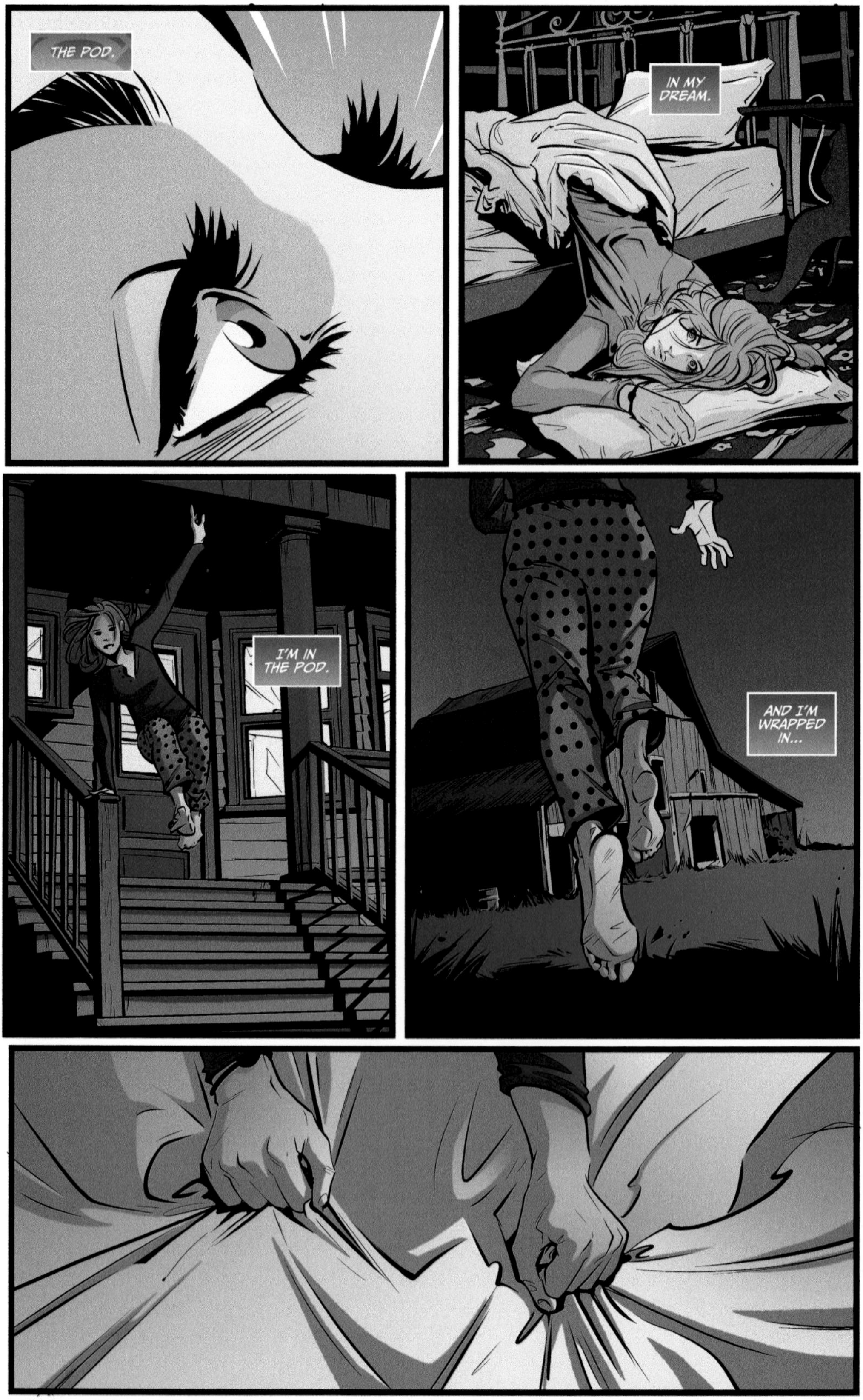
THE POD.
IN MY DREAM.
I'M IN THE POD.
AND I'M WRAPPED IN...

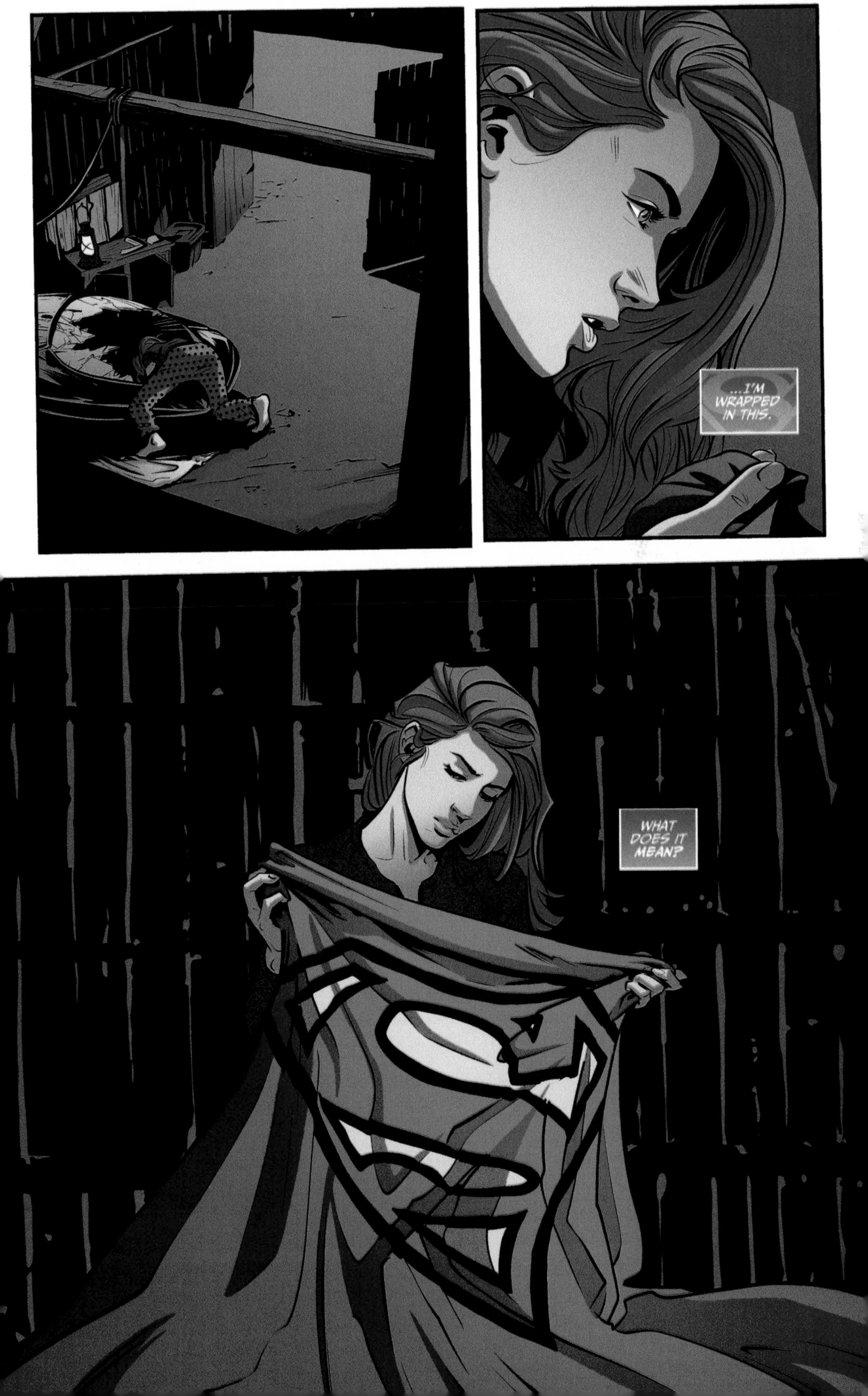
...I'M WRAPPED IN THIS.
WHAT DOES IT MEAN?

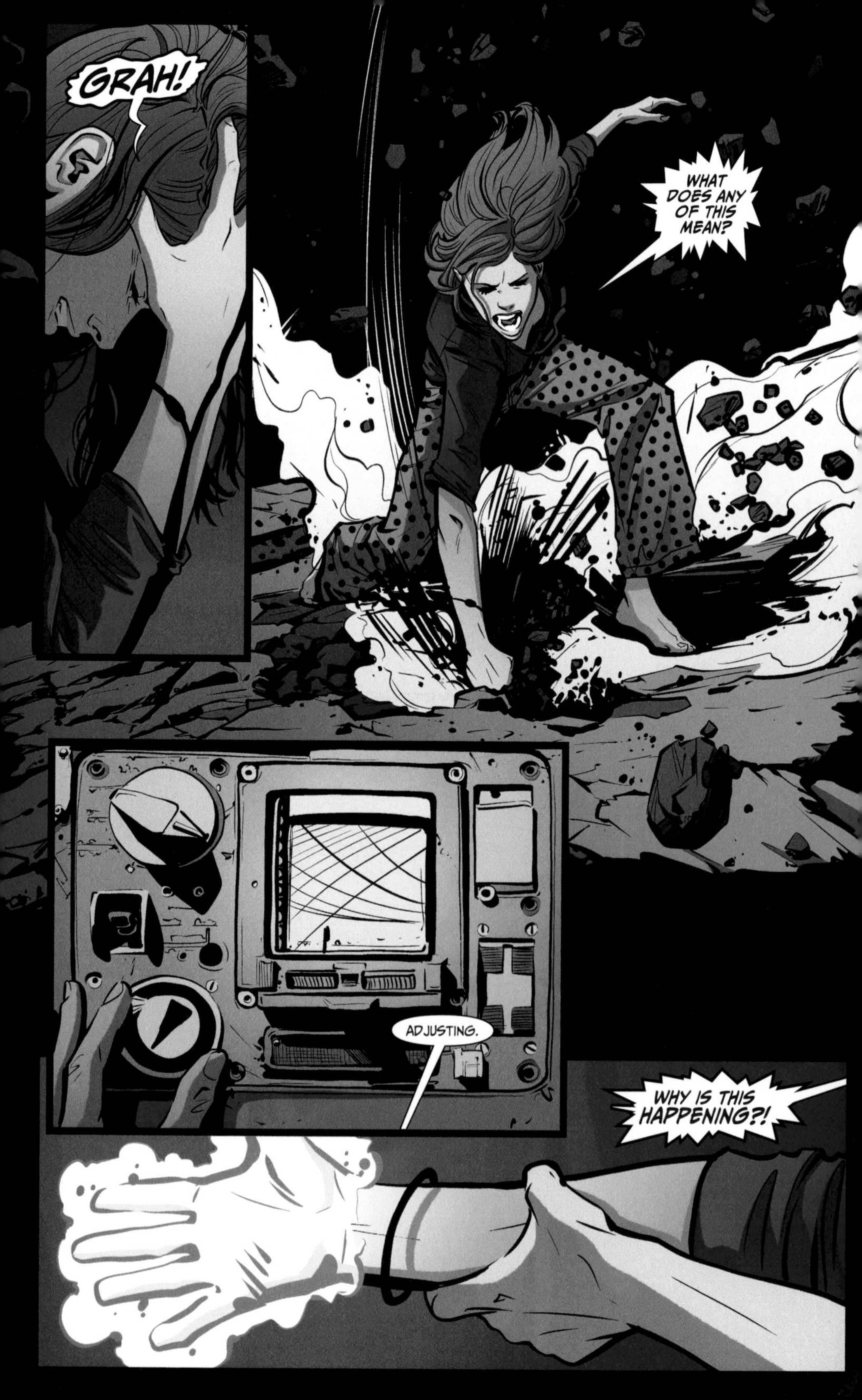
GRAH!
WHAT DOES ANY OF THIS MEAN?
ADJUSTING.
WHY IS THIS HAPPENING?!

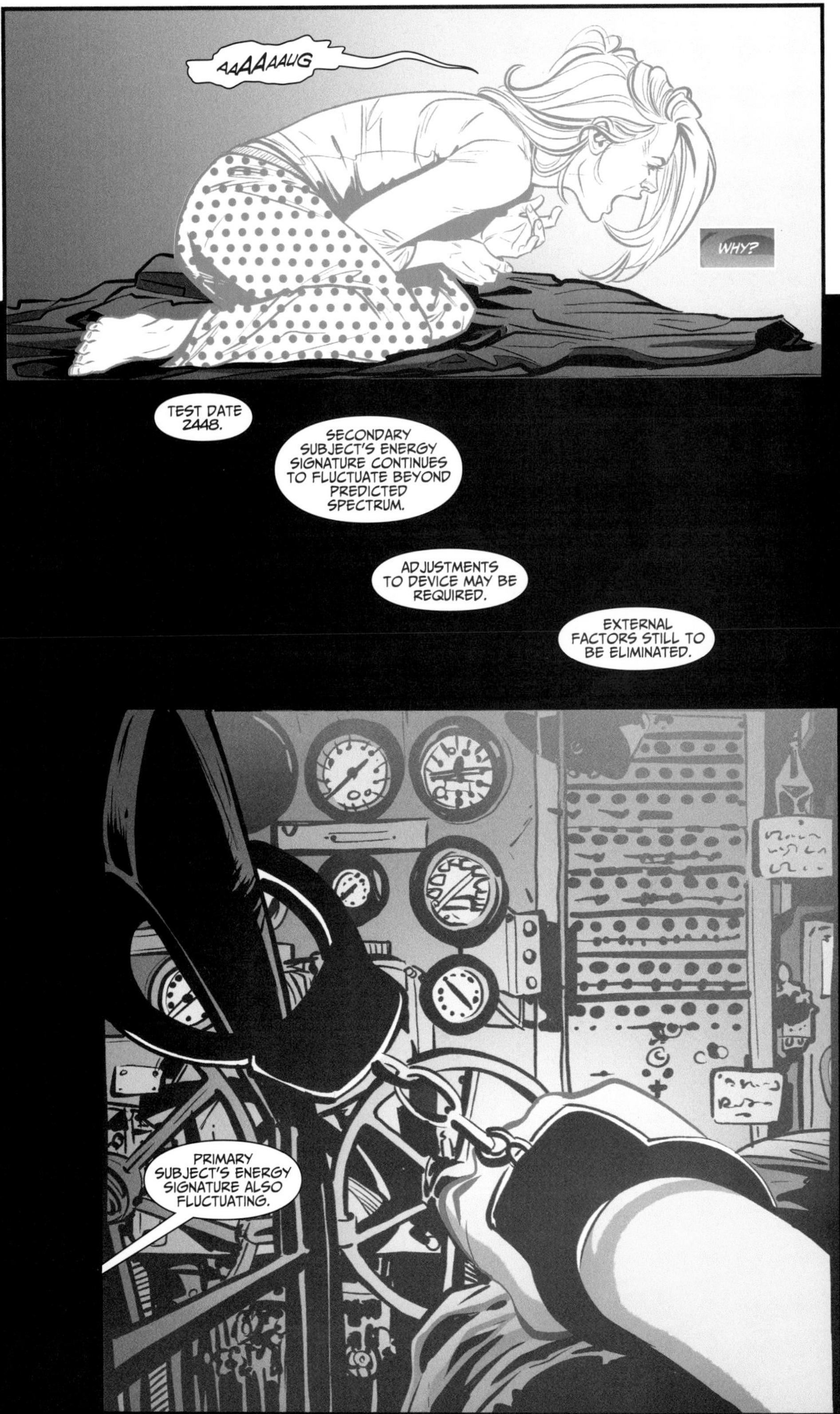
AAAAAAUG
WHY?
TEST DATE 2448.
SECONDARY SUBJECT'S ENERGY SIGNATURE CONTINUES TO FLUCTUATE BEYOND PREDICTED SPECTRUM.
ADJUSTMENTS TO DEVICE MAY BE REQUIRED.
EXTERNAL FACTORS STILL TO BE ELIMINATED.
PRIMARY SUBJECT'S ENERGY SIGNATURE ALSO FLUCTUATING.

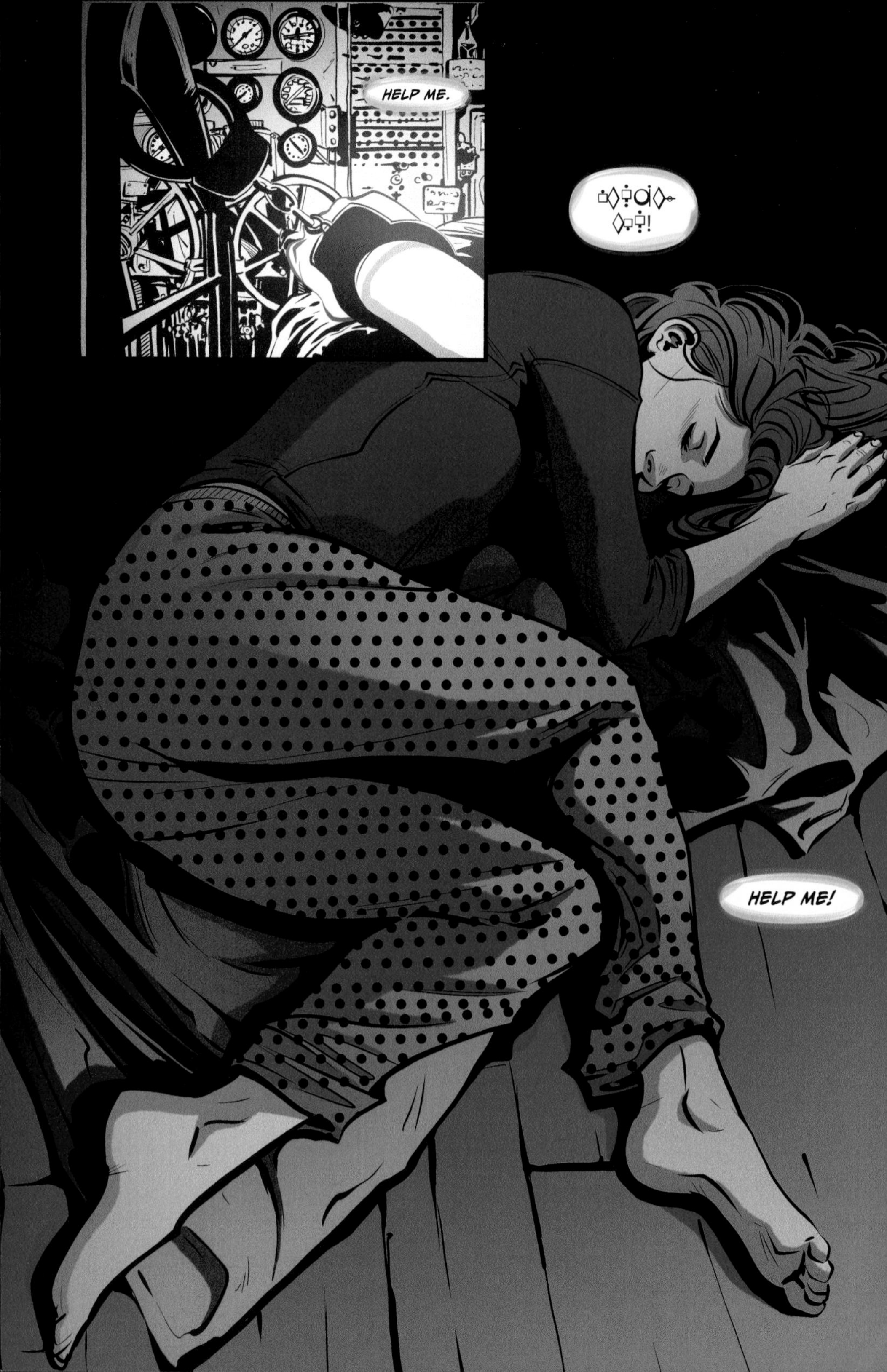
HELP ME.
HELP ME!

CHAPTER THREE: WHO ARE YOU?

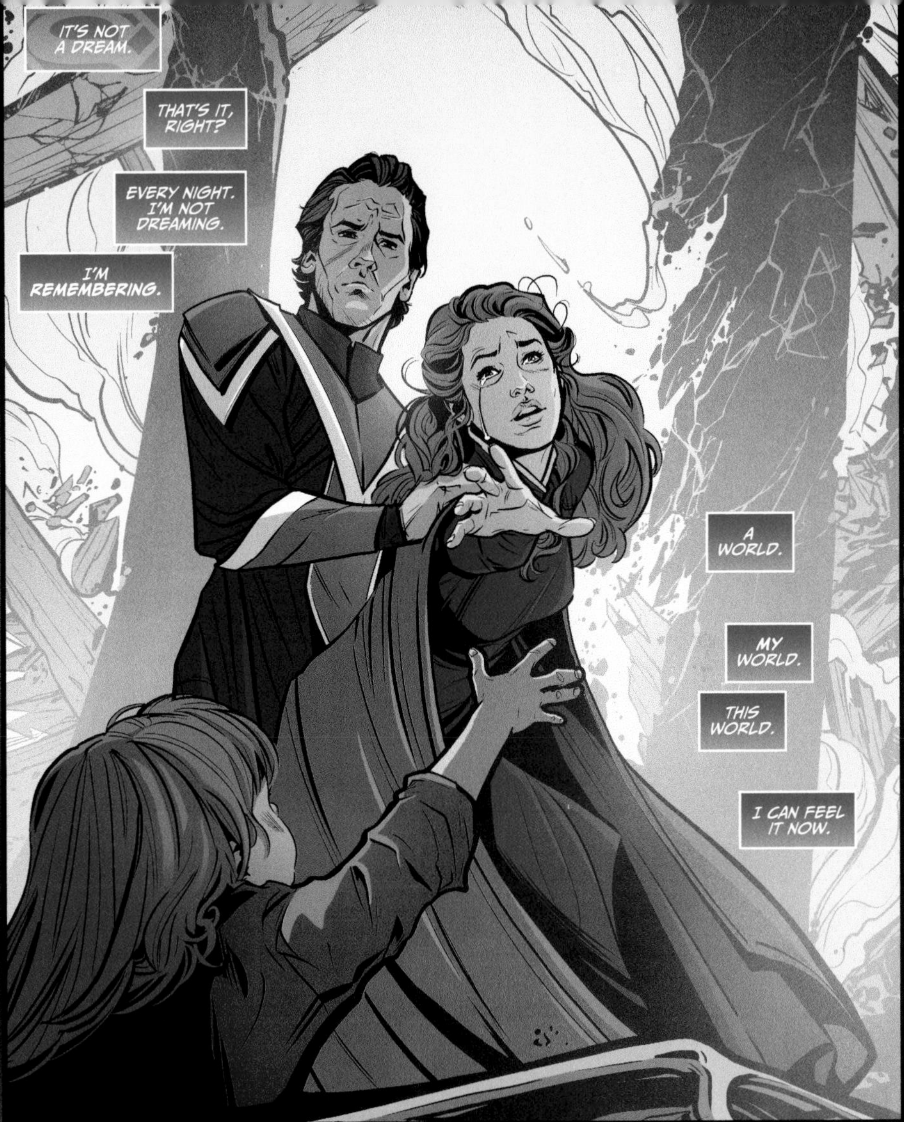
IT'S NOT A DREAM.
THAT'S IT, RIGHT?
EVERY NIGHT. I'M NOT DREAMING.
I'M REMEMBERING.
A WORLD.
MY WORLD.
THIS WORLD.
I CAN FEEL IT NOW.

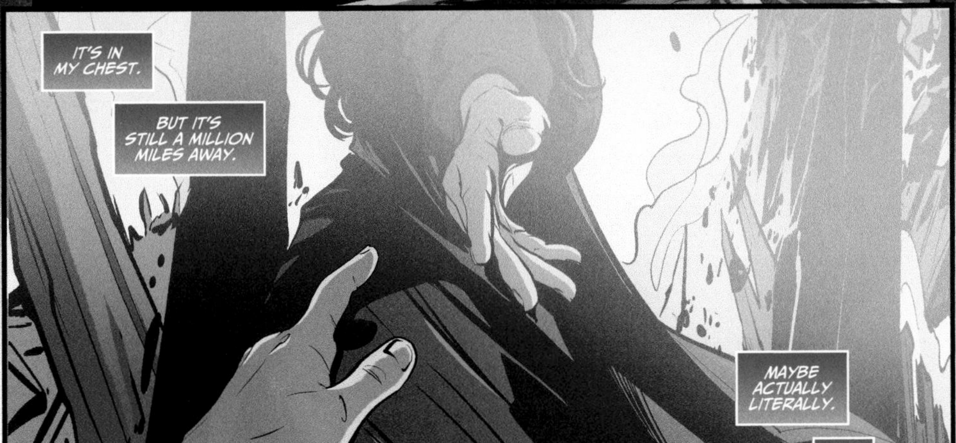
IT'S IN MY CHEST.
BUT IT'S STILL A MILLION MILES AWAY.
MAYBE ACTUALLY LITERALLY.
SO...

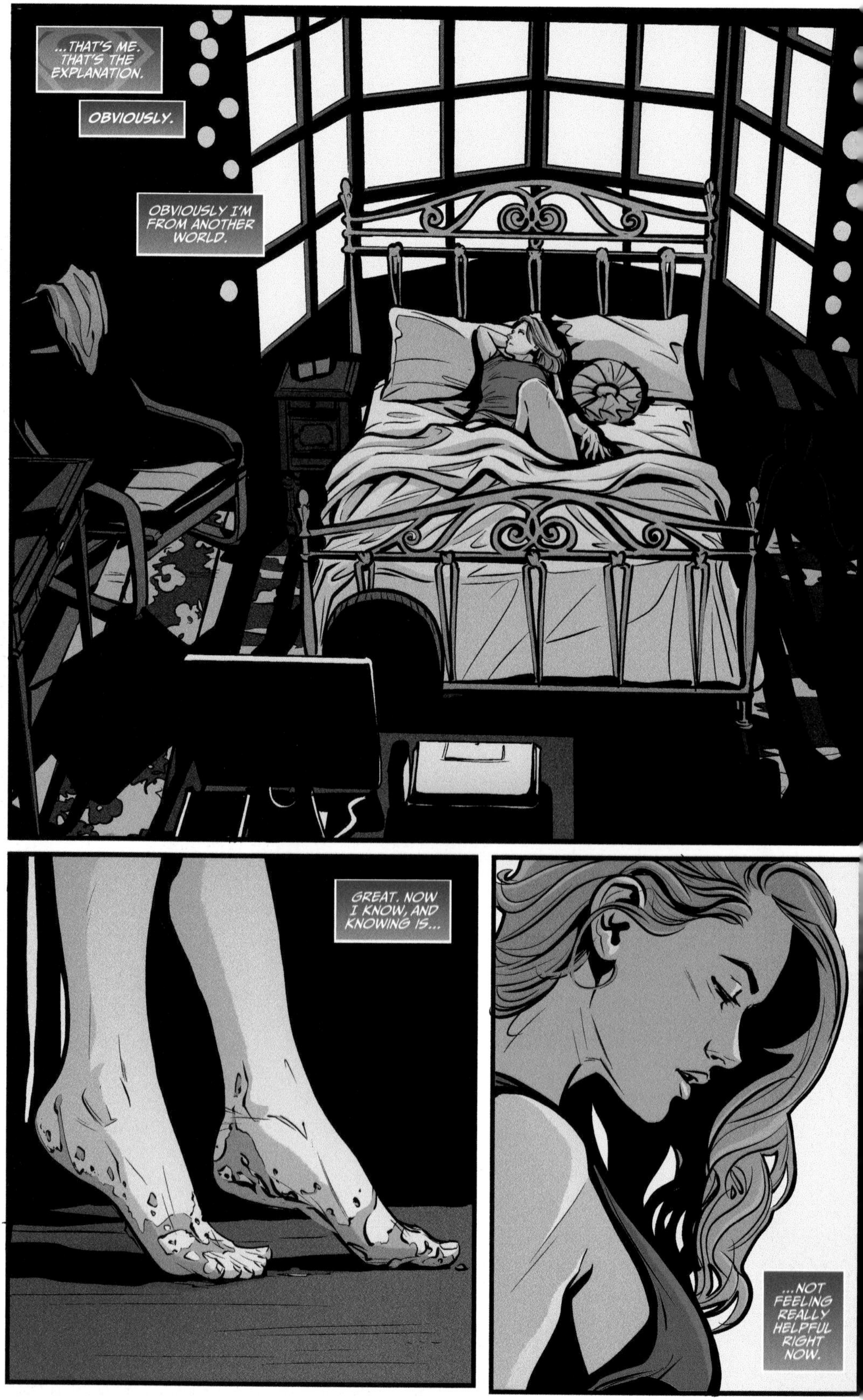
...THAT'S ME. THAT'S THE EXPLANATION.
OBVIOUSLY.
OBVIOUSLY I'M FROM ANOTHER WORLD.
GREAT. NOW I KNOW, AND KNOWING IS...
...NOT FEELING REALLY HELPFUL RIGHT NOW.

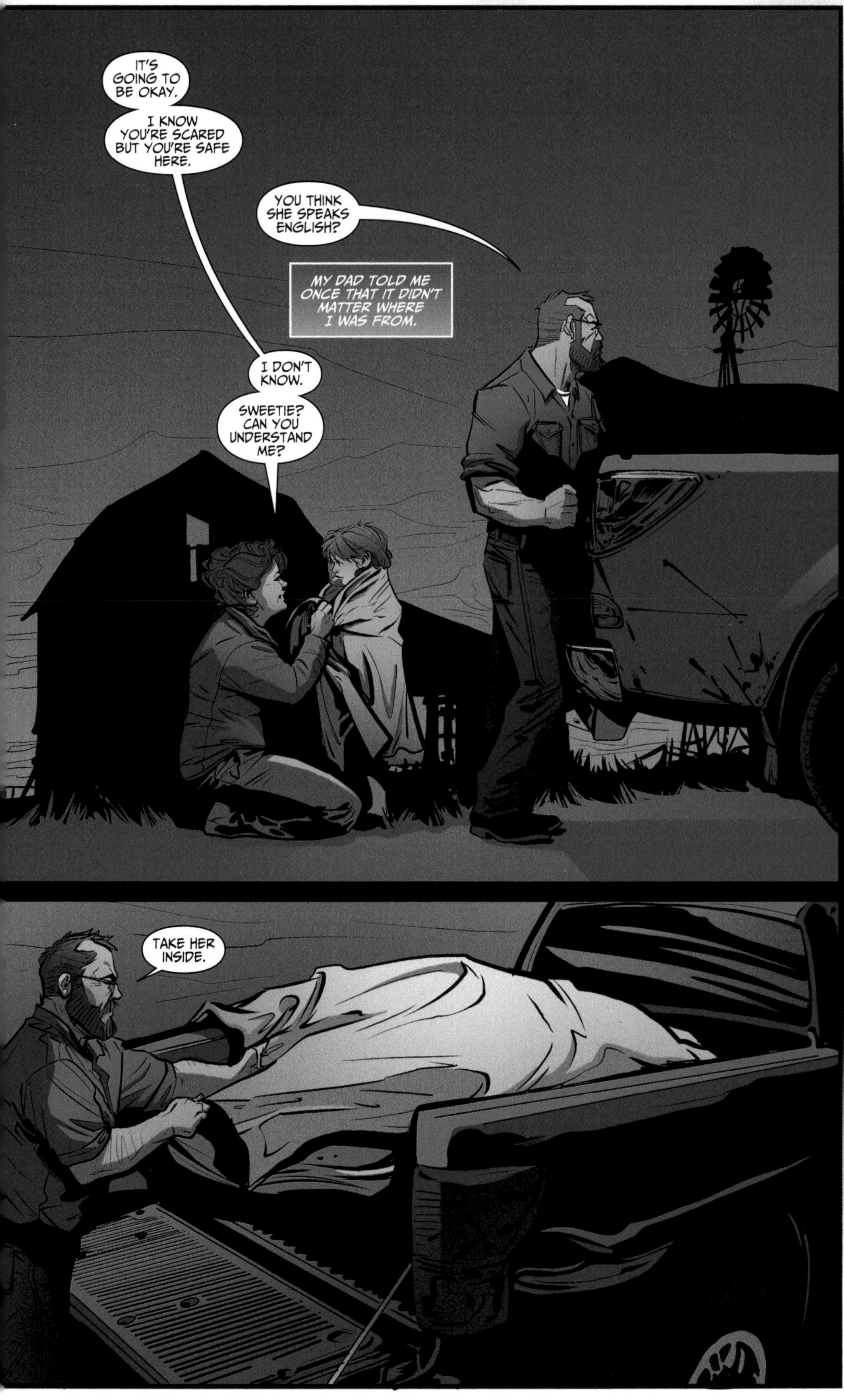
IT'S GOING TO BE OKAY.
I KNOW YOU'RE SCARED BUT YOU'RE SAFE HERE.
YOU THINK SHE SPEAKS ENGLISH?
MY DAD TOLD ME ONCE THAT IT DIDN'T MATTER WHERE I WAS FROM.
I DON'T KNOW.
SWEETIE? CAN YOU UNDERSTAND ME?
TAKE HER INSIDE.

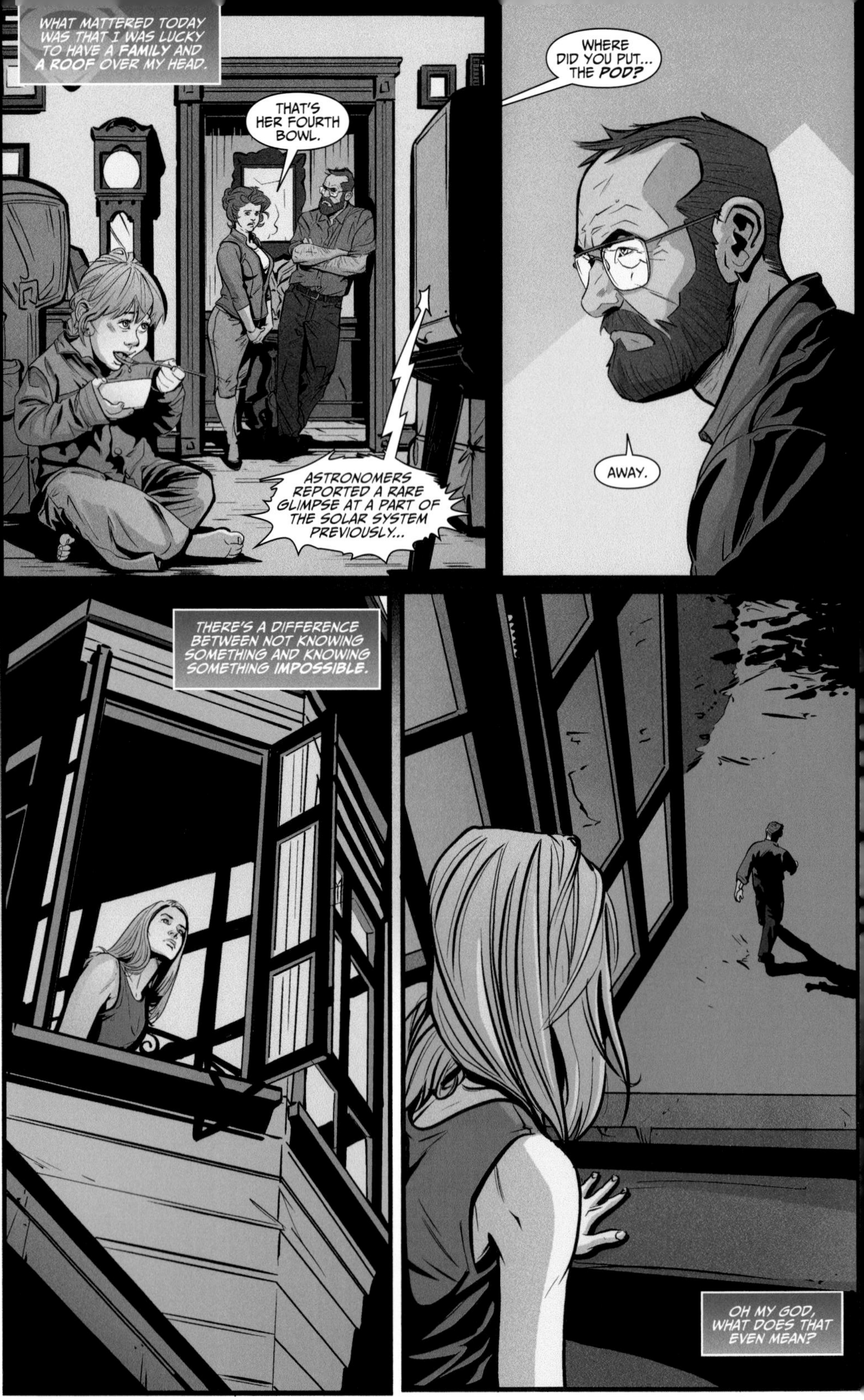
WHAT MATTERED TODAY WAS THAT I WAS LUCKY TO HAVE A FAMILY AND A ROOF OVER MY HEAD.
THAT'S HER FOURTH BOWL.
ASTRONOMERS REPORTED A RARE GLIMPSE AT A PART OF THE SOLAR SYSTEM PREVIOUSLY...
WHERE DID YOU PUT... THE POD?
AWAY.
THERE'S A DIFFERENCE BETWEEN NOT KNOWING SOMETHING AND KNOWING SOMETHING IMPOSSIBLE.
OH MY GOD, WHAT DOES THAT EVEN MEAN?

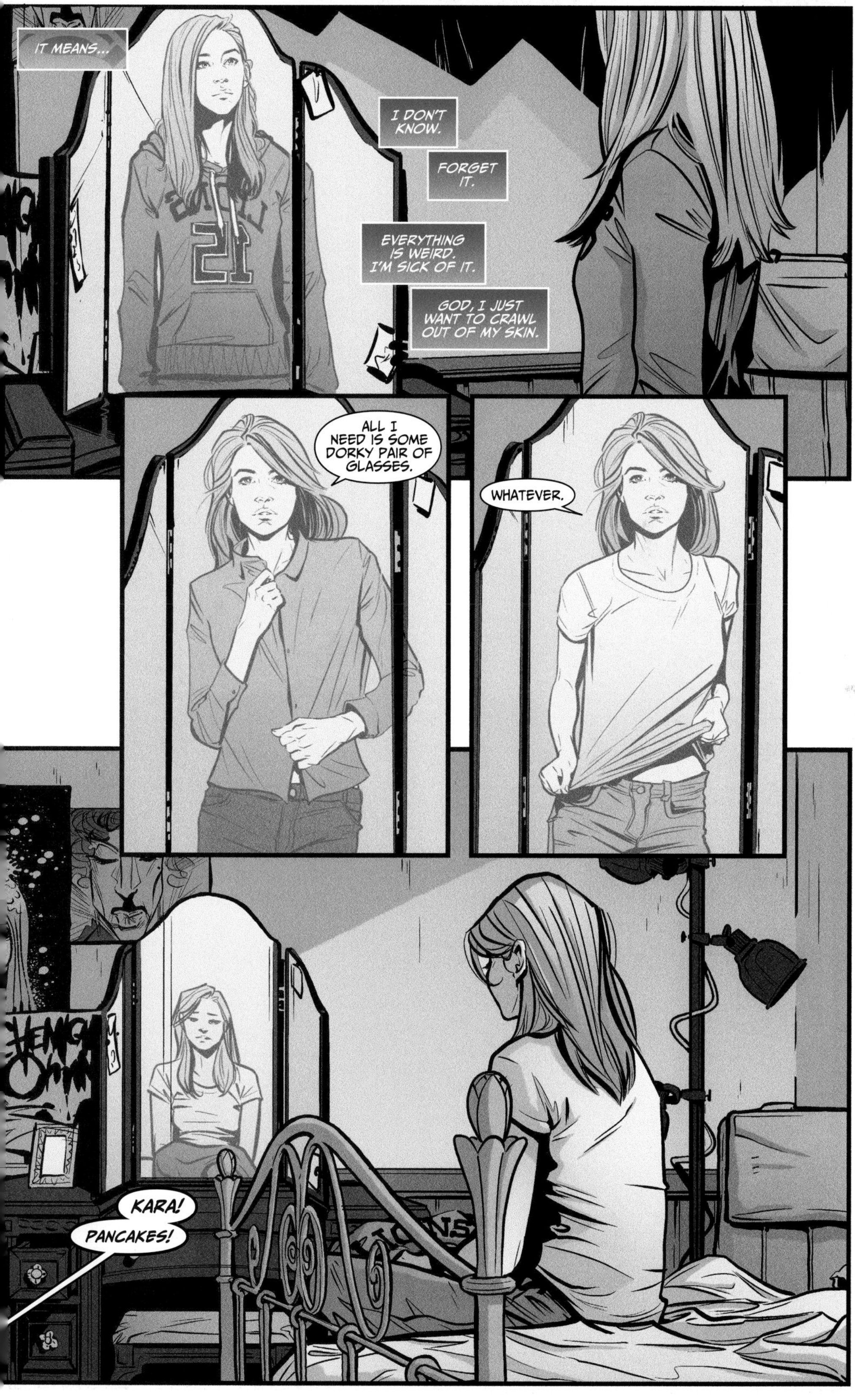
IT MEANS...
I DON'T KNOW.
FORGET IT.
EVERYTHING IS WEIRD. I'M SICK OF IT.
GOD, I JUST WANT TO CRAWL OUT OF MY SKIN.
ALL I NEED IS SOME DORKY PAIR OF GLASSES.
WHATEVER.
KARA!
PANCAKES!

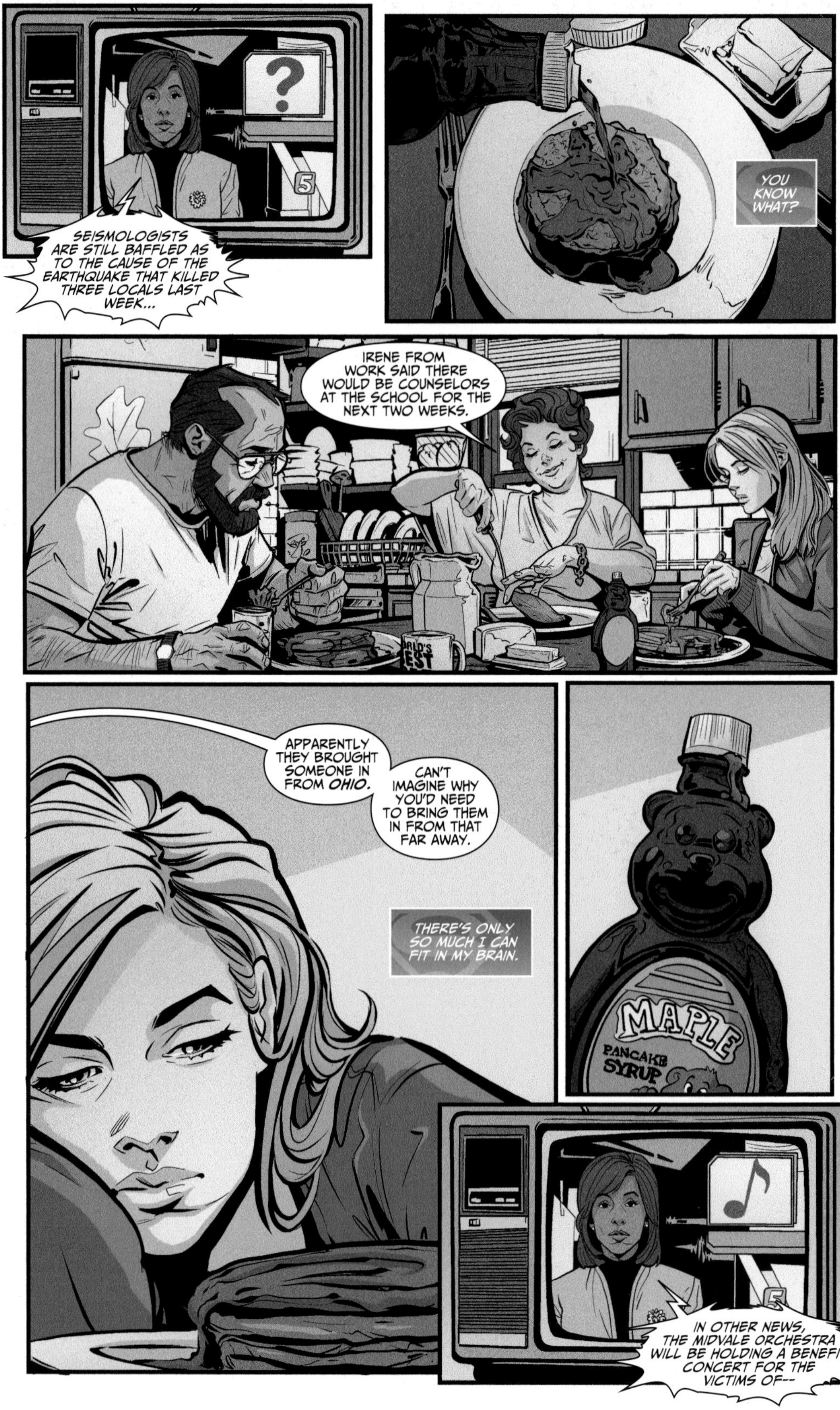
SEISMOLOGISTS ARE STILL BAFFLED AS TO THE CAUSE OF THE EARTHQUAKE THAT KILLED THREE LOCALS LAST WEEK...
YOU KNOW WHAT?
IRENE FROM WORK SAID THERE WOULD BE COUNSELORS AT THE SCHOOL FOR THE NEXT TWO WEEKS.
APPARENTLY THEY BROUGHT SOMEONE IN FROM OHIO.
CAN'T IMAGINE WHY YOU'D NEED TO BRING THEM IN FROM THAT FAR AWAY.
THERE'S ONLY SO MUCH I CAN FIT IN MY BRAIN.
MAPLE
PANCAKE SYRUP
IN OTHER NEWS, THE MIDVALE ORCHESTRA WILL BE HOLDING A BENEFIT CONCERT FOR THE VICTIMS OF--

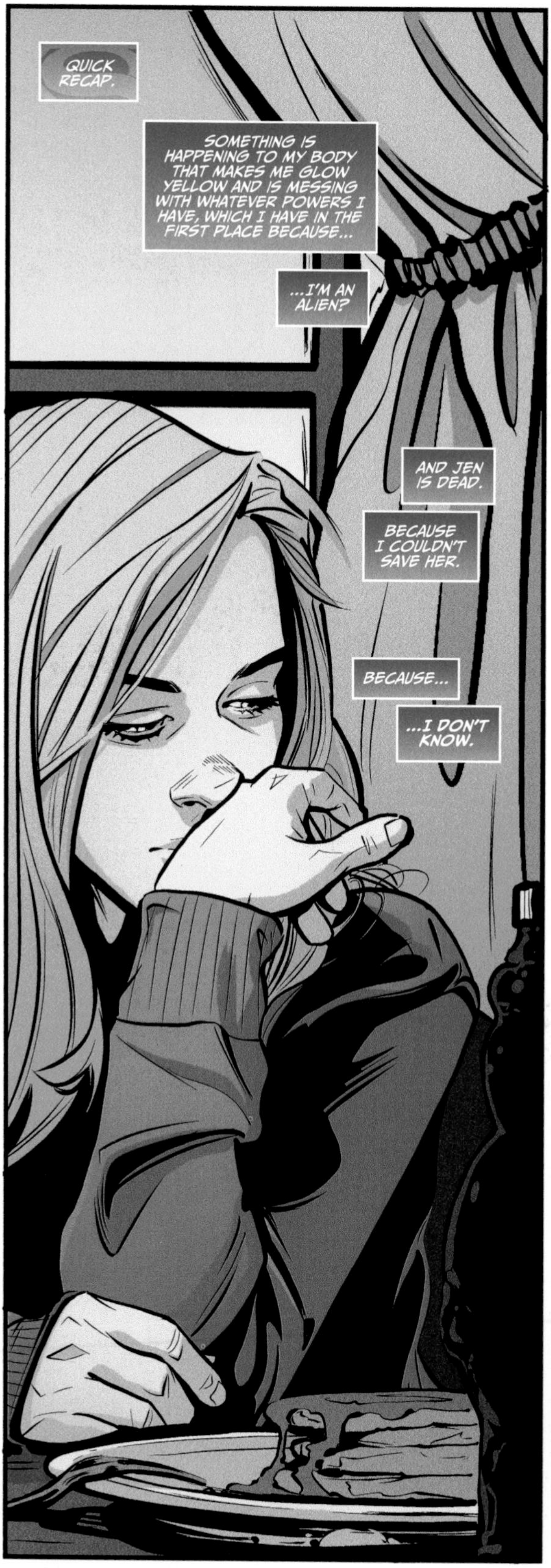
QUICK RECAP.
SOMETHING IS HAPPENING TO MY BODY THAT MAKES ME GLOW YELLOW AND IS MESSING WITH WHATEVER POWERS I HAVE, WHICH I HAVE IN THE FIRST PLACE BECAUSE...
...I'M AN ALIEN?
AND JEN IS DEAD.
BECAUSE I COULDN'T SAVE HER.
BECAUSE...
...I DON'T KNOW.

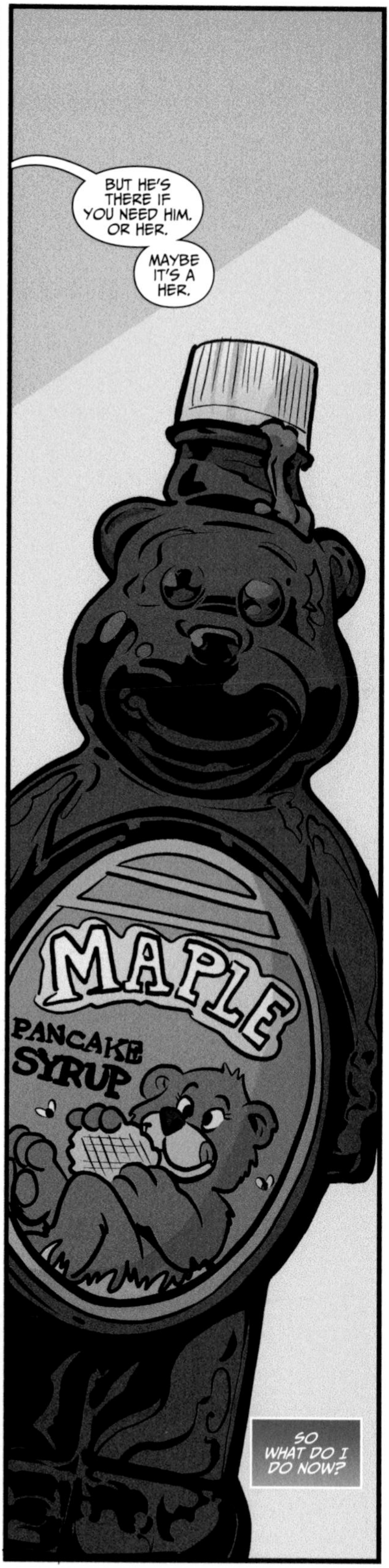
BUT HE'S THERE IF YOU NEED HIM. OR HER.
MAYBE IT'S A HER.
MAPLE
PANCAKE SYRUP
SO WHAT DO I DO NOW?

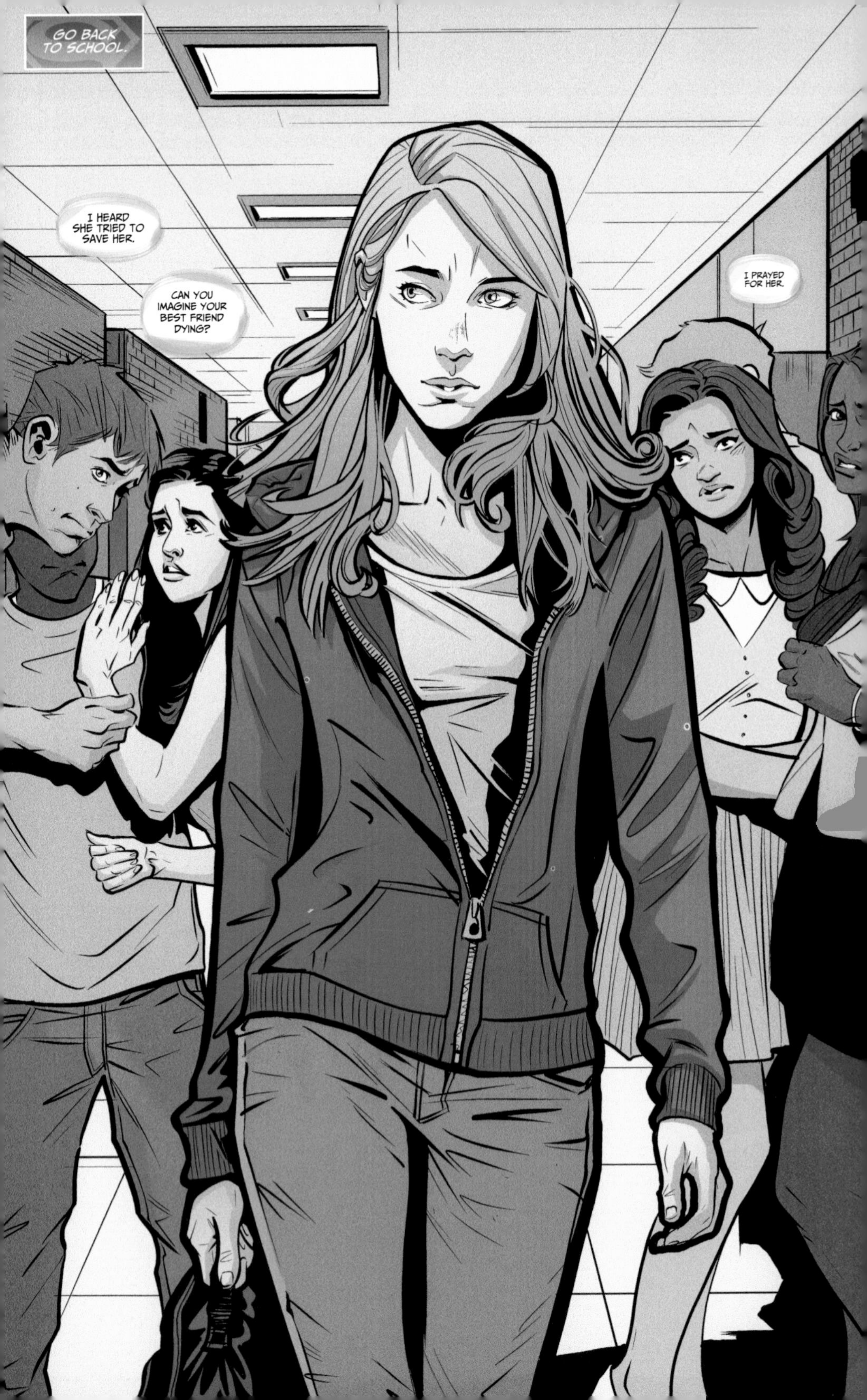
GO BACK TO SCHOOL.
I HEARD SHE TRIED TO SAVE HER.
CAN YOU IMAGINE YOUR BEST FRIEND DYING?
I PRAYED FOR HER.

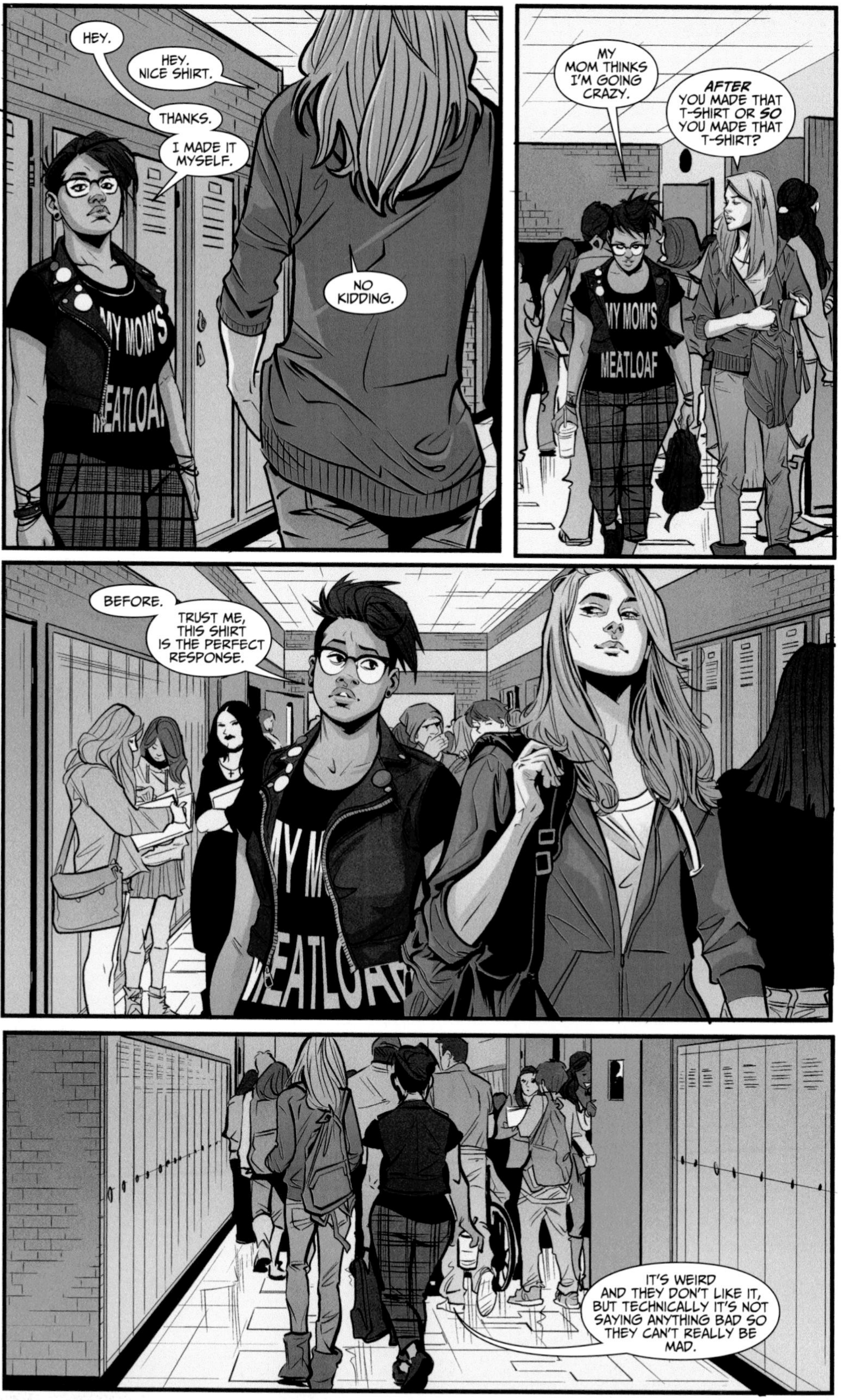
HEY.
HEY. NICE SHIRT.
THANKS.
I MADE IT MYSELF.
MY MOM'S MEATLOAF
NO KIDDING.
MY MOM THINKS I'M GOING CRAZY.
AFTER YOU MADE THAT T-SHIRT OR SO YOU MADE THAT T-SHIRT?
MY MOM'S MEATLOAF
BEFORE.
TRUST ME, THIS SHIRT IS THE PERFECT RESPONSE.
IT'S WEIRD AND THEY DON'T LIKE IT, BUT TECHNICALLY IT'S NOT SAYING ANYTHING BAD SO THEY CAN'T REALLY BE MAD.

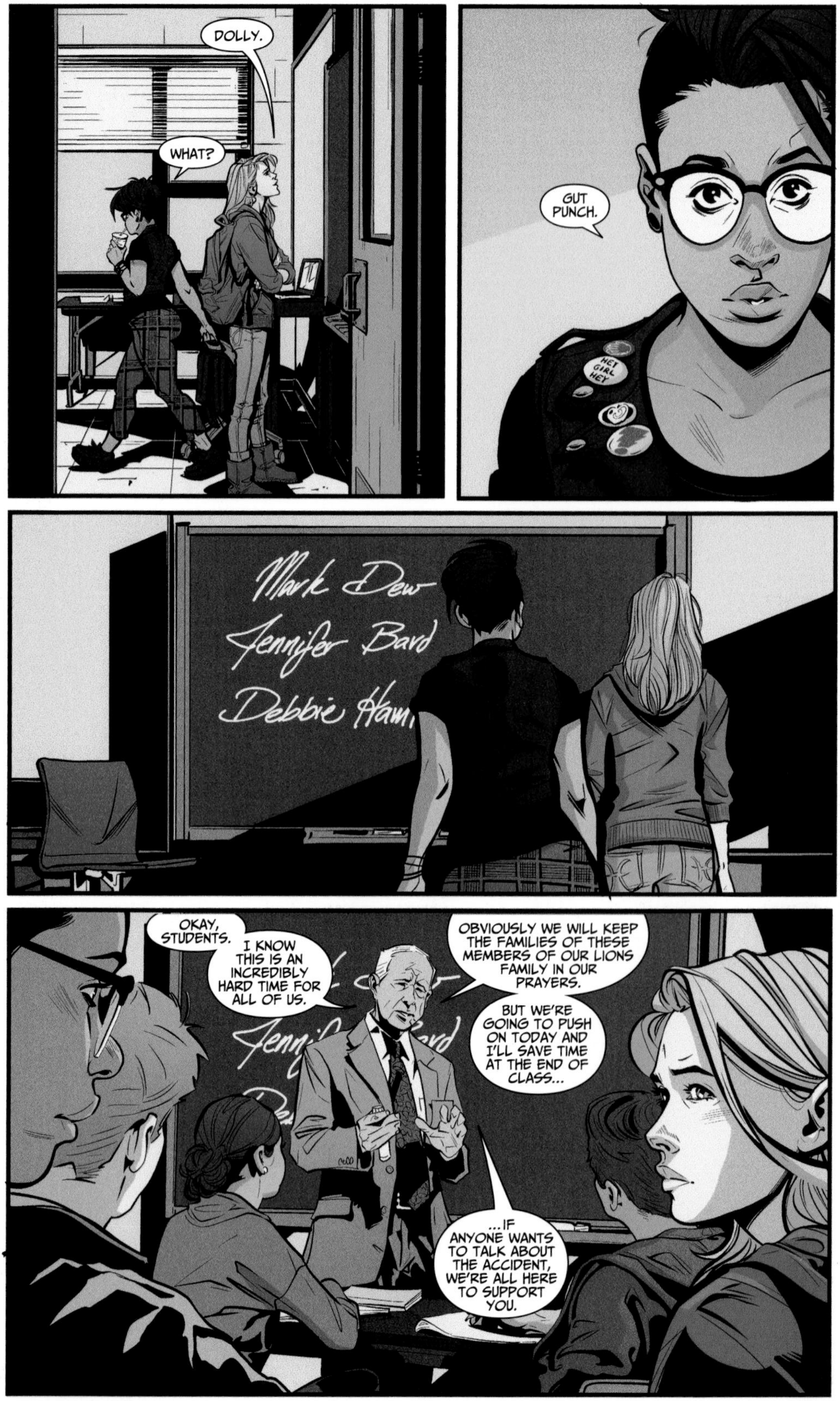
DOLLY.
WHAT?
GUT PUNCH.
Mark Dew
Jennifer Bard
Debbie Ham
OKAY, STUDENTS.
I KNOW THIS IS AN INCREDIBLY HARD TIME FOR ALL OF US.
OBVIOUSLY WE WILL KEEP THE FAMILIES OF THESE MEMBERS OF OUR LIONS FAMILY IN OUR PRAYERS.
BUT WE'RE GOING TO PUSH ON TODAY AND I'LL SAVE TIME AT THE END OF CLASS...
...IF ANYONE WANTS TO TALK ABOUT THE ACCIDENT, WE'RE ALL HERE TO SUPPORT YOU.

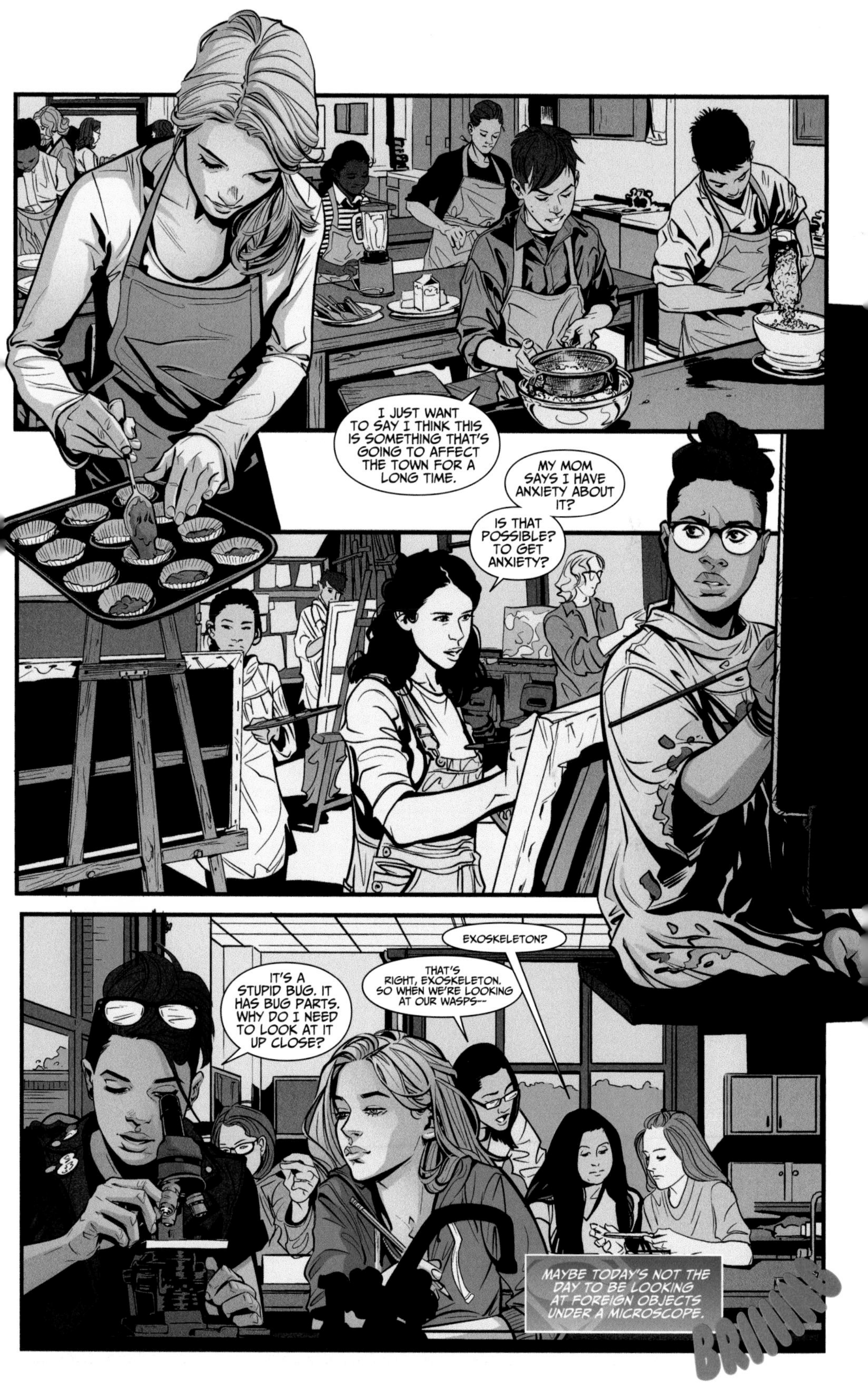
I JUST WANT TO SAY I THINK THIS IS SOMETHING THAT'S GOING TO AFFECT THE TOWN FOR A LONG TIME.
MY MOM SAYS I HAVE ANXIETY ABOUT IT?
IS THAT POSSIBLE? TO GET ANXIETY?
EXOSKELETON?
THAT'S RIGHT, EXOSKELETON. SO WHEN WE'RE LOOKING AT OUR WASPS--
IT'S A STUPID BUG. IT HAS BUG PARTS. WHY DO I NEED TO LOOK AT IT UP CLOSE?
MAYBE TODAY'S NOT THE DAY TO BE LOOKING AT FOREIGN OBJECTS UNDER A MICROSCOPE.
BRIIIING

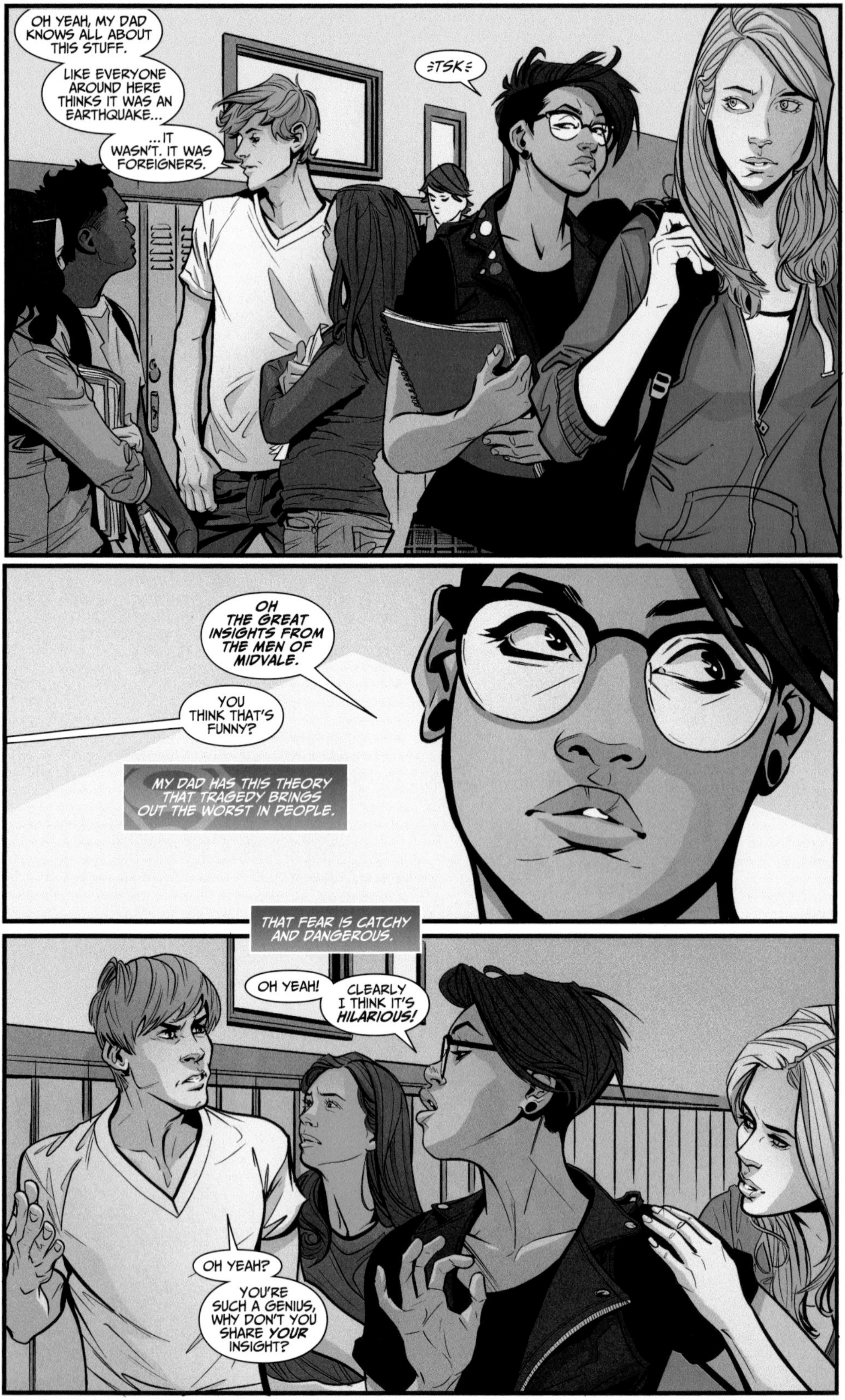
OH YEAH, MY DAD KNOWS ALL ABOUT THIS STUFF.
LIKE EVERYONE AROUND HERE THINKS IT WAS AN EARTHQUAKE...
...IT WASN'T. IT WAS FOREIGNERS.
TSK
OH THE GREAT INSIGHTS FROM THE MEN OF MIDVALE.
YOU THINK THAT'S FUNNY?
MY DAD HAS THIS THEORY THAT TRAGEDY BRINGS OUT THE WORST IN PEOPLE.
THAT FEAR IS CATCHY AND DANGEROUS.
OH YEAH!
CLEARLY I THINK IT'S HILARIOUS!
OH YEAH?
YOU'RE SUCH A GENIUS, WHY DON'T YOU SHARE YOUR INSIGHT?

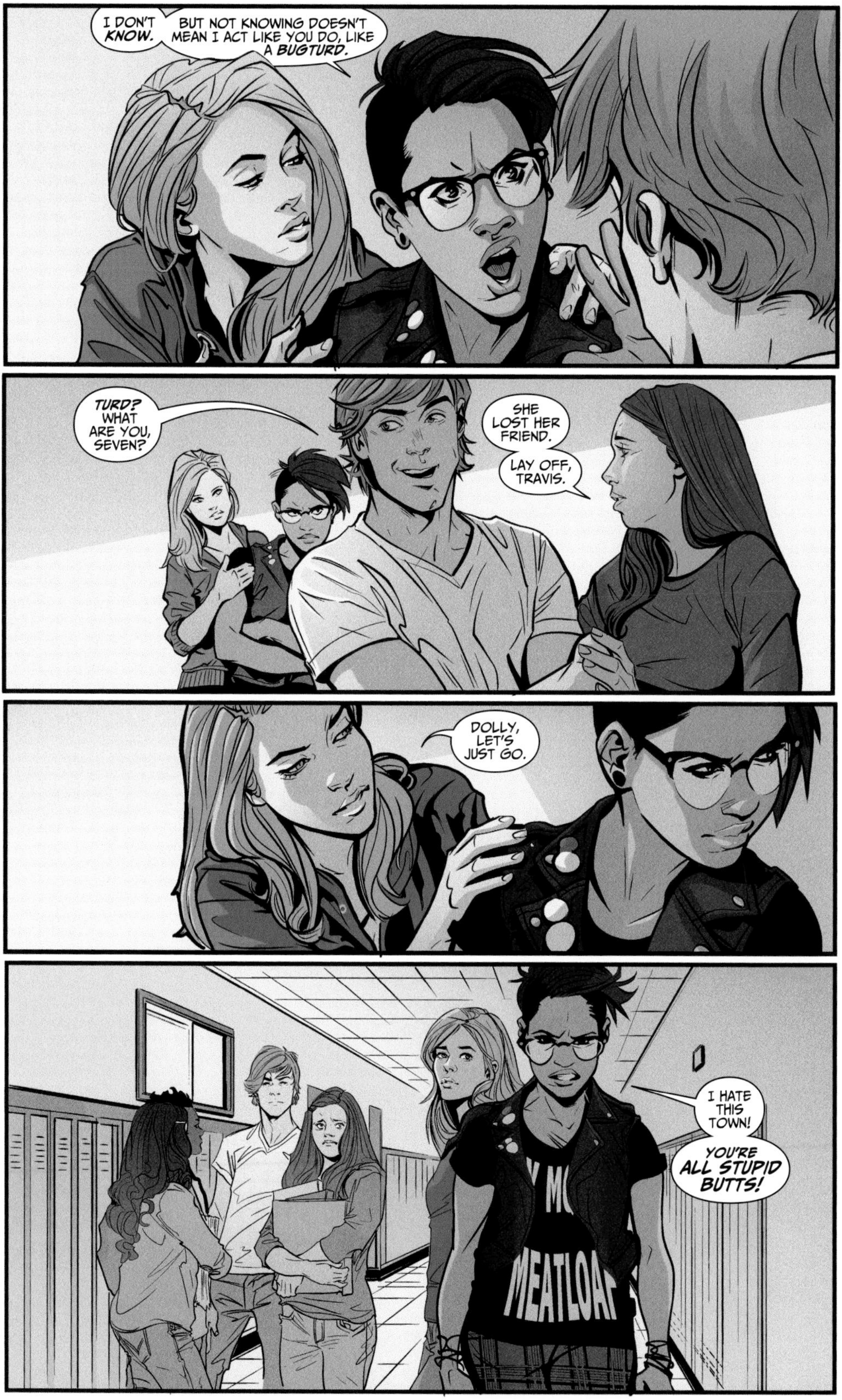
I DON'T *KNOW.*
BUT NOT KNOWING DOESN'T MEAN I ACT LIKE YOU DO, LIKE A *BUGTURD.*
TURD? WHAT ARE YOU, SEVEN?
SHE LOST HER FRIEND.
LAY OFF, TRAVIS.
DOLLY, LET'S JUST GO.
I HATE THIS TOWN!
YOU'RE ALL STUPID BUTTS!
MEATLOAF

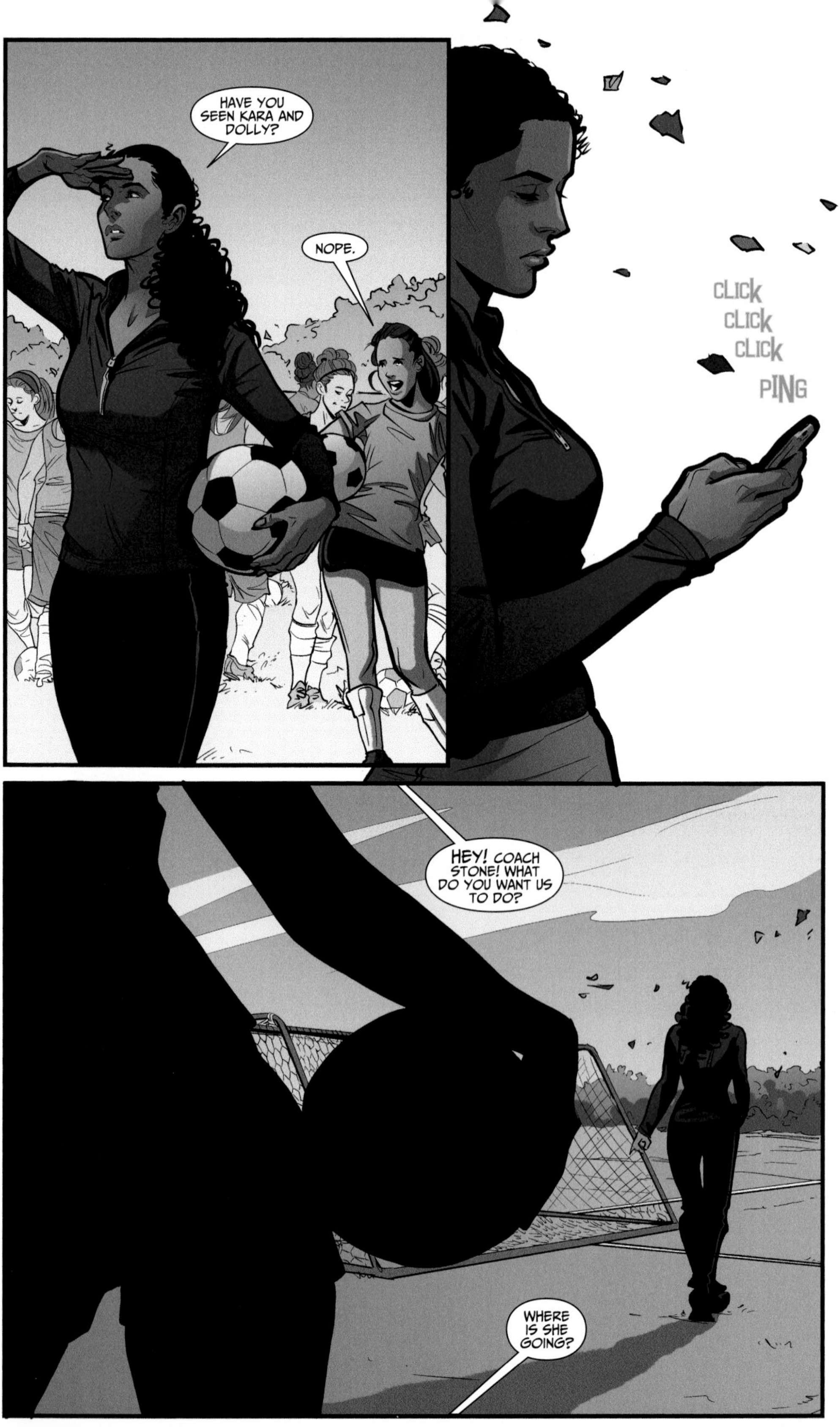
HAVE YOU SEEN KARA AND DOLLY?
NOPE.
CLICK
CLICK
CLICK
PING
HEY! COACH STONE! WHAT DO YOU WANT US TO DO?
WHERE IS SHE GOING?

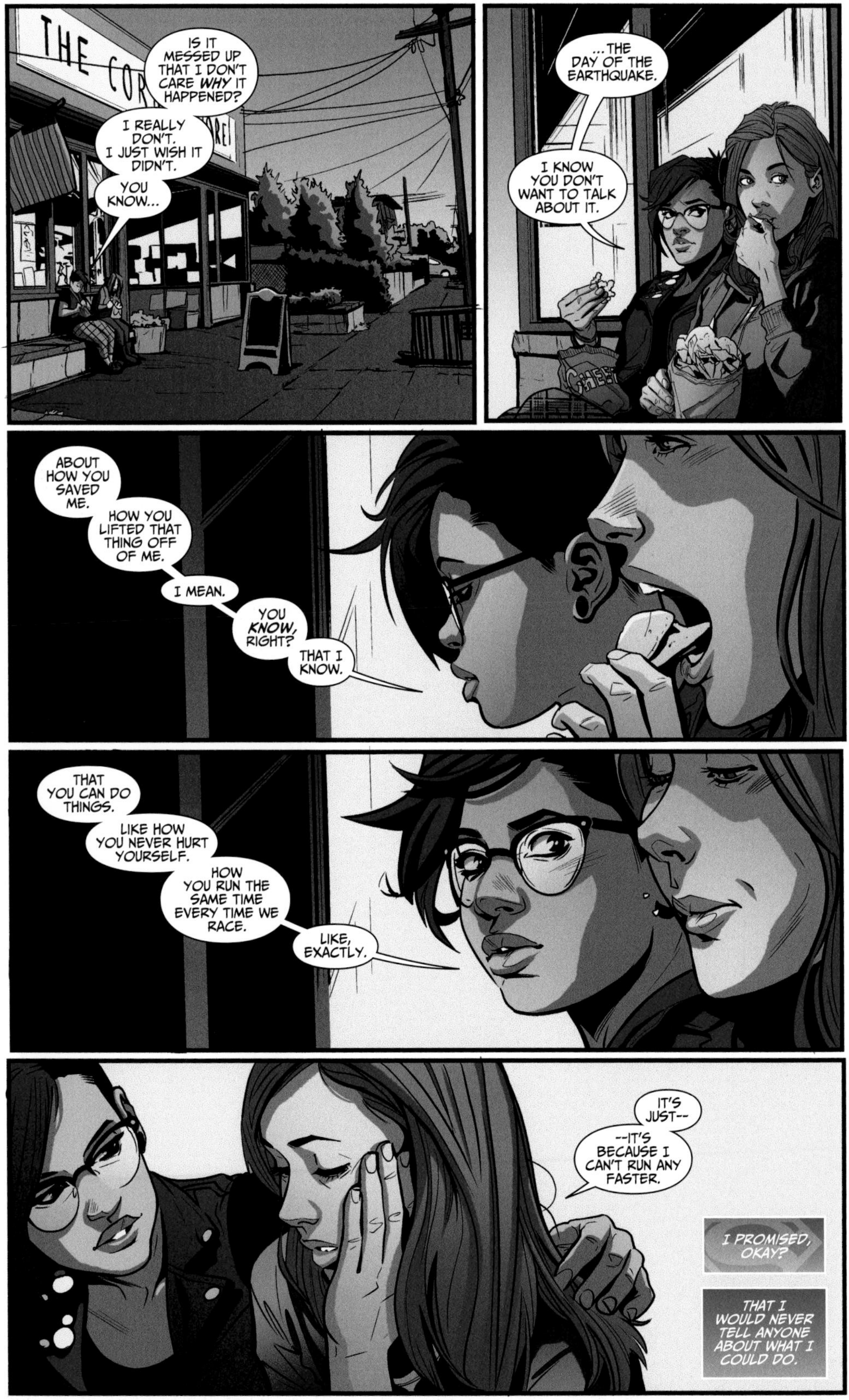
THE COR
STORE
IS IT MESSED UP THAT I DON'T CARE WHY IT HAPPENED?
I REALLY DON'T. I JUST WISH IT DIDN'T.
YOU KNOW...
...THE DAY OF THE EARTHQUAKE.
I KNOW YOU DON'T WANT TO TALK ABOUT IT.
ABOUT HOW YOU SAVED ME.
HOW YOU LIFTED THAT THING OFF OF ME.
I MEAN.
YOU KNOW, RIGHT?
THAT I KNOW.
THAT YOU CAN DO THINGS.
LIKE HOW YOU NEVER HURT YOURSELF.
HOW YOU RUN THE SAME TIME EVERY TIME WE RACE.
LIKE, EXACTLY.
IT'S JUST--
--IT'S BECAUSE I CAN'T RUN ANY FASTER.
I PROMISED, OKAY?
THAT I WOULD NEVER TELL ANYONE ABOUT WHAT I COULD DO.

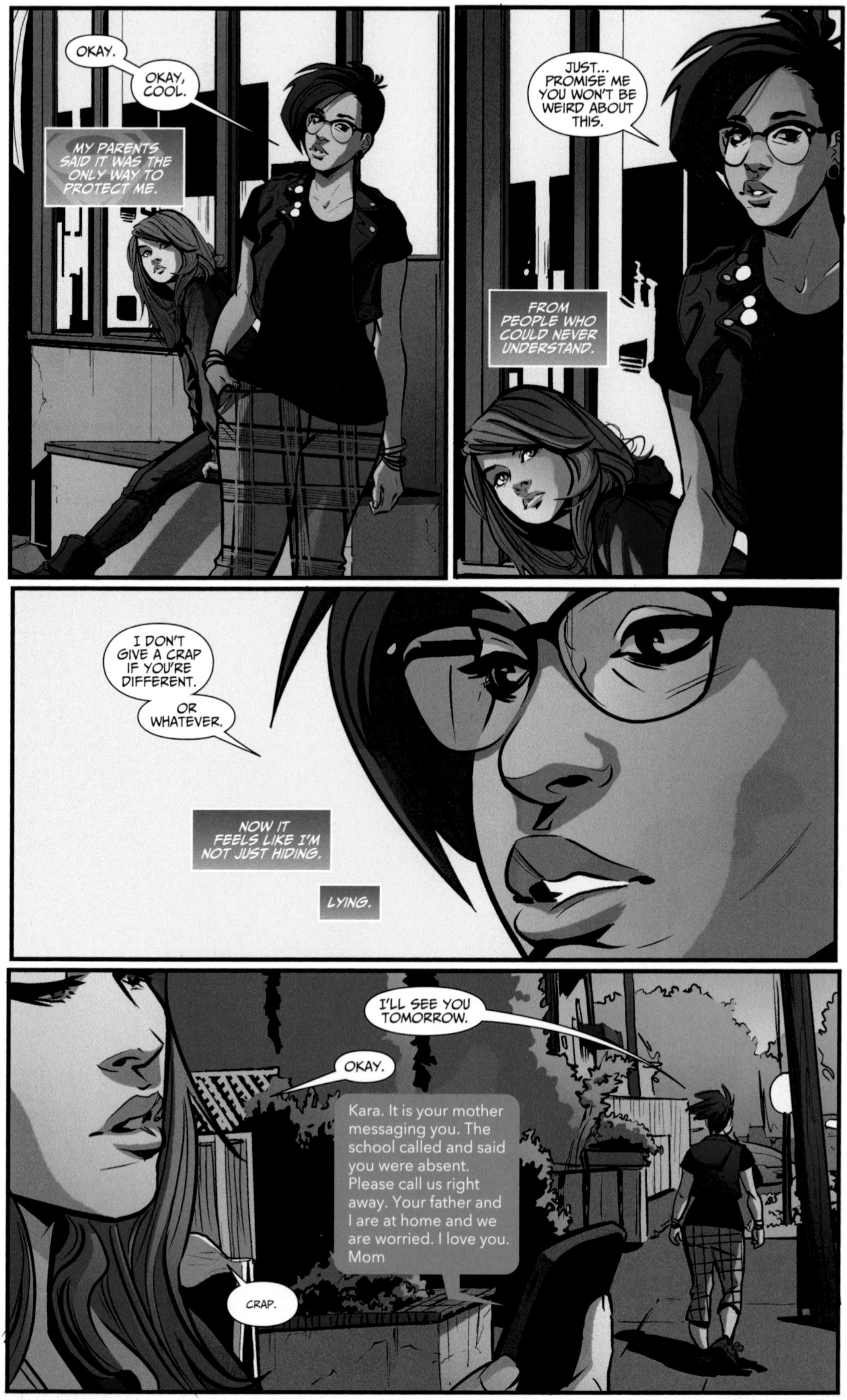
OKAY.
OKAY, COOL.
MY PARENTS SAID IT WAS THE ONLY WAY TO PROTECT ME.
JUST... PROMISE ME YOU WON'T BE WEIRD ABOUT THIS.
FROM PEOPLE WHO COULD NEVER UNDERSTAND.
I DON'T GIVE A CRAP IF YOU'RE DIFFERENT.
OR WHATEVER.
NOW IT FEELS LIKE I'M NOT JUST HIDING.
LYING.
I'LL SEE YOU TOMORROW.
OKAY.
Kara. It is your mother messaging you. The school called and said you were absent. Please call us right away. Your father and I are at home and we are worried. I love you. Mom
CRAP.

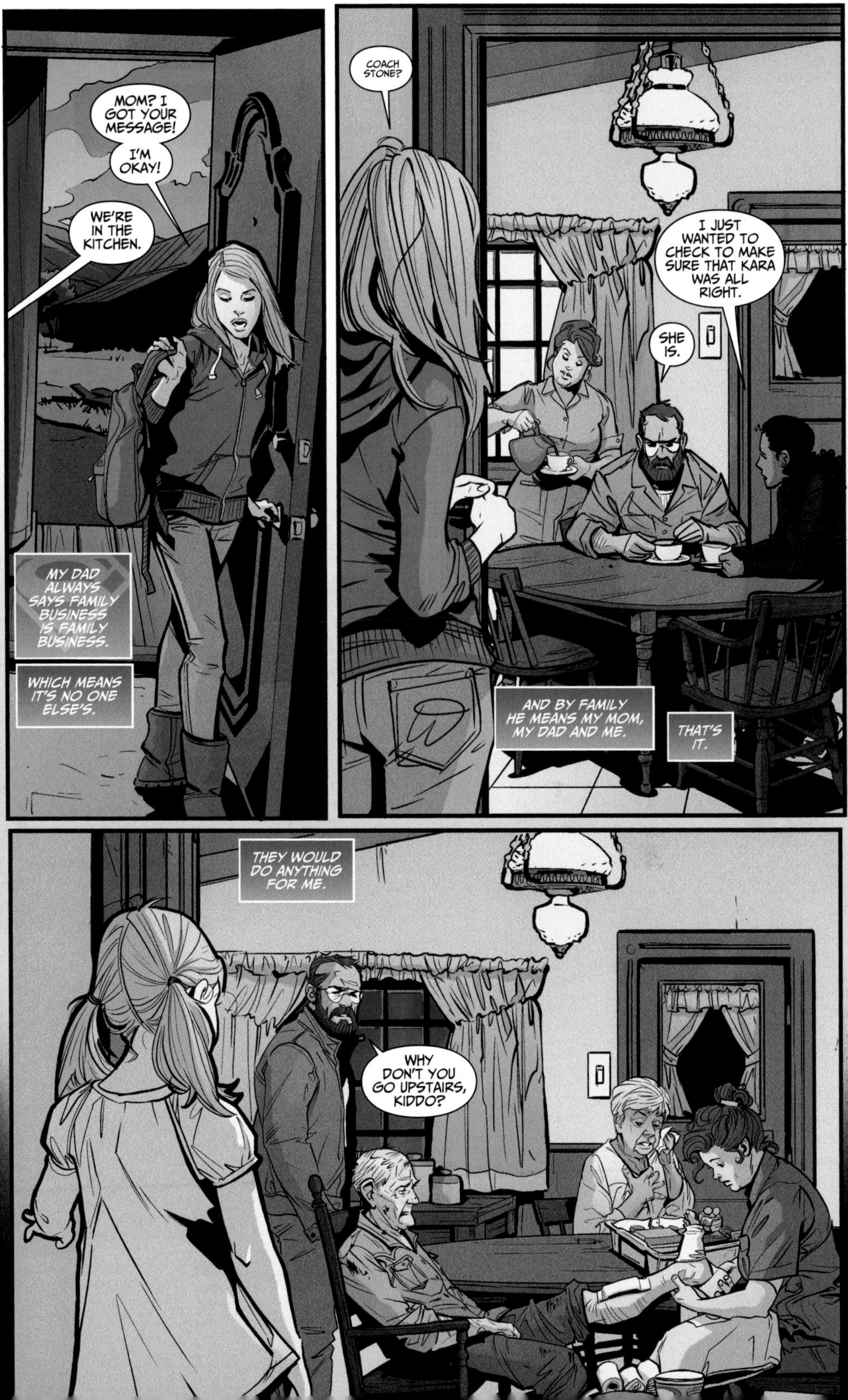
MOM? I GOT YOUR MESSAGE!
I'M OKAY!
WE'RE IN THE KITCHEN.
MY DAD ALWAYS SAYS FAMILY BUSINESS IS FAMILY BUSINESS.
WHICH MEANS IT'S NO ONE ELSE'S.
COACH STONE?
I JUST WANTED TO CHECK TO MAKE SURE THAT KARA WAS ALL RIGHT.
SHE IS.
AND BY FAMILY HE MEANS MY MOM, MY DAD AND ME.
THAT'S IT.
THEY WOULD DO ANYTHING FOR ME.
WHY DON'T YOU GO UPSTAIRS, KIDDO?

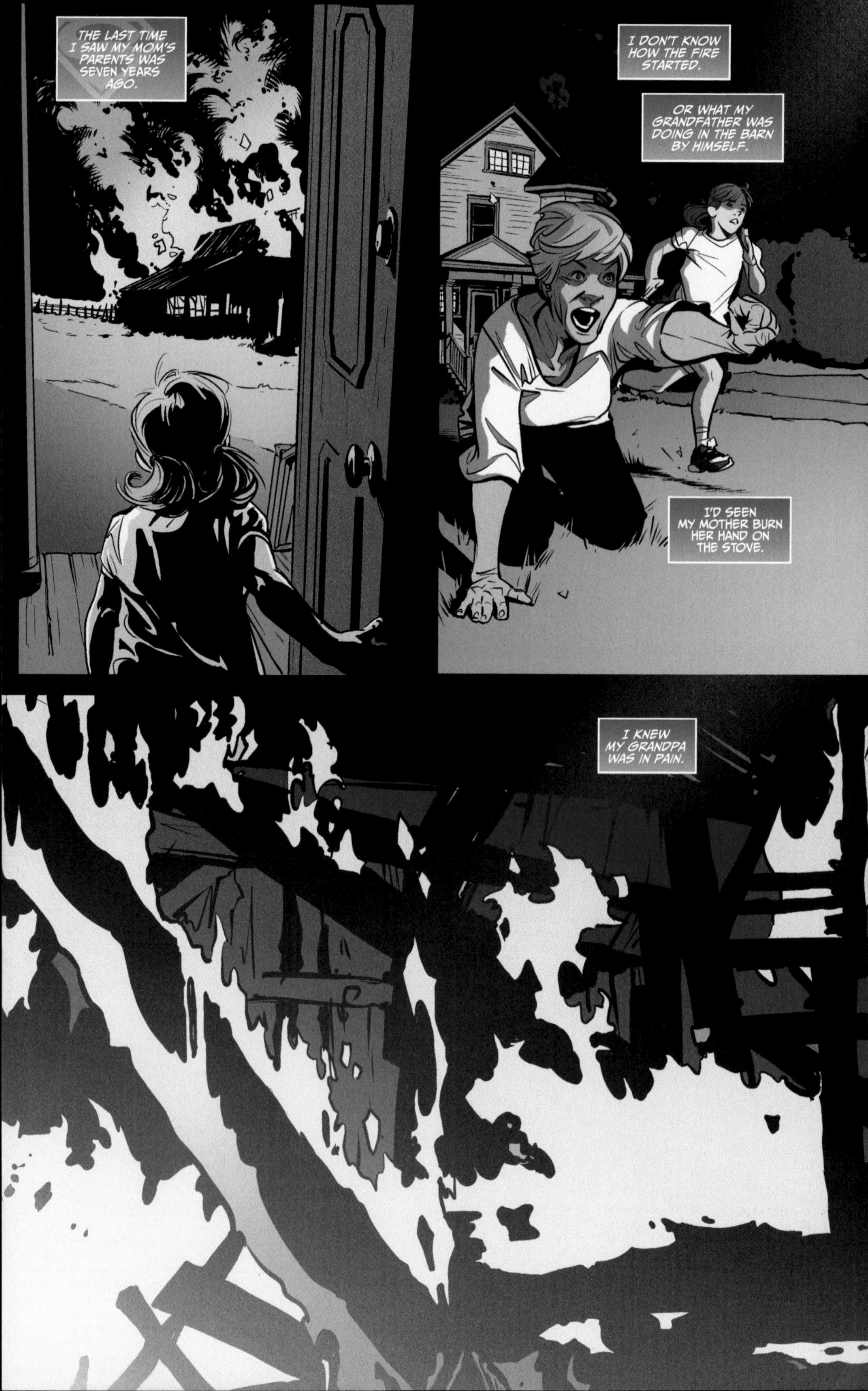
THE LAST TIME I SAW MY MOM'S PARENTS WAS SEVEN YEARS AGO.
I DON'T KNOW HOW THE FIRE STARTED.
OR WHAT MY GRANDFATHER WAS DOING IN THE BARN BY HIMSELF.
I'D SEEN MY MOTHER BURN HER HAND ON THE STOVE.
I KNEW MY GRANDPA WAS IN PAIN.

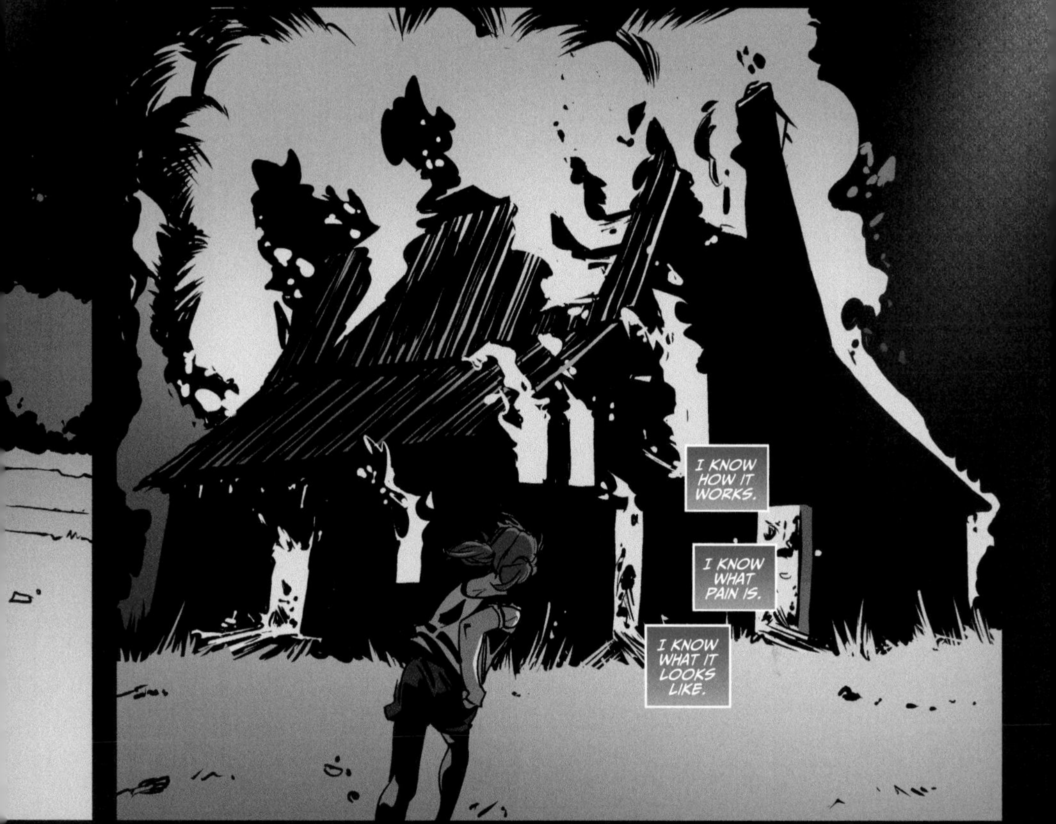
I KNOW HOW IT WORKS.
I KNOW WHAT PAIN IS.
I KNOW WHAT IT LOOKS LIKE.

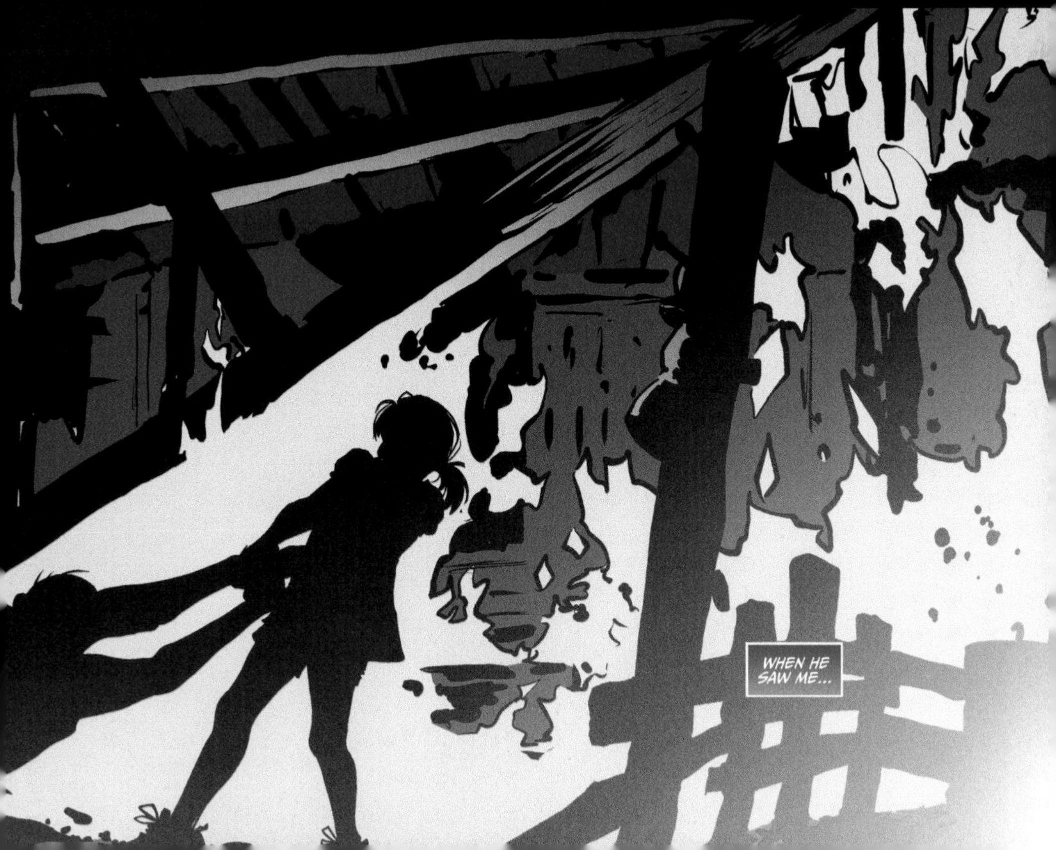
WHEN HE SAW ME...

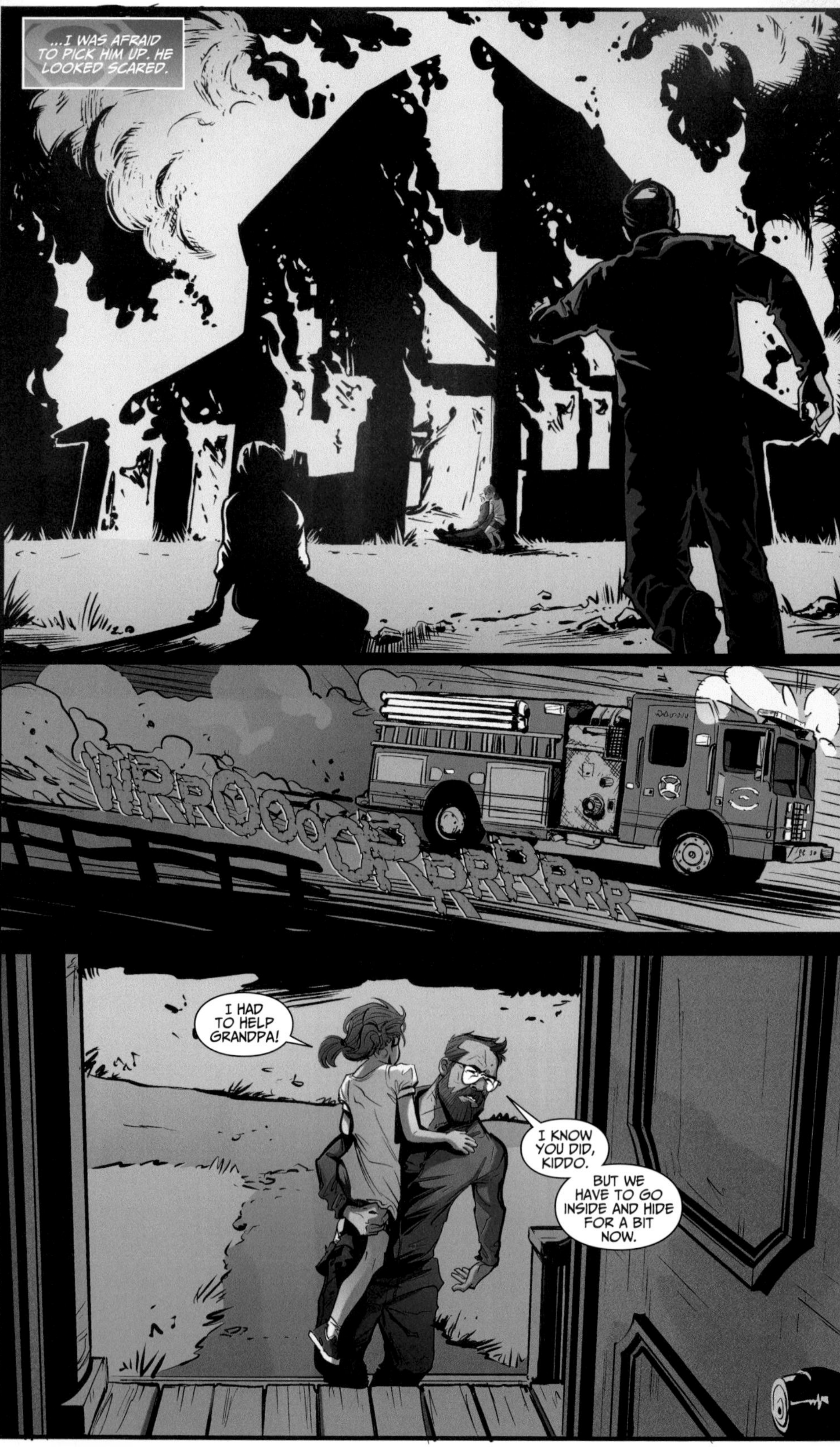
...I WAS AFRAID TO PICK HIM UP. HE LOOKED SCARED.
WRROOOOORRRRRR
I HAD TO HELP GRANDPA!
I KNOW YOU DID, KIDDO.
BUT WE HAVE TO GO INSIDE AND HIDE FOR A BIT NOW.

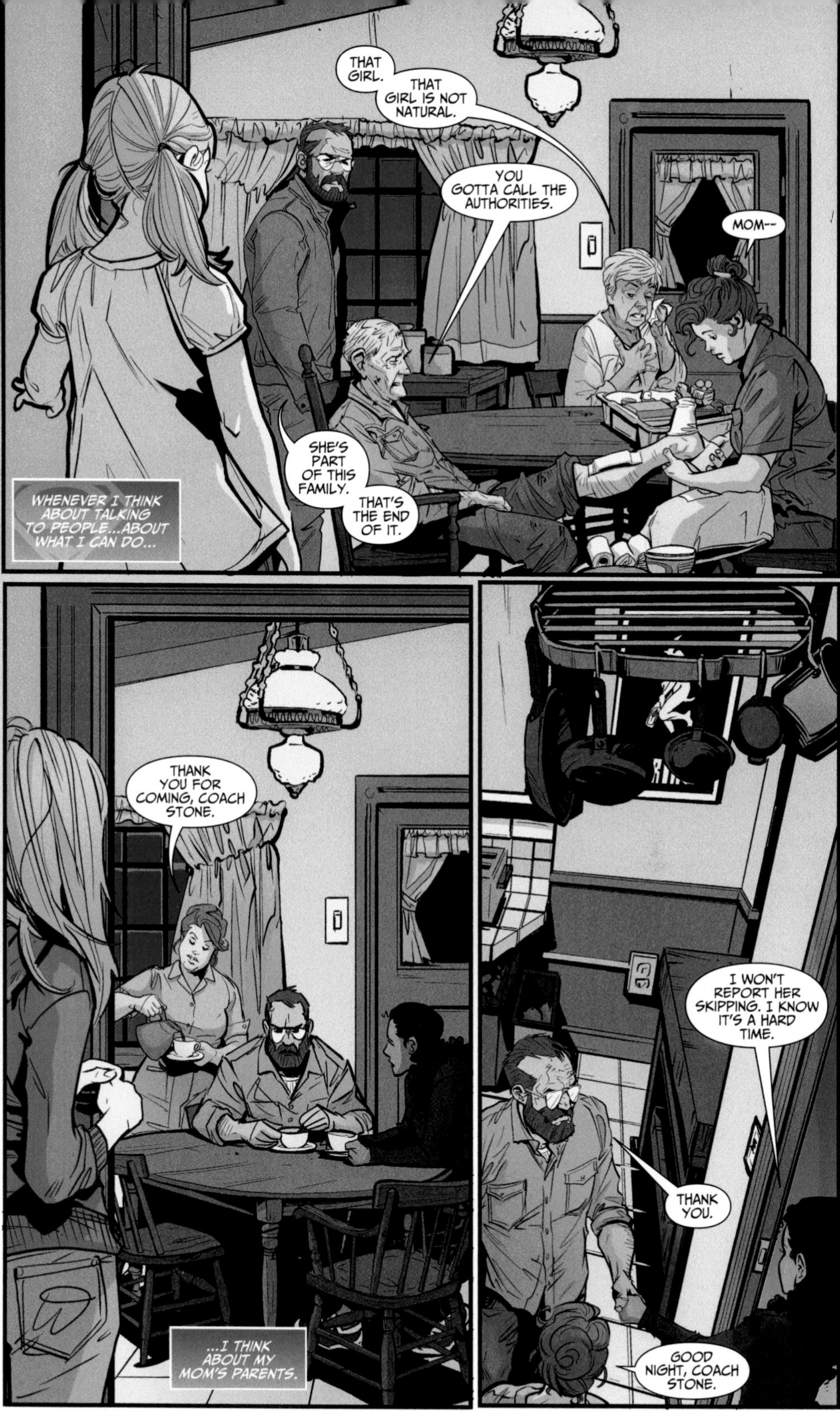
THAT GIRL.
THAT GIRL IS NOT NATURAL.
YOU GOTTA CALL THE AUTHORITIES.
MOM--
SHE'S PART OF THIS FAMILY.
THAT'S THE END OF IT.
WHENEVER I THINK ABOUT TALKING TO PEOPLE...ABOUT WHAT I CAN DO...
THANK YOU FOR COMING, COACH STONE.
...I THINK ABOUT MY MOM'S PARENTS.
I WON'T REPORT HER SKIPPING. I KNOW IT'S A HARD TIME.
THANK YOU.
GOOD NIGHT, COACH STONE.

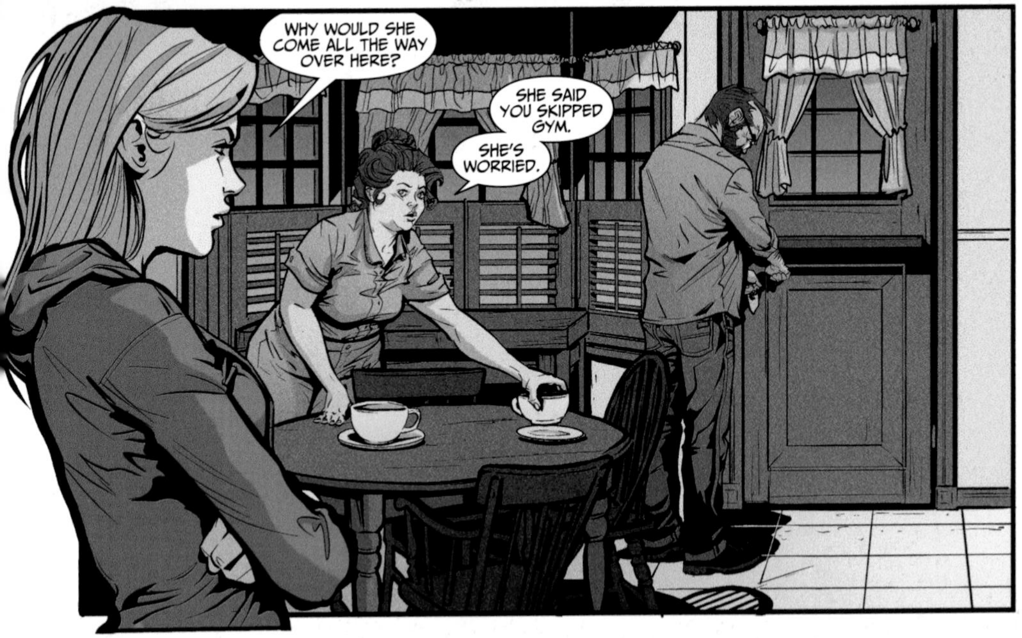
WHY WOULD SHE COME ALL THE WAY OVER HERE?
SHE SAID YOU SKIPPED GYM.
SHE'S WORRIED.

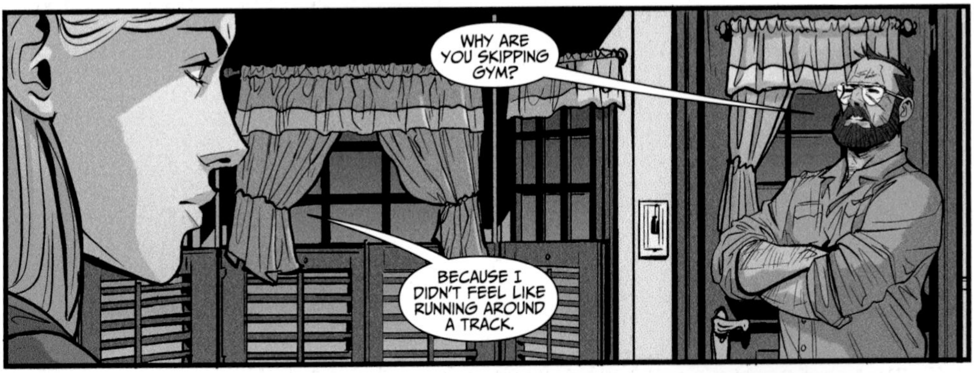
WHY ARE YOU SKIPPING GYM?
BECAUSE I DIDN'T FEEL LIKE RUNNING AROUND A TRACK.

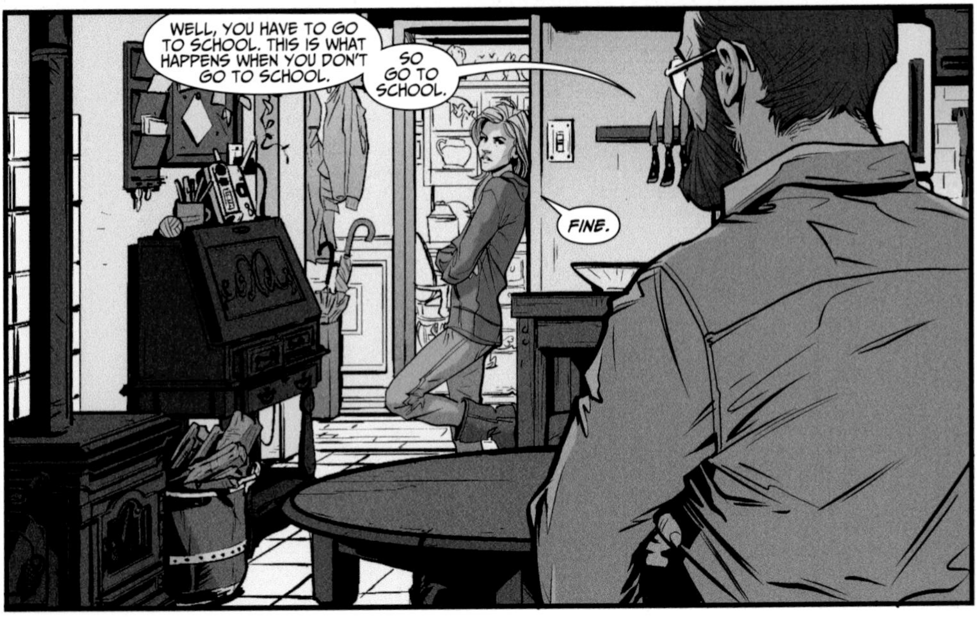
WELL, YOU HAVE TO GO TO SCHOOL. THIS IS WHAT HAPPENS WHEN YOU DON'T GO TO SCHOOL.
SO GO TO SCHOOL.
FINE.

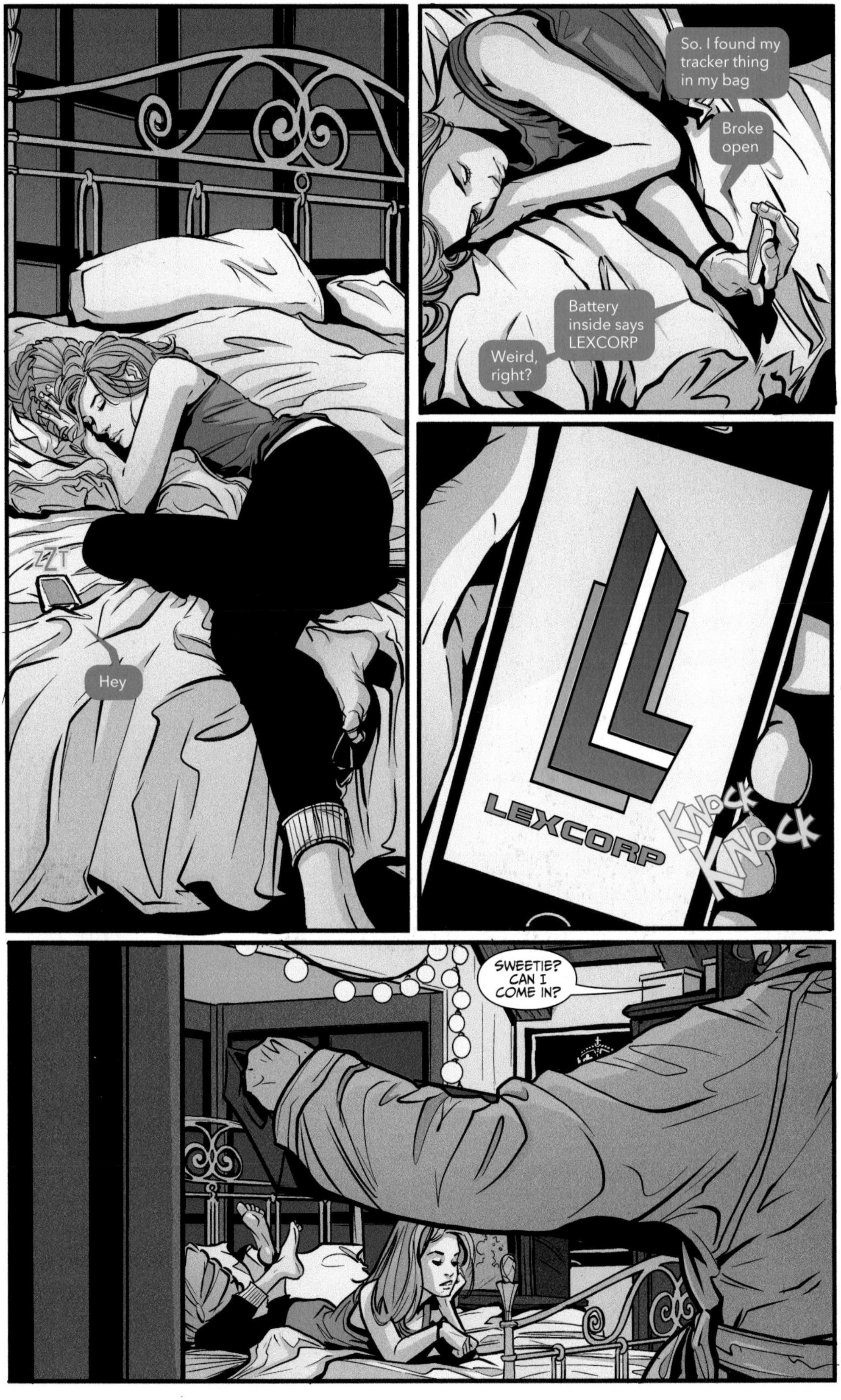

ZZZT
Hey
So. I found my tracker thing in my bag
Broke open
Battery inside says LEXCORP
Weird, right?
LEXCORP
KNOCK KNOCK
SWEETIE? CAN I COME IN?

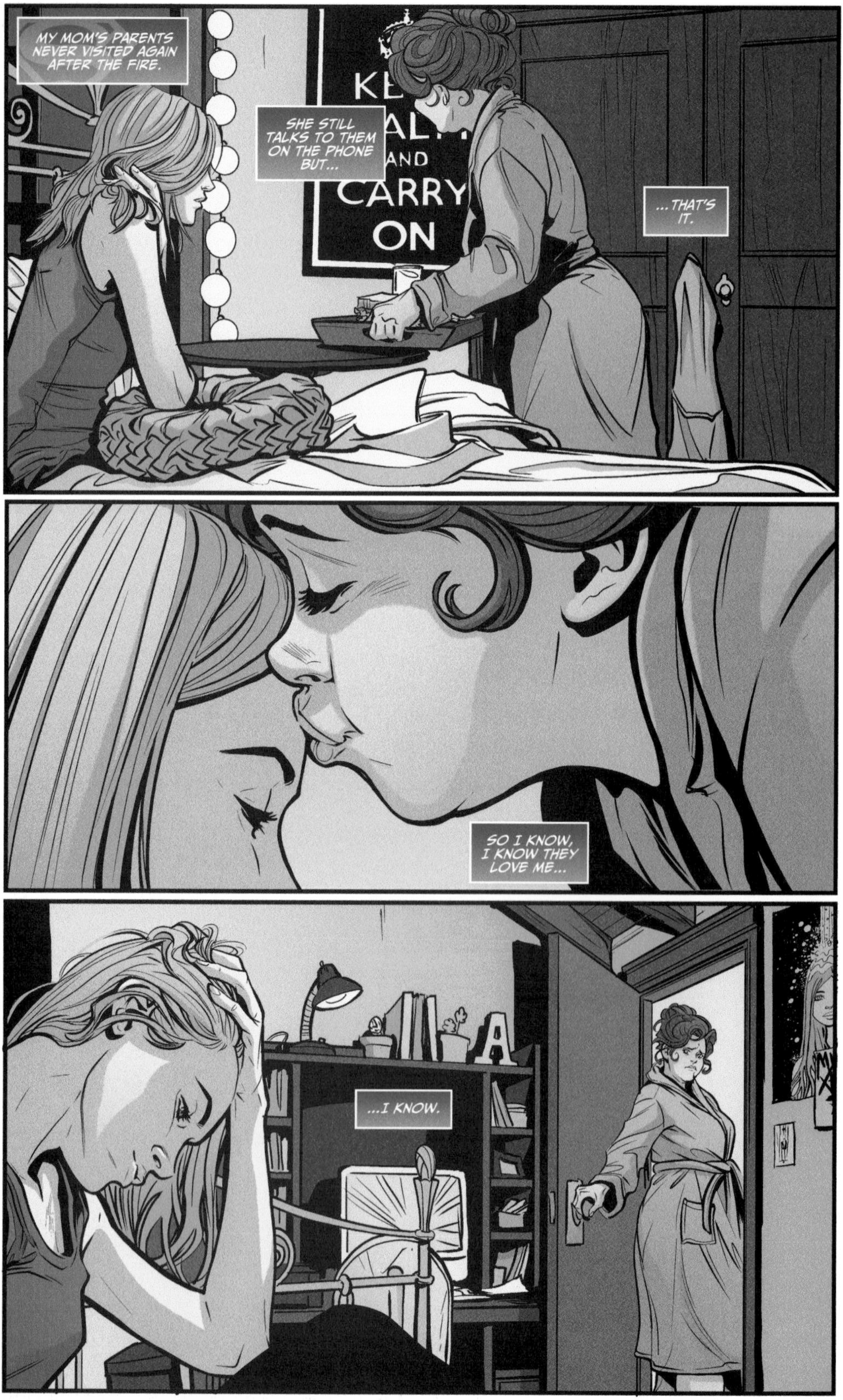
MY MOM'S PARENTS NEVER VISITED AGAIN AFTER THE FIRE.
SHE STILL TALKS TO THEM ON THE PHONE BUT...
KEEP CALM AND CARRY ON
...THAT'S IT.
SO I KNOW, I KNOW THEY LOVE ME...
...I KNOW.

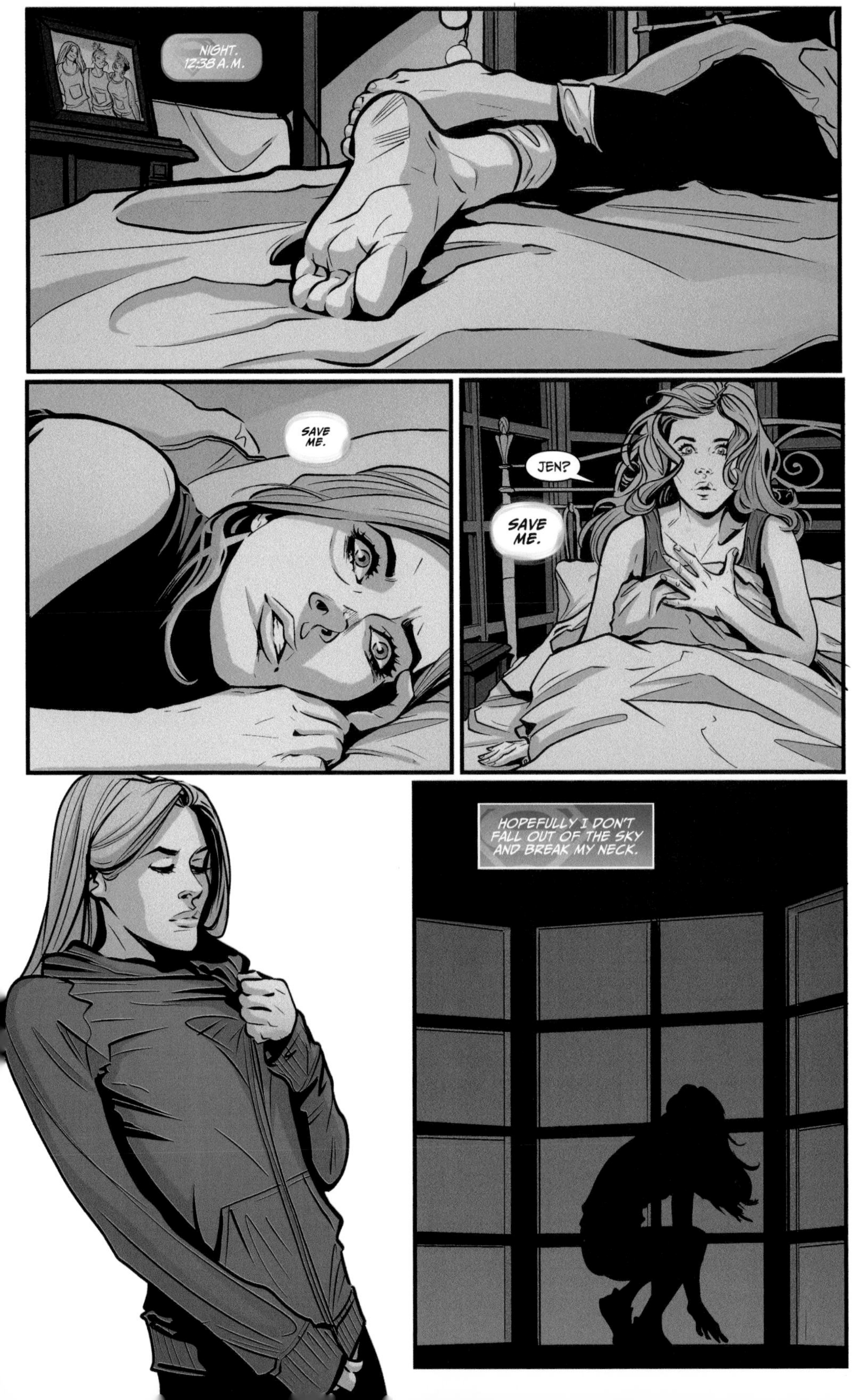
NIGHT. 12:38 A.M.
SAVE ME.
JEN?
SAVE ME.
HOPEFULLY I DON'T FALL OUT OF THE SKY AND BREAK MY NECK.

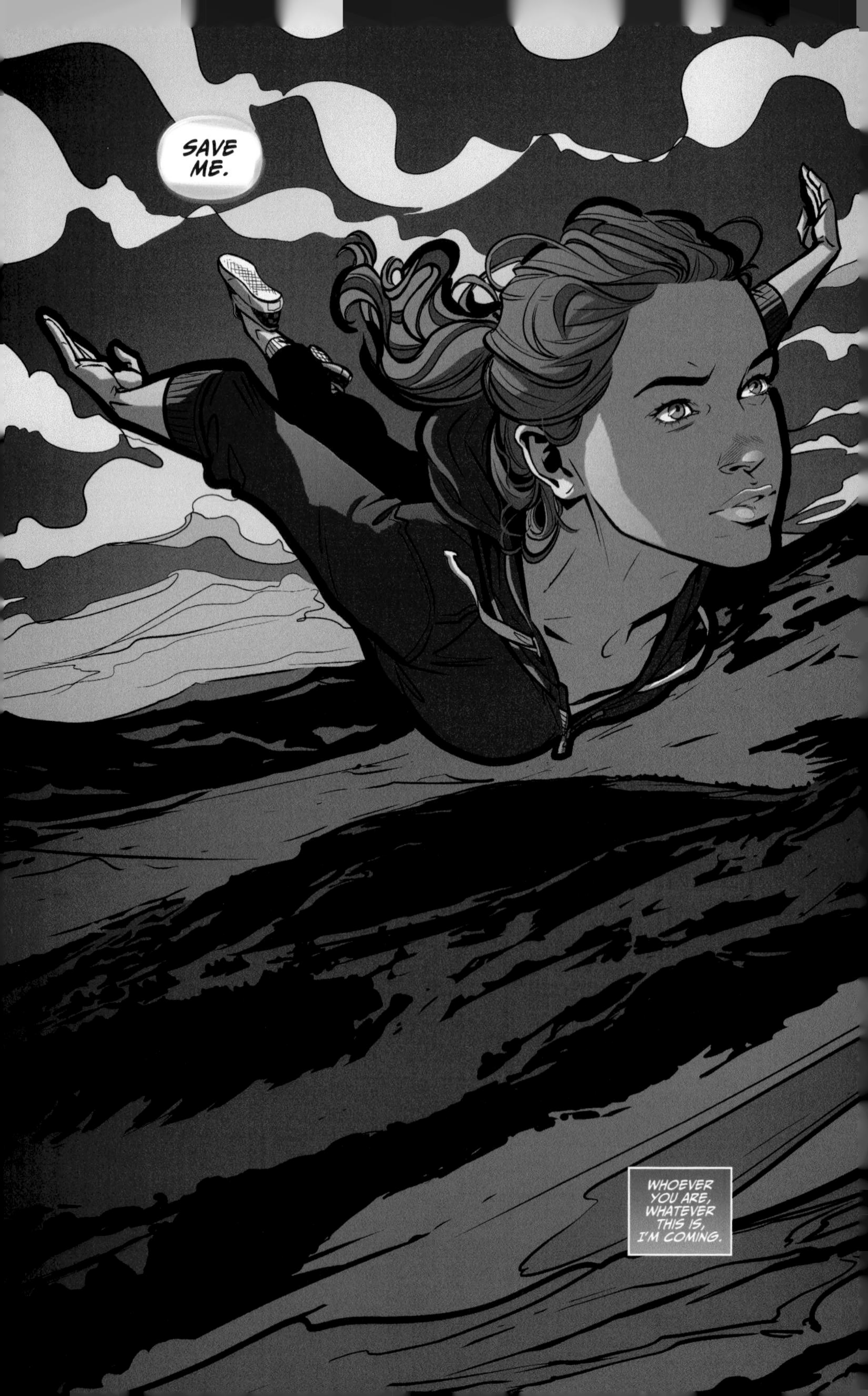
SAVE ME.
WHOEVER YOU ARE, WHATEVER THIS IS, I'M COMING.

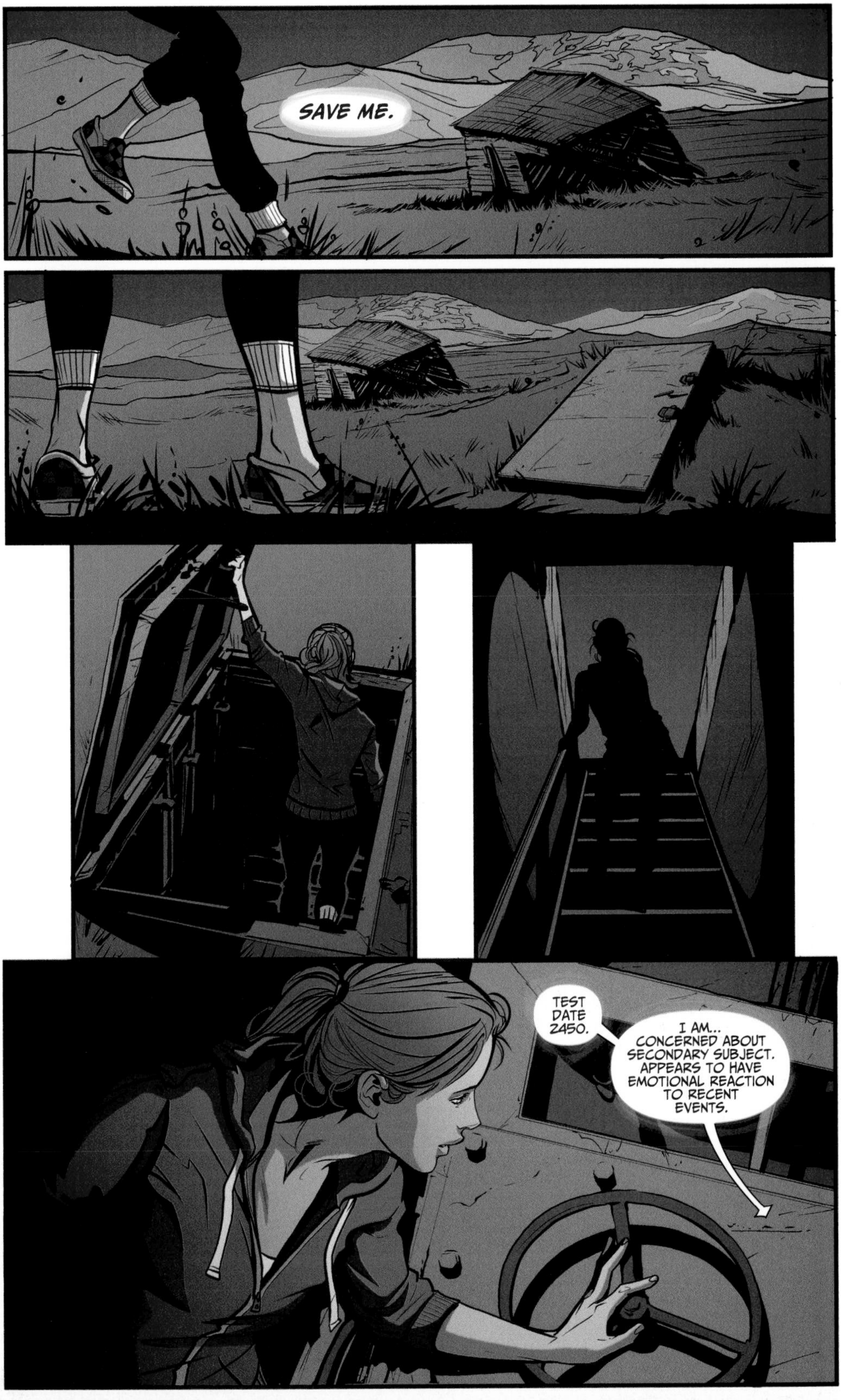
SAVE ME.
TEST DATE 2450.
I AM... CONCERNED ABOUT SECONDARY SUBJECT. APPEARS TO HAVE EMOTIONAL REACTION TO RECENT EVENTS.

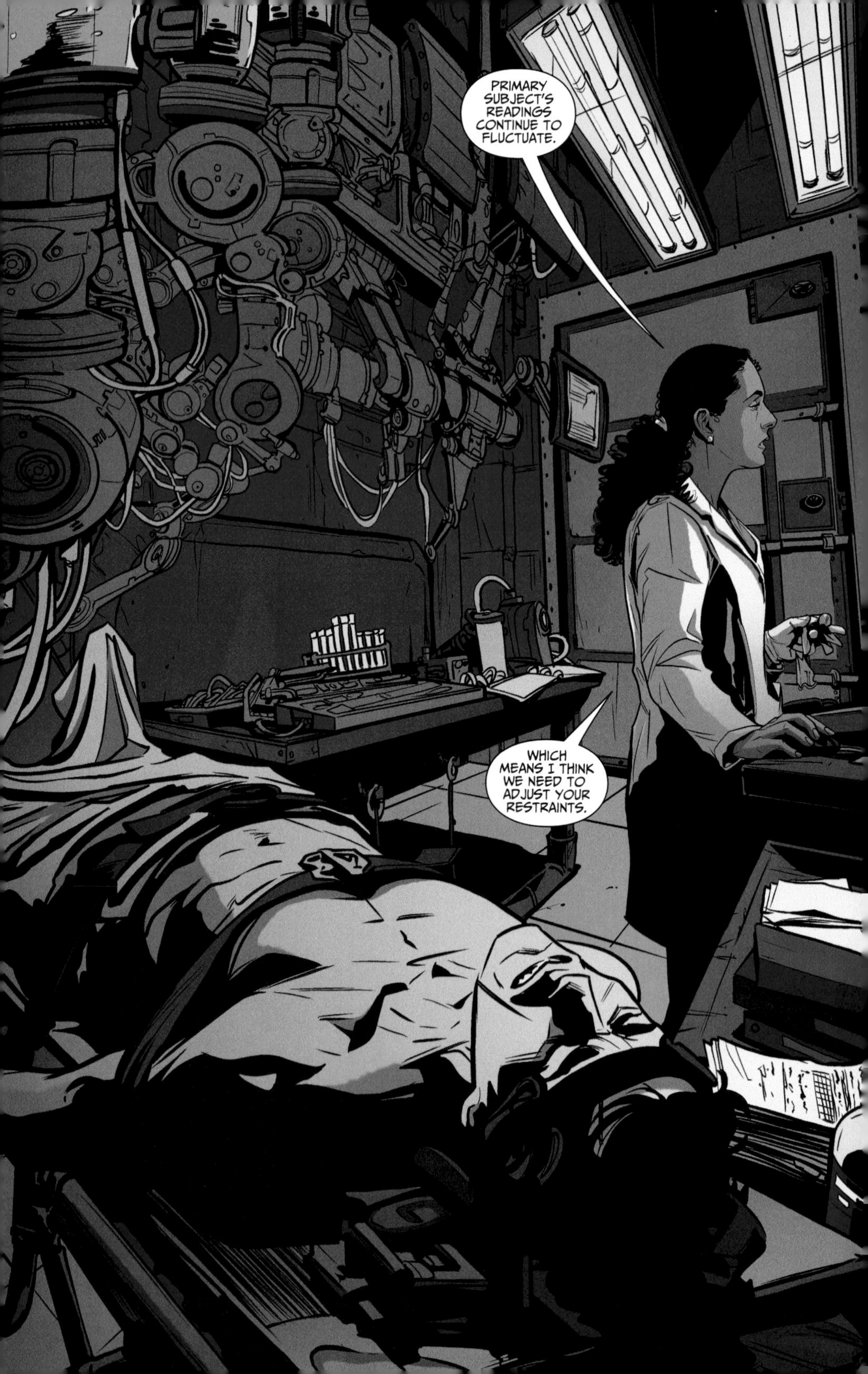
PRIMARY SUBJECT'S READINGS CONTINUE TO FLUCTUATE.
WHICH MEANS I THINK WE NEED TO ADJUST YOUR RESTRAINTS.

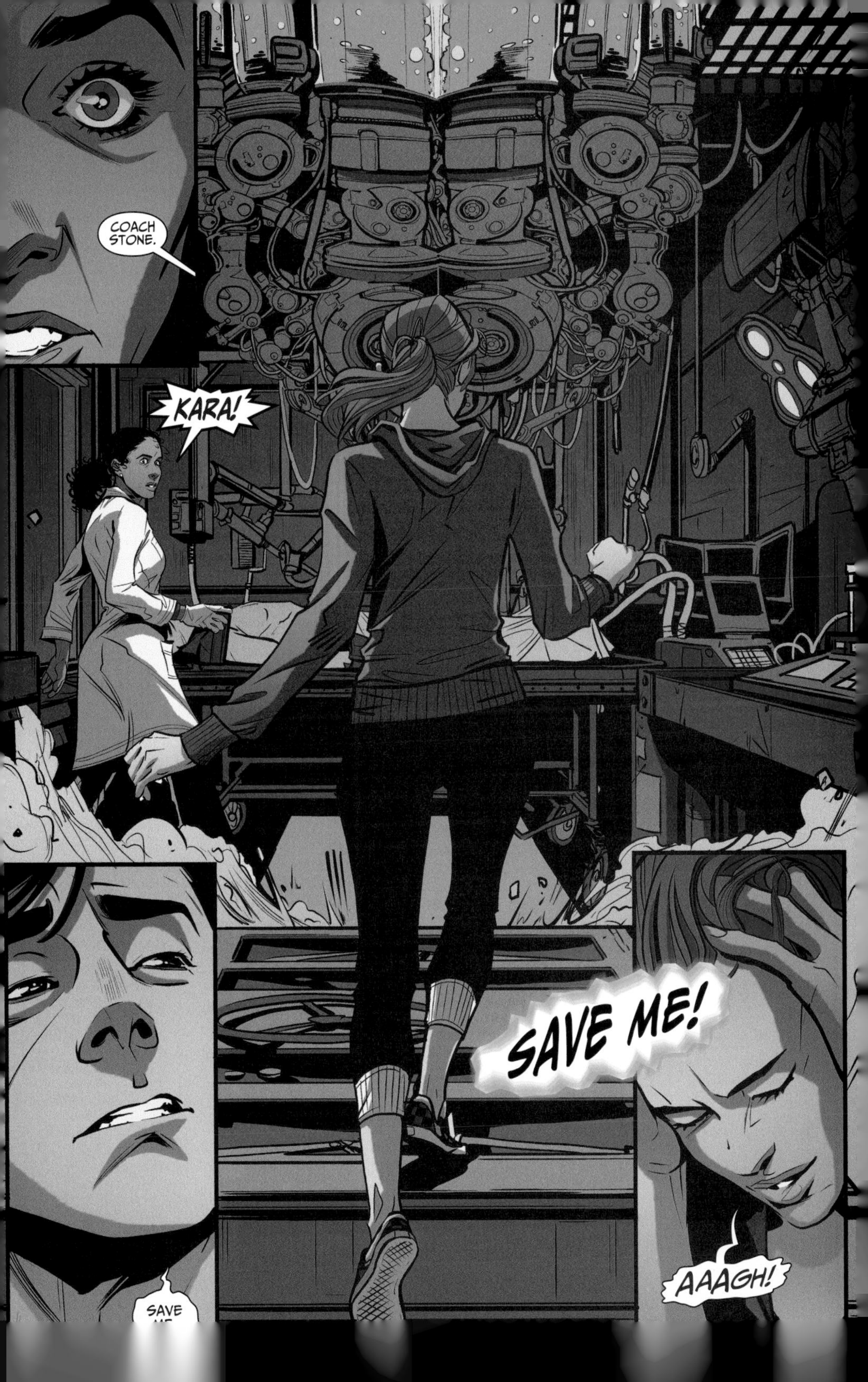
COACH STONE.
KARA!
SAVE
SAVE ME!
AAAGH!

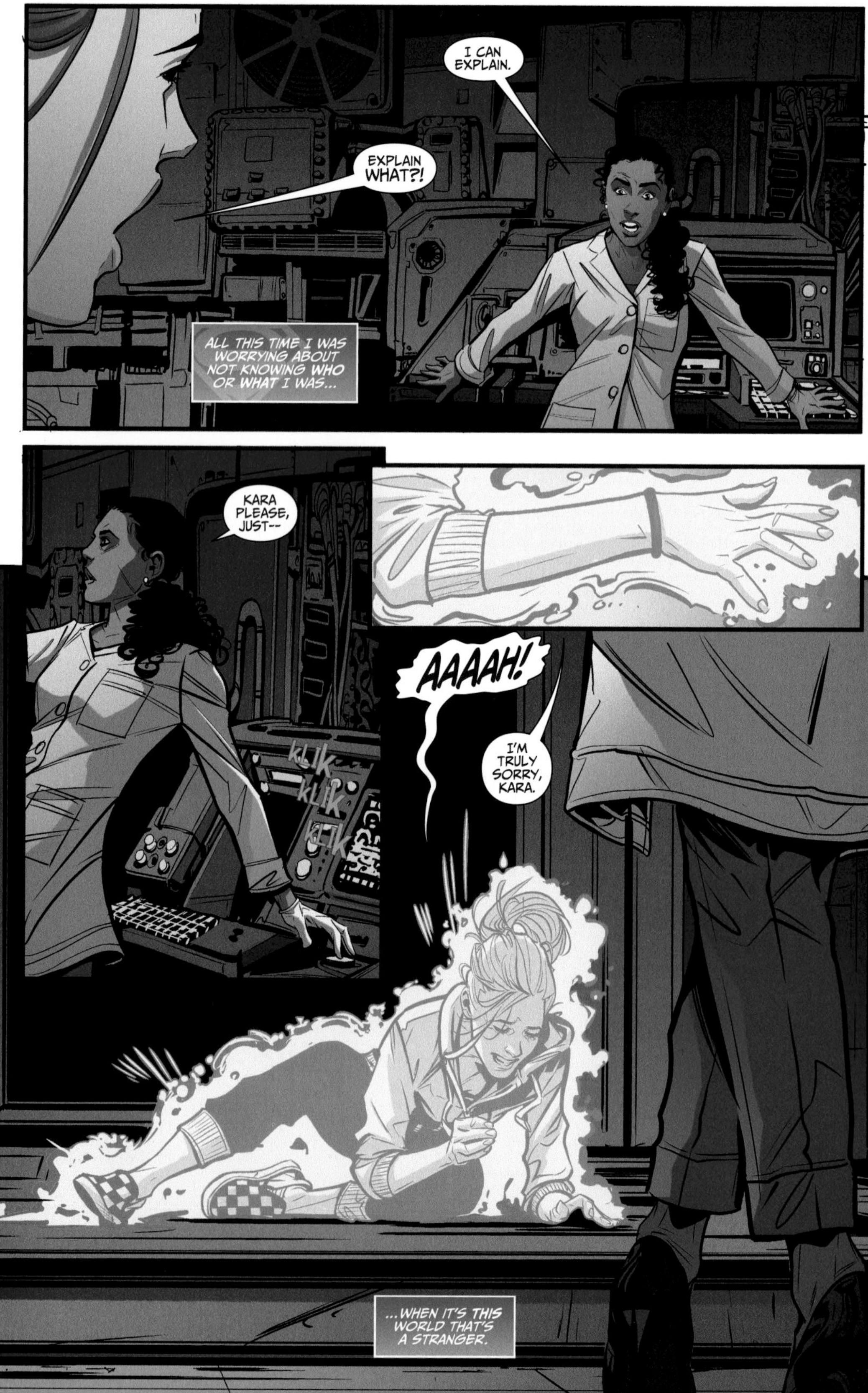
I CAN EXPLAIN.
EXPLAIN WHAT?!
ALL THIS TIME I WAS WORRYING ABOUT NOT KNOWING WHO OR WHAT I WAS...
KARA PLEASE, JUST--
KLIK KLIK KLIK
AAAAH!
I'M TRULY SORRY, KARA.
...WHEN IT'S THIS WORLD THAT'S A STRANGER.

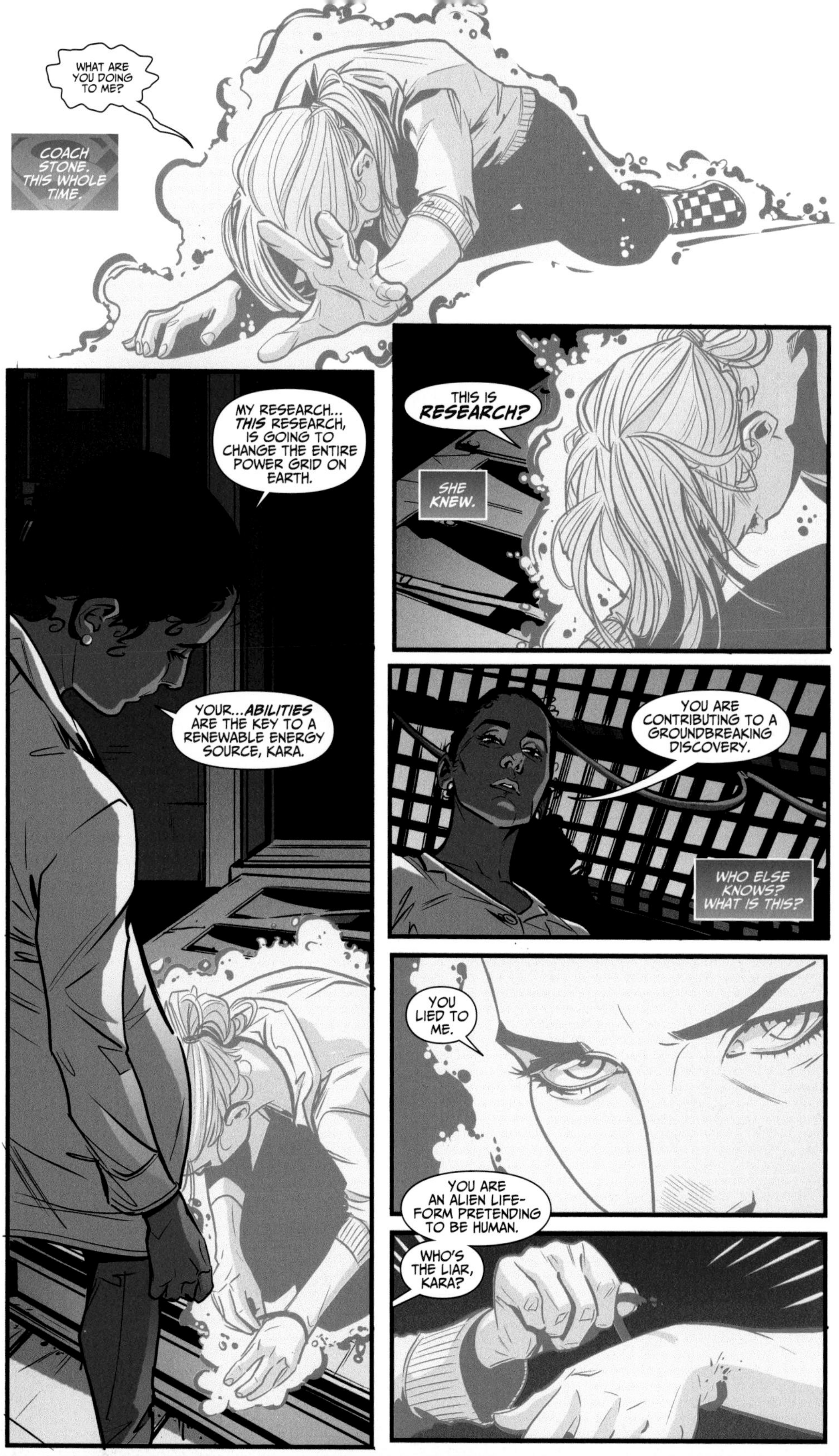
WHAT ARE YOU DOING TO ME?
COACH STONE. THIS WHOLE TIME.
MY RESEARCH... THIS RESEARCH, IS GOING TO CHANGE THE ENTIRE POWER GRID ON EARTH.
THIS IS RESEARCH?
SHE KNEW.
YOUR...ABILITIES ARE THE KEY TO A RENEWABLE ENERGY SOURCE, KARA.
YOU ARE CONTRIBUTING TO A GROUNDBREAKING DISCOVERY.
WHO ELSE KNOWS? WHAT IS THIS?
YOU LIED TO ME.
YOU ARE AN ALIEN LIFE-FORM PRETENDING TO BE HUMAN.
WHO'S THE LIAR, KARA?

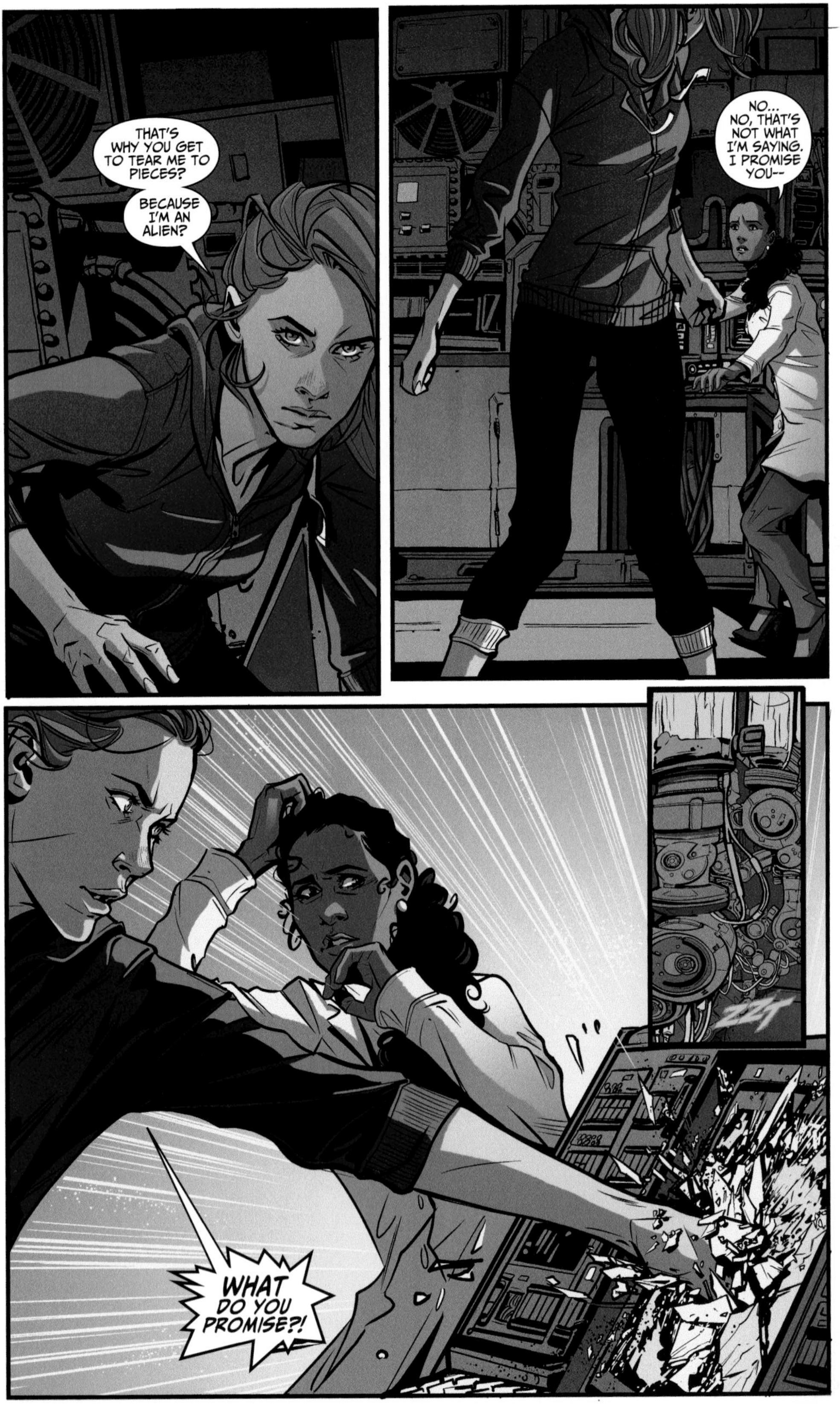
THAT'S WHY YOU GET TO TEAR ME TO PIECES?
BECAUSE I'M AN ALIEN?
NO... NO, THAT'S NOT WHAT I'M SAYING. I PROMISE YOU--
WHAT DO YOU PROMISE?!

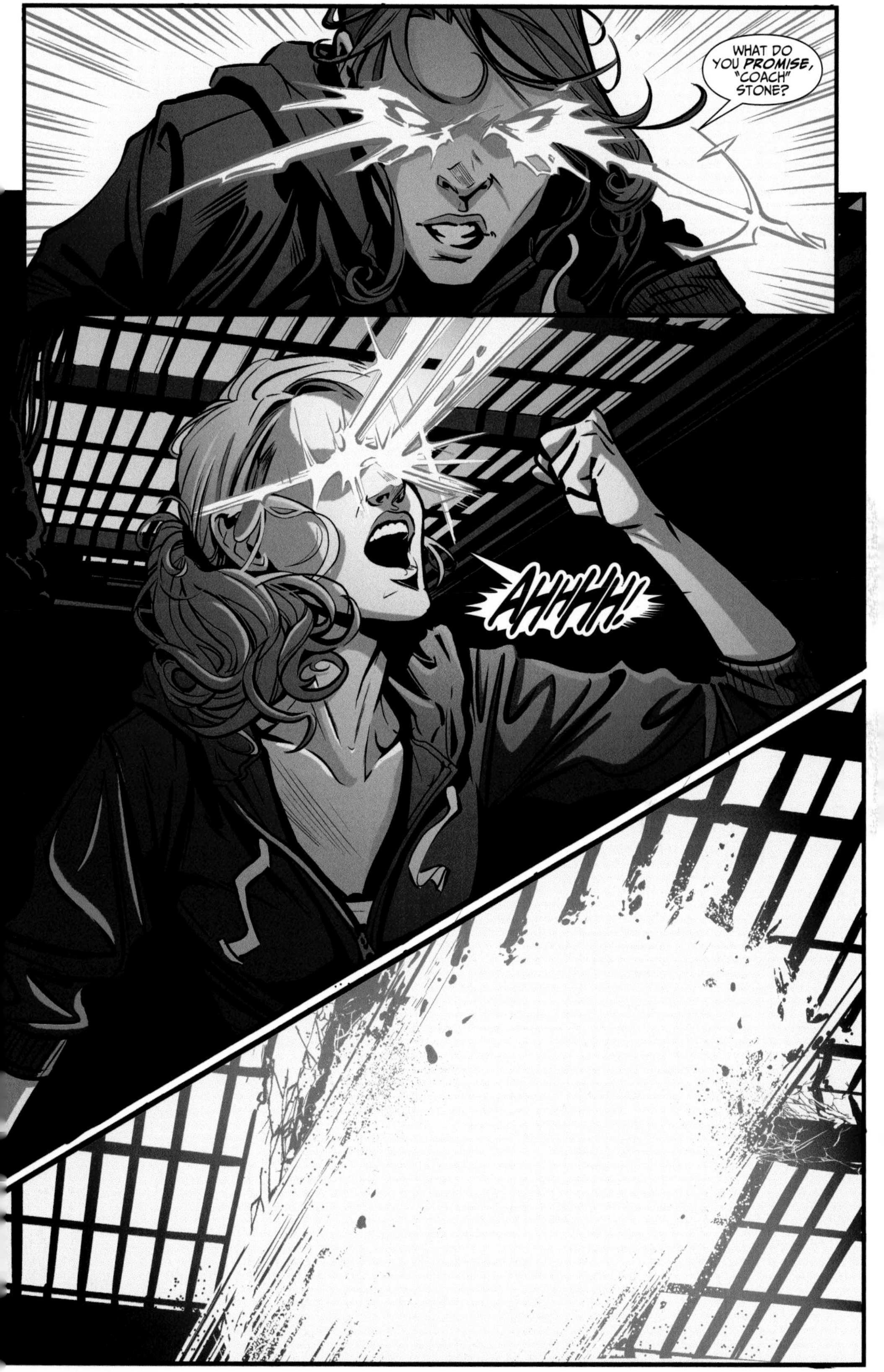
WHAT DO YOU PROMISE, "COACH" STONE?
AHHHH!

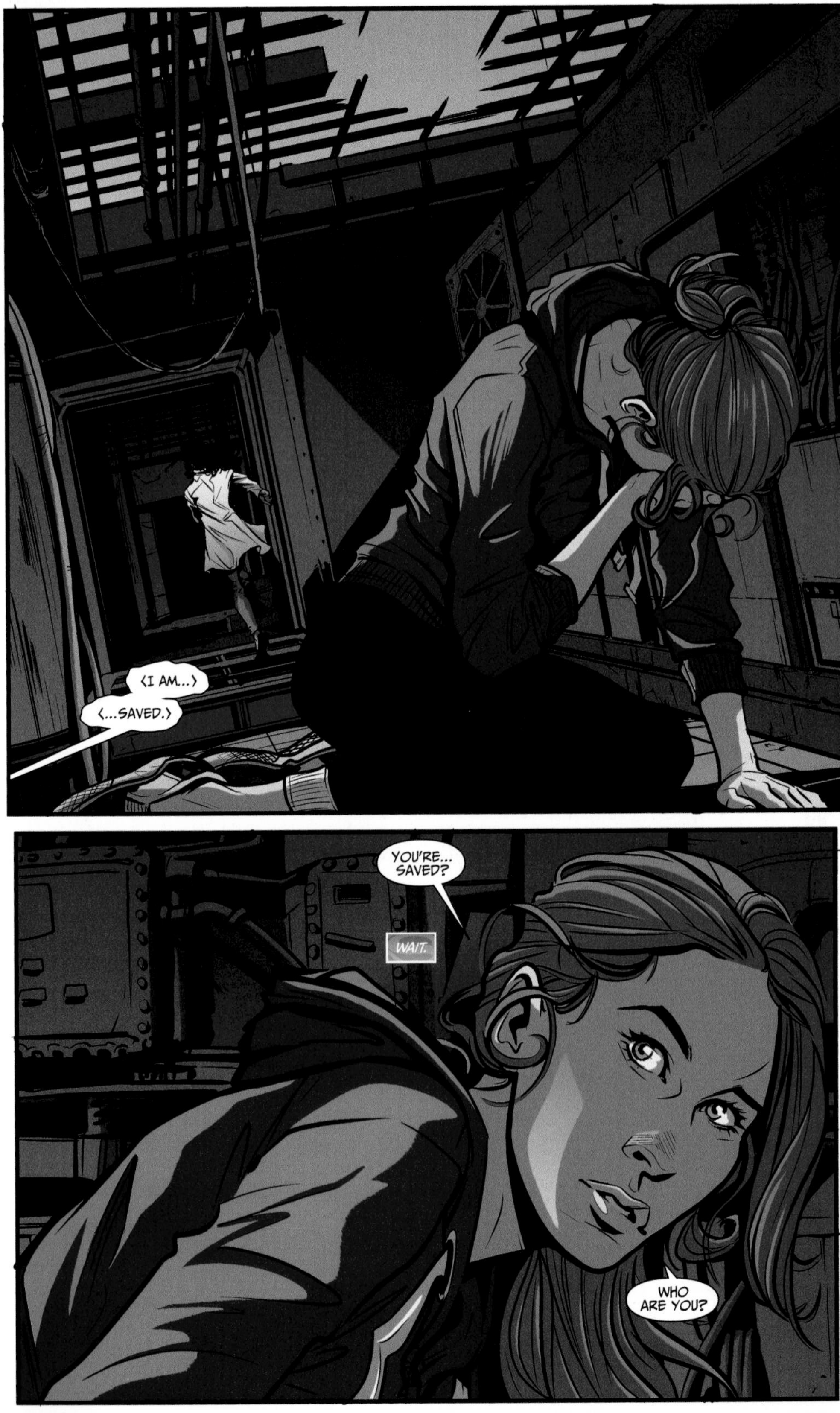

<I AM...>
<...SAVED.>
YOU'RE... SAVED?
WAIT.
WHO ARE YOU?

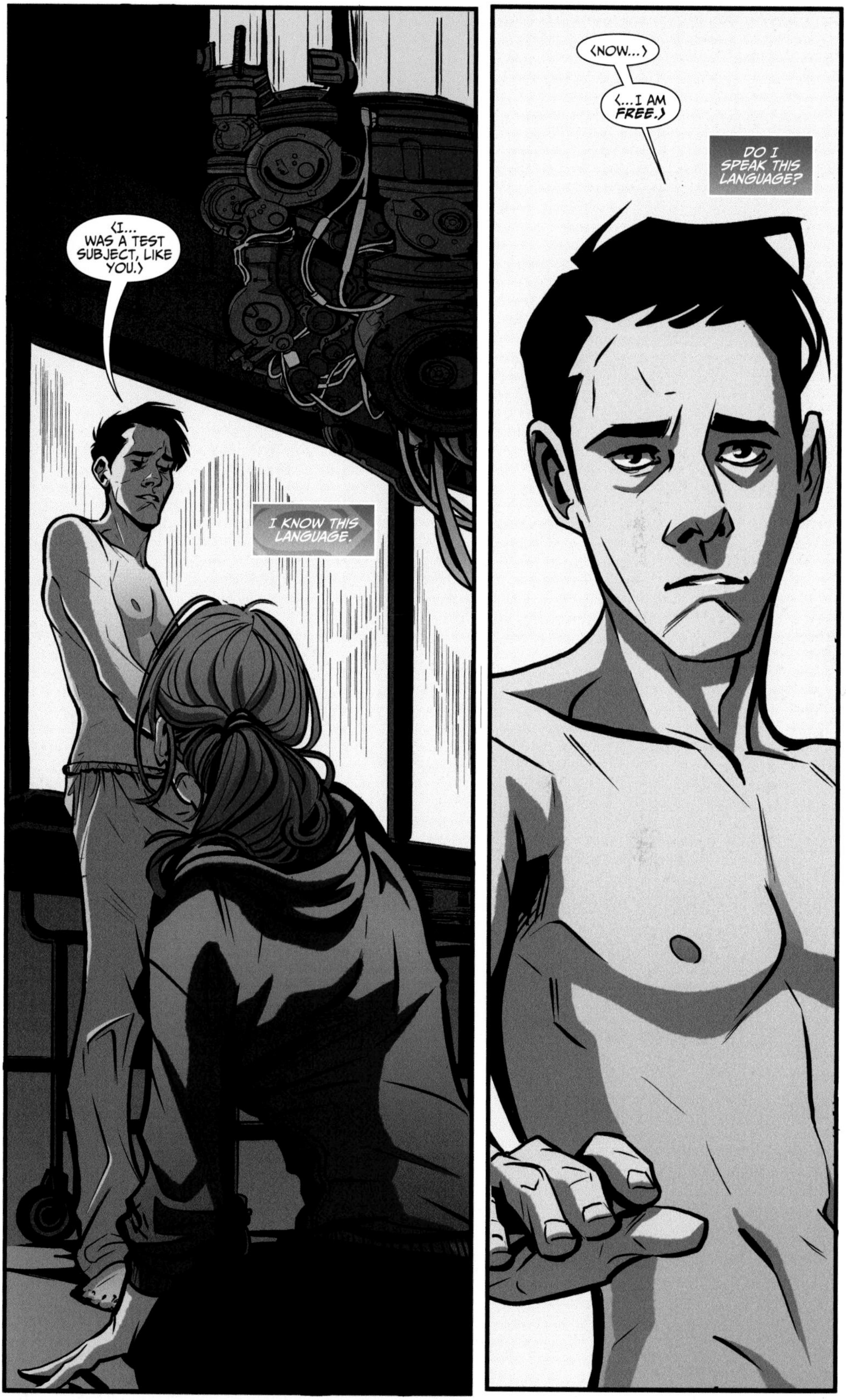
⟨I... WAS A TEST SUBJECT, LIKE YOU.⟩
I KNOW THIS LANGUAGE.
⟨NOW...⟩
⟨...I AM FREE.⟩
DO I SPEAK THIS LANGUAGE?

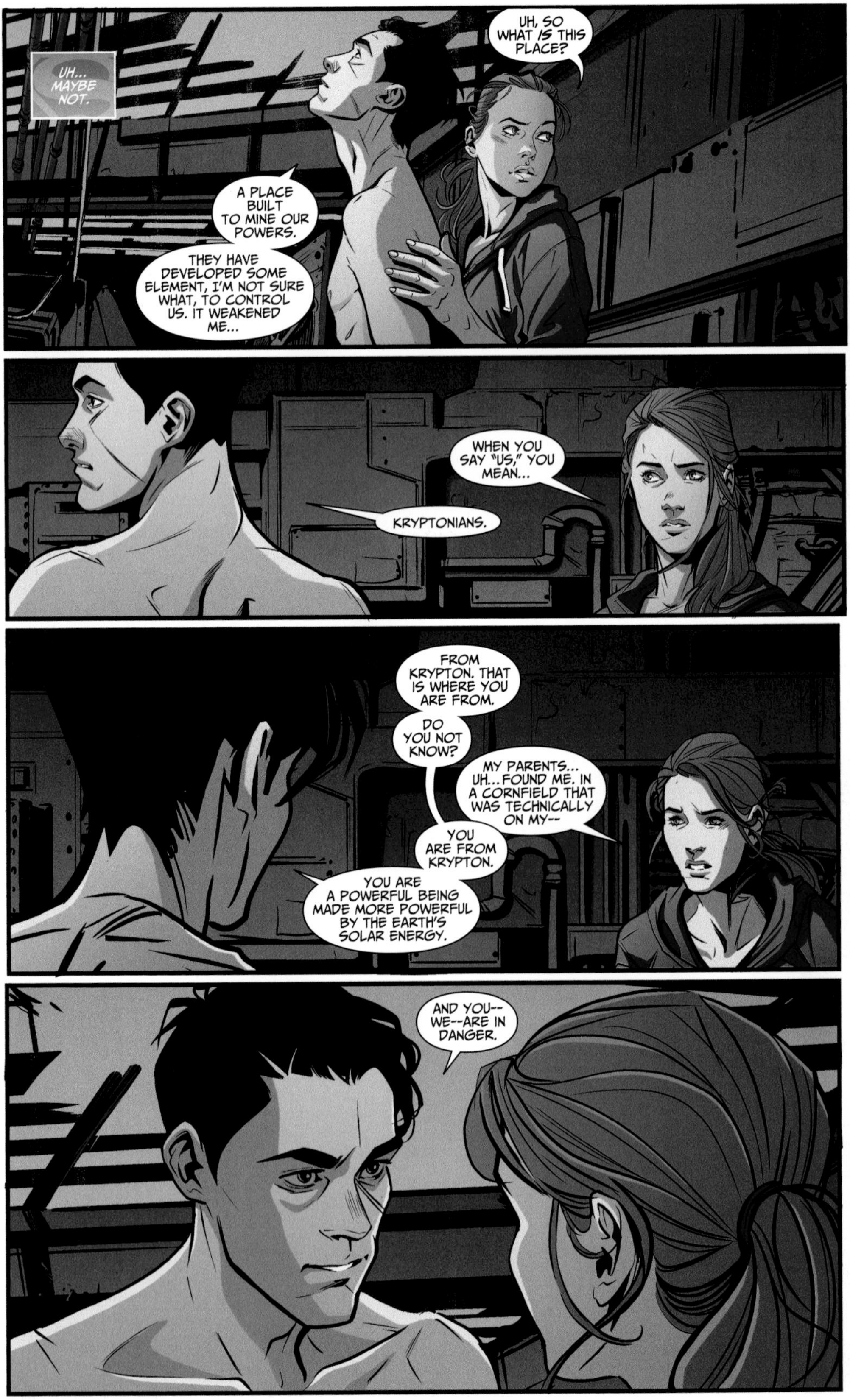
UH... MAYBE NOT.
UH, SO WHAT IS THIS PLACE?
A PLACE BUILT TO MINE OUR POWERS.
THEY HAVE DEVELOPED SOME ELEMENT, I'M NOT SURE WHAT, TO CONTROL US. IT WEAKENED ME...
WHEN YOU SAY "US," YOU MEAN...
KRYPTONIANS.
FROM KRYPTON. THAT IS WHERE YOU ARE FROM.
DO YOU NOT KNOW?
MY PARENTS... UH...FOUND ME. IN A CORNFIELD THAT WAS TECHNICALLY ON MY--
YOU ARE FROM KRYPTON.
YOU ARE A POWERFUL BEING MADE MORE POWERFUL BY THE EARTH'S SOLAR ENERGY.
AND YOU-- WE--ARE IN DANGER.

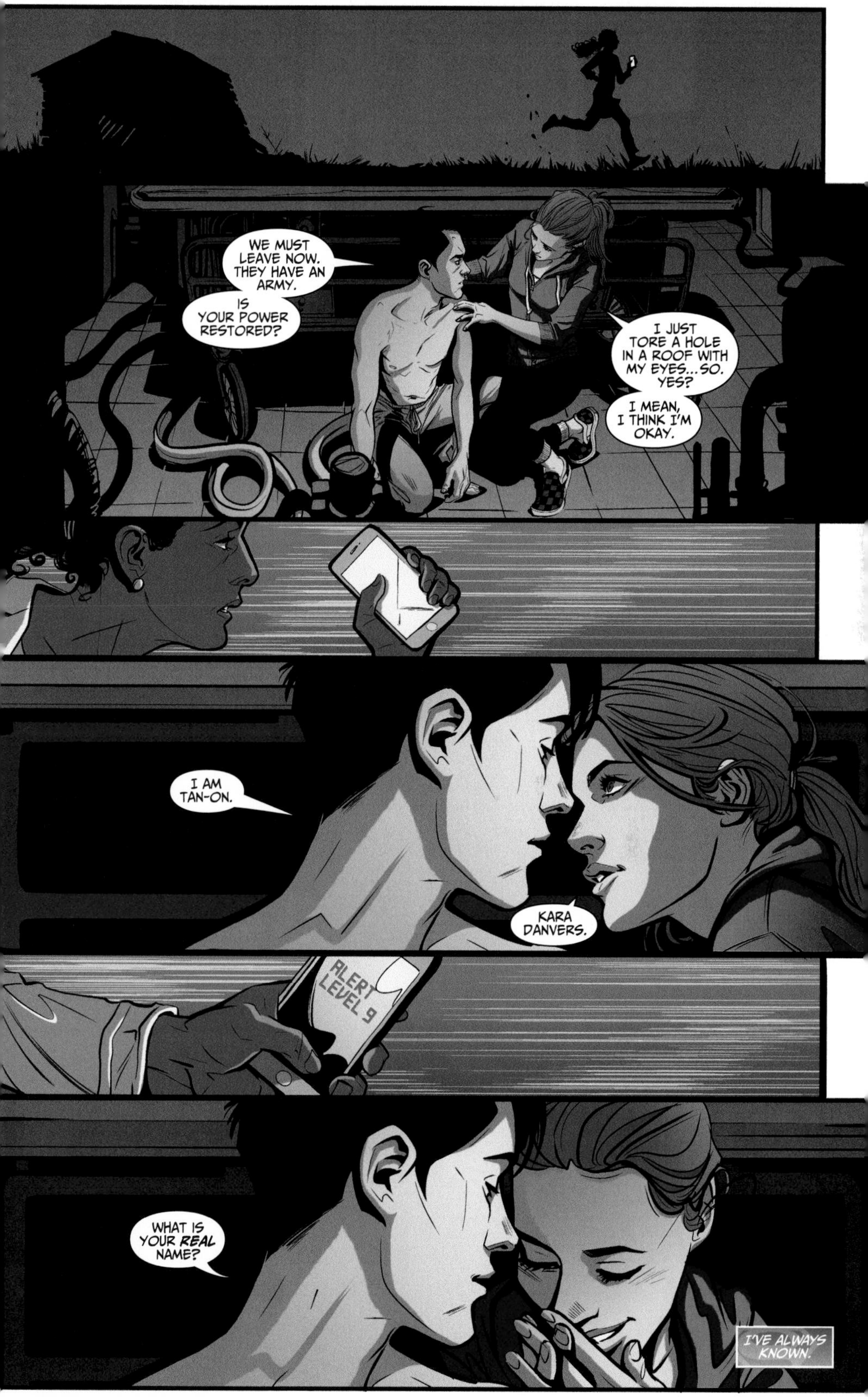
WE MUST LEAVE NOW. THEY HAVE AN ARMY.
IS YOUR POWER RESTORED?
I JUST TORE A HOLE IN A ROOF WITH MY EYES...SO. YES?
I MEAN, I THINK I'M OKAY.
I AM TAN-ON.
KARA DANVERS.
ALERT LEVEL 9
WHAT IS YOUR *REAL* NAME?
I'VE ALWAYS KNOWN.

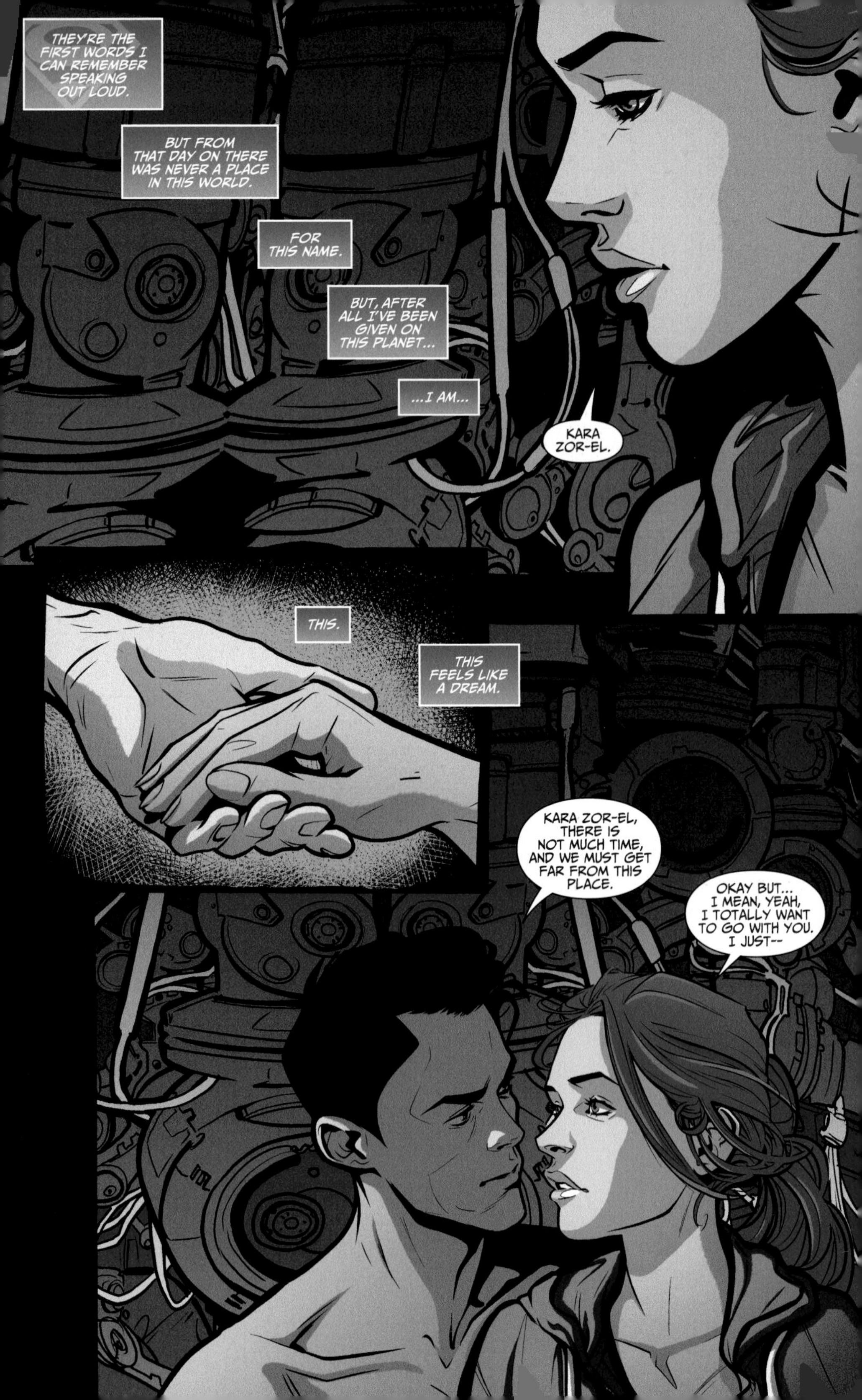
THEY'RE THE FIRST WORDS I CAN REMEMBER SPEAKING OUT LOUD.
BUT FROM THAT DAY ON THERE WAS NEVER A PLACE IN THIS WORLD.
FOR THIS NAME.
BUT, AFTER ALL I'VE BEEN GIVEN ON THIS PLANET...
...I AM...
KARA ZOR-EL.
THIS.
THIS FEELS LIKE A DREAM.
KARA ZOR-EL, THERE IS NOT MUCH TIME, AND WE MUST GET FAR FROM THIS PLACE.
OKAY BUT... I MEAN, YEAH, I TOTALLY WANT TO GO WITH YOU. I JUST--

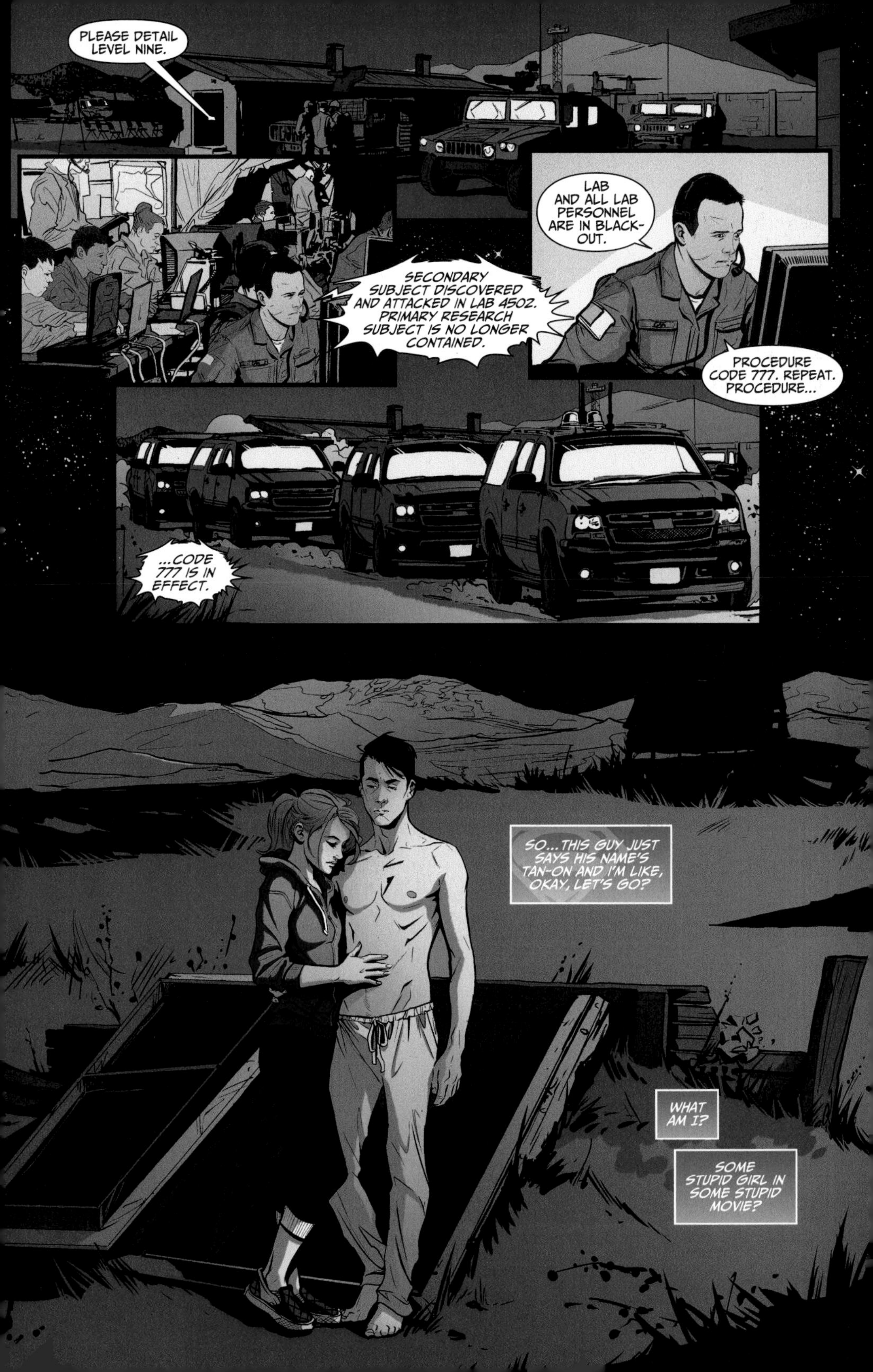
PLEASE DETAIL LEVEL NINE.
SECONDARY SUBJECT DISCOVERED AND ATTACKED IN LAB 4502. PRIMARY RESEARCH SUBJECT IS NO LONGER CONTAINED.
LAB AND ALL LAB PERSONNEL ARE IN BLACK-OUT.
PROCEDURE CODE 777. REPEAT. PROCEDURE...
...CODE 777 IS IN EFFECT.
SO...THIS GUY JUST SAYS HIS NAME'S TAN-ON AND I'M LIKE, OKAY, LET'S GO?
WHAT AM I?
SOME STUPID GIRL IN SOME STUPID MOVIE?

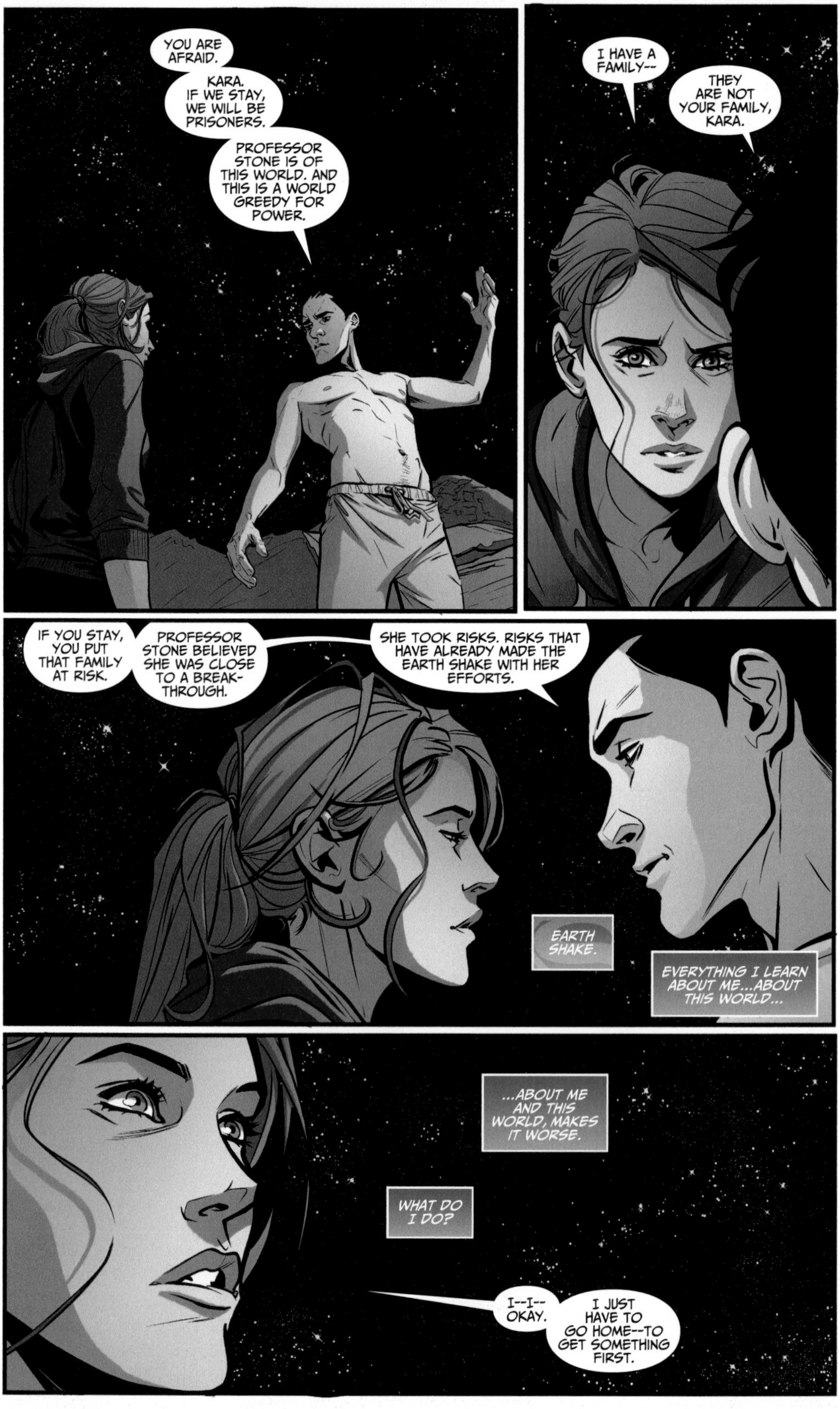

YOU ARE AFRAID.
KARA. IF WE STAY, WE WILL BE PRISONERS.
PROFESSOR STONE IS OF THIS WORLD. AND THIS IS A WORLD GREEDY FOR POWER.
I HAVE A FAMILY--
THEY ARE NOT YOUR FAMILY, KARA.
IF YOU STAY, YOU PUT THAT FAMILY AT RISK.
PROFESSOR STONE BELIEVED SHE WAS CLOSE TO A BREAK-THROUGH.
SHE TOOK RISKS. RISKS THAT HAVE ALREADY MADE THE EARTH SHAKE WITH HER EFFORTS.
EARTH SHAKE.
EVERYTHING I LEARN ABOUT ME...ABOUT THIS WORLD...
...ABOUT ME AND THIS WORLD, MAKES IT WORSE.
WHAT DO I DO?
I--I-- OKAY.
I JUST HAVE TO GO HOME--TO GET SOMETHING FIRST.

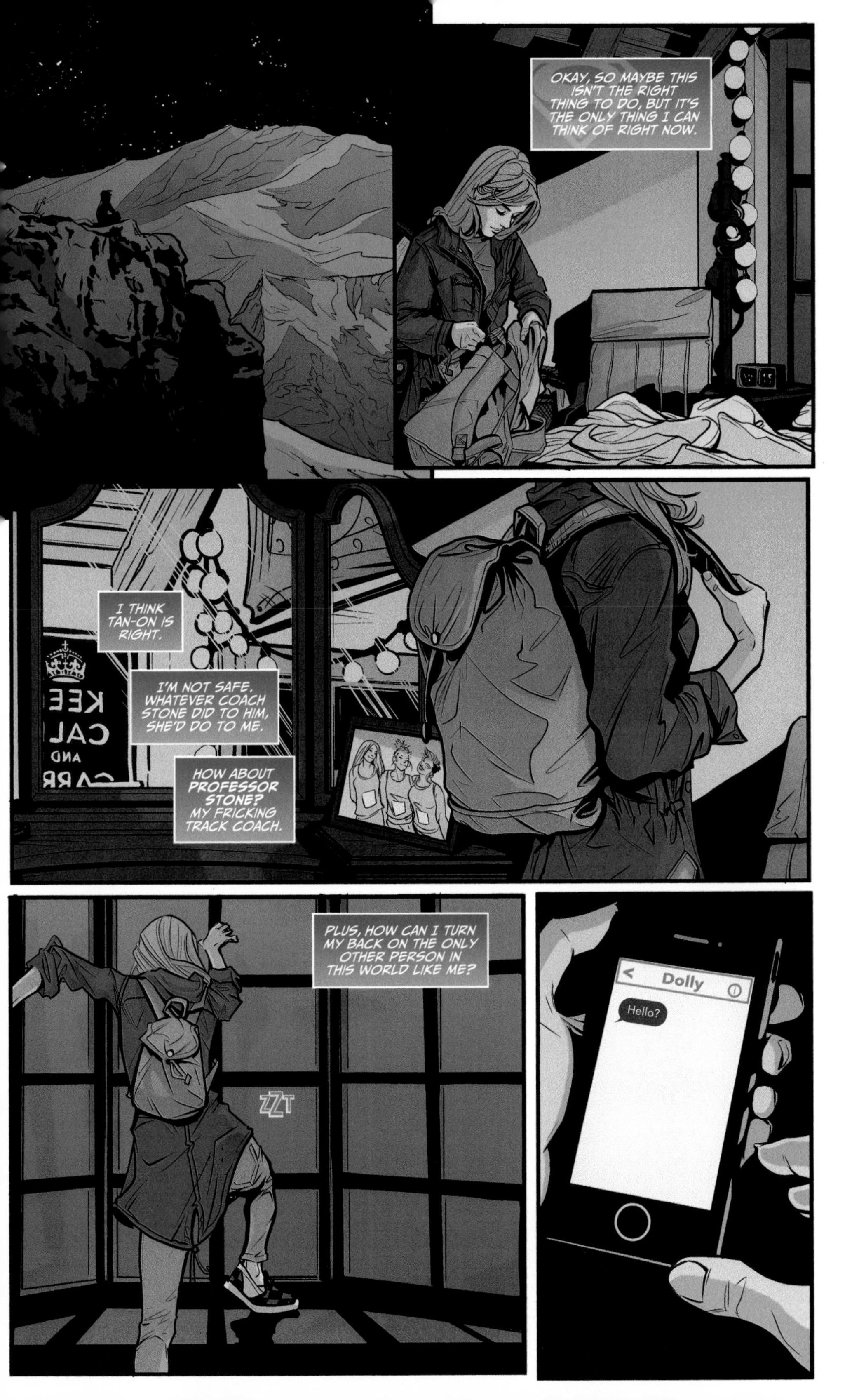
OKAY, SO MAYBE THIS ISN'T THE RIGHT THING TO DO, BUT IT'S THE ONLY THING I CAN THINK OF RIGHT NOW.
I THINK TAN-ON IS RIGHT.
I'M NOT SAFE. WHATEVER COACH STONE DID TO HIM, SHE'D DO TO ME.
HOW ABOUT PROFESSOR STONE? MY FRICKING TRACK COACH.
PLUS, HOW CAN I TURN MY BACK ON THE ONLY OTHER PERSON IN THIS WORLD LIKE ME?
ZZT
Dolly
Hello?

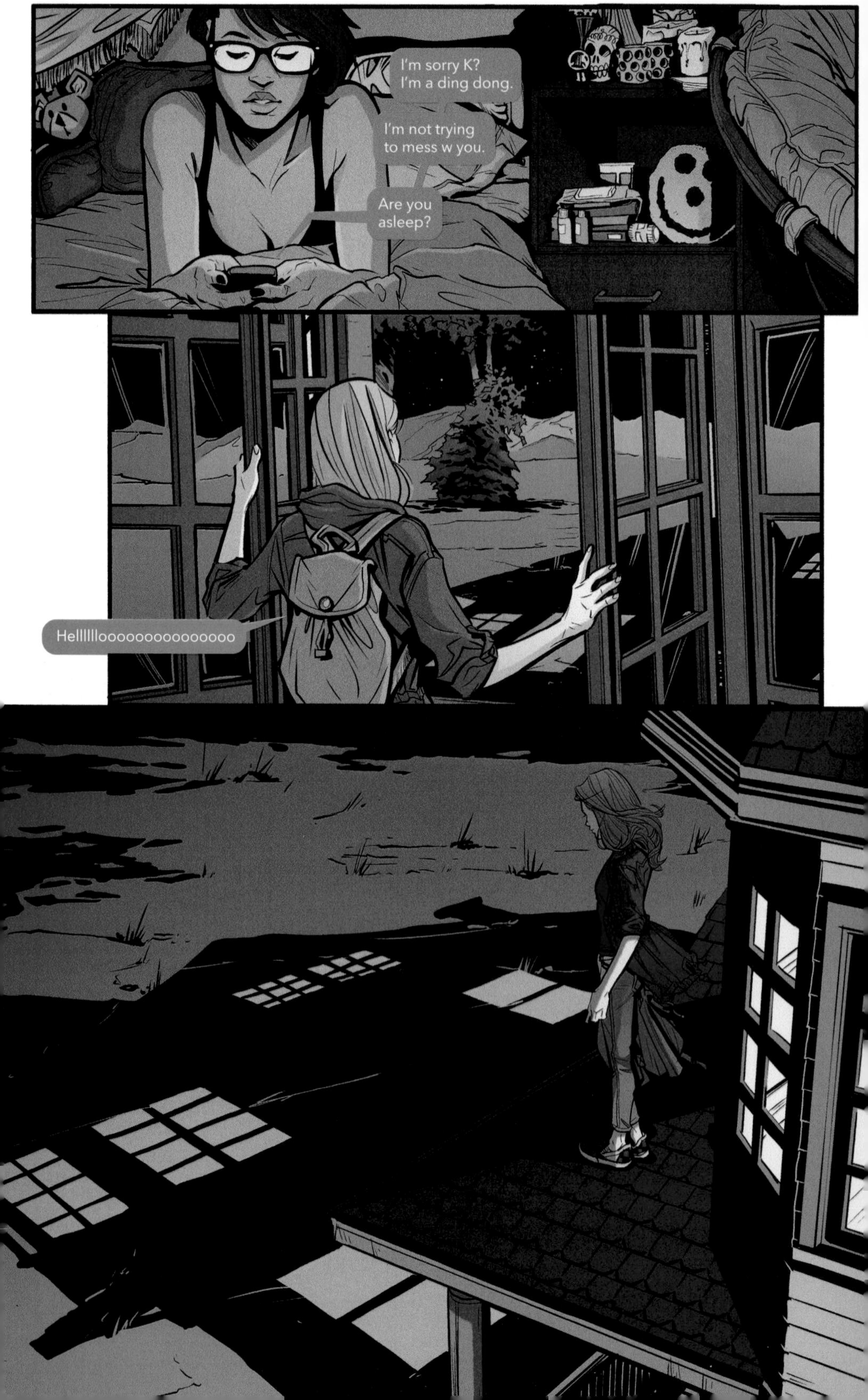
I'm sorry K?
I'm a ding dong.
I'm not trying to mess w you.
Are you asleep?
Hellllllooooooooooooooo

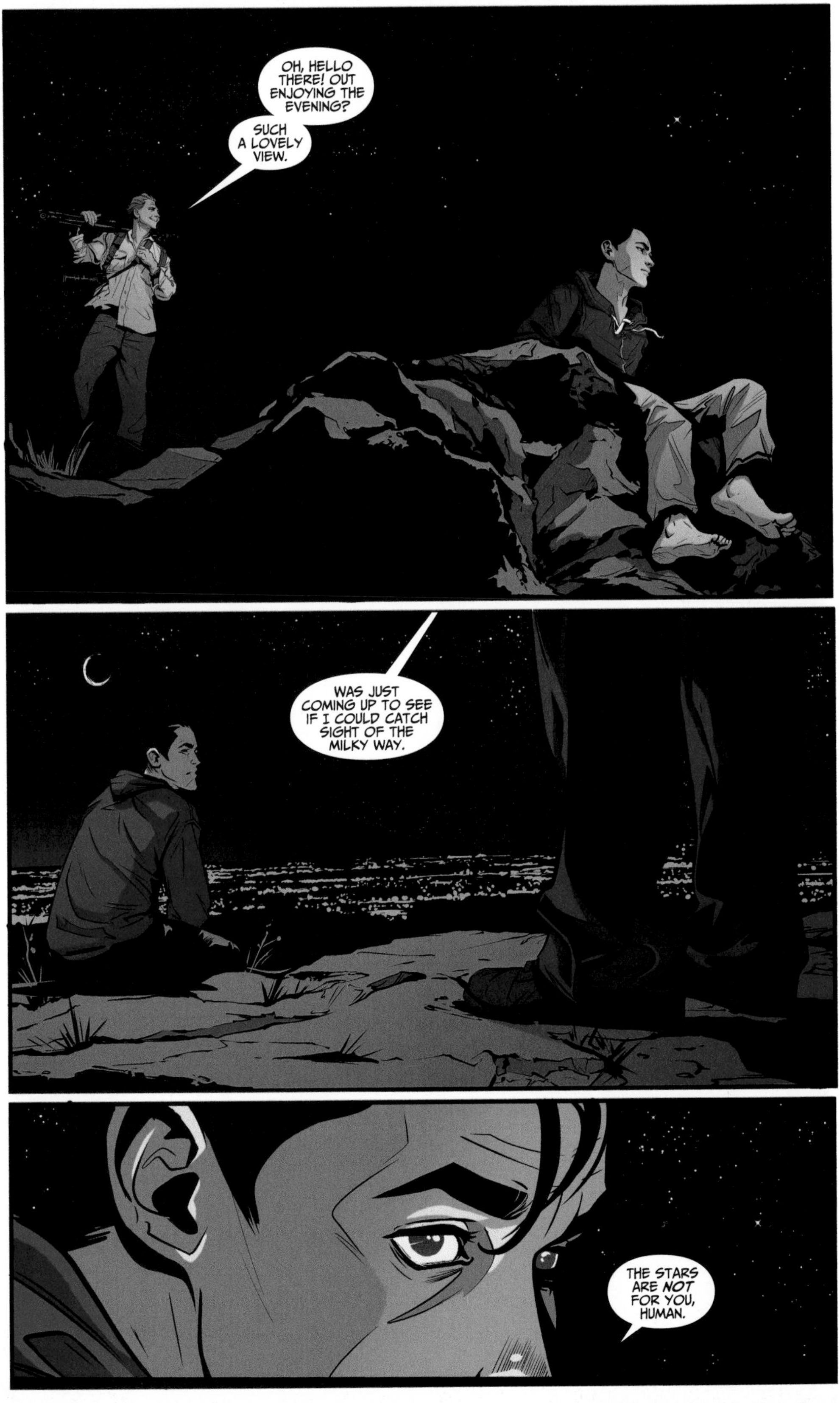
OH, HELLO THERE! OUT ENJOYING THE EVENING?
SUCH A LOVELY VIEW.
WAS JUST COMING UP TO SEE IF I COULD CATCH SIGHT OF THE MILKY WAY.
THE STARS ARE *NOT* FOR YOU, HUMAN.

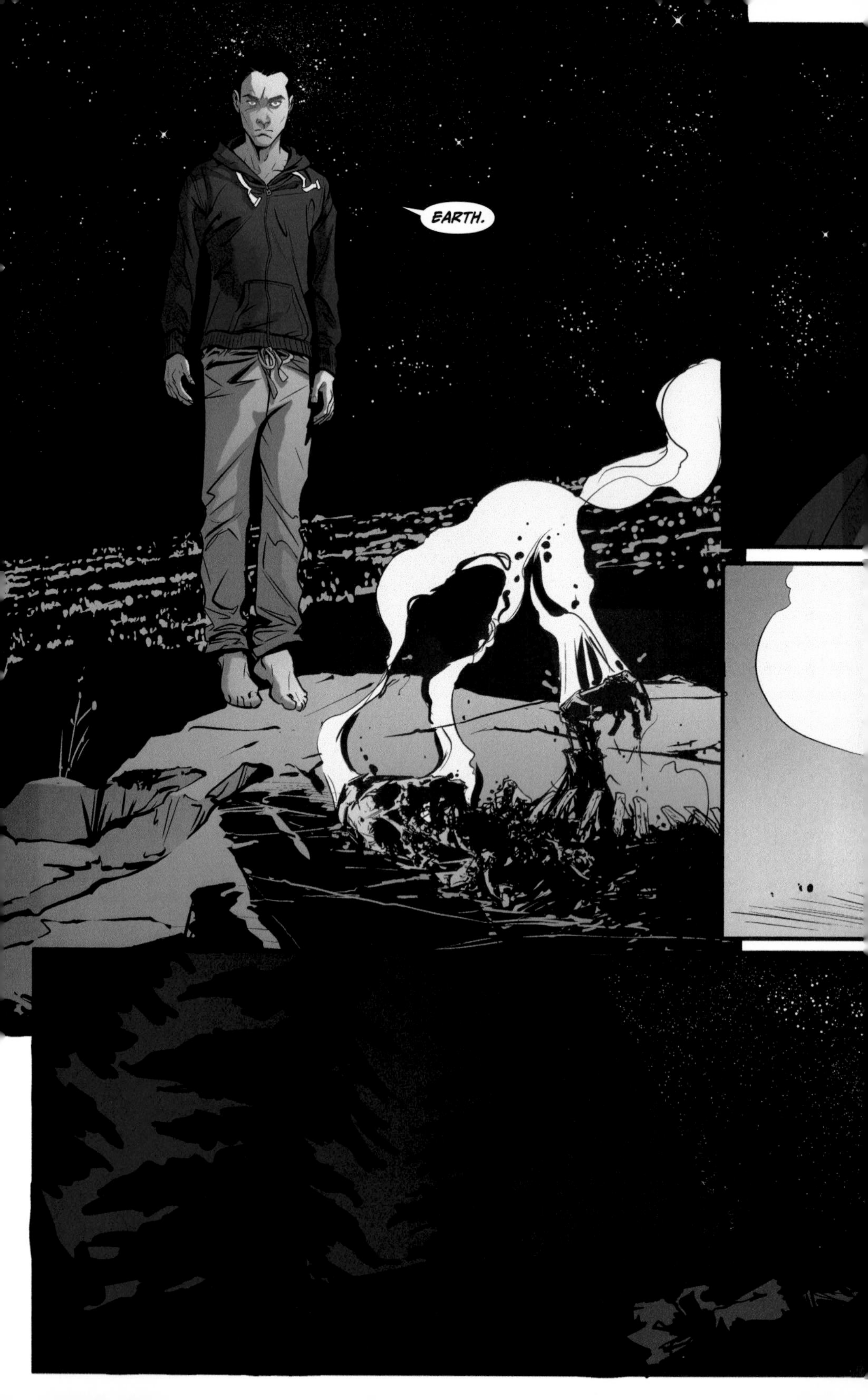
EARTH.

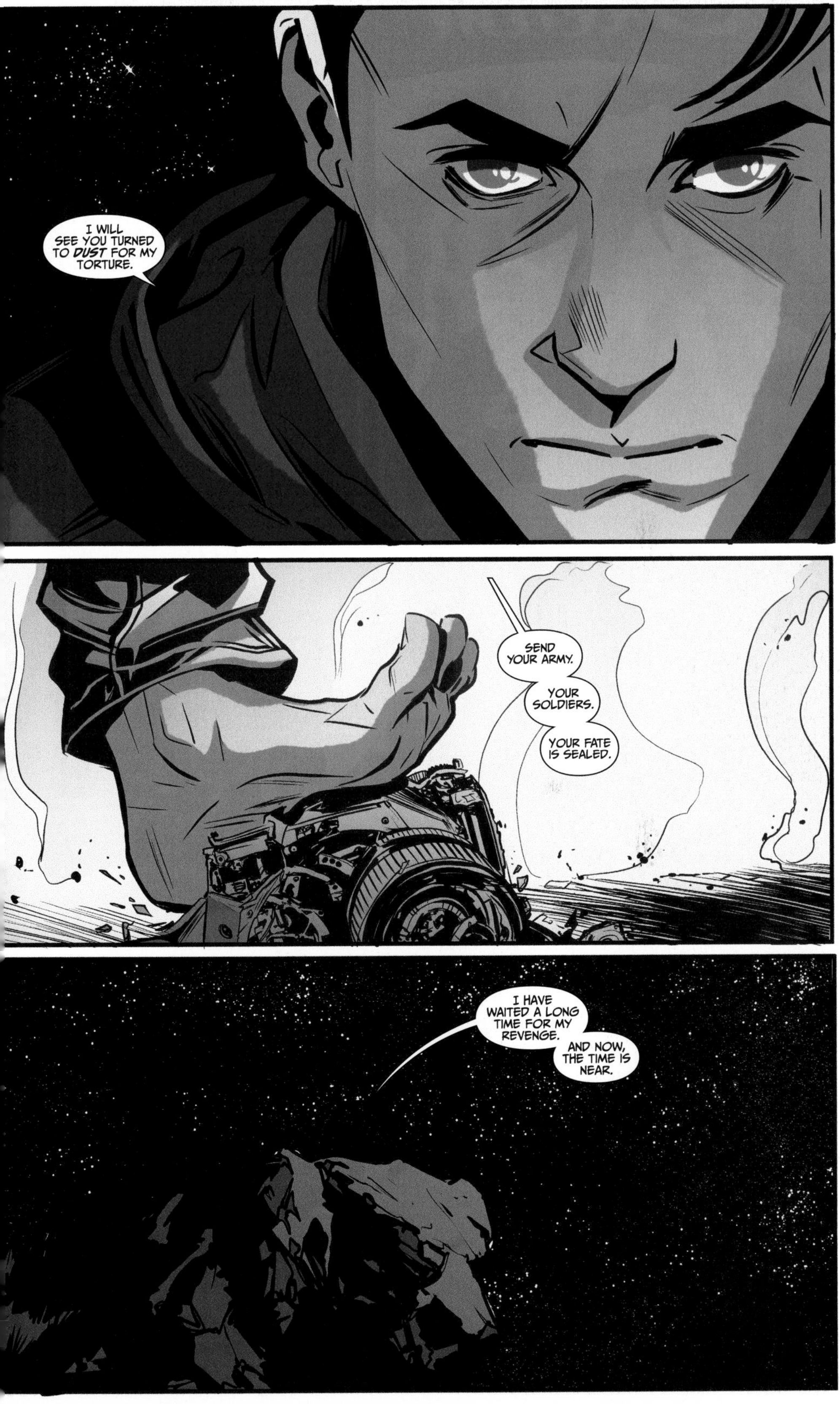
I WILL SEE YOU TURNED TO *DUST* FOR MY TORTURE.
SEND YOUR ARMY.
YOUR SOLDIERS.
YOUR FATE IS SEALED.
I HAVE WAITED A LONG TIME FOR MY REVENGE.
AND NOW, THE TIME IS NEAR.

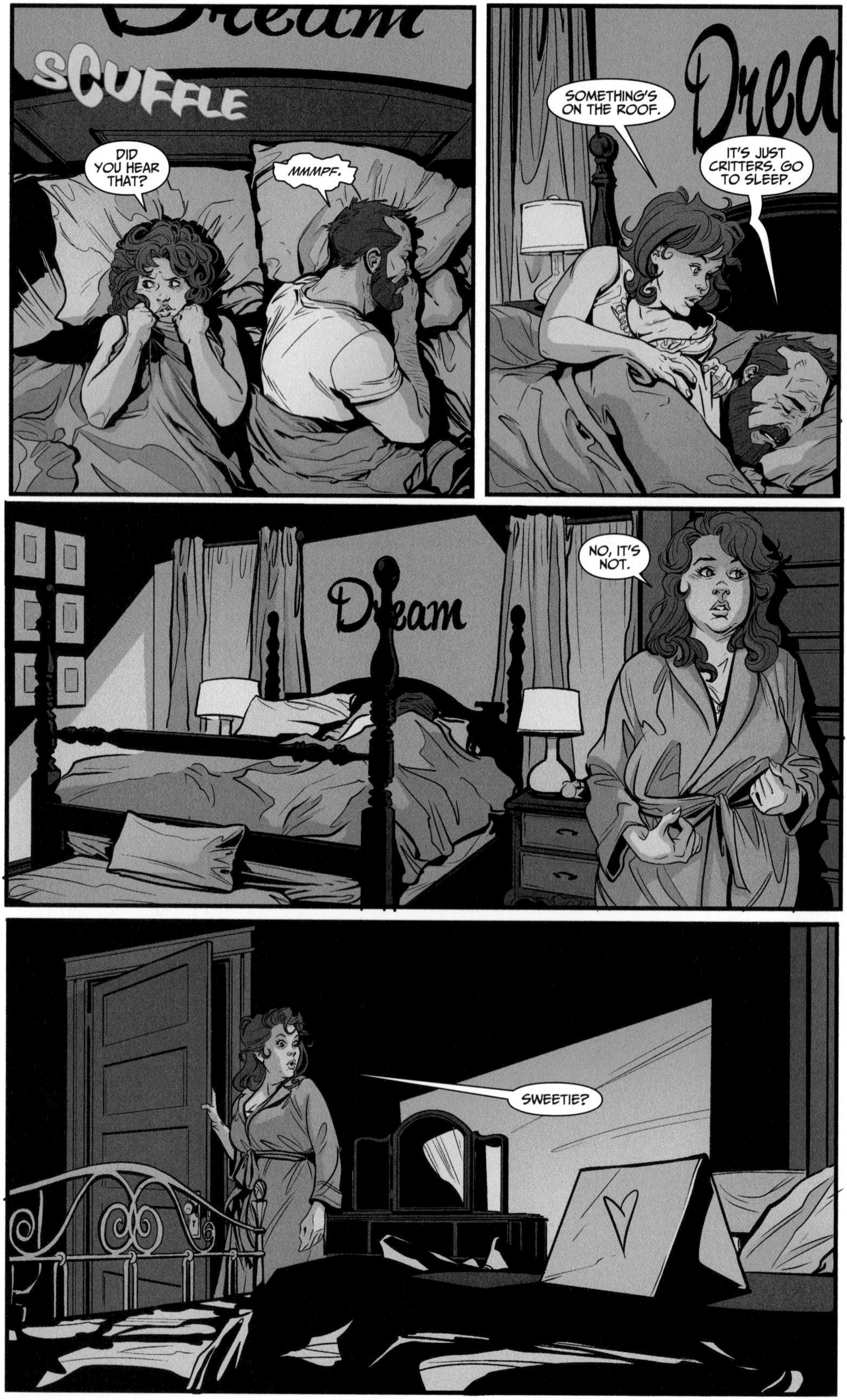
Dream
SCUFFLE
DID YOU HEAR THAT?
MMMPF.
Drea
SOMETHING'S ON THE ROOF.
IT'S JUST CRITTERS. GO TO SLEEP.
Dream
NO, IT'S NOT.
SWEETIE?

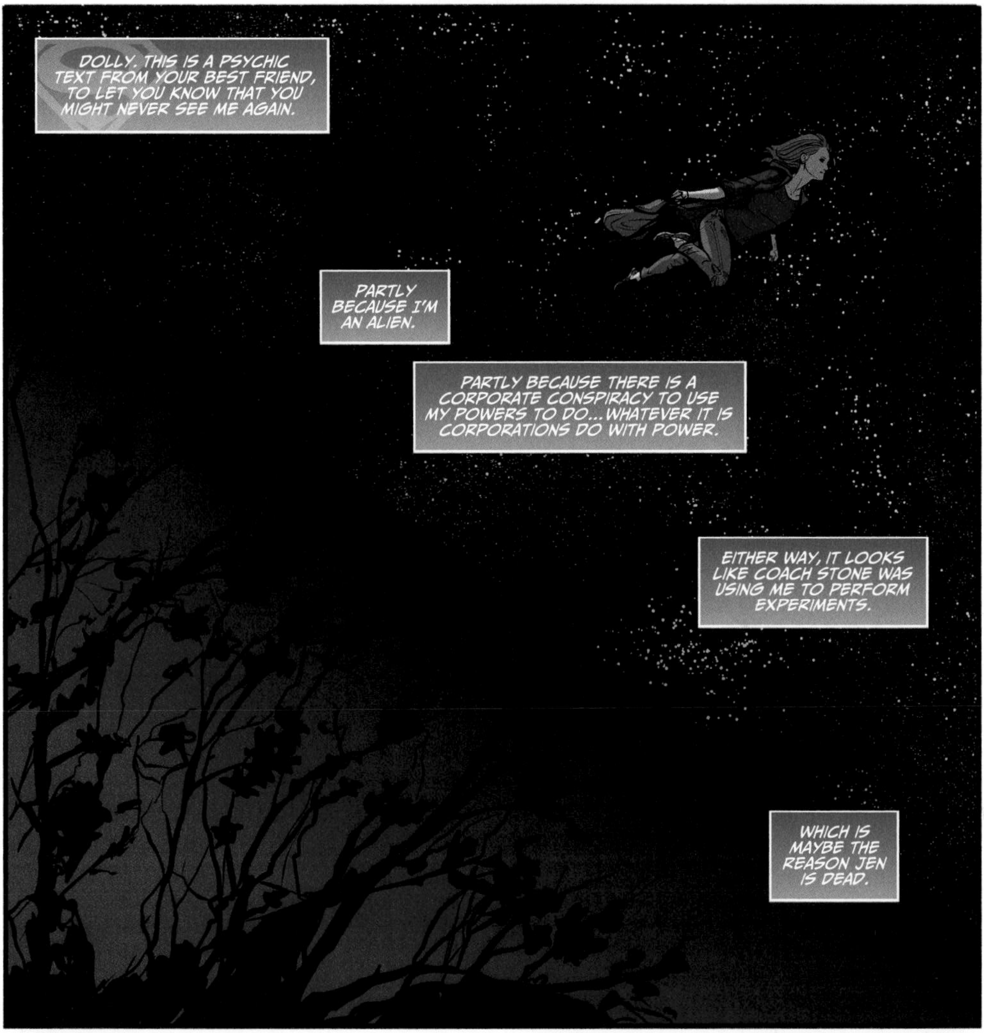
DOLLY. THIS IS A PSYCHIC TEXT FROM YOUR BEST FRIEND, TO LET YOU KNOW THAT YOU MIGHT NEVER SEE ME AGAIN.
PARTLY BECAUSE I'M AN ALIEN.
PARTLY BECAUSE THERE IS A CORPORATE CONSPIRACY TO USE MY POWERS TO DO...WHATEVER IT IS CORPORATIONS DO WITH POWER.
EITHER WAY, IT LOOKS LIKE COACH STONE WAS USING ME TO PERFORM EXPERIMENTS.
WHICH IS MAYBE THE REASON JEN IS DEAD.

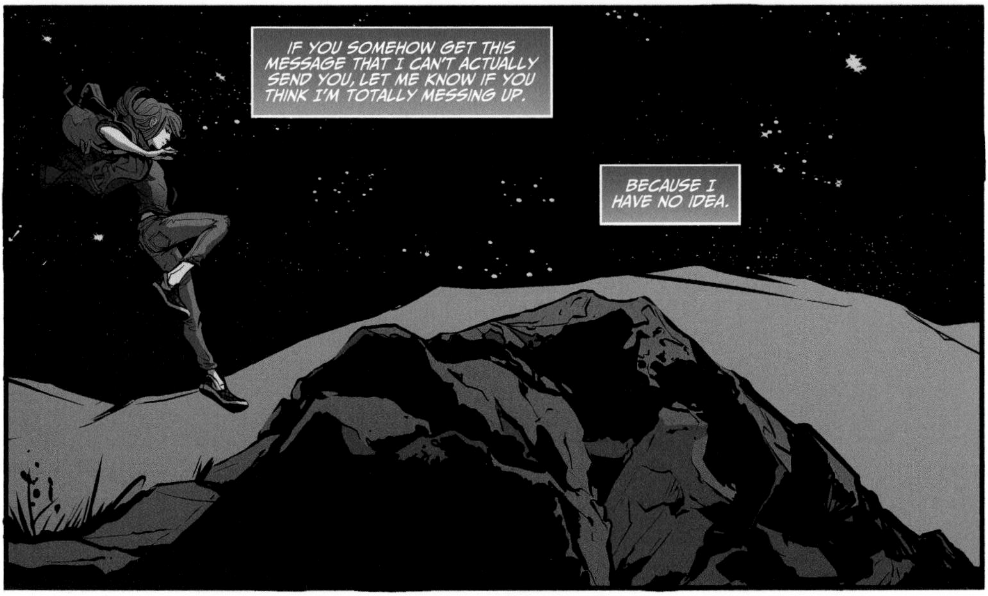
IF YOU SOMEHOW GET THIS MESSAGE THAT I CAN'T ACTUALLY SEND YOU, LET ME KNOW IF YOU THINK I'M TOTALLY MESSING UP.
BECAUSE I HAVE NO IDEA.

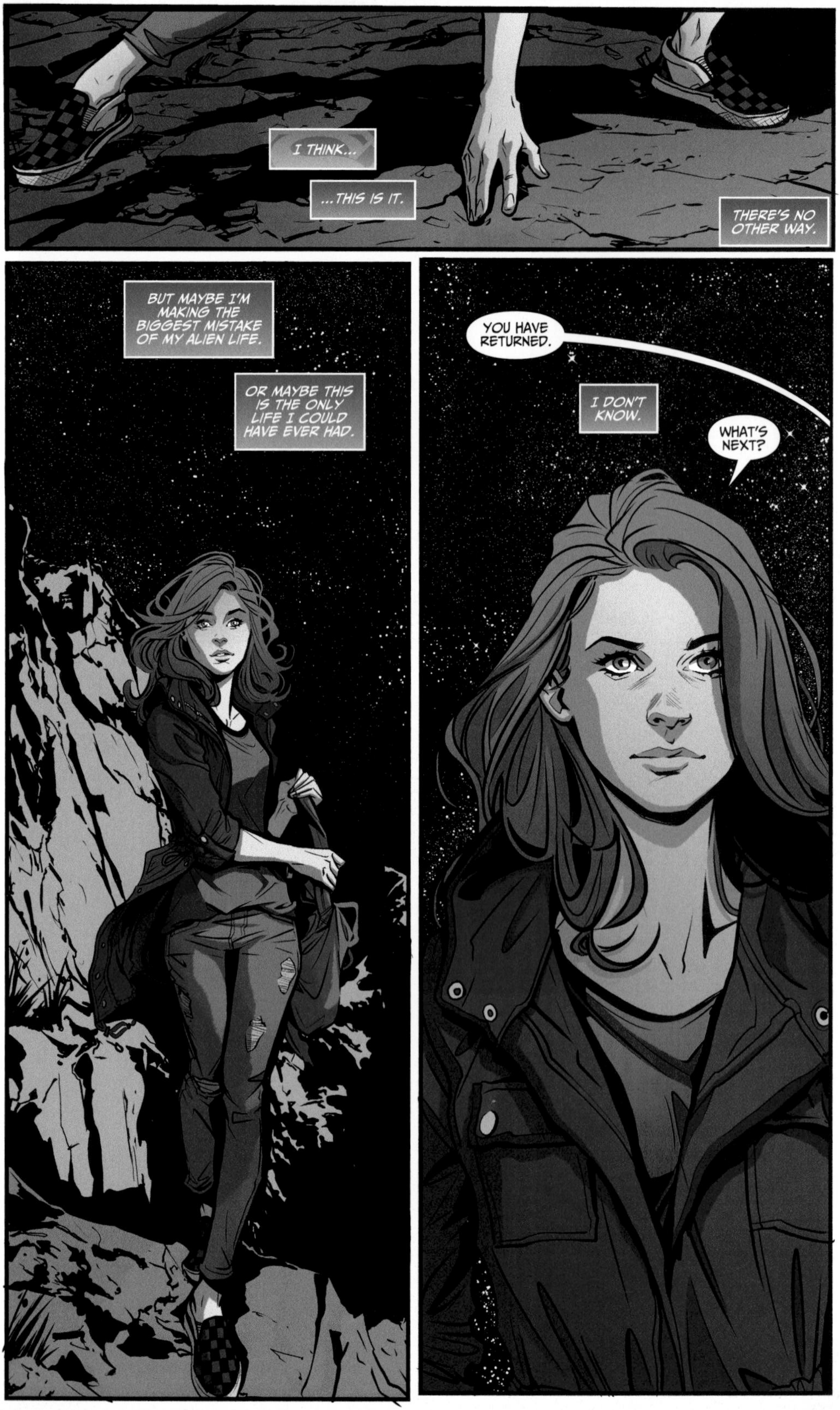
I THINK...
...THIS IS IT.
THERE'S NO OTHER WAY.
BUT MAYBE I'M MAKING THE BIGGEST MISTAKE OF MY ALIEN LIFE.
OR MAYBE THIS IS THE ONLY LIFE I COULD HAVE EVER HAD.
YOU HAVE RETURNED.
I DON'T KNOW.
WHAT'S NEXT?

CHAPTER FOUR:
WHO I AM.

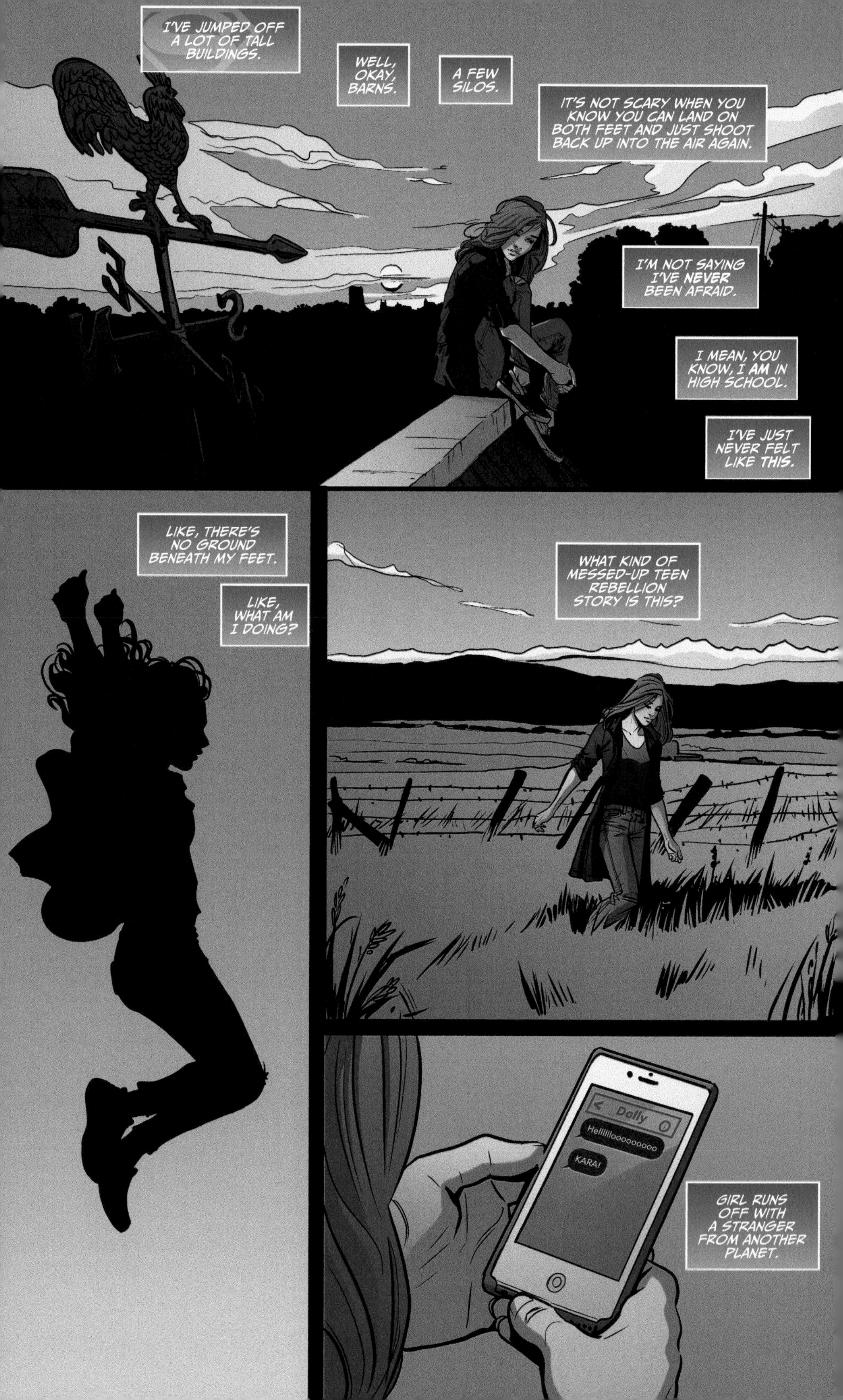
I'VE JUMPED OFF A LOT OF TALL BUILDINGS.
WELL, OKAY, BARNS.
A FEW SILOS.
IT'S NOT SCARY WHEN YOU KNOW YOU CAN LAND ON BOTH FEET AND JUST SHOOT BACK UP INTO THE AIR AGAIN.
I'M NOT SAYING I'VE NEVER BEEN AFRAID.
I MEAN, YOU KNOW, I AM IN HIGH SCHOOL.
I'VE JUST NEVER FELT LIKE THIS.
LIKE, THERE'S NO GROUND BENEATH MY FEET.
LIKE, WHAT AM I DOING?
WHAT KIND OF MESSED-UP TEEN REBELLION STORY IS THIS?
Dolly
Hellllllooooooooo
KARA!
GIRL RUNS OFF WITH A STRANGER FROM ANOTHER PLANET.

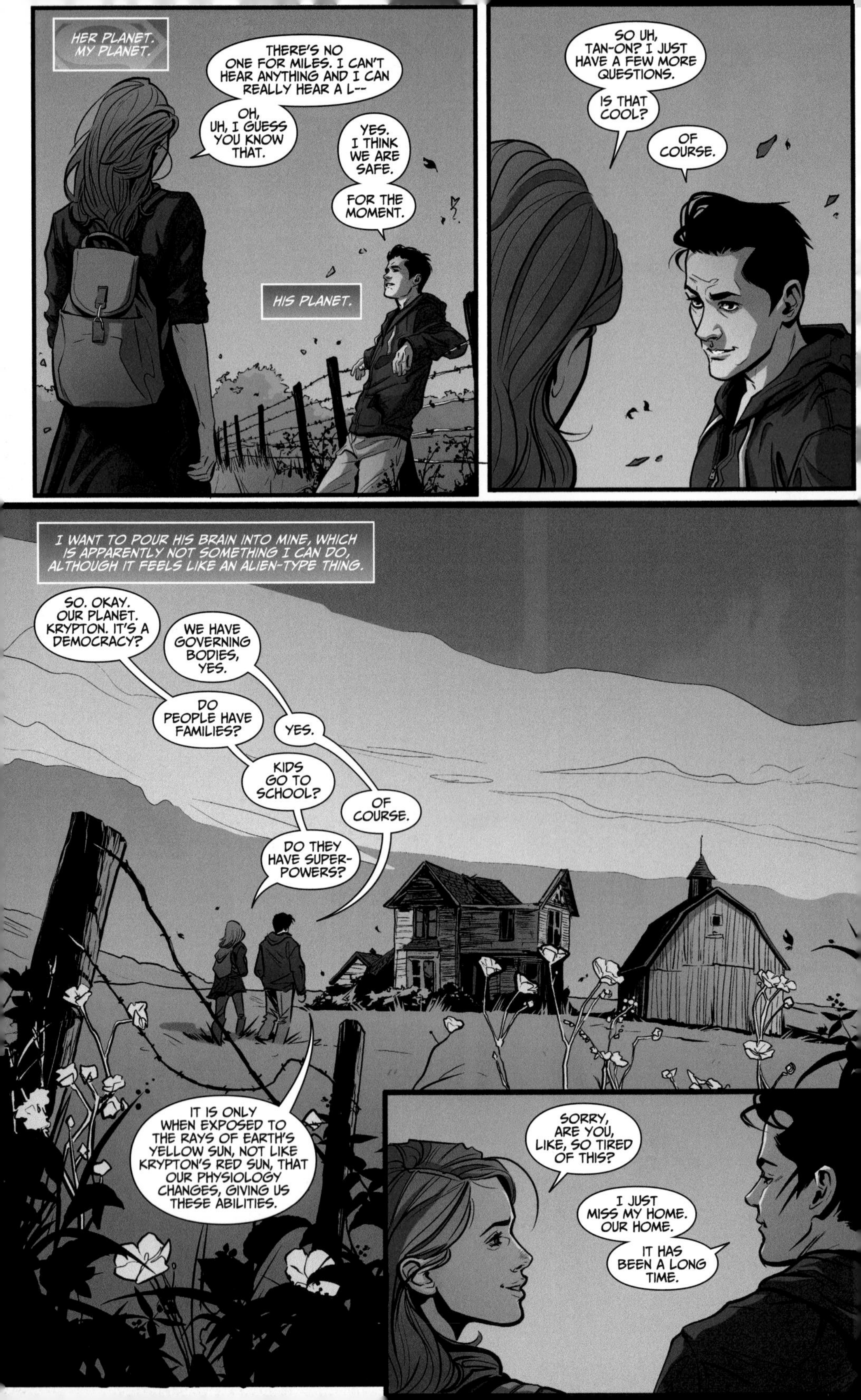
HER PLANET. MY PLANET.
THERE'S NO ONE FOR MILES. I CAN'T HEAR ANYTHING AND I CAN REALLY HEAR A L--
OH, UH, I GUESS YOU KNOW THAT.
YES. I THINK WE ARE SAFE.
FOR THE MOMENT.
HIS PLANET.
SO UH, TAN-ON? I JUST HAVE A FEW MORE QUESTIONS.
IS THAT COOL?
OF COURSE.
I WANT TO POUR HIS BRAIN INTO MINE, WHICH IS APPARENTLY NOT SOMETHING I CAN DO, ALTHOUGH IT FEELS LIKE AN ALIEN-TYPE THING.
SO. OKAY. OUR PLANET. KRYPTON. IT'S A DEMOCRACY?
WE HAVE GOVERNING BODIES, YES.
DO PEOPLE HAVE FAMILIES?
YES.
KIDS GO TO SCHOOL?
OF COURSE.
DO THEY HAVE SUPER-POWERS?
IT IS ONLY WHEN EXPOSED TO THE RAYS OF EARTH'S YELLOW SUN, NOT LIKE KRYPTON'S RED SUN, THAT OUR PHYSIOLOGY CHANGES, GIVING US THESE ABILITIES.
SORRY, ARE YOU, LIKE, SO TIRED OF THIS?
I JUST MISS MY HOME. OUR HOME.
IT HAS BEEN A LONG TIME.

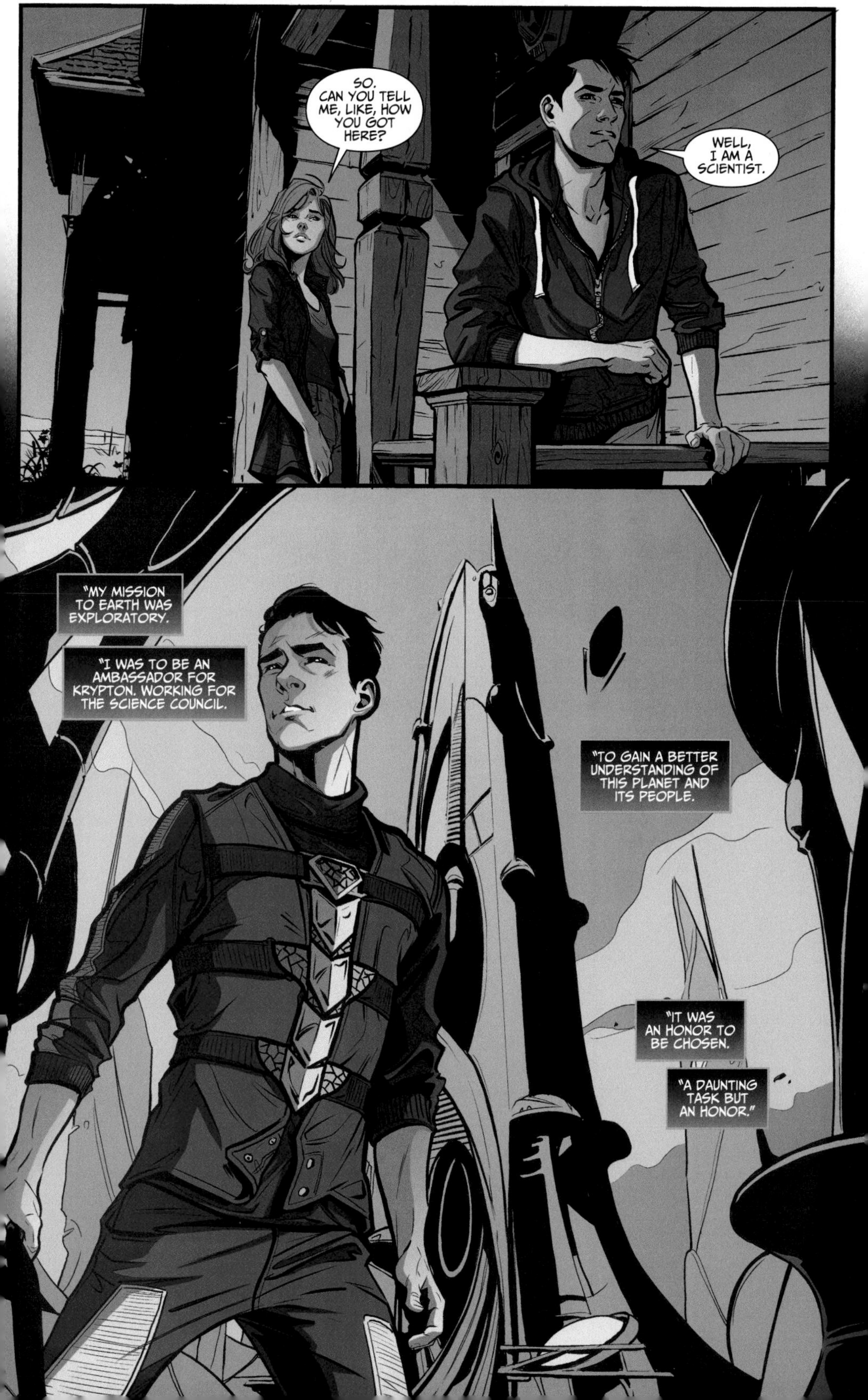
SO. CAN YOU TELL ME, LIKE, HOW YOU GOT HERE?
WELL, I AM A SCIENTIST.
"MY MISSION TO EARTH WAS EXPLORATORY.
"I WAS TO BE AN AMBASSADOR FOR KRYPTON. WORKING FOR THE SCIENCE COUNCIL.
"TO GAIN A BETTER UNDERSTANDING OF THIS PLANET AND ITS PEOPLE.
"IT WAS AN HONOR TO BE CHOSEN.
"A DAUNTING TASK BUT AN HONOR."

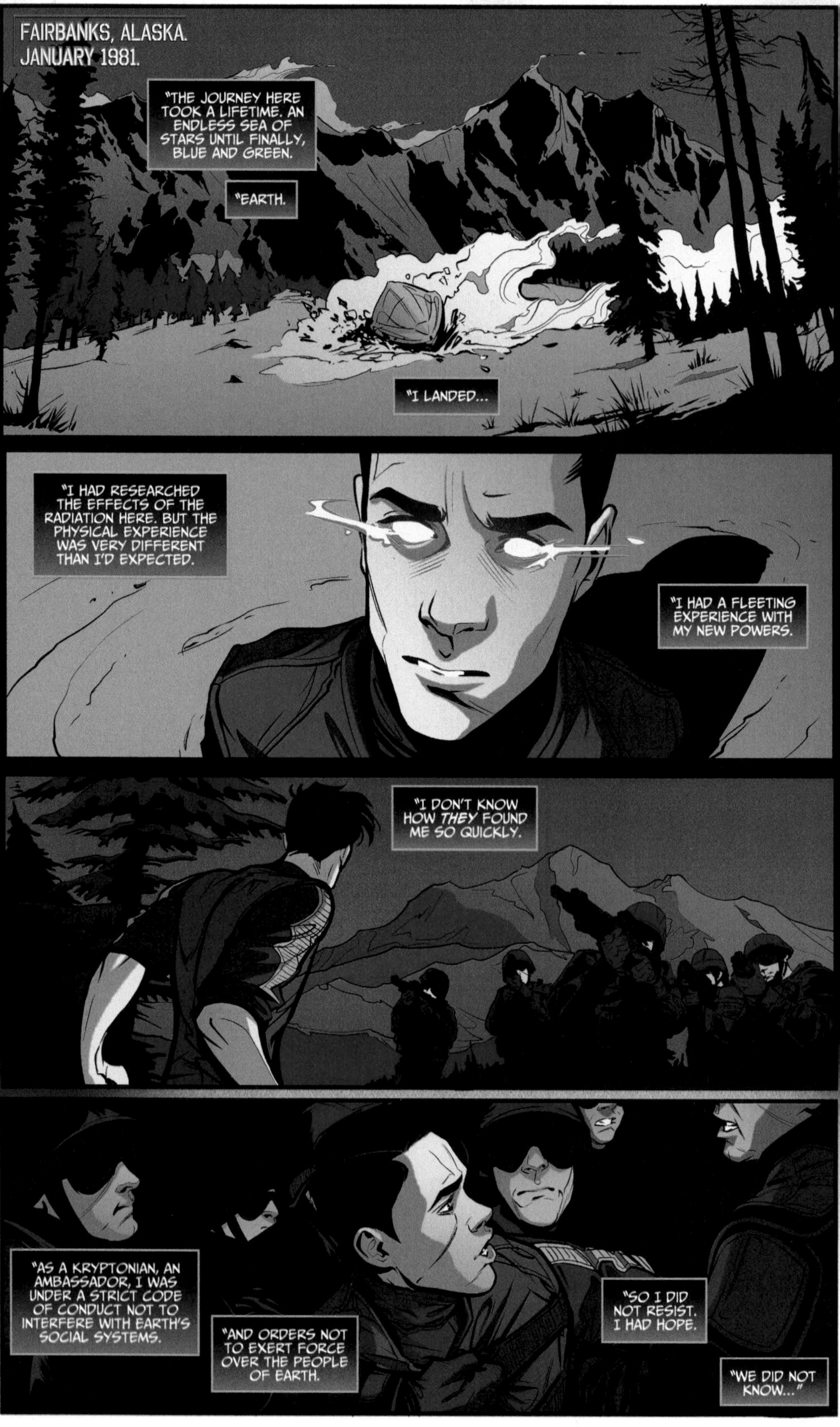
FAIRBANKS, ALASKA.
JANUARY 1981.
"THE JOURNEY HERE TOOK A LIFETIME. AN ENDLESS SEA OF STARS UNTIL FINALLY, BLUE AND GREEN.
"EARTH.
"I LANDED...
"I HAD RESEARCHED THE EFFECTS OF THE RADIATION HERE. BUT THE PHYSICAL EXPERIENCE WAS VERY DIFFERENT THAN I'D EXPECTED.
"I HAD A FLEETING EXPERIENCE WITH MY NEW POWERS.
"I DON'T KNOW HOW *THEY* FOUND ME SO QUICKLY.
"AS A KRYPTONIAN, AN AMBASSADOR, I WAS UNDER A STRICT CODE OF CONDUCT NOT TO INTERFERE WITH EARTH'S SOCIAL SYSTEMS.
"AND ORDERS NOT TO EXERT FORCE OVER THE PEOPLE OF EARTH.
"SO I DID NOT RESIST. I HAD HOPE.
"WE DID NOT KNOW..."

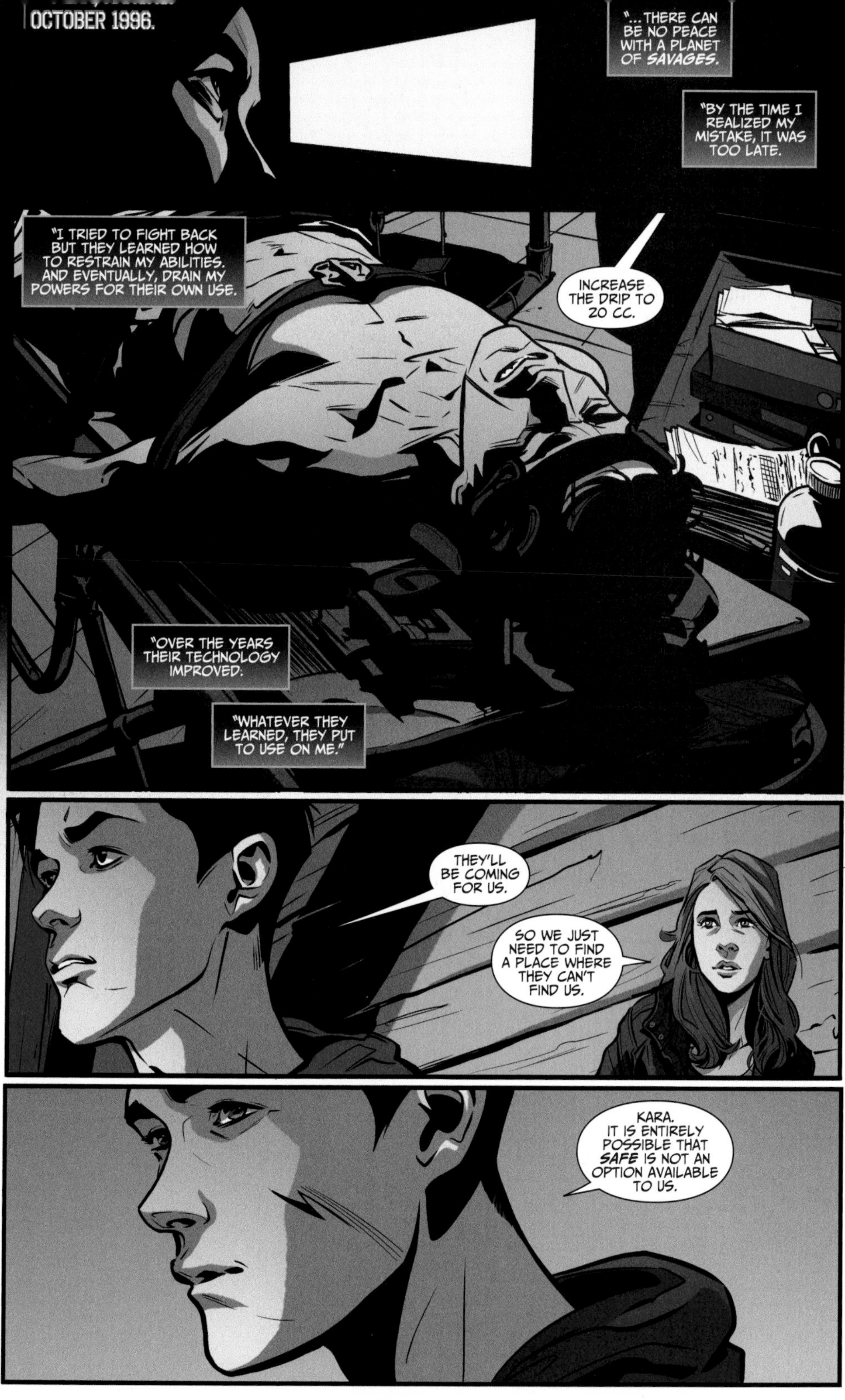
OCTOBER 1996.
"...THERE CAN BE NO PEACE WITH A PLANET OF *SAVAGES.*
"BY THE TIME I REALIZED MY MISTAKE, IT WAS TOO LATE.
"I TRIED TO FIGHT BACK BUT THEY LEARNED HOW TO RESTRAIN MY ABILITIES. AND EVENTUALLY, DRAIN MY POWERS FOR THEIR OWN USE.
INCREASE THE DRIP TO 20 CC.
"OVER THE YEARS THEIR TECHNOLOGY IMPROVED.
"WHATEVER THEY LEARNED, THEY PUT TO USE ON ME."
THEY'LL BE COMING FOR US.
SO WE JUST NEED TO FIND A PLACE WHERE THEY CAN'T FIND US.
KARA. IT IS ENTIRELY POSSIBLE THAT *SAFE* IS NOT AN OPTION AVAILABLE TO US.

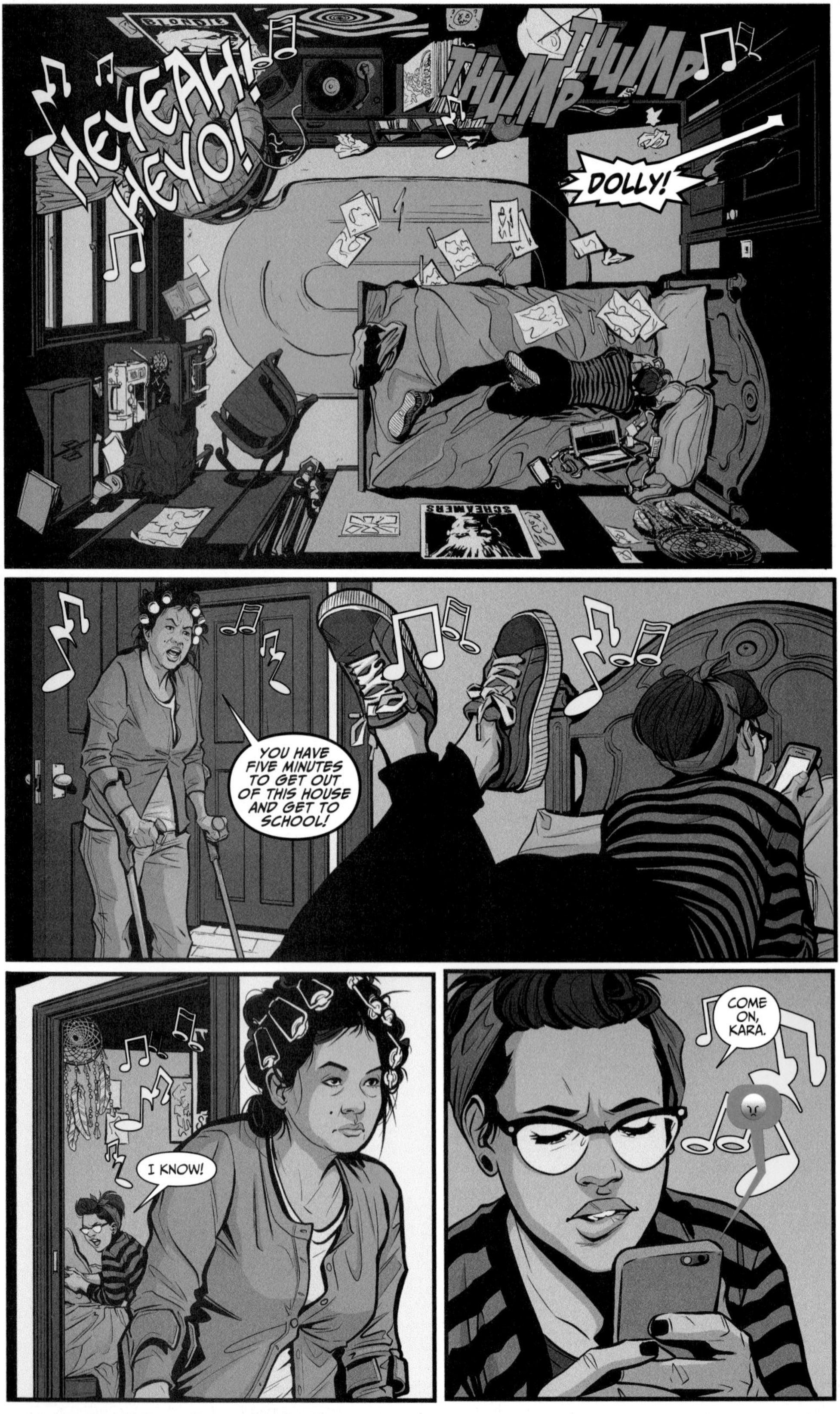
BLONDIE
HEYEAH! HEYO!
THUMP THUMP
DOLLY!
SCREAMERS
YOU HAVE FIVE MINUTES TO GET OUT OF THIS HOUSE AND GET TO SCHOOL!
I KNOW!
COME ON, KARA.

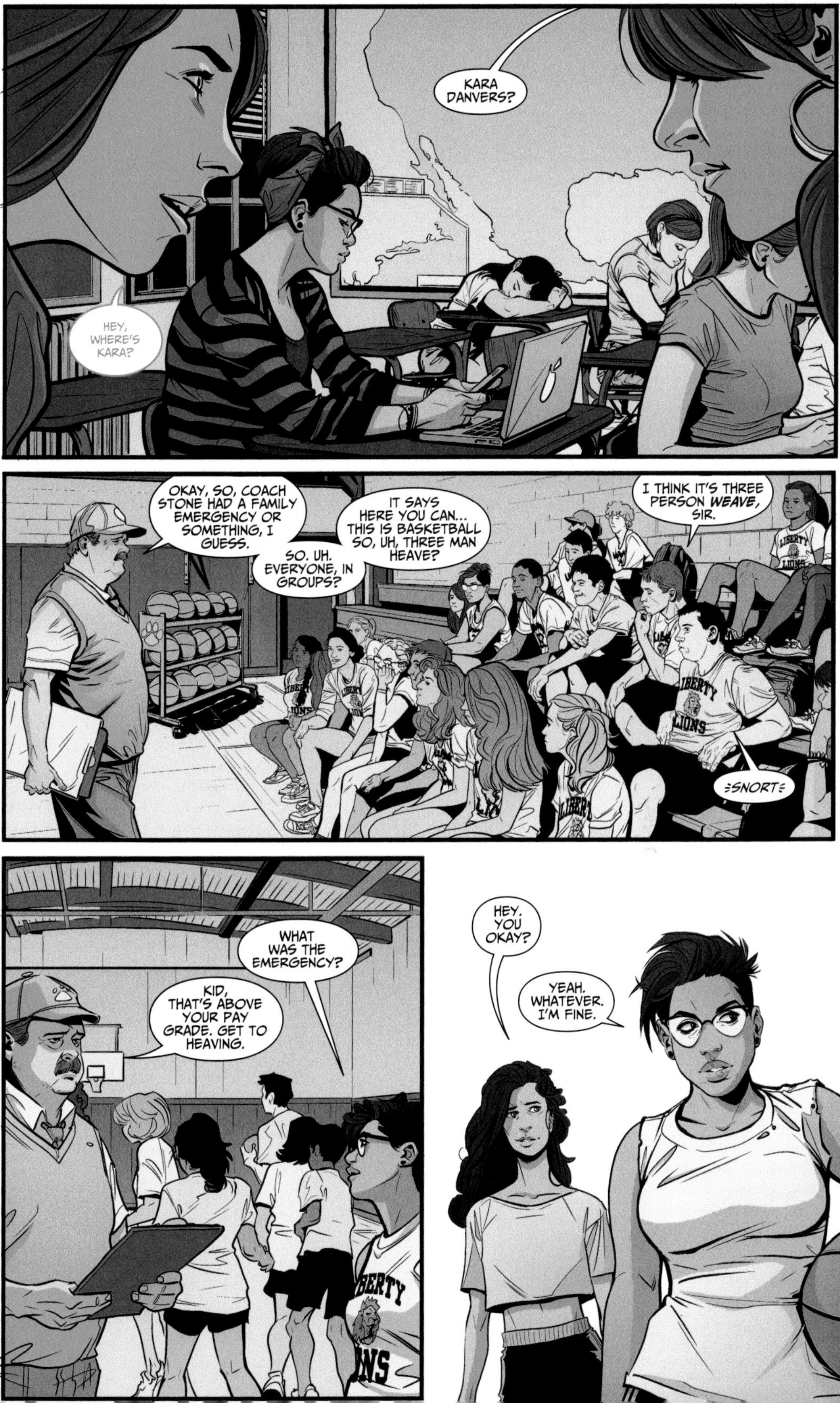

KARA DANVERS?
HEY, WHERE'S KARA?
OKAY, SO, COACH STONE HAD A FAMILY EMERGENCY OR SOMETHING, I GUESS.
SO. UH. EVERYONE, IN GROUPS?
IT SAYS HERE YOU CAN... THIS IS BASKETBALL SO, UH, THREE MAN HEAVE?
I THINK IT'S THREE PERSON WEAVE, SIR.
SNORT
WHAT WAS THE EMERGENCY?
KID, THAT'S ABOVE YOUR PAY GRADE. GET TO HEAVING.
HEY. YOU OKAY?
YEAH. WHATEVER. I'M FINE.

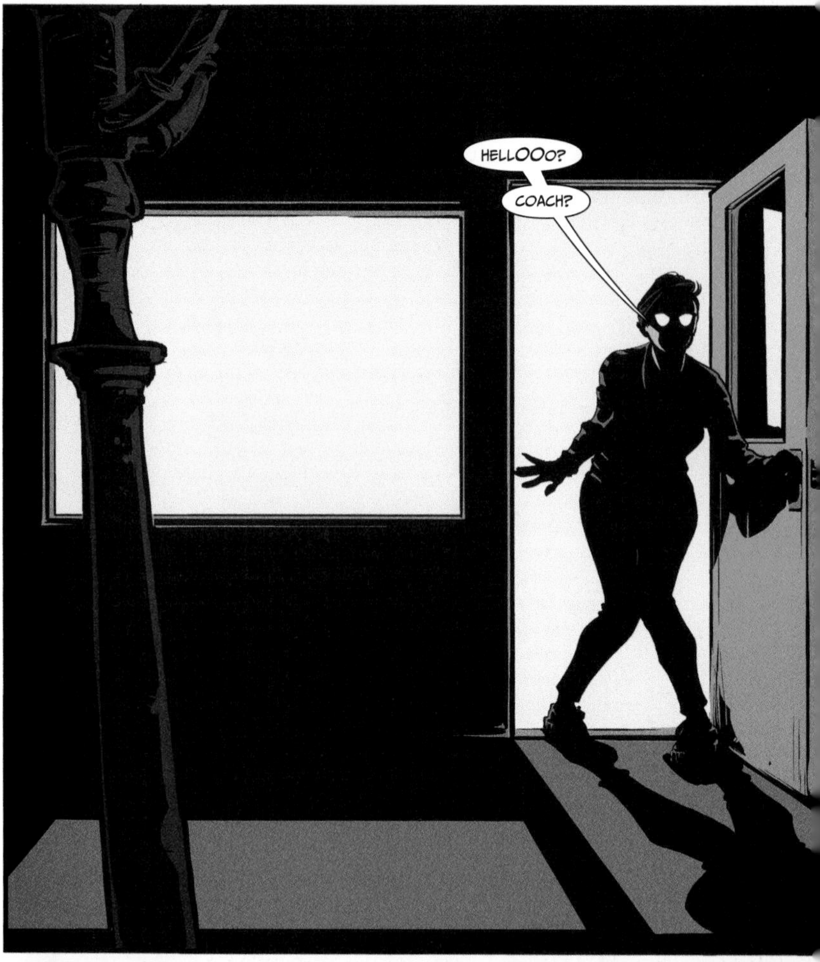
HELLOOOo?
COACH?

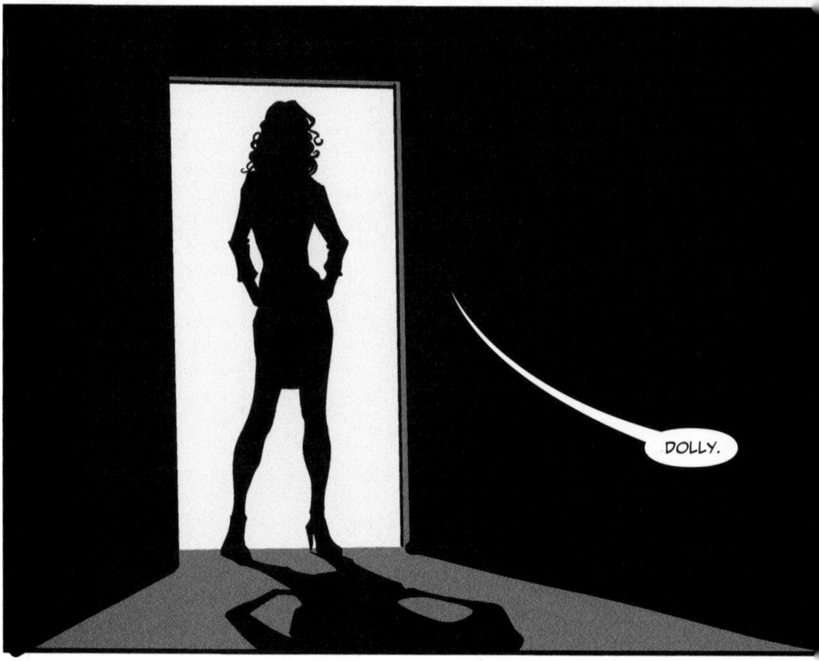
DOLLY.

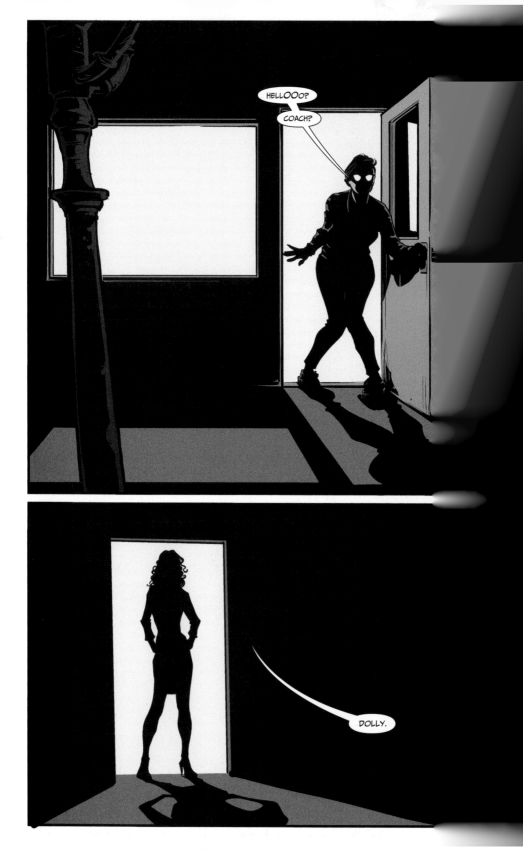

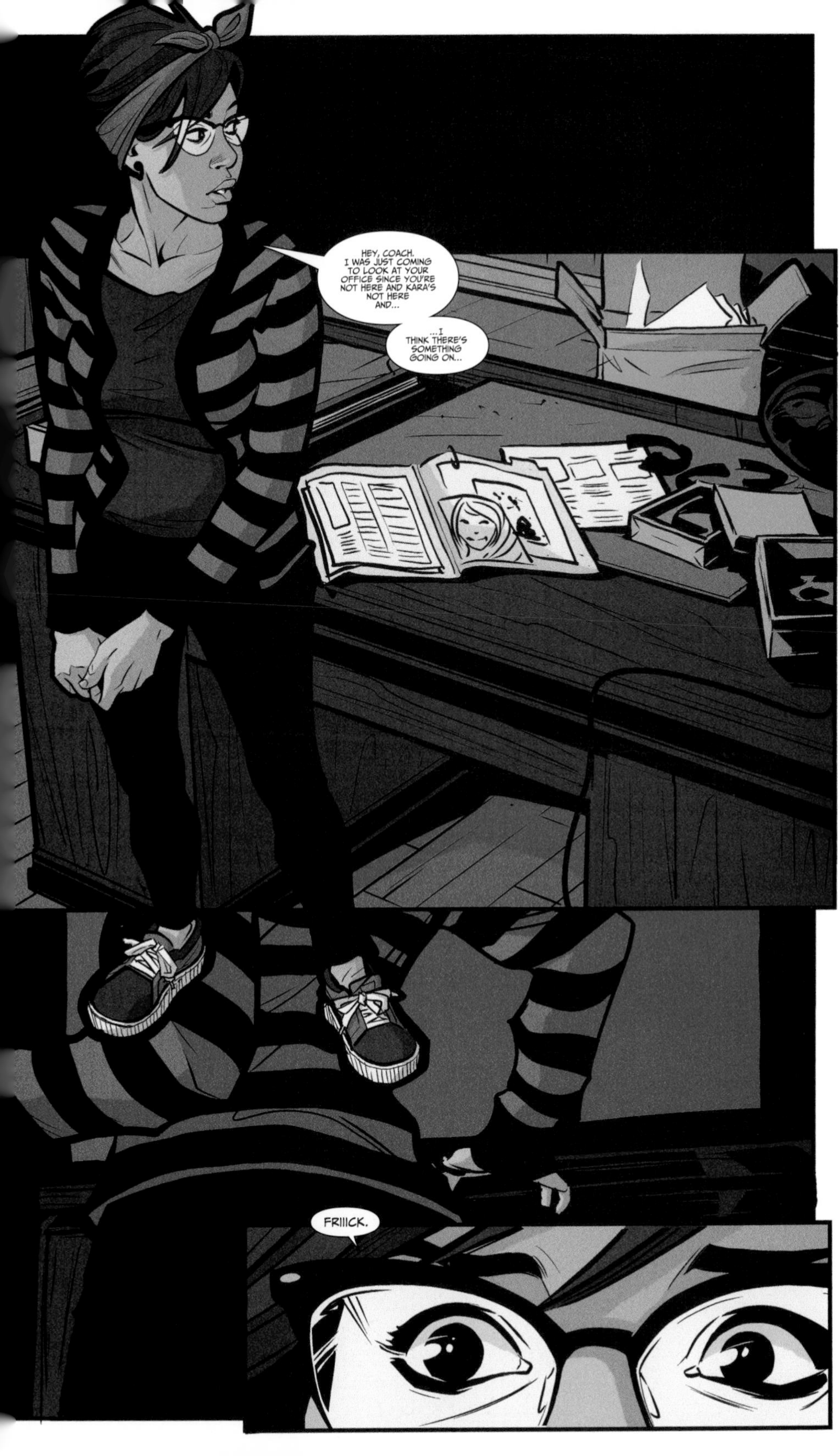
HEY, COACH. I WAS JUST COMING TO LOOK AT YOUR OFFICE SINCE YOU'RE NOT HERE AND KARA'S NOT HERE AND...
...I THINK THERE'S SOMETHING GOING ON...
FRIIICK.

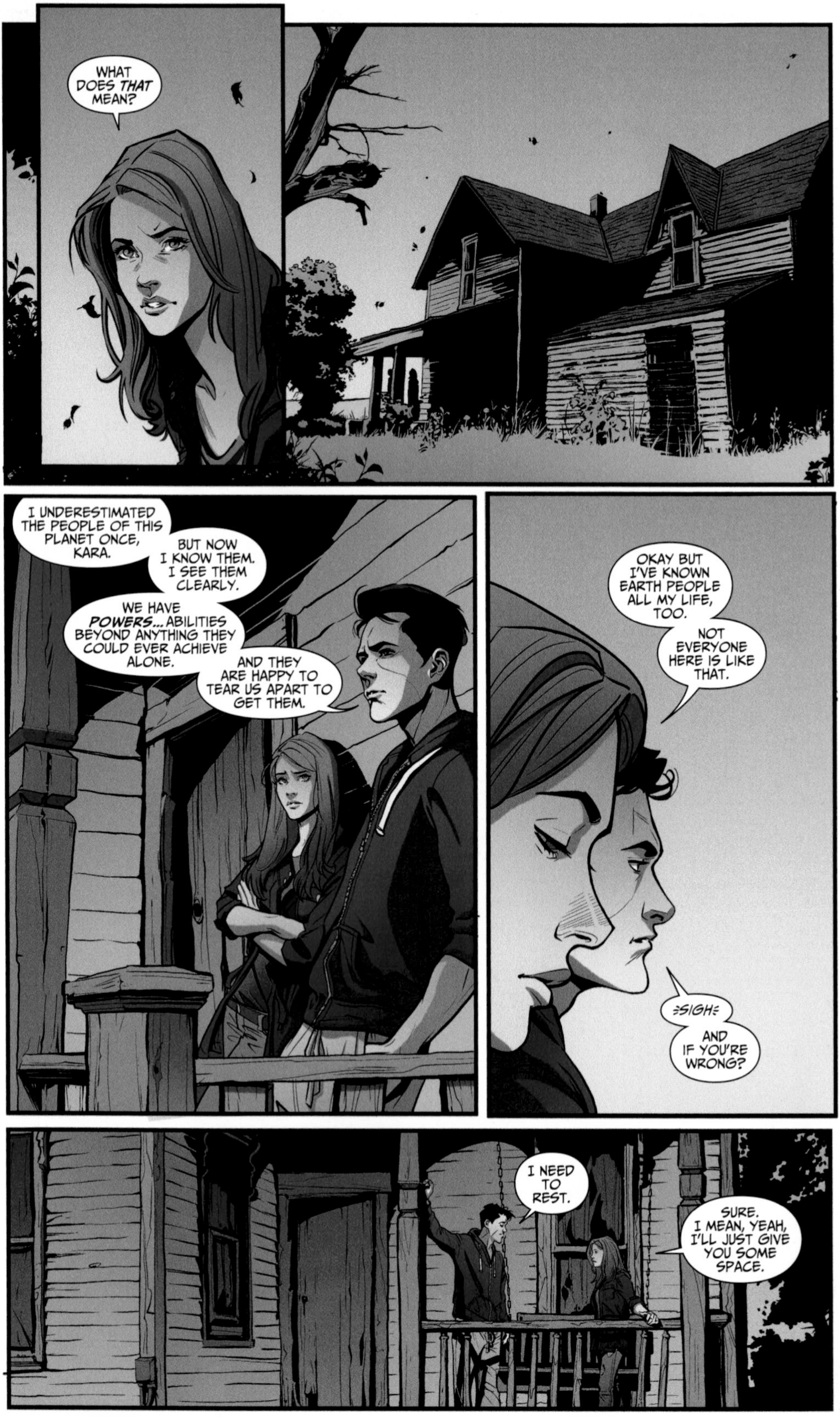
WHAT DOES *THAT* MEAN?
I UNDERESTIMATED THE PEOPLE OF THIS PLANET ONCE, KARA.
BUT NOW I KNOW THEM. I SEE THEM CLEARLY.
WE HAVE ***POWERS...*** ABILITIES BEYOND ANYTHING THEY COULD EVER ACHIEVE ALONE.
AND THEY ARE HAPPY TO TEAR US APART TO GET THEM.
OKAY BUT I'VE KNOWN EARTH PEOPLE ALL MY LIFE, TOO.
NOT EVERYONE HERE IS LIKE THAT.
SIGH
AND IF YOU'RE WRONG?
I NEED TO REST.
SURE. I MEAN, YEAH, I'LL JUST GIVE YOU SOME SPACE.

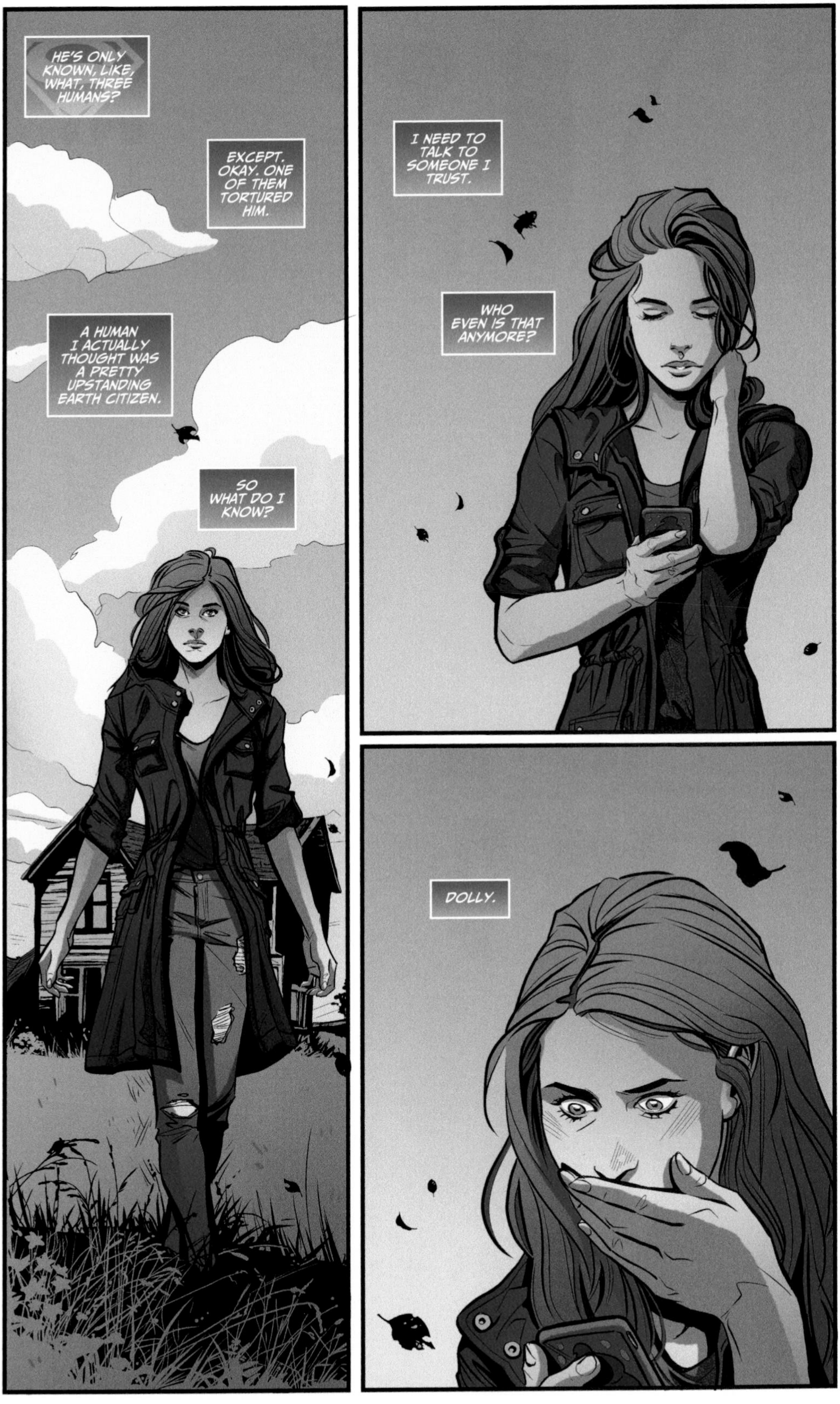
HE'S ONLY KNOWN, LIKE, WHAT, THREE HUMANS?
EXCEPT. OKAY. ONE OF THEM TORTURED HIM.
A HUMAN I ACTUALLY THOUGHT WAS A PRETTY UPSTANDING EARTH CITIZEN.
SO WHAT DO I KNOW?
I NEED TO TALK TO SOMEONE I TRUST.
WHO EVEN IS THAT ANYMORE?
DOLLY.

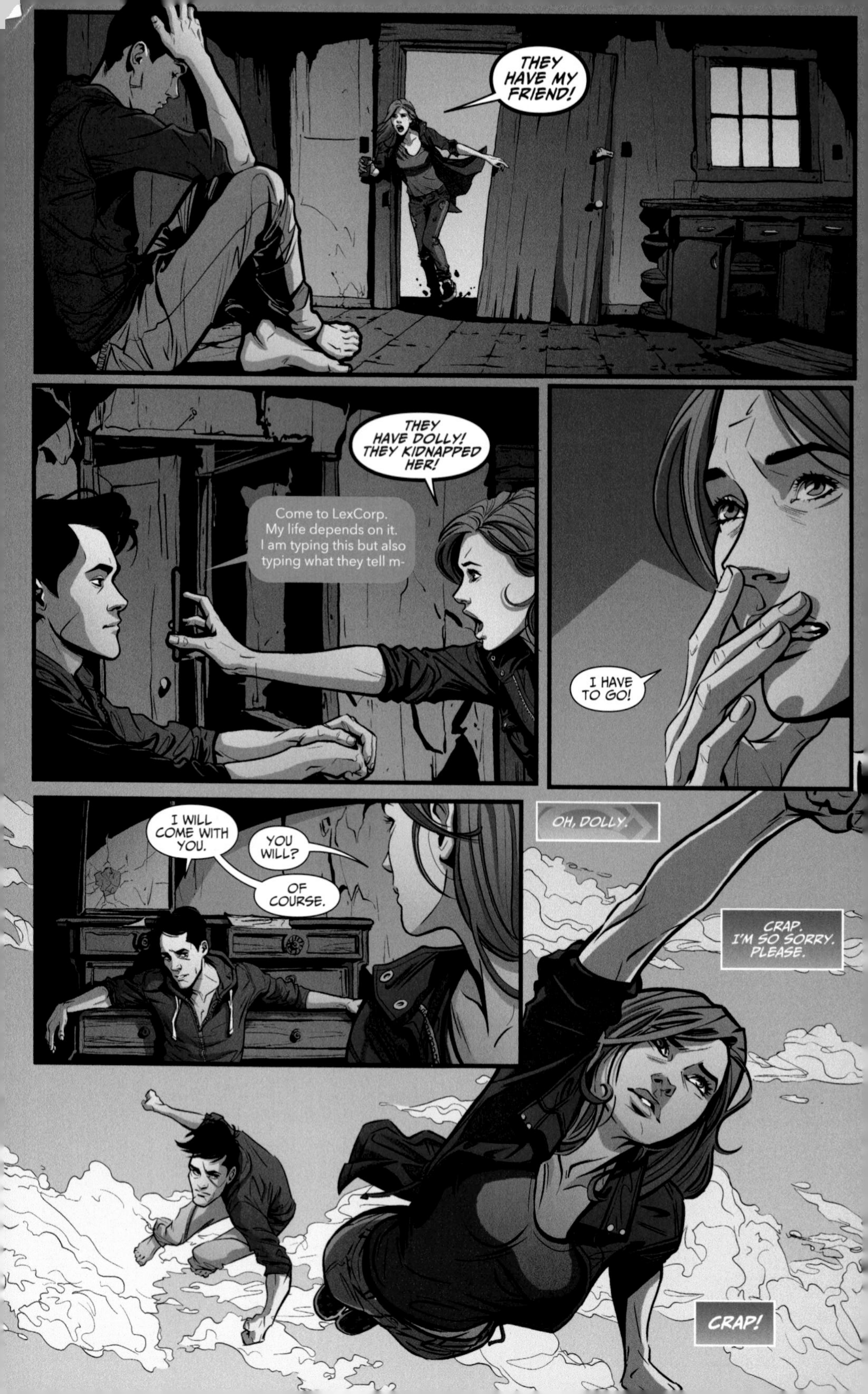
THEY HAVE MY FRIEND!
THEY HAVE DOLLY! THEY KIDNAPPED HER!
Come to LexCorp. My life depends on it. I am typing this but also typing what they tell m-
I HAVE TO GO!
I WILL COME WITH YOU.
YOU WILL?
OF COURSE.
OH, DOLLY.
CRAP. I'M SO SORRY. PLEASE.
CRAP!

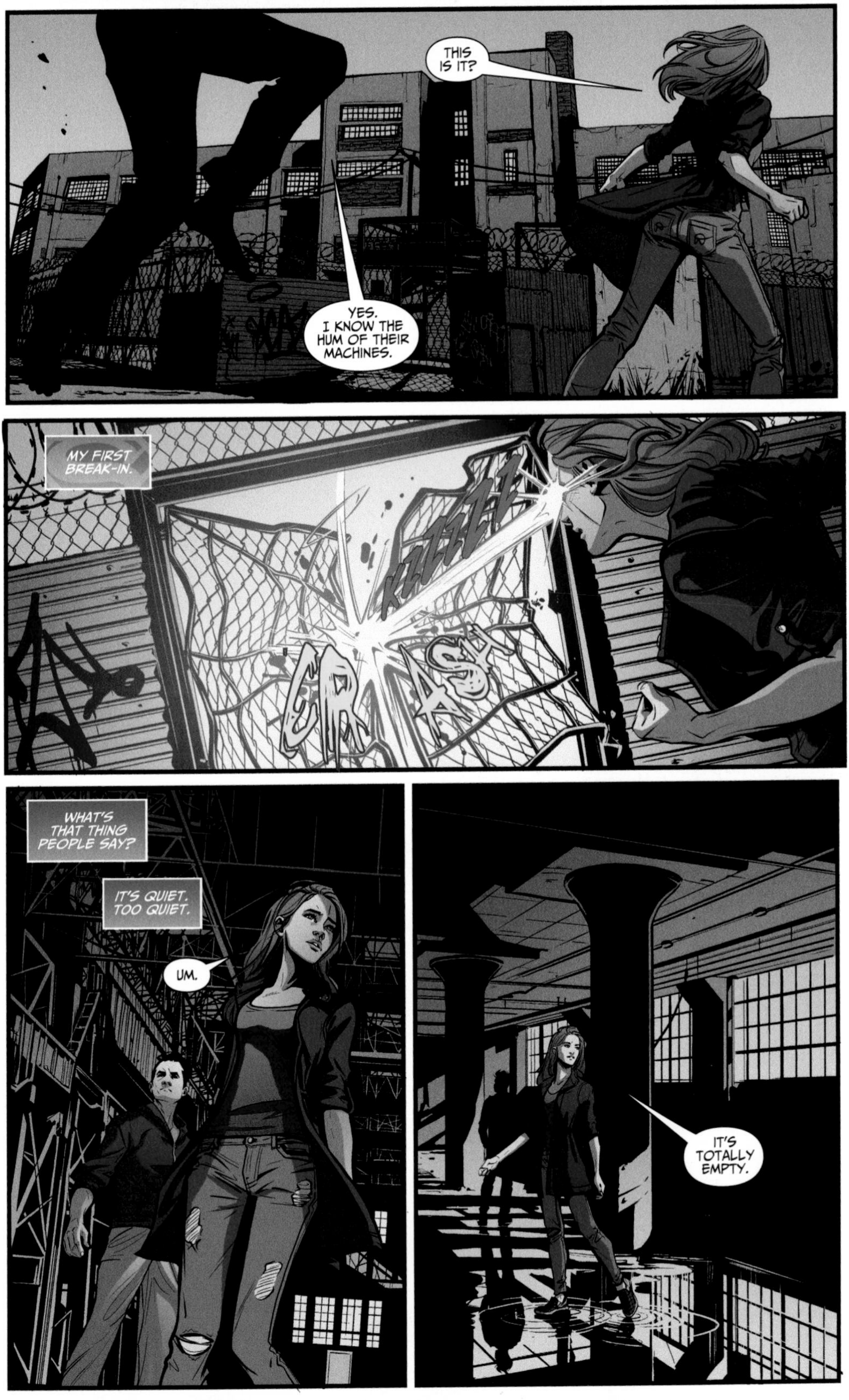
THIS IS IT?
YES. I KNOW THE HUM OF THEIR MACHINES.
MY FIRST BREAK-IN.
KZZZZZT
CRASH
WHAT'S THAT THING PEOPLE SAY?
IT'S QUIET. TOO QUIET.
UM.
IT'S TOTALLY EMPTY.

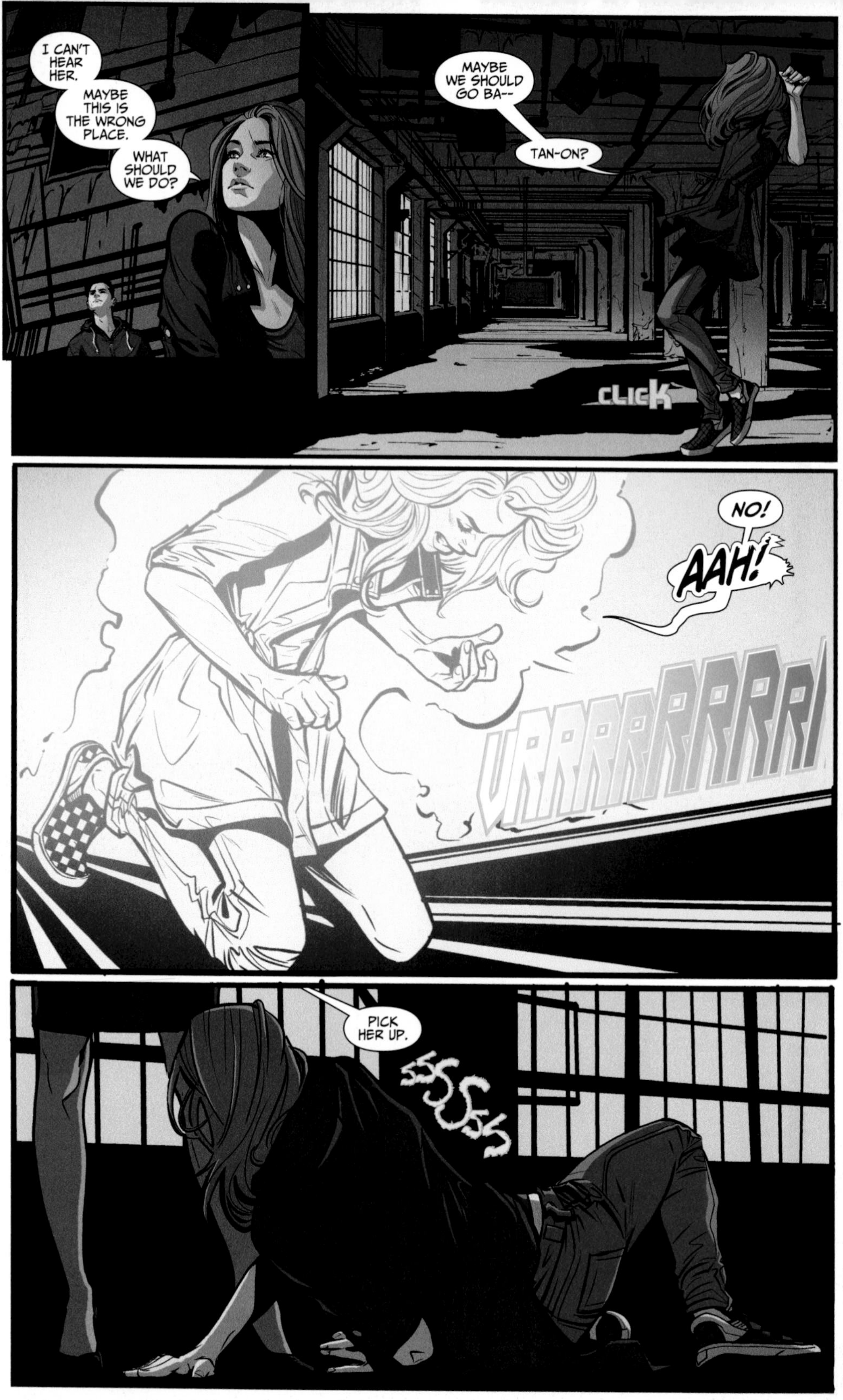
I CAN'T HEAR HER.
MAYBE THIS IS THE WRONG PLACE.
WHAT SHOULD WE DO?
MAYBE WE SHOULD GO BA--
TAN-ON?
CLICK
NO!
AAH!
URRRRRRRRR!
PICK HER UP.
SSSSSSS

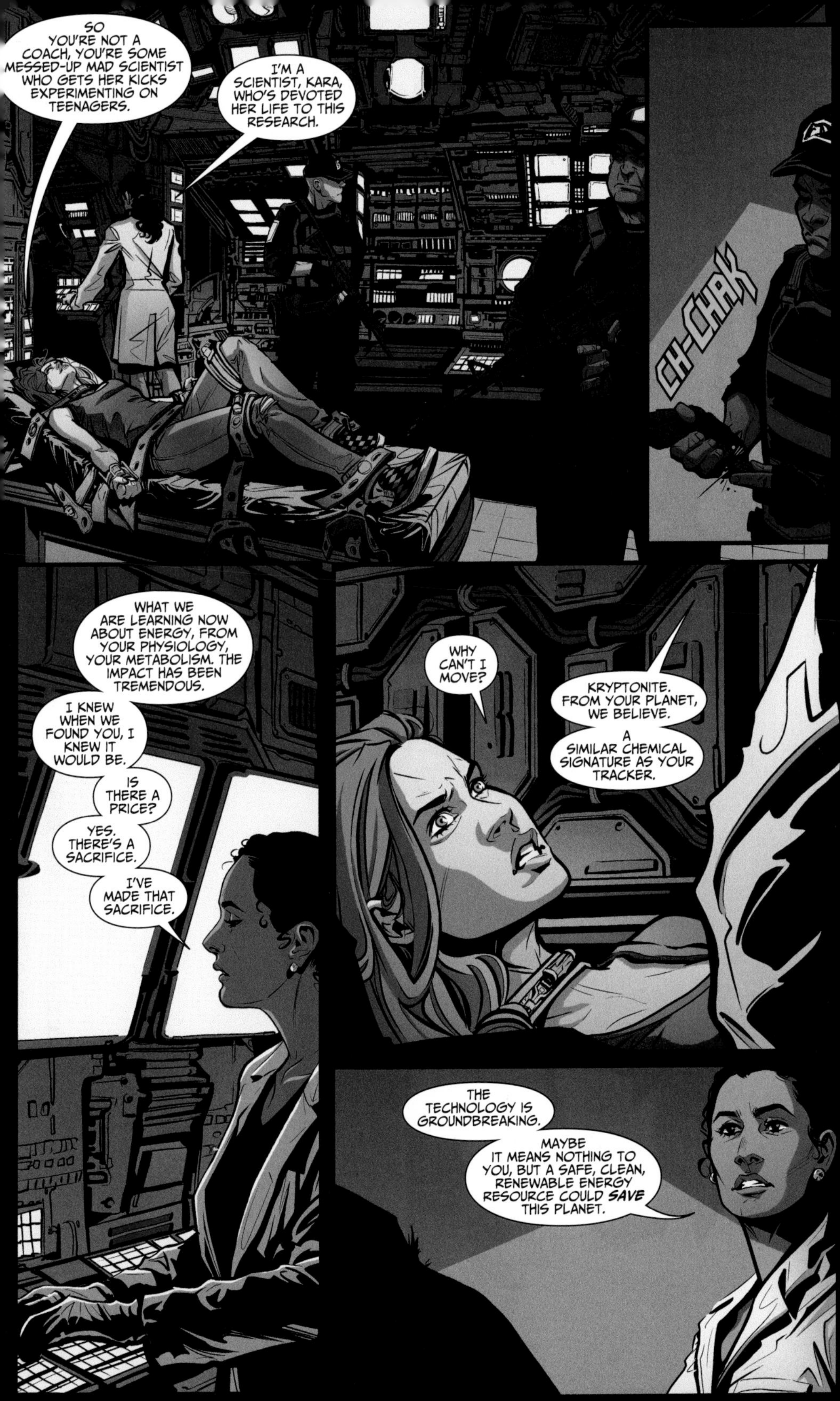

SO YOU'RE NOT A COACH, YOU'RE SOME MESSED-UP MAD SCIENTIST WHO GETS HER KICKS EXPERIMENTING ON TEENAGERS.
I'M A SCIENTIST, KARA, WHO'S DEVOTED HER LIFE TO THIS RESEARCH.
CH-CHAK
WHAT WE ARE LEARNING NOW ABOUT ENERGY, FROM YOUR PHYSIOLOGY, YOUR METABOLISM. THE IMPACT HAS BEEN TREMENDOUS.
I KNEW WHEN WE FOUND YOU, I KNEW IT WOULD BE.
IS THERE A PRICE?
YES. THERE'S A SACRIFICE.
I'VE MADE THAT SACRIFICE.
WHY CAN'T I MOVE?
KRYPTONITE. FROM YOUR PLANET, WE BELIEVE.
A SIMILAR CHEMICAL SIGNATURE AS YOUR TRACKER.
THE TECHNOLOGY IS GROUNDBREAKING.
MAYBE IT MEANS NOTHING TO YOU, BUT A SAFE, CLEAN, RENEWABLE ENERGY RESOURCE COULD SAVE THIS PLANET.

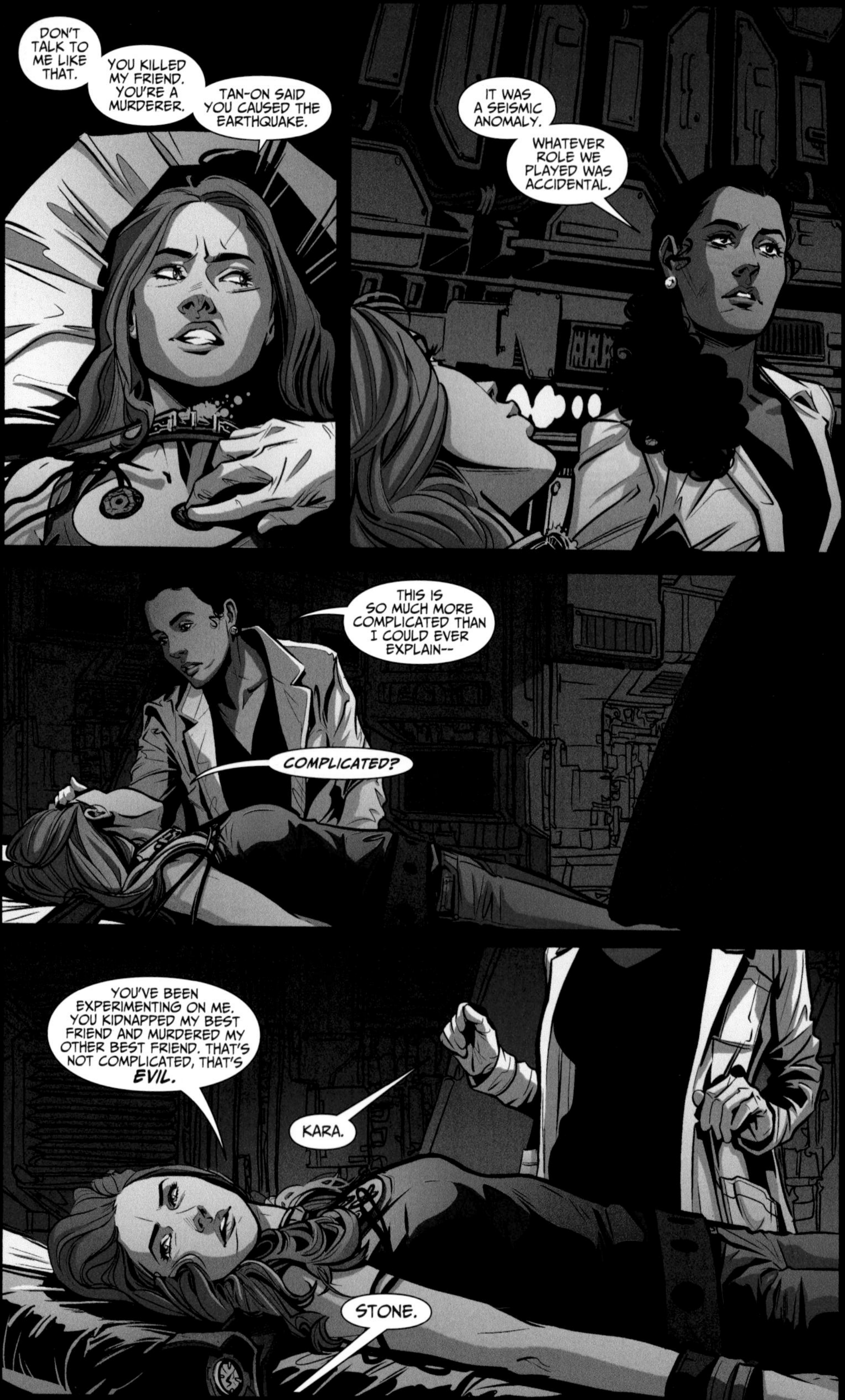
DON'T TALK TO ME LIKE THAT.
YOU KILLED MY FRIEND. YOU'RE A MURDERER.
TAN-ON SAID YOU CAUSED THE EARTHQUAKE.
IT WAS A SEISMIC ANOMALY.
WHATEVER ROLE WE PLAYED WAS ACCIDENTAL.
THIS IS SO MUCH MORE COMPLICATED THAN I COULD EVER EXPLAIN--
COMPLICATED?
YOU'VE BEEN EXPERIMENTING ON ME. YOU KIDNAPPED MY BEST FRIEND AND MURDERED MY OTHER BEST FRIEND. THAT'S NOT COMPLICATED, THAT'S EVIL.
KARA.
STONE.

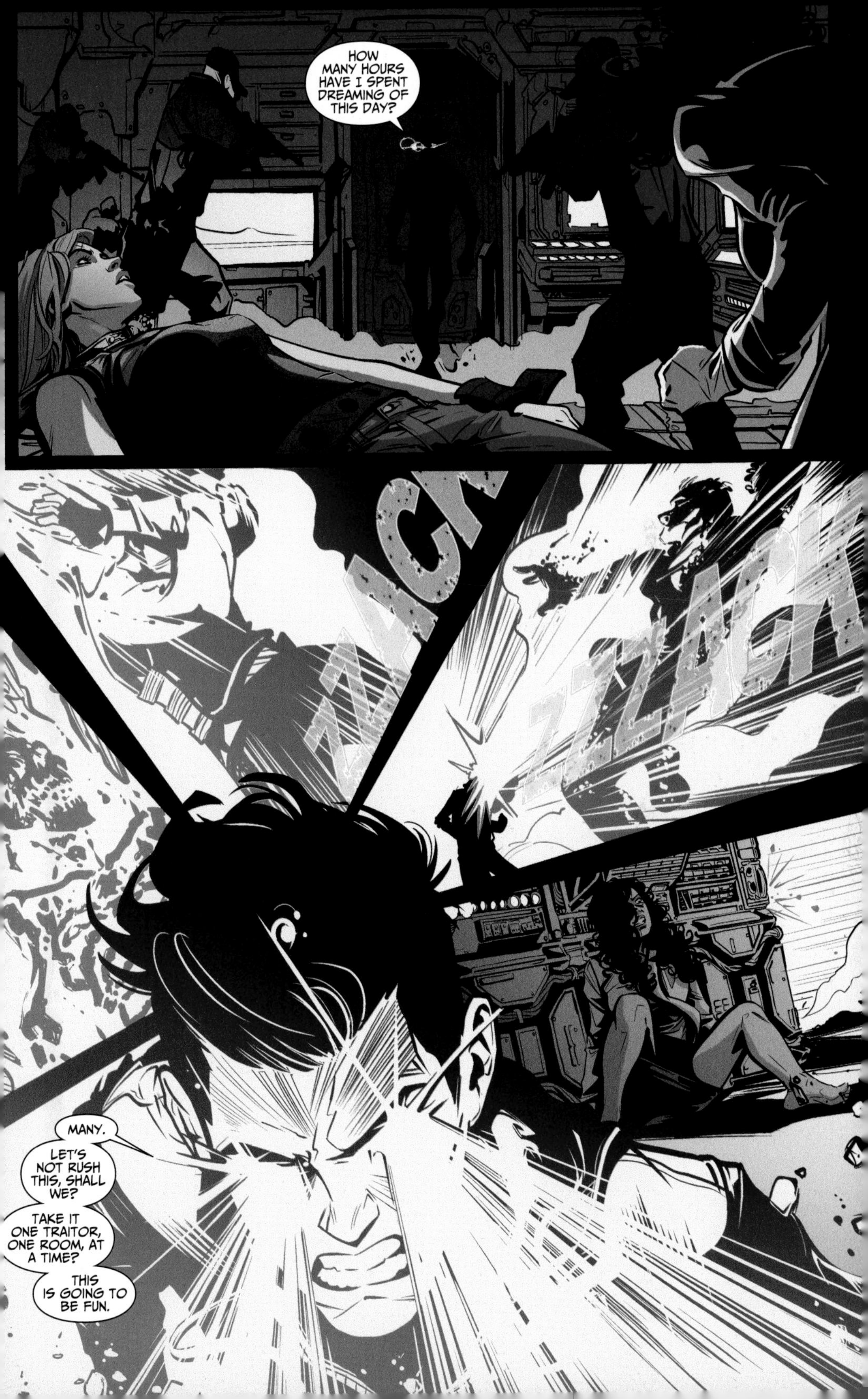
HOW MANY HOURS HAVE I SPENT DREAMING OF THIS DAY?
ZZACK
ZZZACK
MANY.
LET'S NOT RUSH THIS, SHALL WE?
TAKE IT ONE TRAITOR, ONE ROOM, AT A TIME?
THIS IS GOING TO BE FUN.

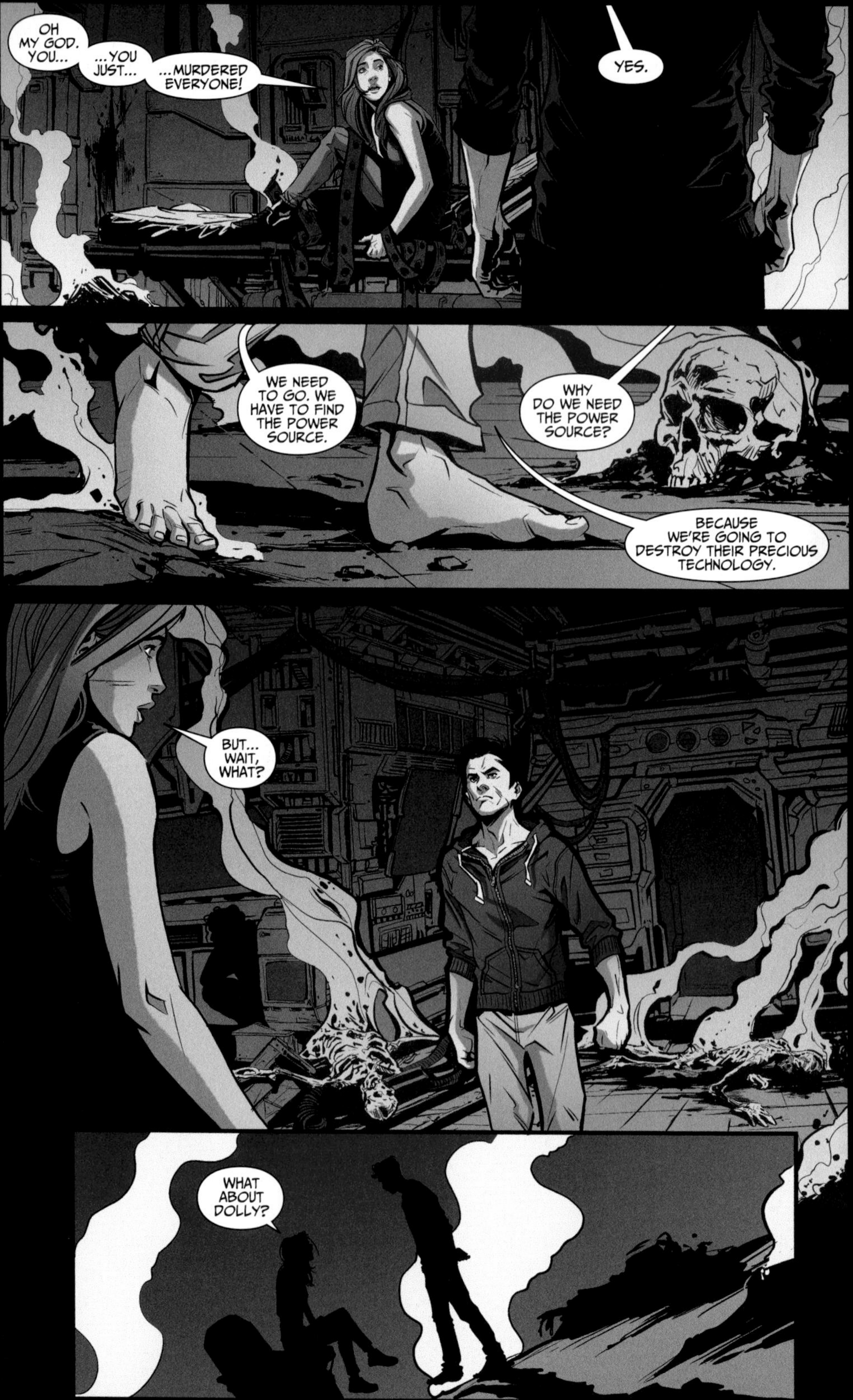
OH MY GOD. YOU...
...YOU JUST...
...MURDERED EVERYONE!
YES.
WE NEED TO GO. WE HAVE TO FIND THE POWER SOURCE.
WHY DO WE NEED THE POWER SOURCE?
BECAUSE WE'RE GOING TO DESTROY THEIR PRECIOUS TECHNOLOGY.
BUT... WAIT, WHAT?
WHAT ABOUT DOLLY?

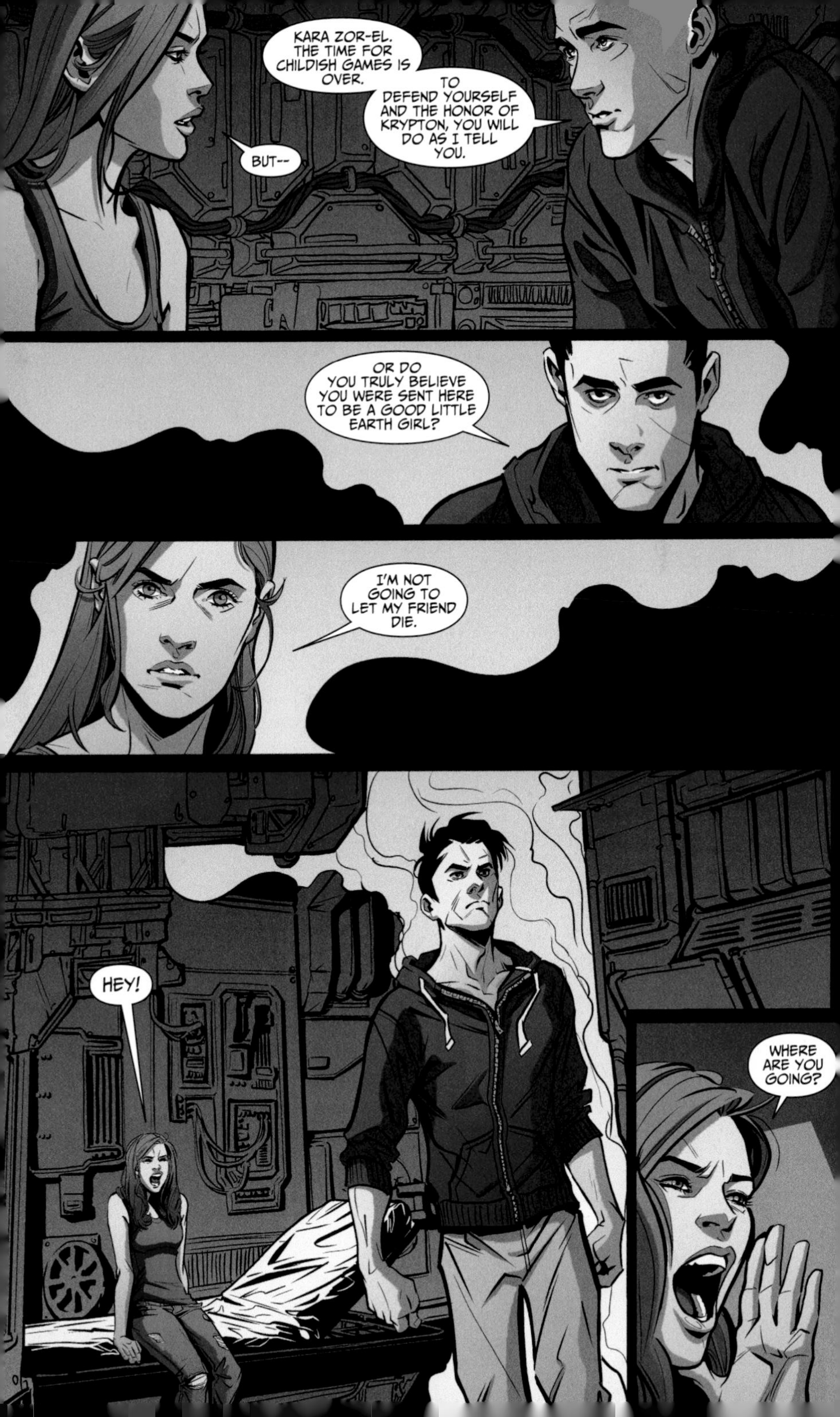
KARA ZOR-EL. THE TIME FOR CHILDISH GAMES IS OVER.
BUT--
TO DEFEND YOURSELF AND THE HONOR OF KRYPTON, YOU WILL DO AS I TELL YOU.
OR DO YOU TRULY BELIEVE YOU WERE SENT HERE TO BE A GOOD LITTLE EARTH GIRL?
I'M NOT GOING TO LET MY FRIEND DIE.
HEY!
WHERE ARE YOU GOING?

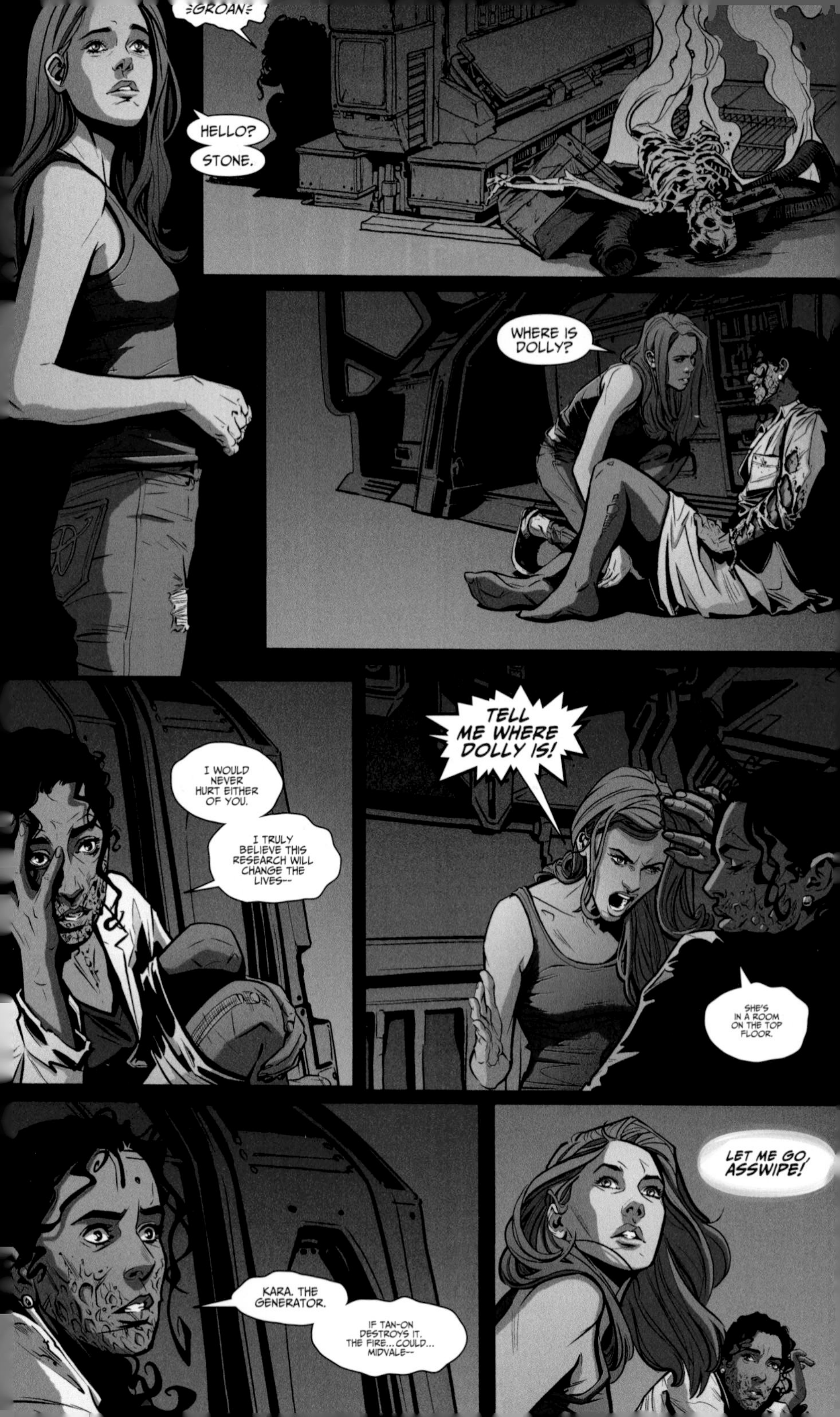
GROAN
HELLO?
STONE.
WHERE IS DOLLY?
I WOULD NEVER HURT EITHER OF YOU.
I TRULY BELIEVE THIS RESEARCH WILL CHANGE THE LIVES--
TELL ME WHERE DOLLY IS!
SHE'S IN A ROOM ON THE TOP FLOOR.
KARA. THE GENERATOR.
IF TAN-ON DESTROYS IT. THE FIRE... COULD... MIDVALE--
LET ME GO, ASSWIPE!

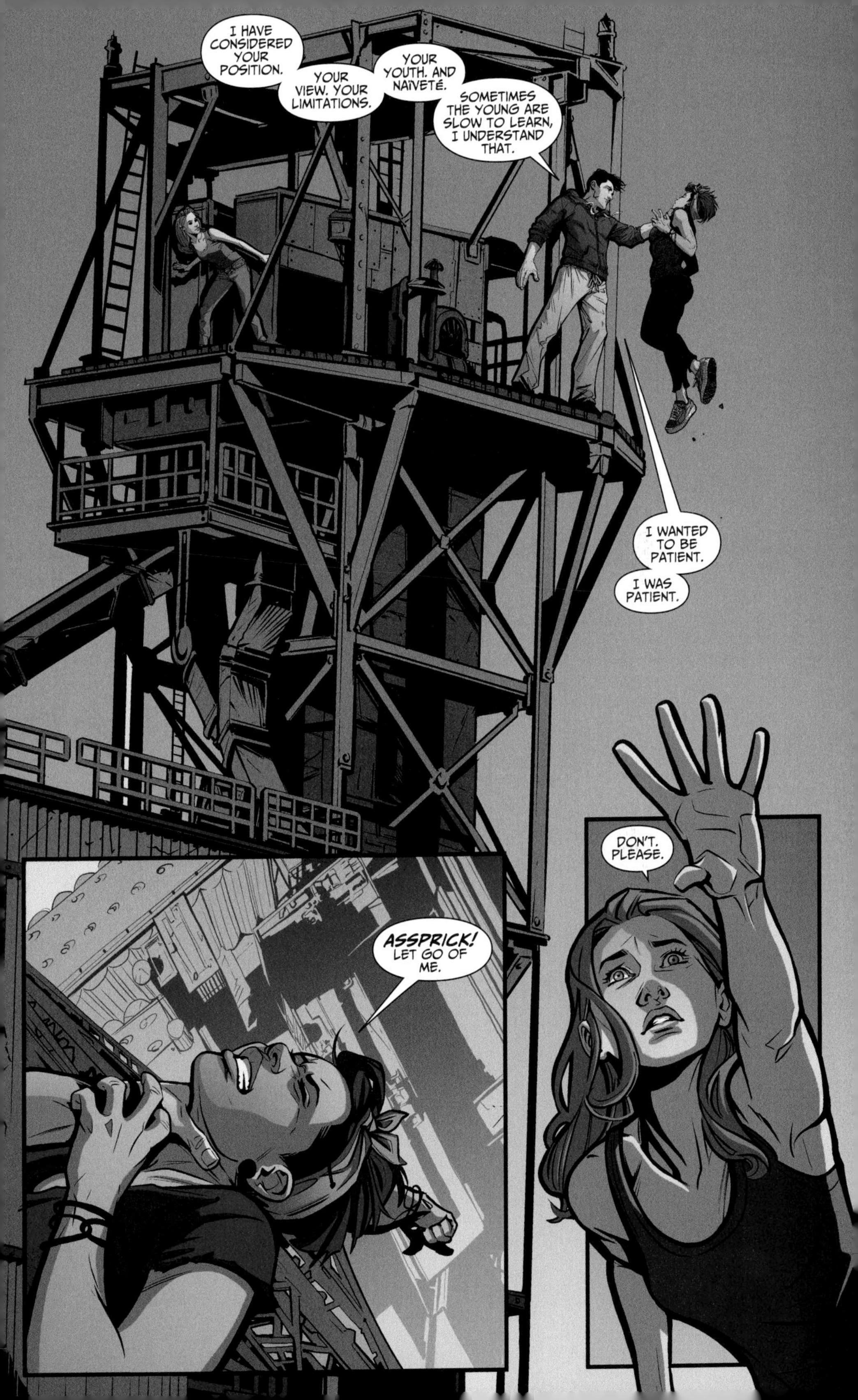
I HAVE CONSIDERED YOUR POSITION.
YOUR VIEW. YOUR LIMITATIONS.
YOUR YOUTH. AND NAÏVETÉ.
SOMETIMES THE YOUNG ARE SLOW TO LEARN, I UNDERSTAND THAT.
I WANTED TO BE PATIENT.
I WAS PATIENT.
ASSPRICK! LET GO OF ME.
DON'T. PLEASE.

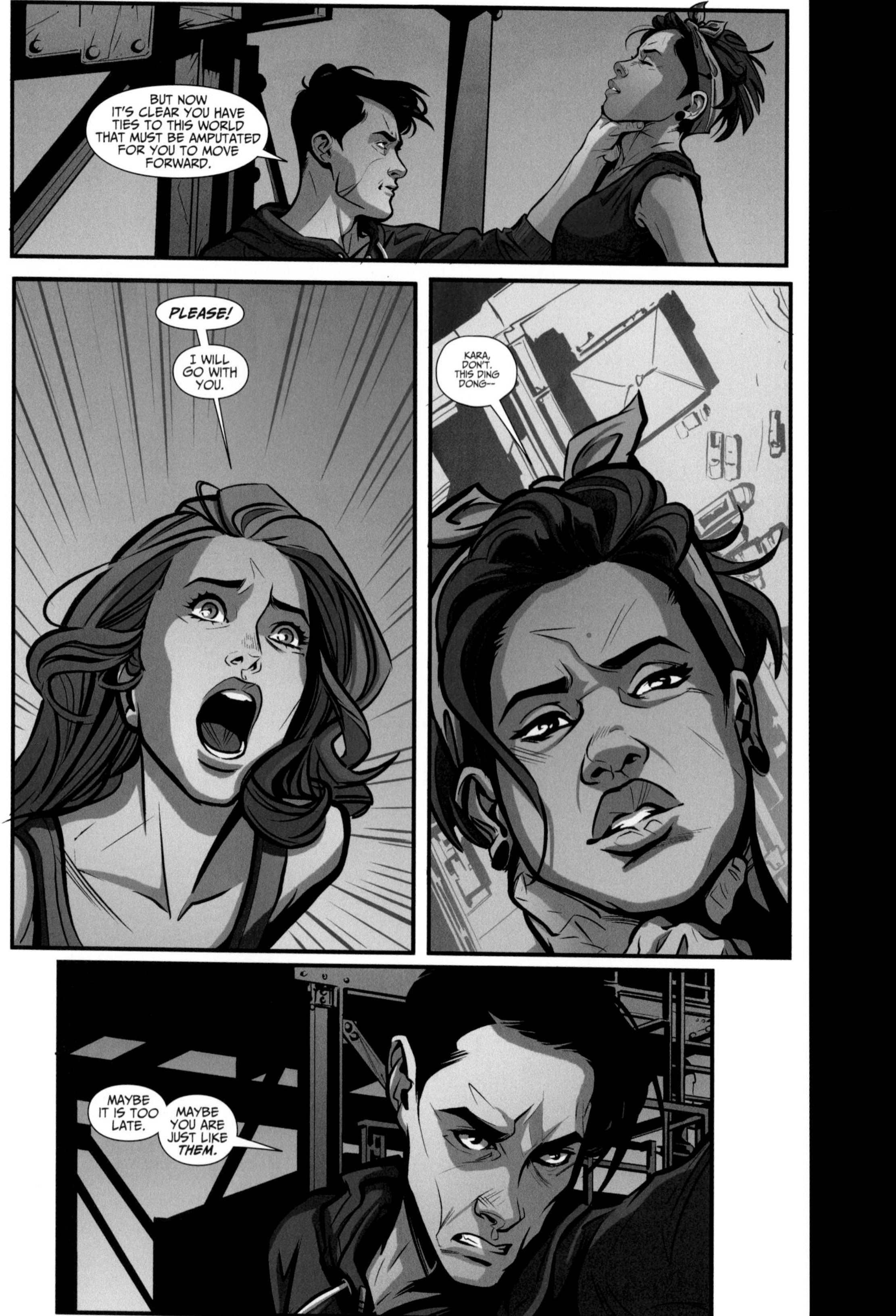
BUT NOW IT'S CLEAR YOU HAVE TIES TO THIS WORLD THAT MUST BE AMPUTATED FOR YOU TO MOVE FORWARD.
PLEASE!
I WILL GO WITH YOU.
KARA, DON'T. THIS DING DONG--
MAYBE IT IS TOO LATE.
MAYBE YOU ARE JUST LIKE THEM.

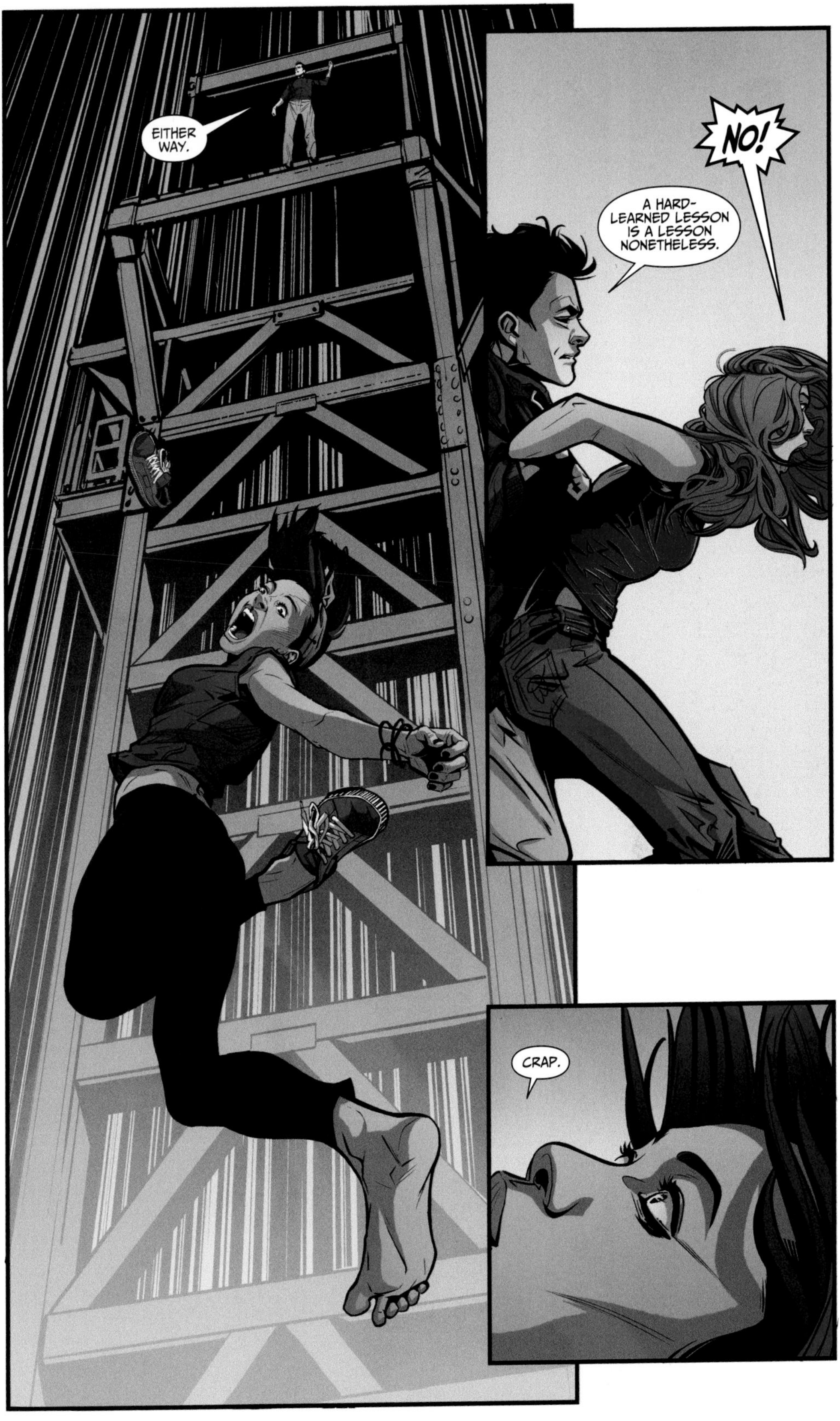
EITHER WAY.
NO!
A HARD-LEARNED LESSON IS A LESSON NONETHELESS.
CRAP.

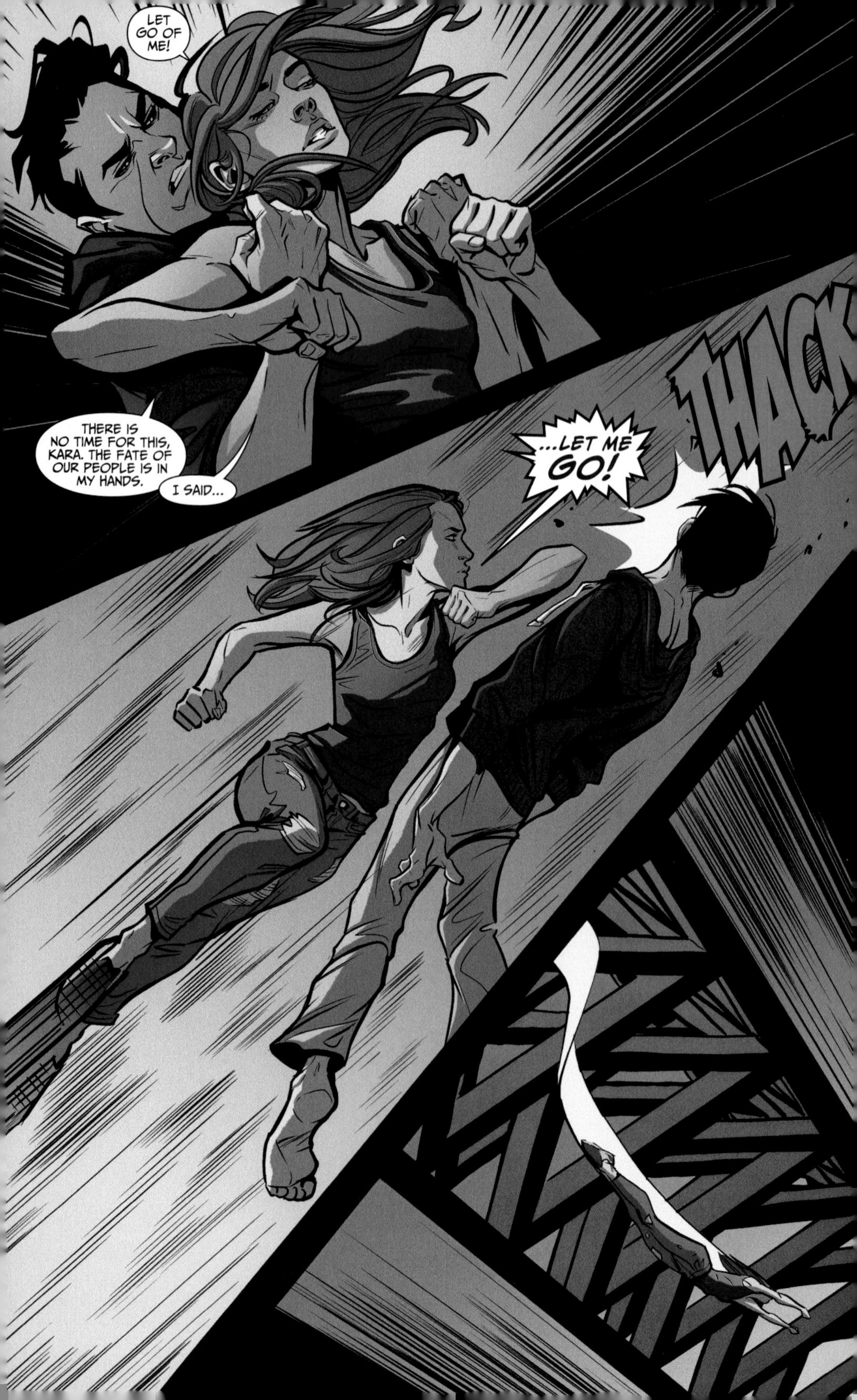
LET GO OF ME!
THERE IS NO TIME FOR THIS, KARA. THE FATE OF OUR PEOPLE IS IN MY HANDS.
I SAID...
...LET ME GO!
THACK

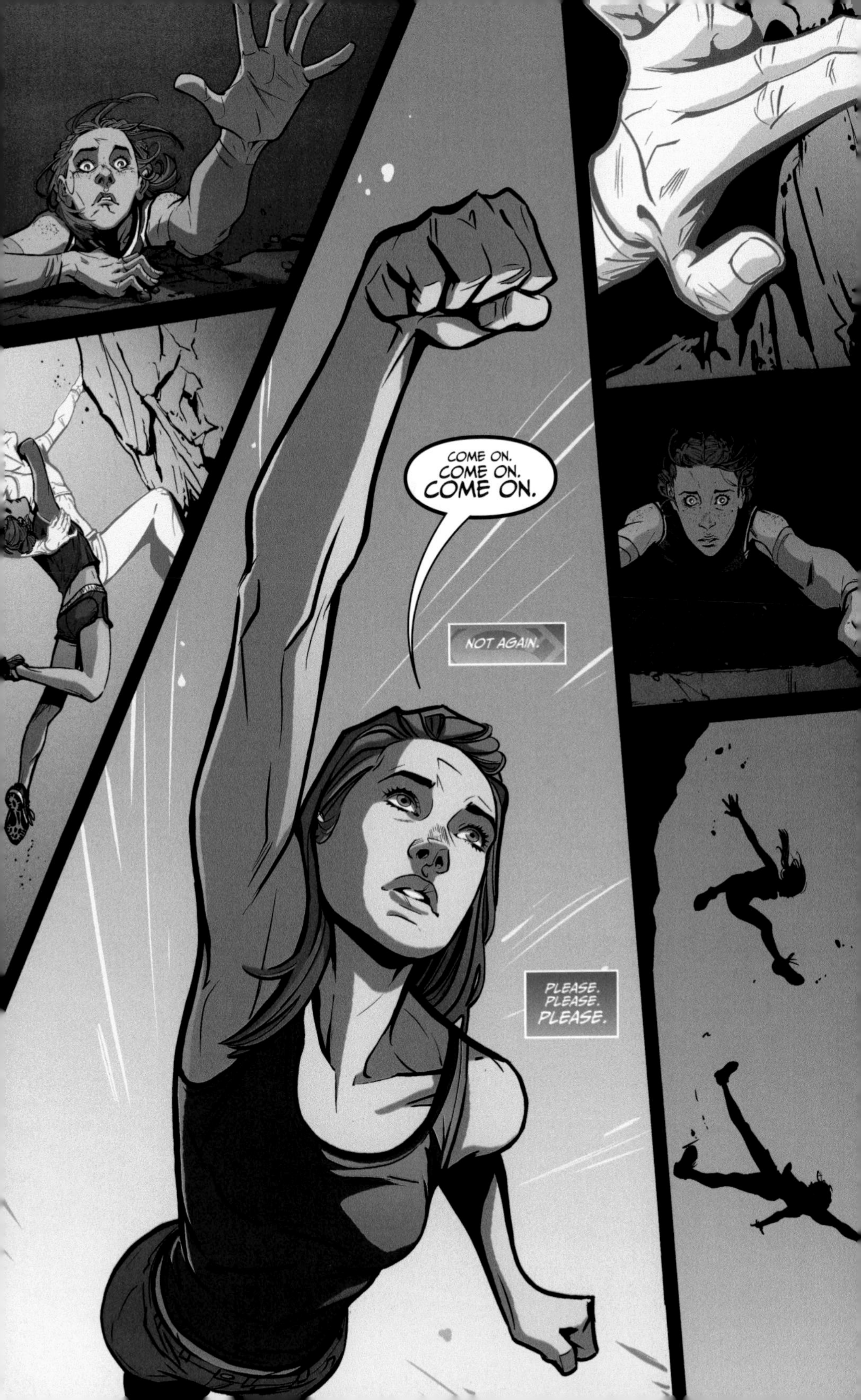
COME ON.
COME ON.
COME ON.
NOT AGAIN.
PLEASE.
PLEASE.
PLEASE.

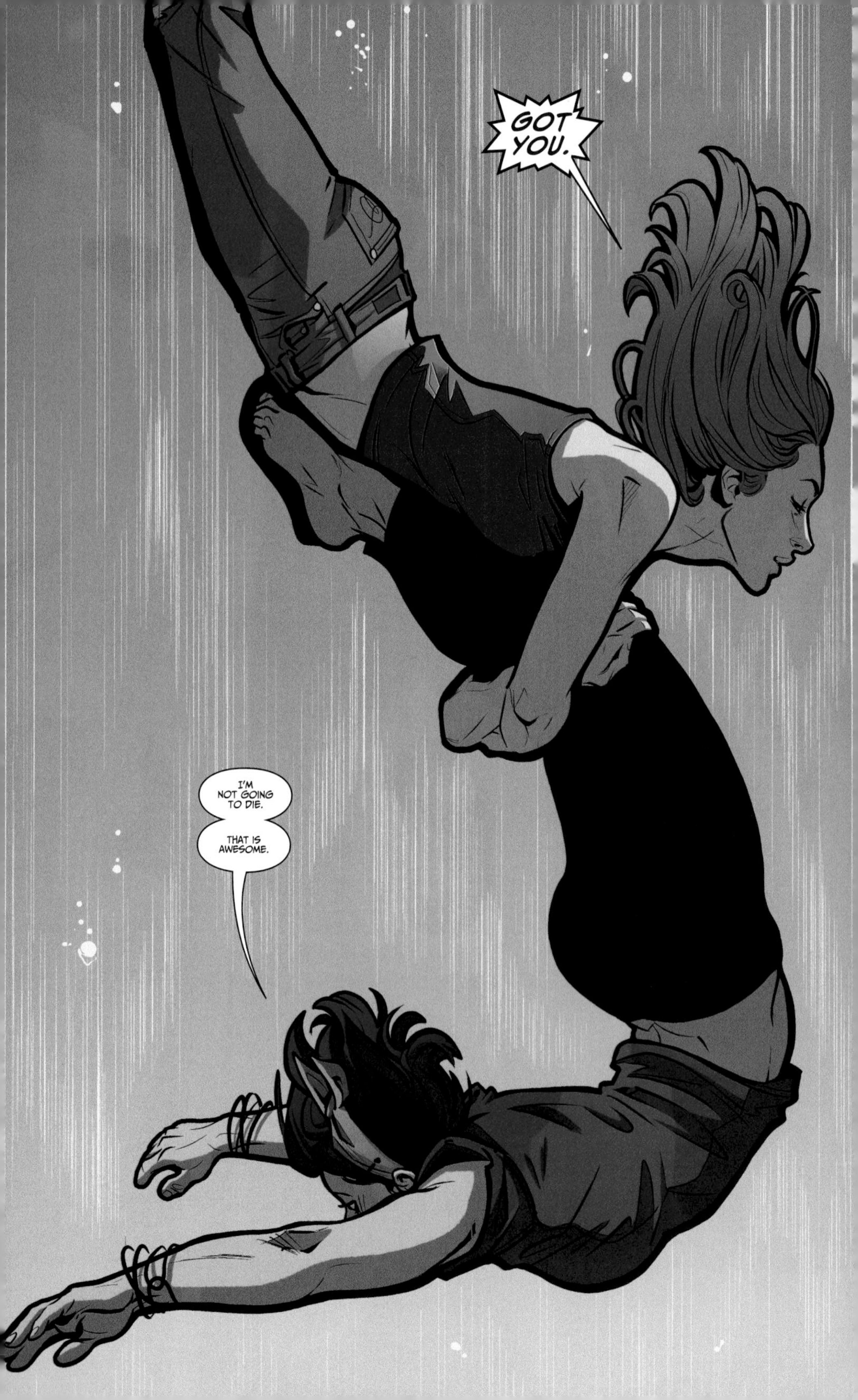
GOT YOU.
I'M NOT GOING TO DIE.
THAT IS AWESOME.

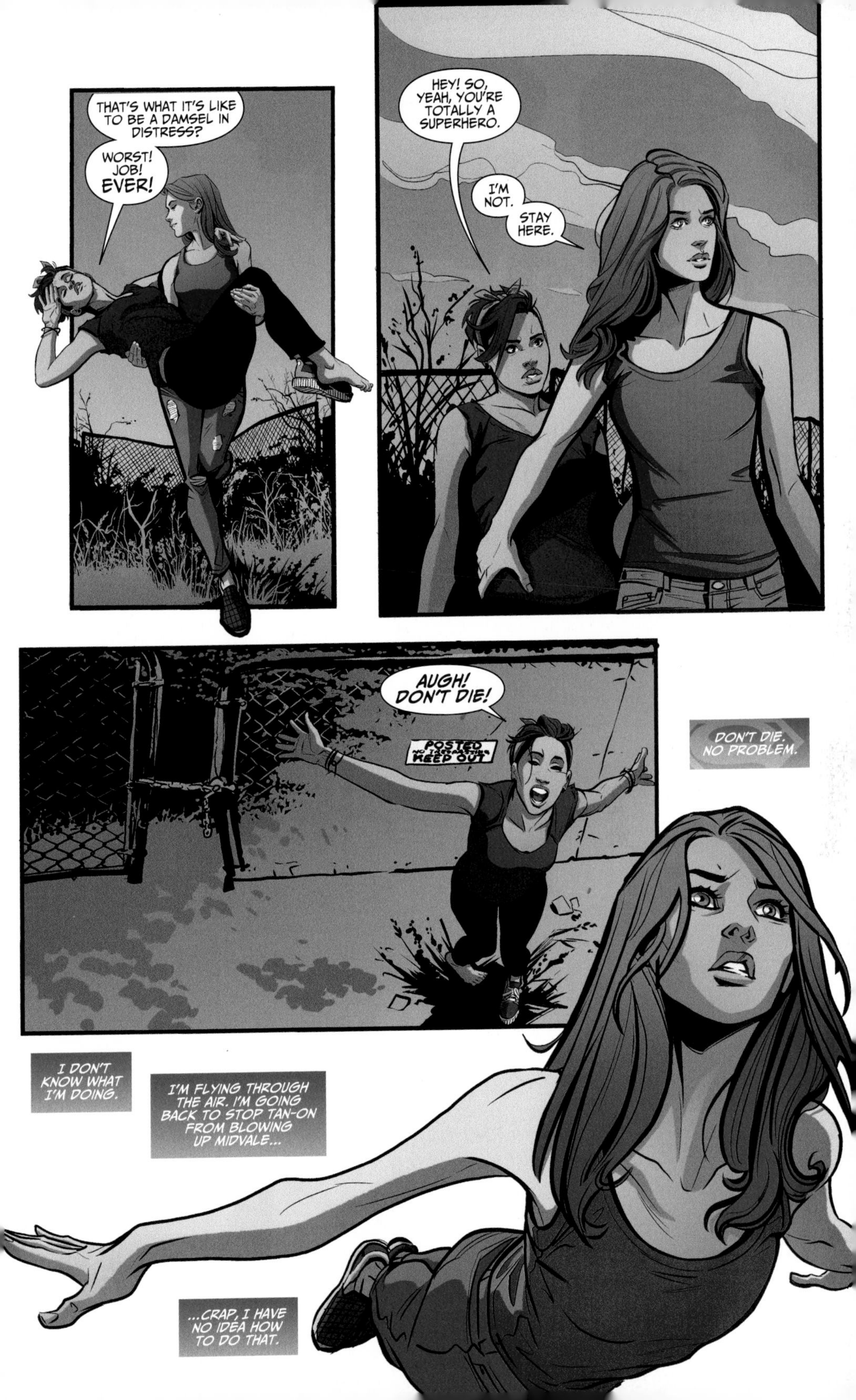

THAT'S WHAT IT'S LIKE TO BE A DAMSEL IN DISTRESS?
WORST! JOB! EVER!
HEY! SO, YEAH, YOU'RE TOTALLY A SUPERHERO.
I'M NOT.
STAY HERE.
AUGH! DON'T DIE!
POSTED
KEEP OUT
DON'T DIE. NO PROBLEM.
I DON'T KNOW WHAT I'M DOING.
I'M FLYING THROUGH THE AIR. I'M GOING BACK TO STOP TAN-ON FROM BLOWING UP MIDVALE...
...CRAP, I HAVE NO IDEA HOW TO DO THAT.

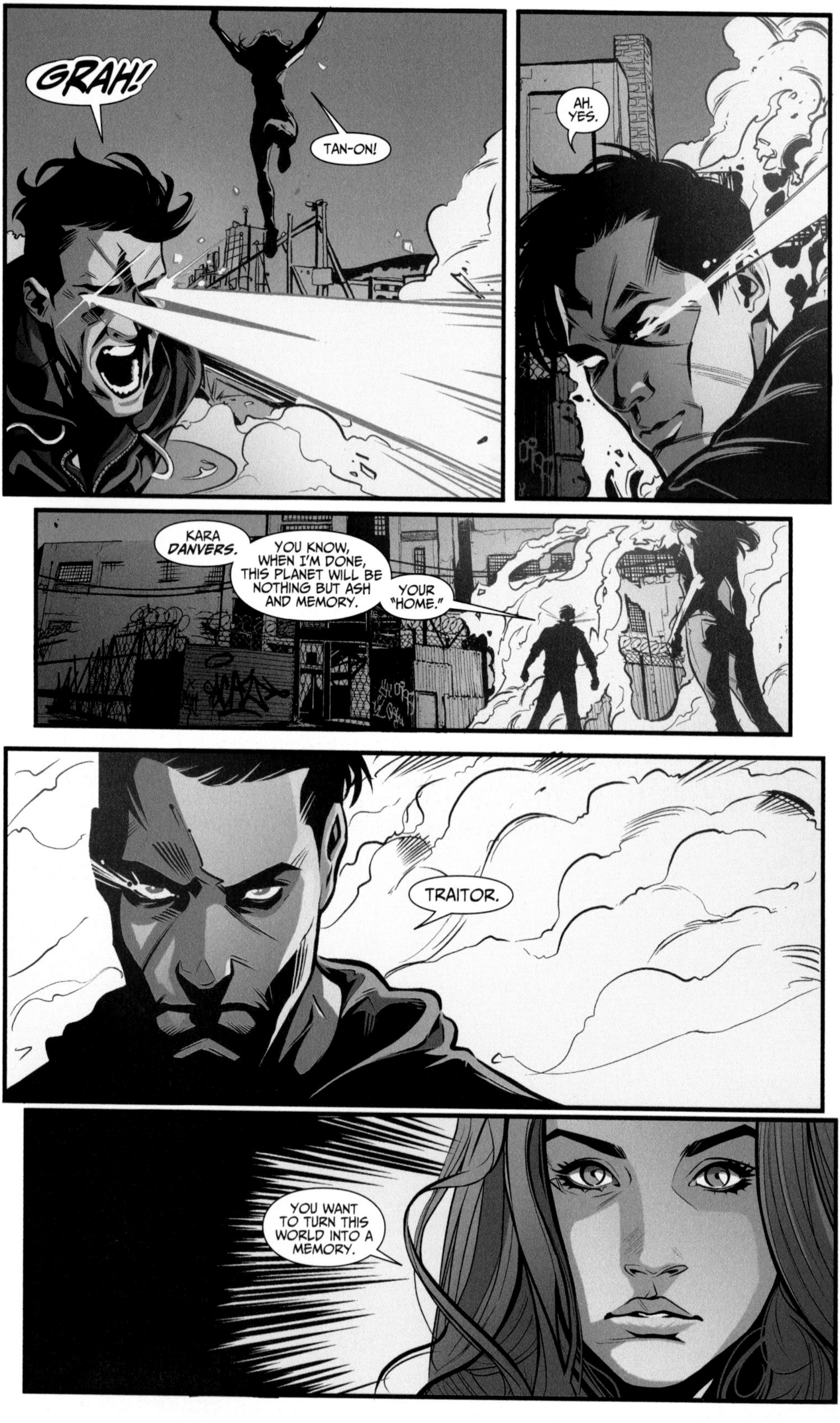
GRAH!
TAN-ON!
AH. YES.
KARA DANVERS.
YOU KNOW, WHEN I'M DONE, THIS PLANET WILL BE NOTHING BUT ASH AND MEMORY.
YOUR "HOME."
TRAITOR.
YOU WANT TO TURN THIS WORLD INTO A MEMORY.

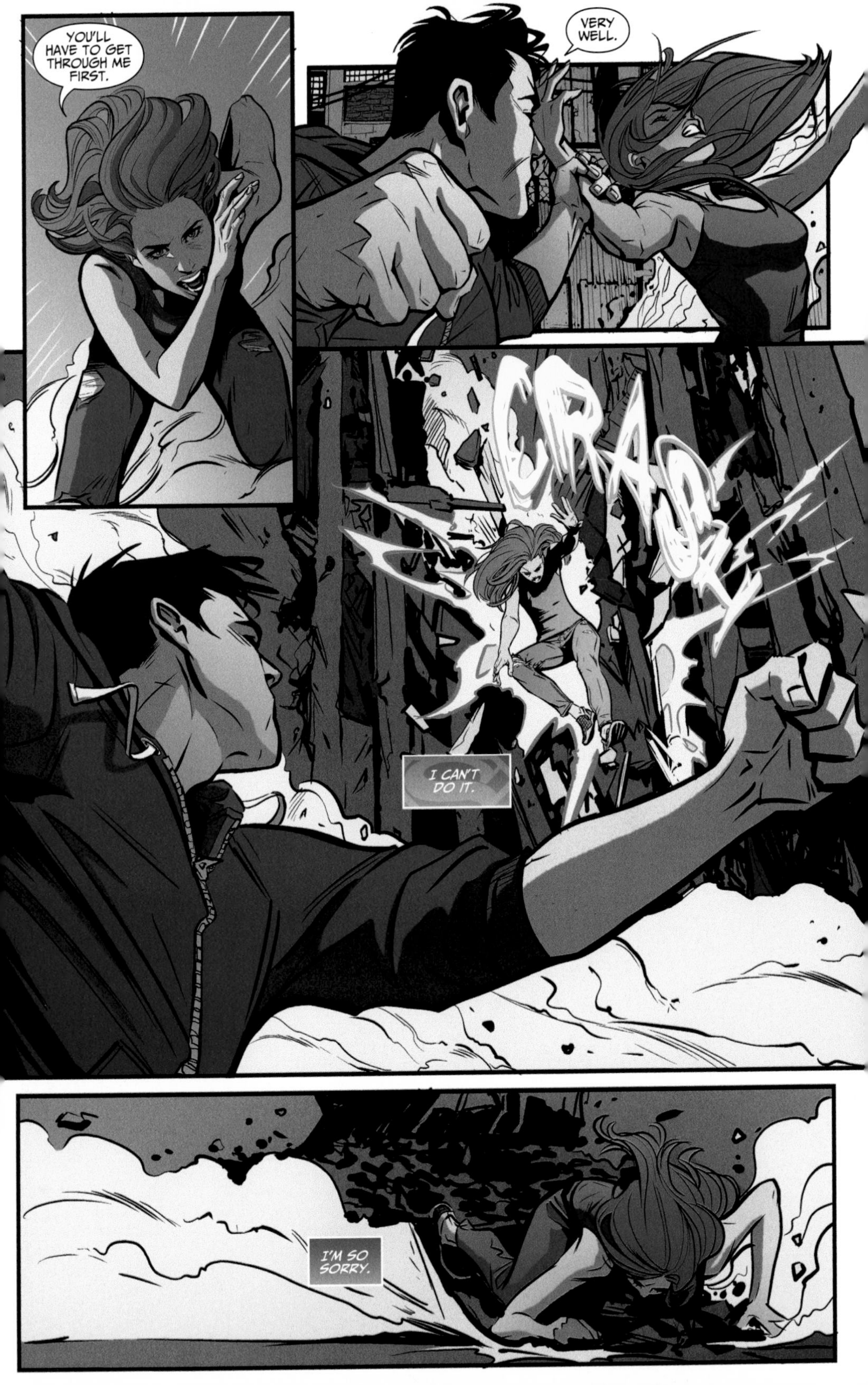
YOU'LL HAVE TO GET THROUGH ME FIRST.
VERY WELL.
CRASH
I CAN'T DO IT.
I'M SO SORRY.

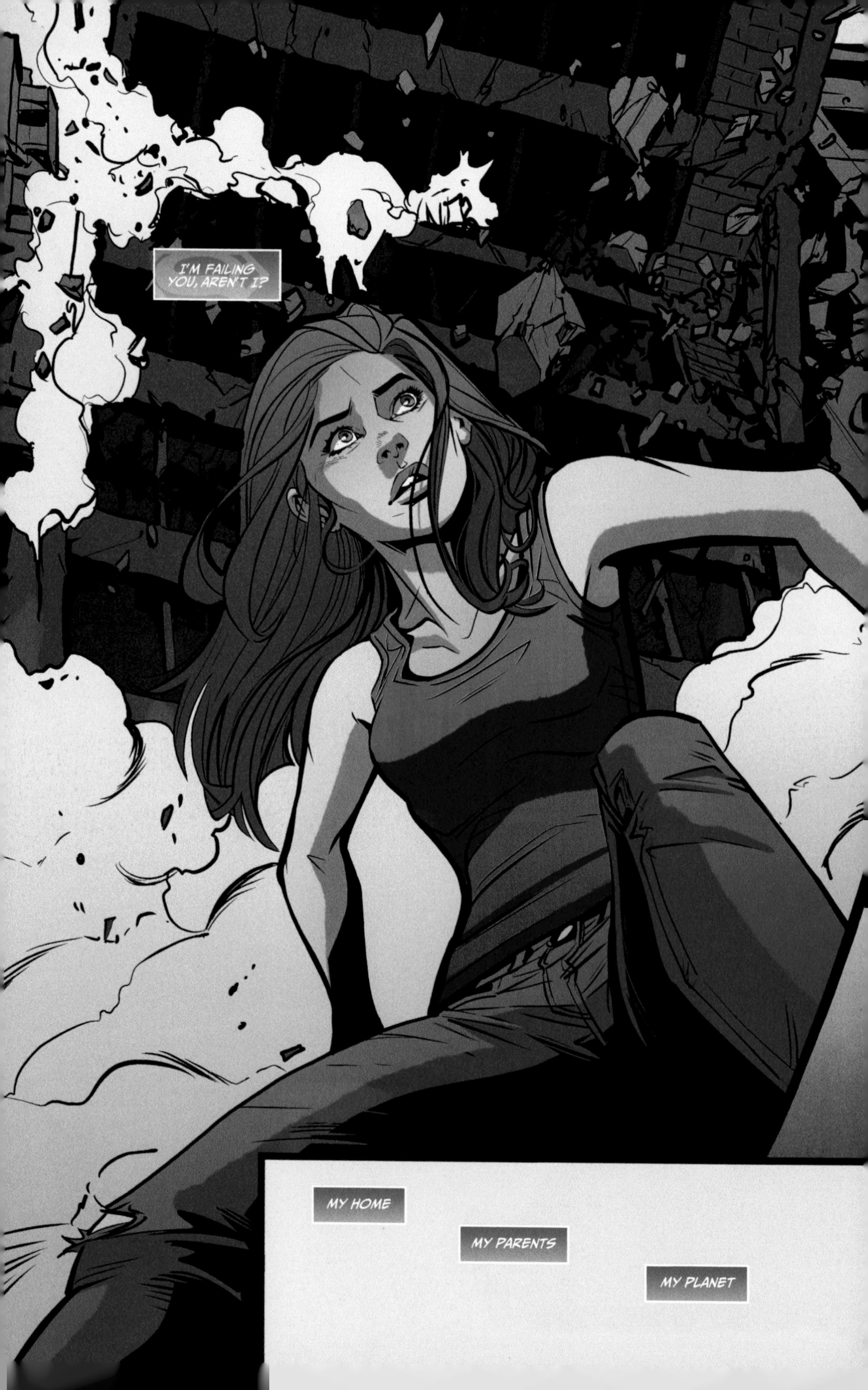
I'M FAILING YOU, AREN'T I?
MY HOME
MY PARENTS
MY PLANET

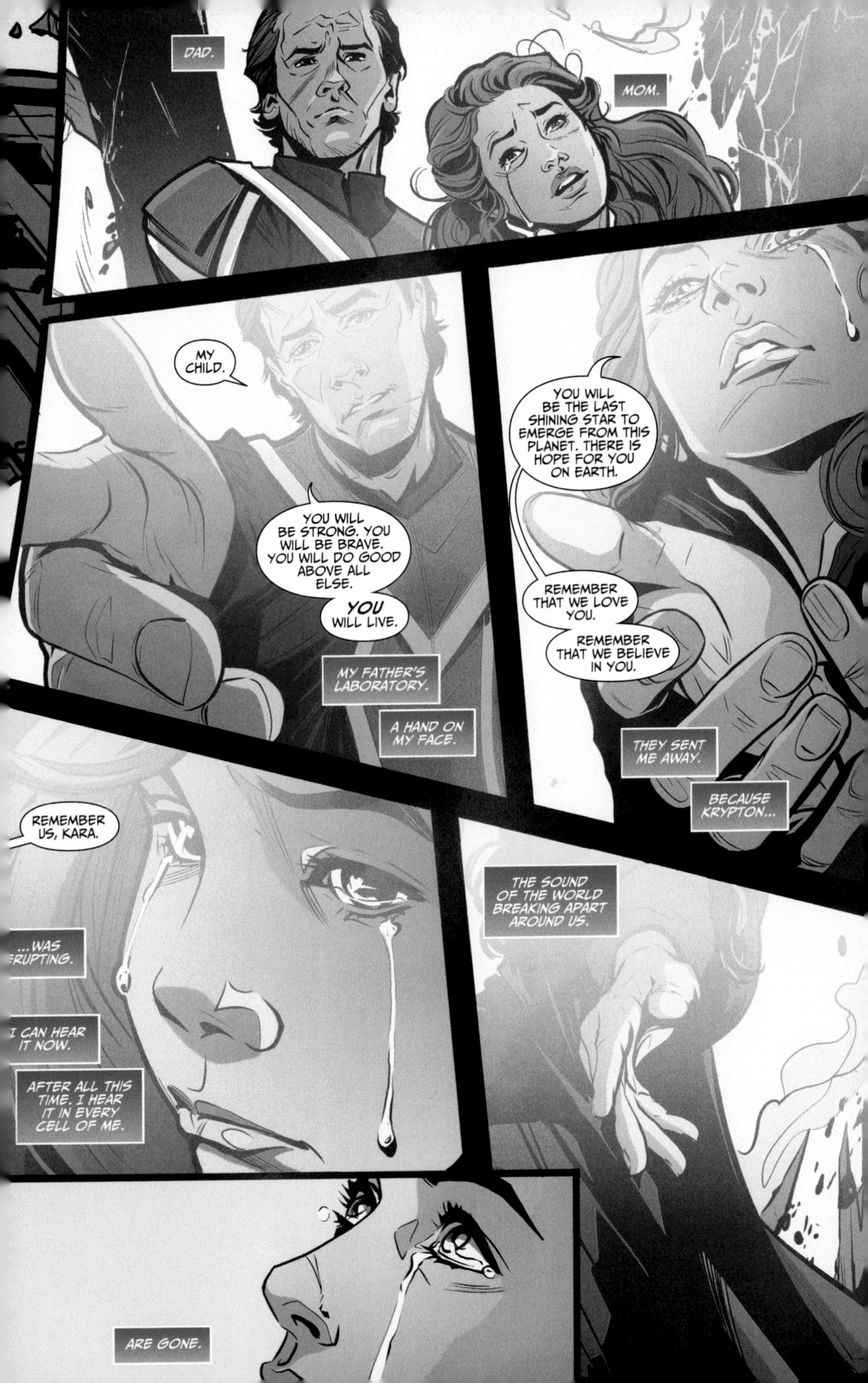
DAD.
MOM.
MY CHILD.
YOU WILL BE STRONG. YOU WILL BE BRAVE. YOU WILL DO GOOD ABOVE ALL ELSE.
YOU WILL LIVE.
MY FATHER'S LABORATORY.
A HAND ON MY FACE.
YOU WILL BE THE LAST SHINING STAR TO EMERGE FROM THIS PLANET. THERE IS HOPE FOR YOU ON EARTH.
REMEMBER THAT WE LOVE YOU.
REMEMBER THAT WE BELIEVE IN YOU.
THEY SENT ME AWAY.
BECAUSE KRYPTON...
REMEMBER US, KARA.
...WAS ERUPTING.
I CAN HEAR IT NOW.
AFTER ALL THIS TIME. I HEAR IT IN EVERY CELL OF ME.
THE SOUND OF THE WORLD BREAKING APART AROUND US.
ARE GONE.

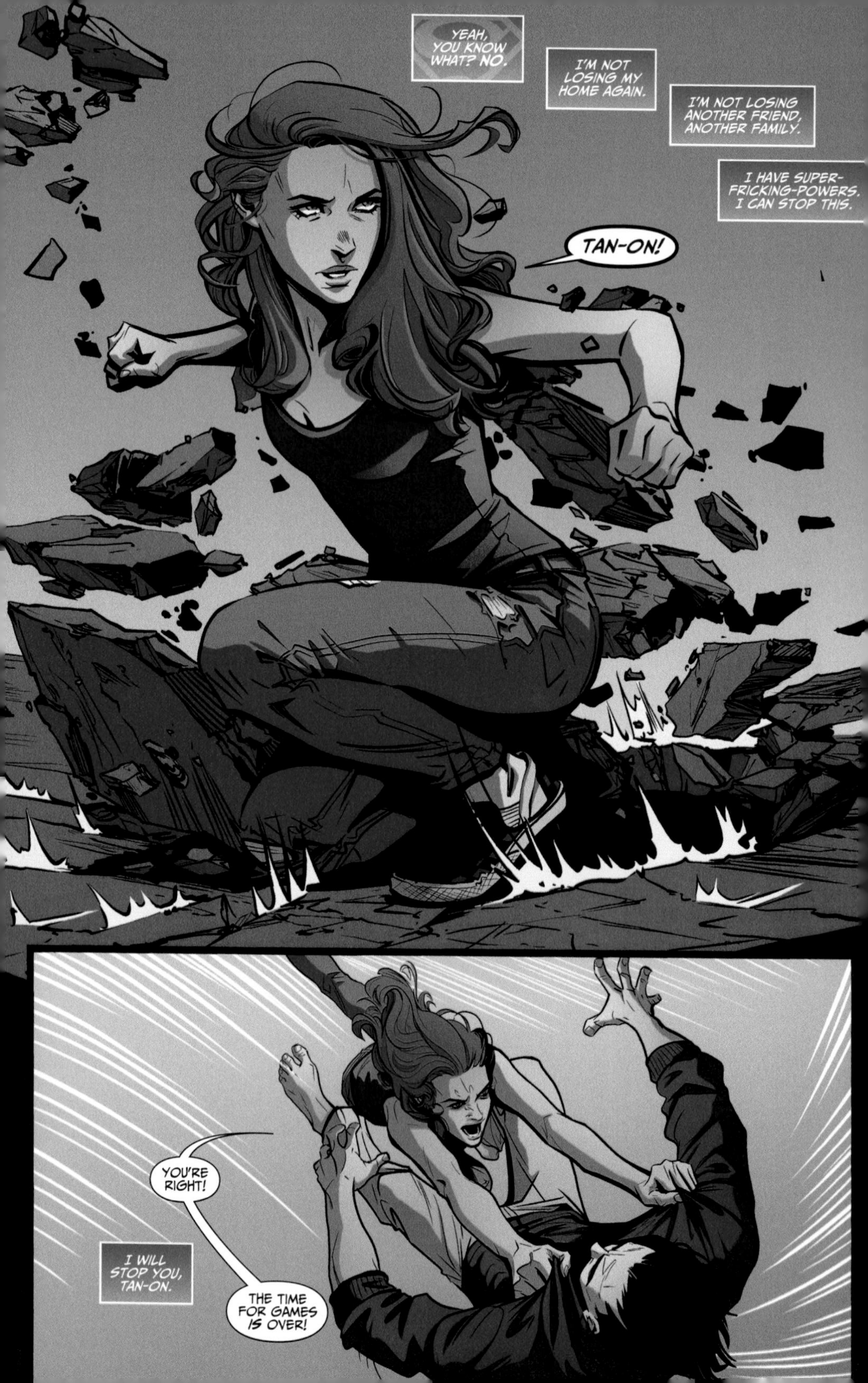

YEAH, YOU KNOW WHAT? NO.
I'M NOT LOSING MY HOME AGAIN.
I'M NOT LOSING ANOTHER FRIEND, ANOTHER FAMILY.
I HAVE SUPER-FRICKING-POWERS. I CAN STOP THIS.
TAN-ON!
I WILL STOP YOU, TAN-ON.
YOU'RE RIGHT!
THE TIME FOR GAMES IS OVER!

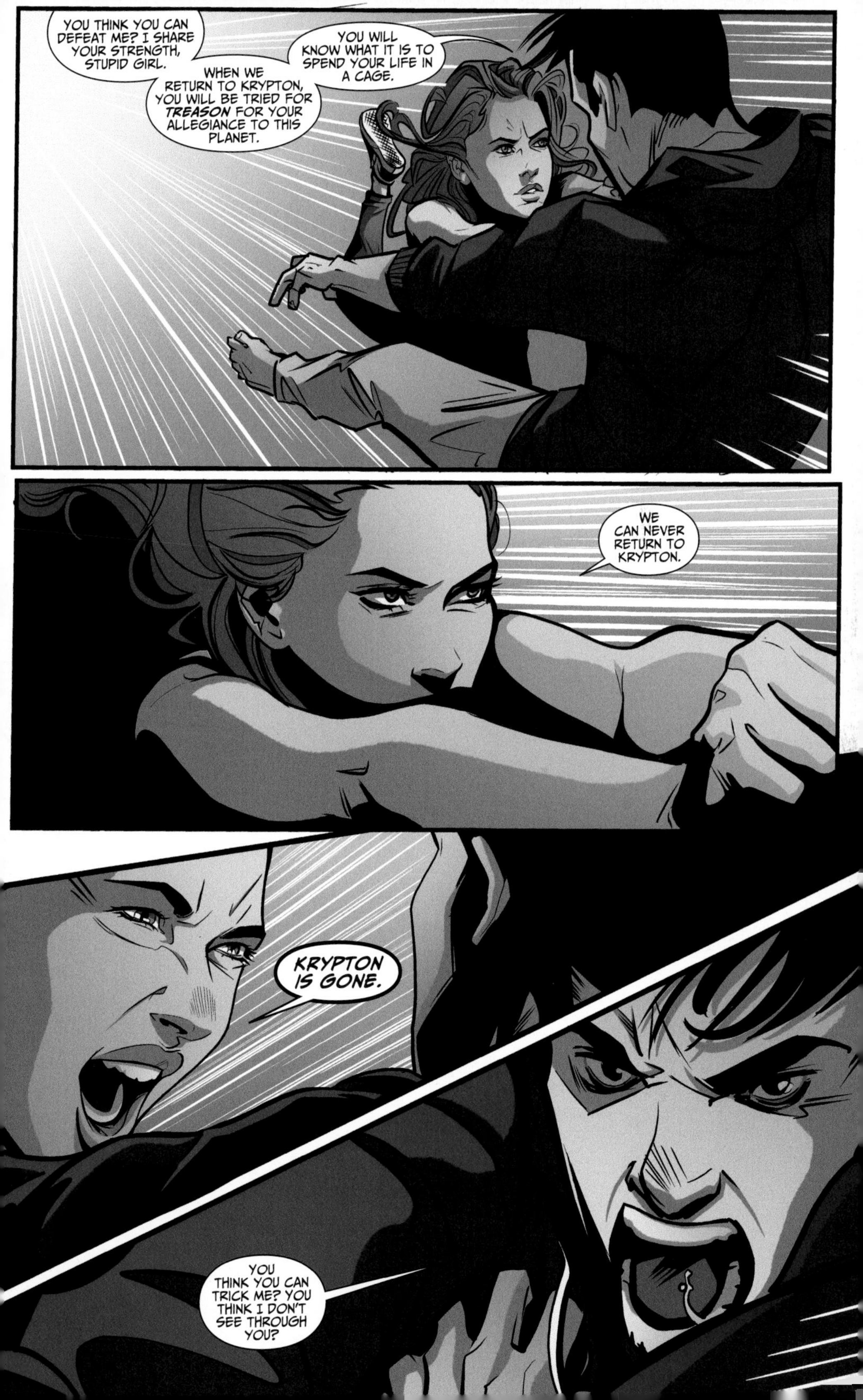
YOU THINK YOU CAN DEFEAT ME? I SHARE YOUR STRENGTH, STUPID GIRL.
WHEN WE RETURN TO KRYPTON, YOU WILL BE TRIED FOR TREASON FOR YOUR ALLEGIANCE TO THIS PLANET.
YOU WILL KNOW WHAT IT IS TO SPEND YOUR LIFE IN A CAGE.
WE CAN NEVER RETURN TO KRYPTON.
KRYPTON IS GONE.
YOU THINK YOU CAN TRICK ME? YOU THINK I DON'T SEE THROUGH YOU?

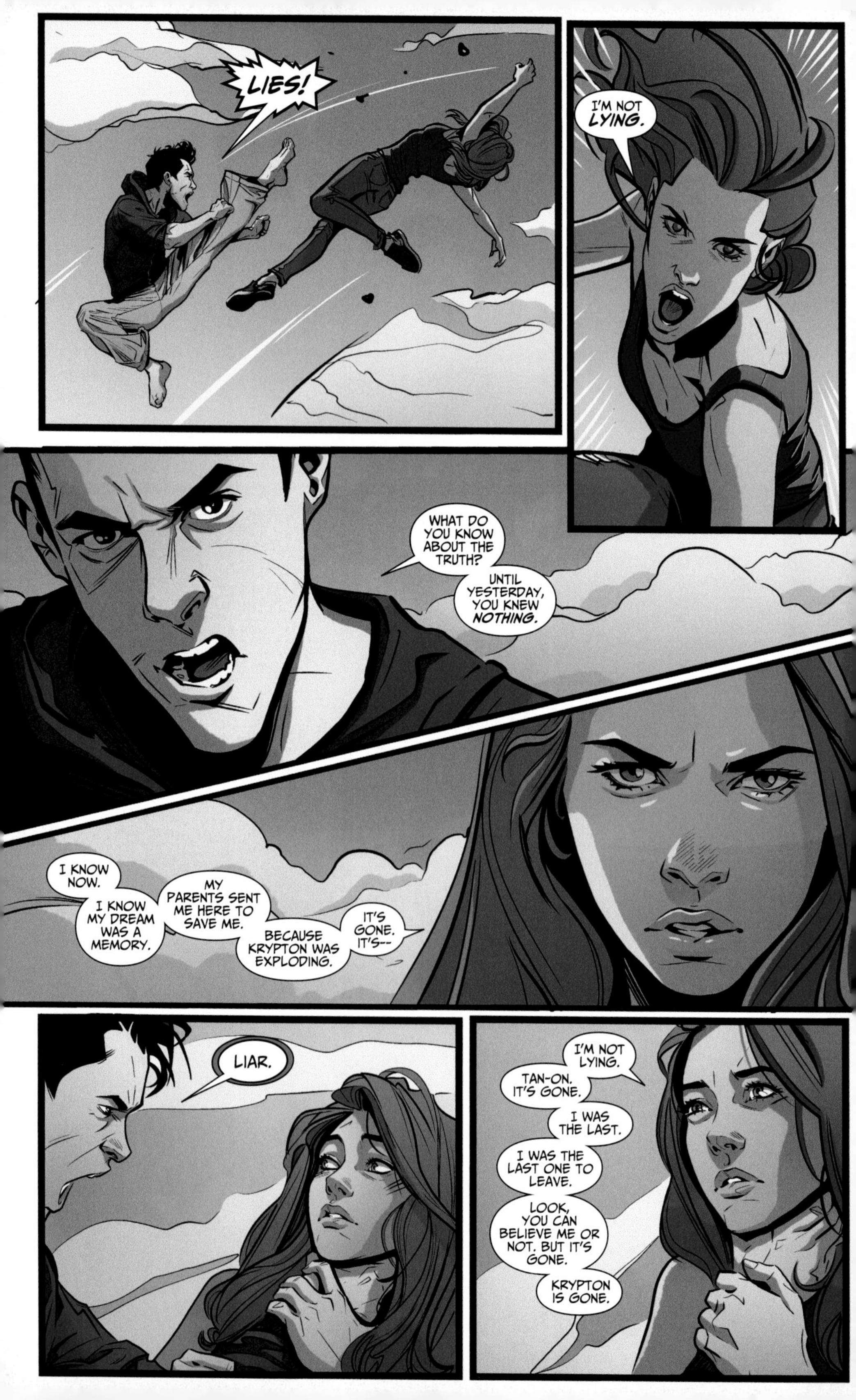
LIES!
I'M NOT LYING.
WHAT DO YOU KNOW ABOUT THE TRUTH?
UNTIL YESTERDAY, YOU KNEW NOTHING.
I KNOW NOW.
I KNOW MY DREAM WAS A MEMORY.
MY PARENTS SENT ME HERE TO SAVE ME.
BECAUSE KRYPTON WAS EXPLODING.
IT'S GONE. IT'S--
LIAR.
I'M NOT LYING.
TAN-ON. IT'S GONE.
I WAS THE LAST.
I WAS THE LAST ONE TO LEAVE.
LOOK, YOU CAN BELIEVE ME OR NOT. BUT IT'S GONE.
KRYPTON IS GONE.

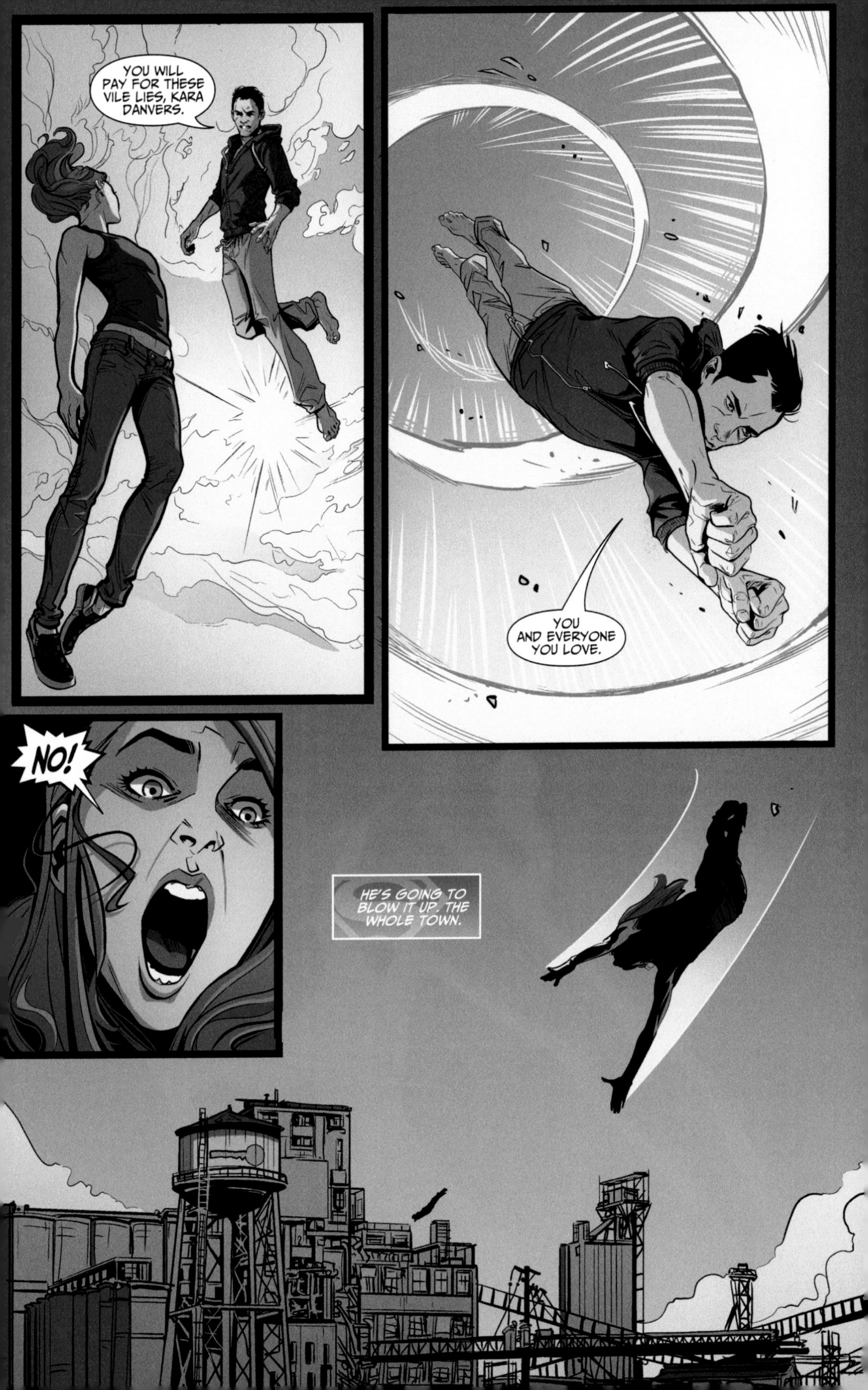

YOU WILL PAY FOR THESE VILE LIES, KARA DANVERS.
YOU AND EVERYONE YOU LOVE.
NO!
HE'S GOING TO BLOW IT UP. THE WHOLE TOWN.

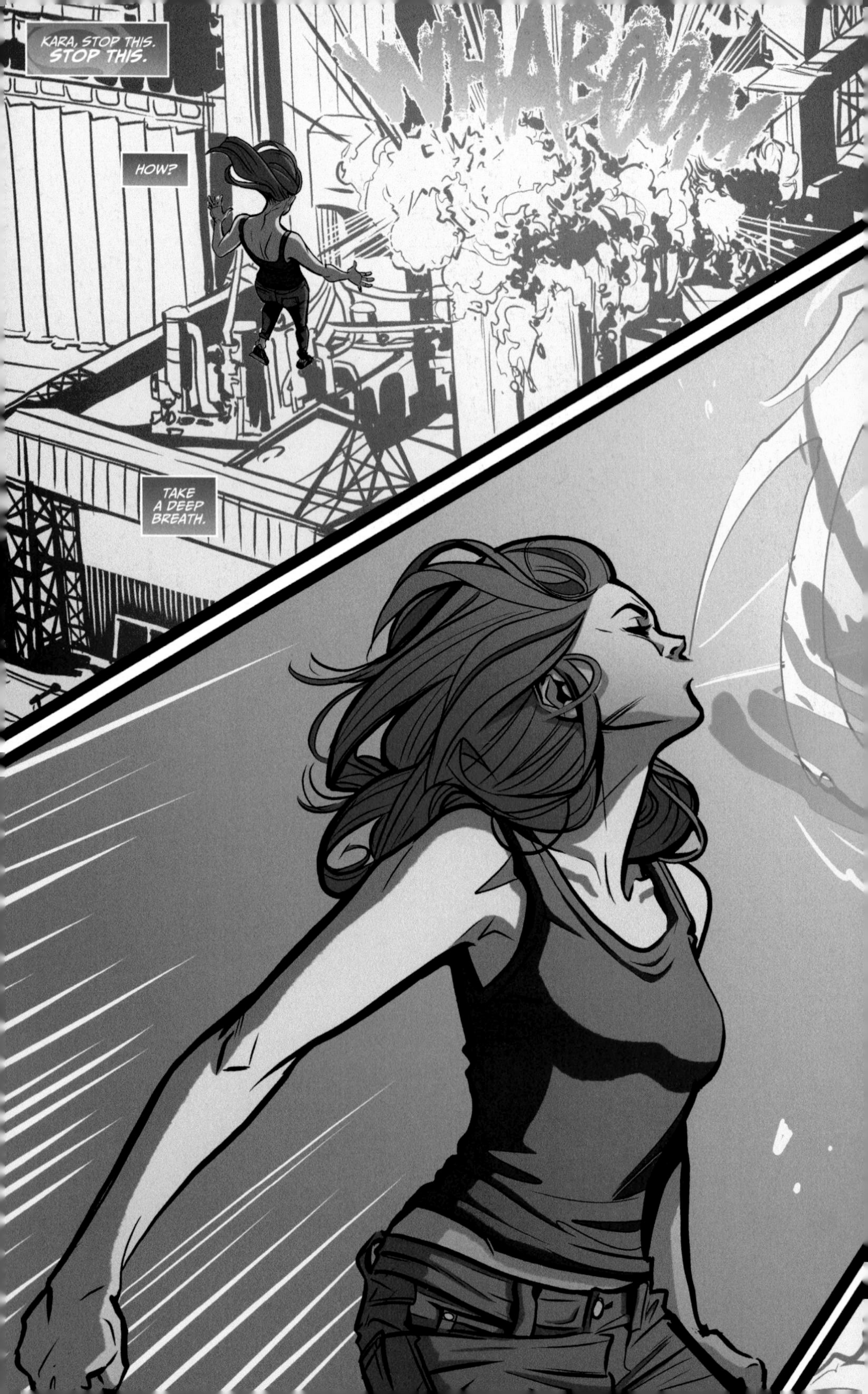
KARA, STOP THIS. STOP THIS.
WHABOOM
HOW?
TAKE A DEEP BREATH.

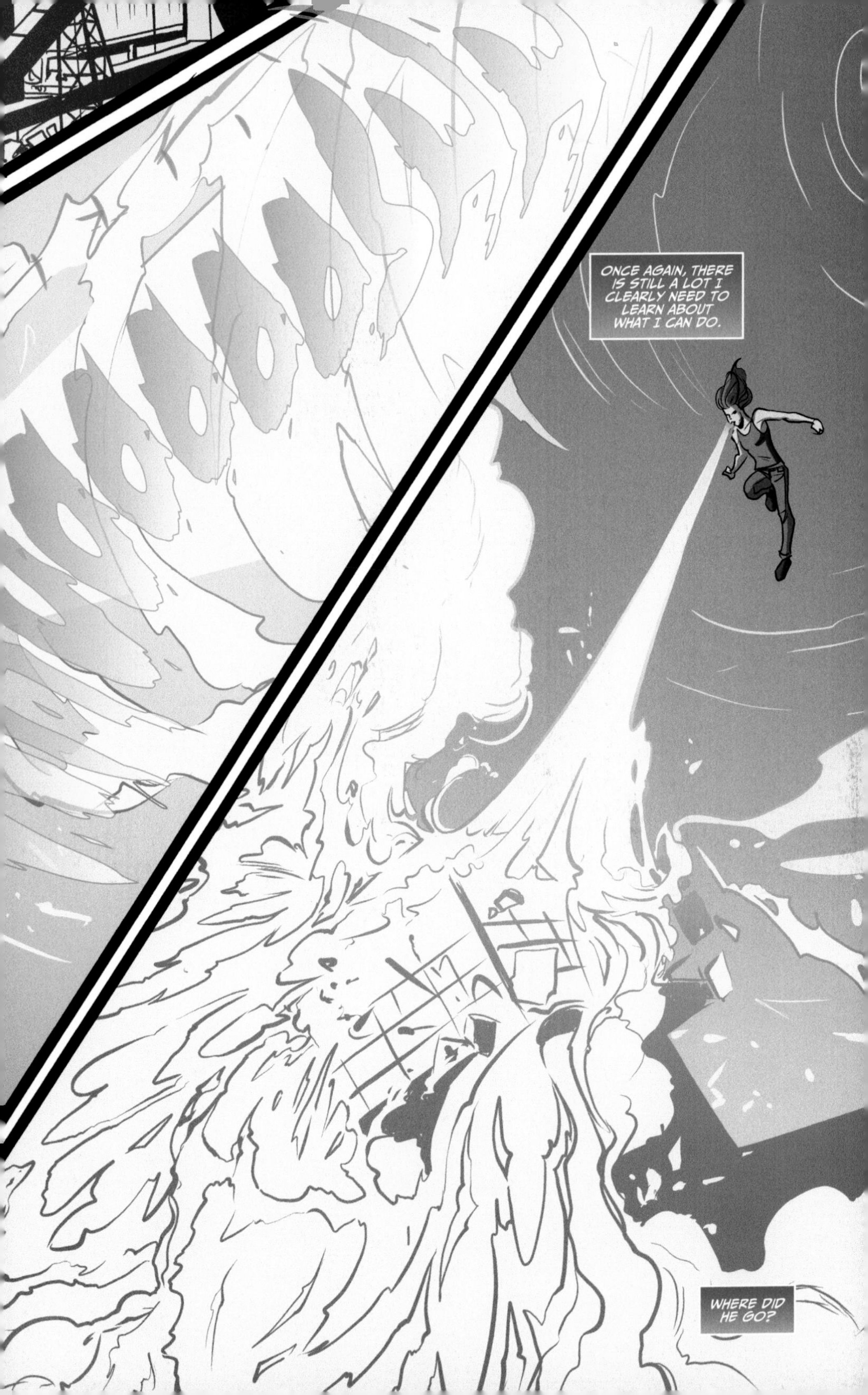
ONCE AGAIN, THERE IS STILL A LOT I CLEARLY NEED TO LEARN ABOUT WHAT I CAN DO.
WHERE DID HE GO?

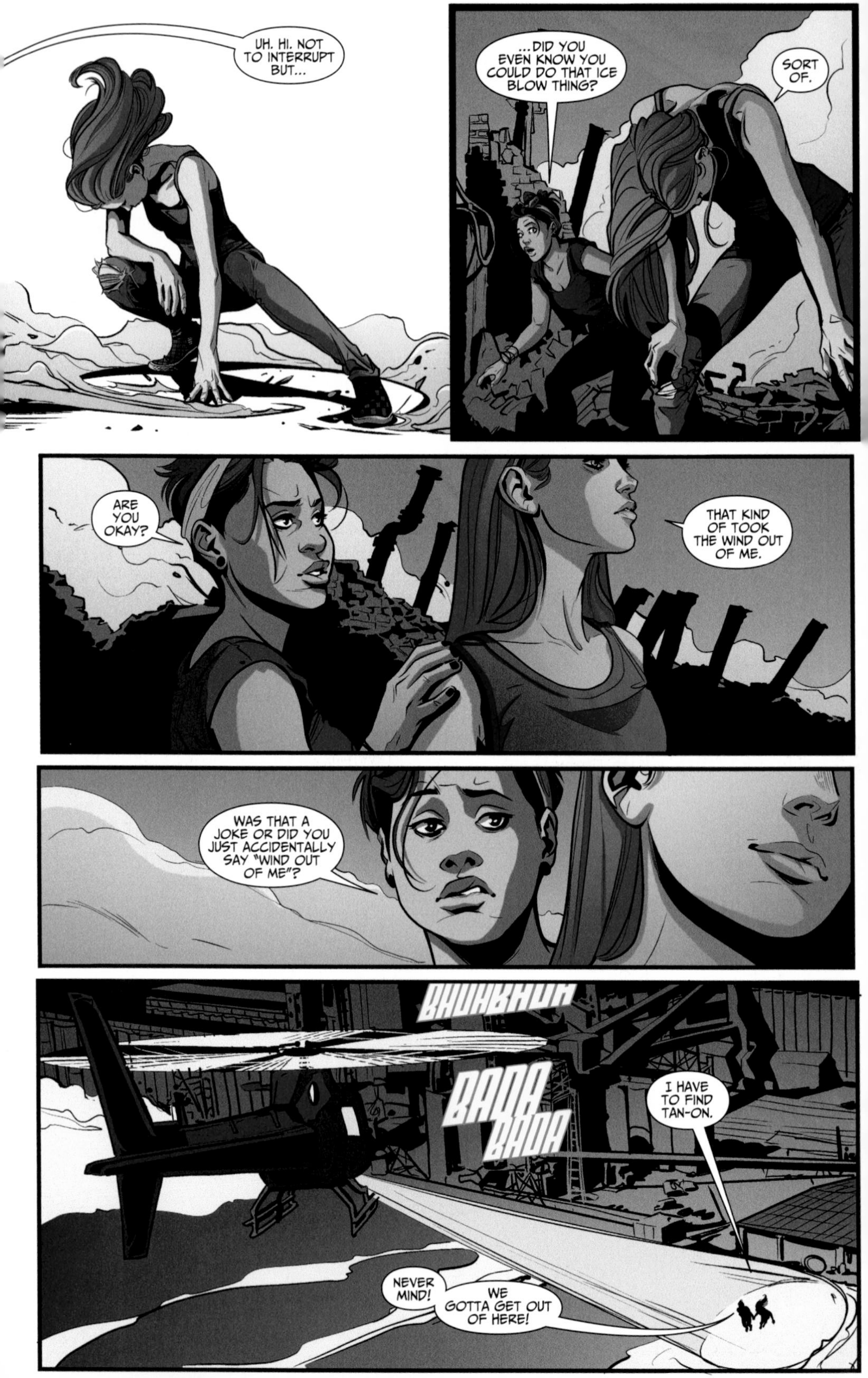
UH. HI. NOT TO INTERRUPT BUT...
...DID YOU EVEN KNOW YOU COULD DO THAT ICE BLOW THING?
SORT OF.
ARE YOU OKAY?
THAT KIND OF TOOK THE WIND OUT OF ME.
WAS THAT A JOKE OR DID YOU JUST ACCIDENTALLY SAY "WIND OUT OF ME"?
BHUHBHUH
BADA BADA
I HAVE TO FIND TAN-ON.
NEVER MIND!
WE GOTTA GET OUT OF HERE!

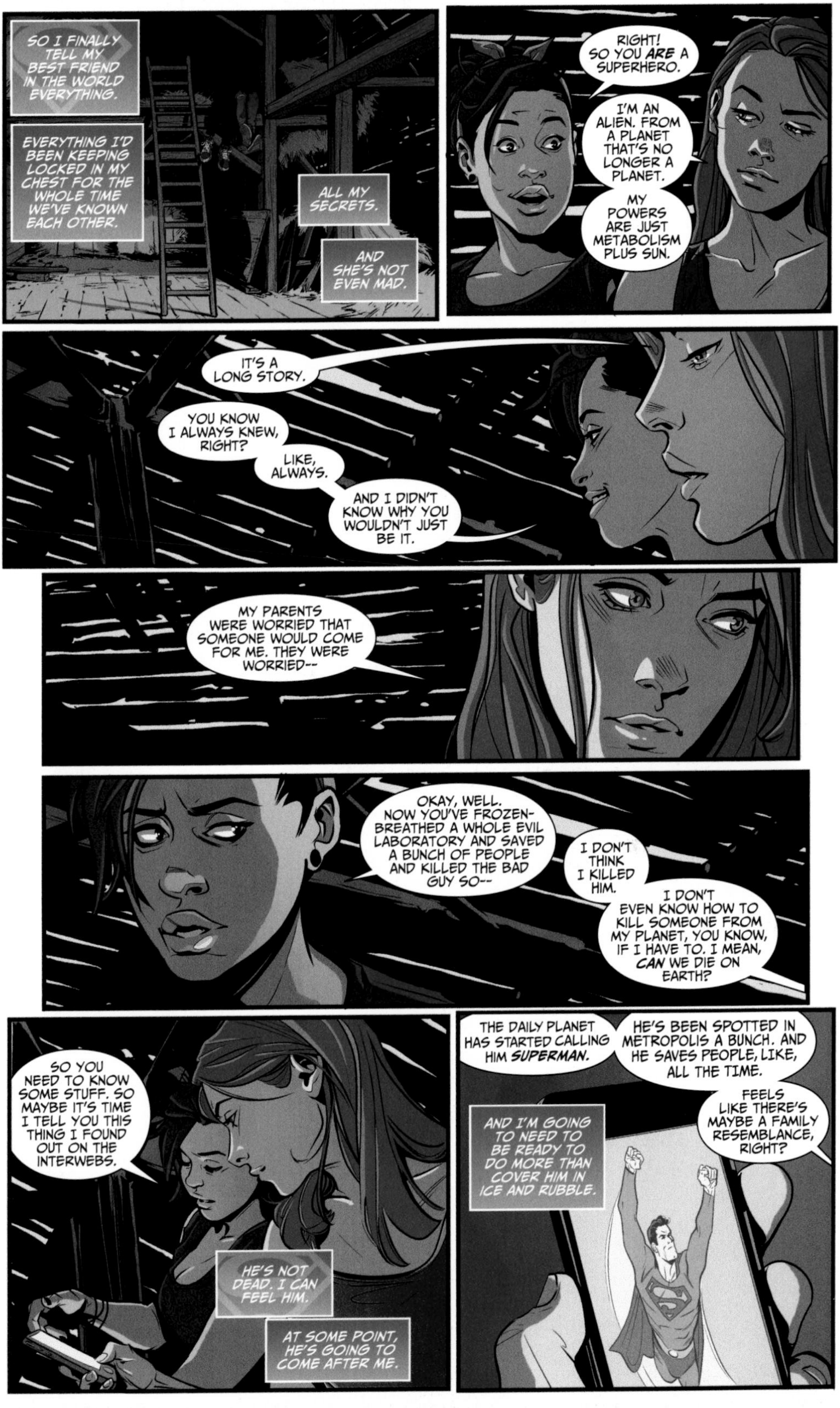
SO I FINALLY TELL MY BEST FRIEND IN THE WORLD EVERYTHING.
EVERYTHING I'D BEEN KEEPING LOCKED IN MY CHEST FOR THE WHOLE TIME WE'VE KNOWN EACH OTHER.
ALL MY SECRETS.
AND SHE'S NOT EVEN MAD.
RIGHT! SO YOU ARE A SUPERHERO.
I'M AN ALIEN. FROM A PLANET THAT'S NO LONGER A PLANET.
MY POWERS ARE JUST METABOLISM PLUS SUN.
IT'S A LONG STORY.
YOU KNOW I ALWAYS KNEW, RIGHT?
LIKE, ALWAYS.
AND I DIDN'T KNOW WHY YOU WOULDN'T JUST BE IT.
MY PARENTS WERE WORRIED THAT SOMEONE WOULD COME FOR ME. THEY WERE WORRIED--
OKAY, WELL. NOW YOU'VE FROZEN-BREATHED A WHOLE EVIL LABORATORY AND SAVED A BUNCH OF PEOPLE AND KILLED THE BAD GUY SO--
I DON'T THINK I KILLED HIM.
I DON'T EVEN KNOW HOW TO KILL SOMEONE FROM MY PLANET, YOU KNOW, IF I HAVE TO. I MEAN, CAN WE DIE ON EARTH?
SO YOU NEED TO KNOW SOME STUFF. SO MAYBE IT'S TIME I TELL YOU THIS THING I FOUND OUT ON THE INTERWEBS.
HE'S NOT DEAD. I CAN FEEL HIM.
AT SOME POINT, HE'S GOING TO COME AFTER ME.
THE DAILY PLANET HAS STARTED CALLING HIM SUPERMAN.
HE'S BEEN SPOTTED IN METROPOLIS A BUNCH. AND HE SAVES PEOPLE, LIKE, ALL THE TIME.
FEELS LIKE THERE'S MAYBE A FAMILY RESEMBLANCE, RIGHT?
AND I'M GOING TO NEED TO BE READY TO DO MORE THAN COVER HIM IN ICE AND RUBBLE.

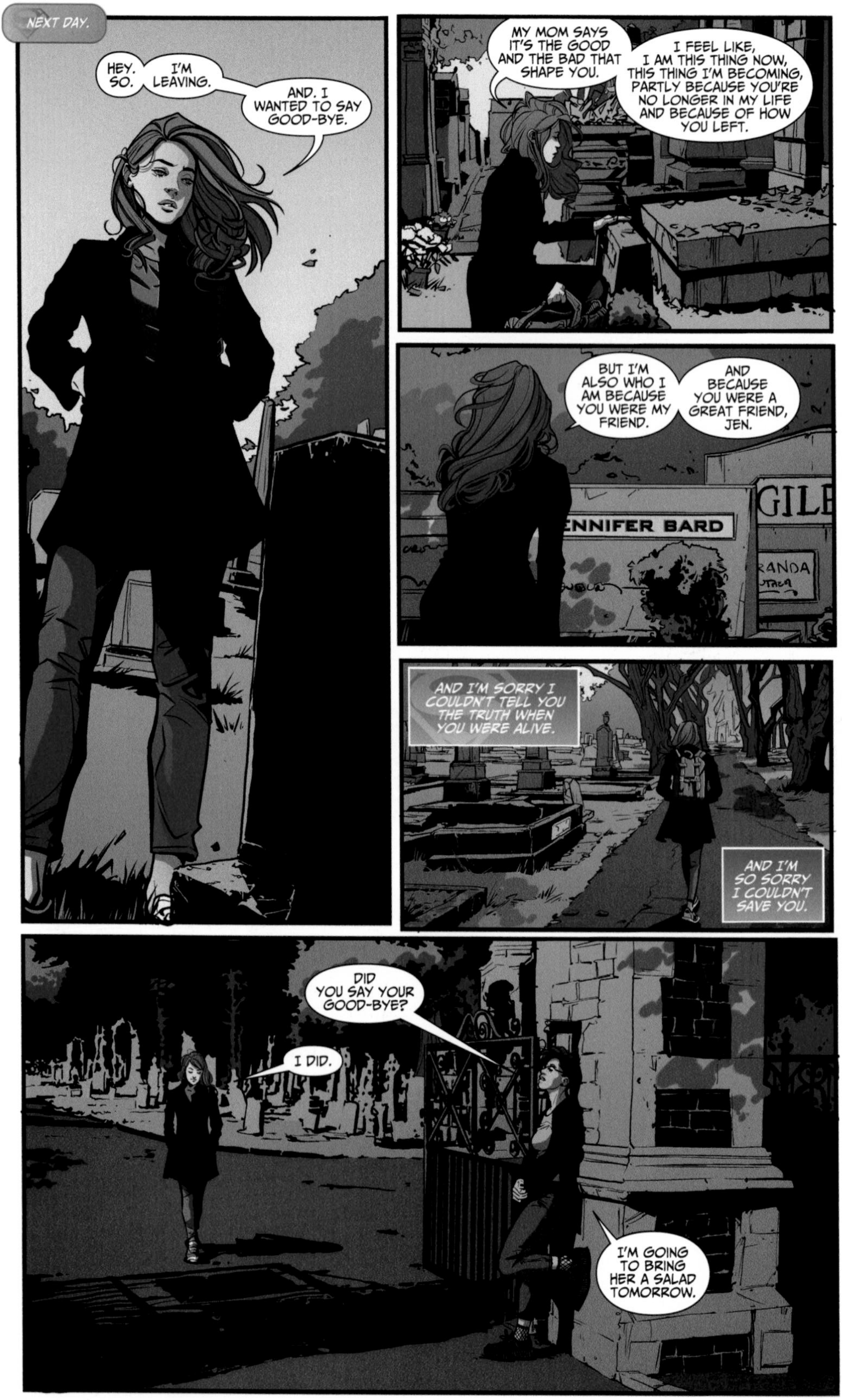
NEXT DAY.
HEY. SO.
I'M LEAVING.
AND. I WANTED TO SAY GOOD-BYE.
MY MOM SAYS IT'S THE GOOD AND THE BAD THAT SHAPE YOU.
I FEEL LIKE, I AM THIS THING NOW, THIS THING I'M BECOMING, PARTLY BECAUSE YOU'RE NO LONGER IN MY LIFE AND BECAUSE OF HOW YOU LEFT.
BUT I'M ALSO WHO I AM BECAUSE YOU WERE MY FRIEND.
AND BECAUSE YOU WERE A GREAT FRIEND, JEN.
ENNIFER BARD
GILB
RANDA
AND I'M SORRY I COULDN'T TELL YOU THE TRUTH WHEN YOU WERE ALIVE.
AND I'M SO SORRY I COULDN'T SAVE YOU.
DID YOU SAY YOUR GOOD-BYE?
I DID.
I'M GOING TO BRING HER A SALAD TOMORROW.

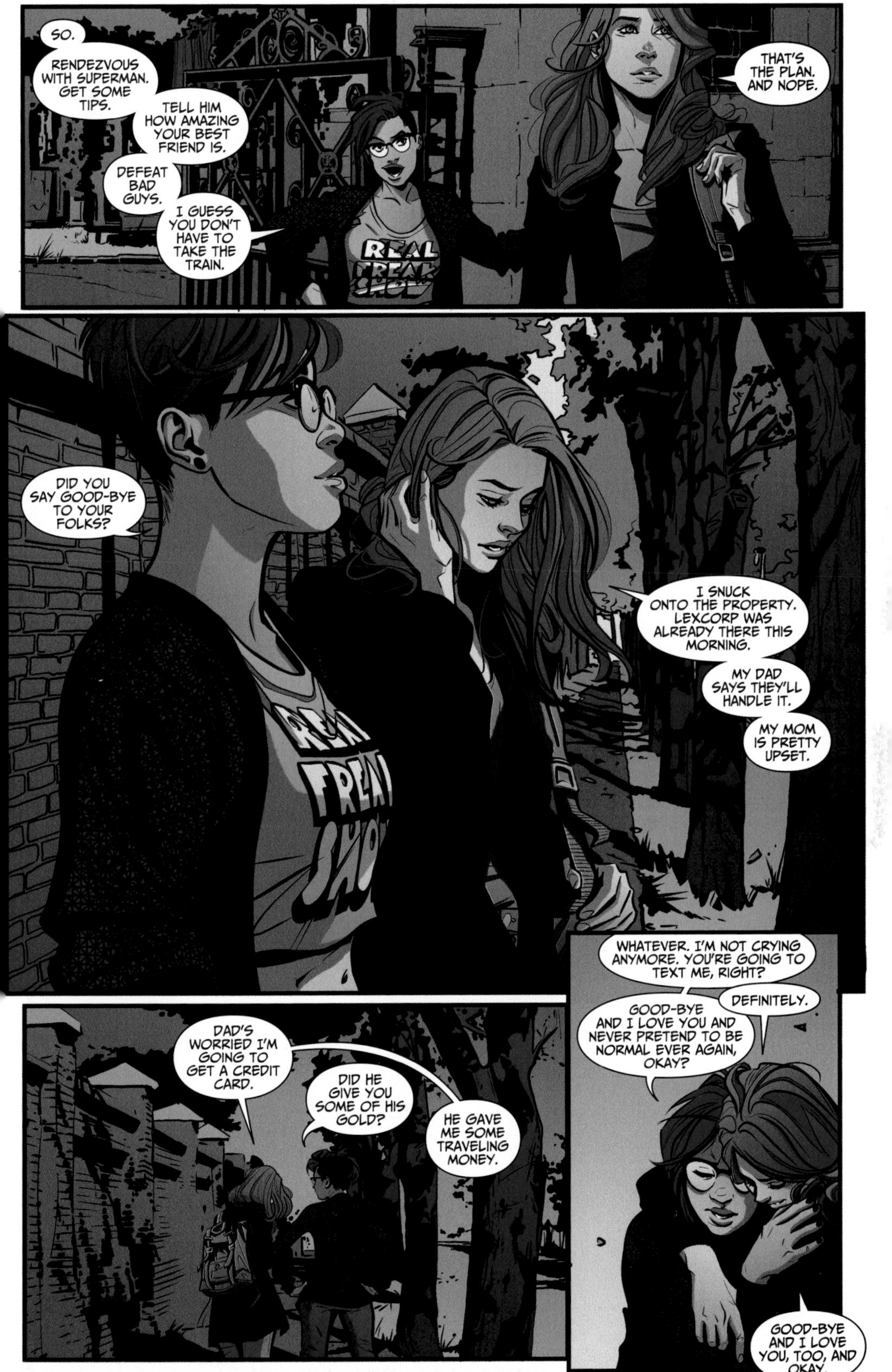
SO.
RENDEZVOUS WITH SUPERMAN. GET SOME TIPS.
TELL HIM HOW AMAZING YOUR BEST FRIEND IS.
DEFEAT BAD GUYS.
I GUESS YOU DON'T HAVE TO TAKE THE TRAIN.
THAT'S THE PLAN. AND NOPE.
REAL FREAK SHOW
DID YOU SAY GOOD-BYE TO YOUR FOLKS?
I SNUCK ONTO THE PROPERTY. LEXCORP WAS ALREADY THERE THIS MORNING.
MY DAD SAYS THEY'LL HANDLE IT.
MY MOM IS PRETTY UPSET.
DAD'S WORRIED I'M GOING TO GET A CREDIT CARD.
DID HE GIVE YOU SOME OF HIS GOLD?
HE GAVE ME SOME TRAVELING MONEY.
WHATEVER. I'M NOT CRYING ANYMORE. YOU'RE GOING TO TEXT ME, RIGHT?
DEFINITELY.
GOOD-BYE AND I LOVE YOU AND NEVER PRETEND TO BE NORMAL EVER AGAIN, OKAY?
GOOD-BYE AND I LOVE YOU, TOO, AND OKAY.

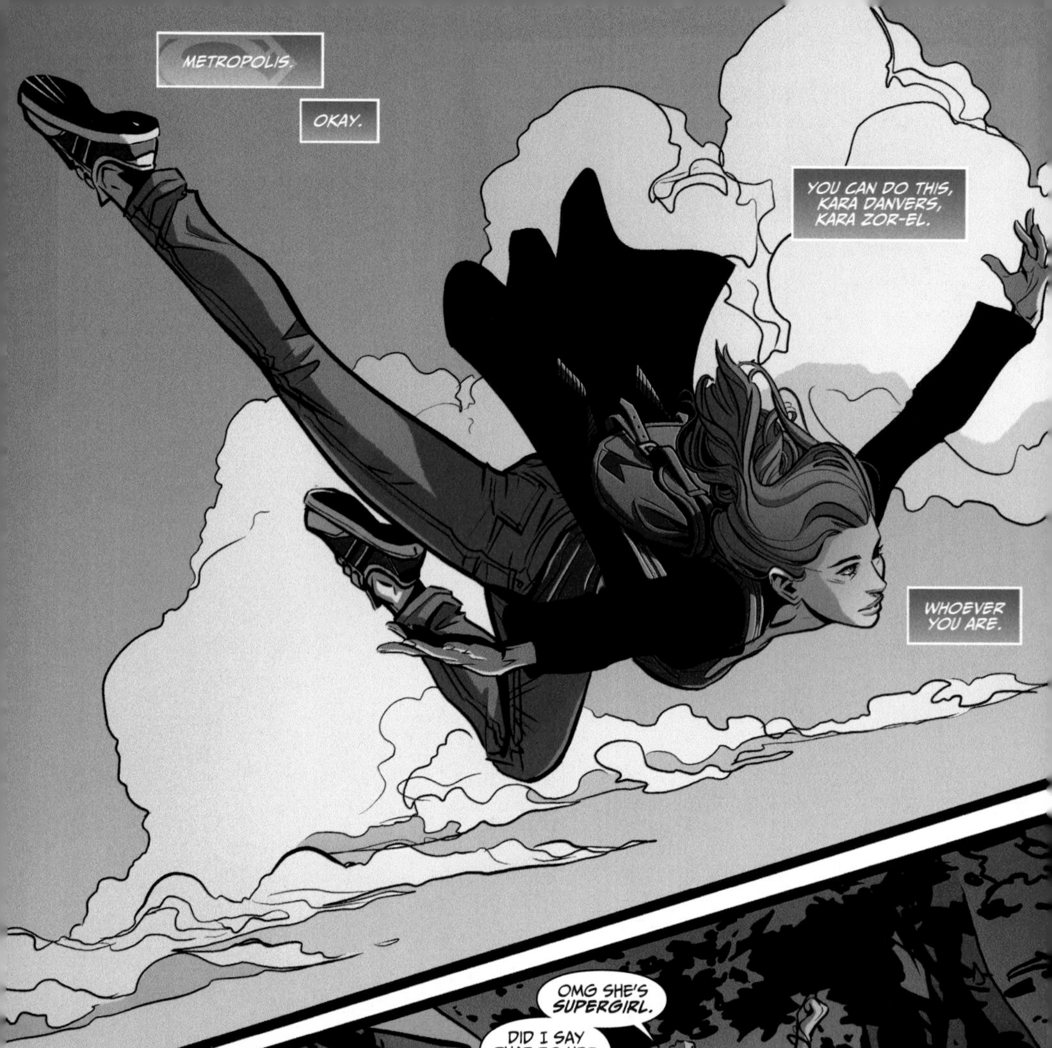
METROPOLIS.
OKAY.
YOU CAN DO THIS, KARA DANVERS, KARA ZOR-EL.
WHOEVER YOU ARE.

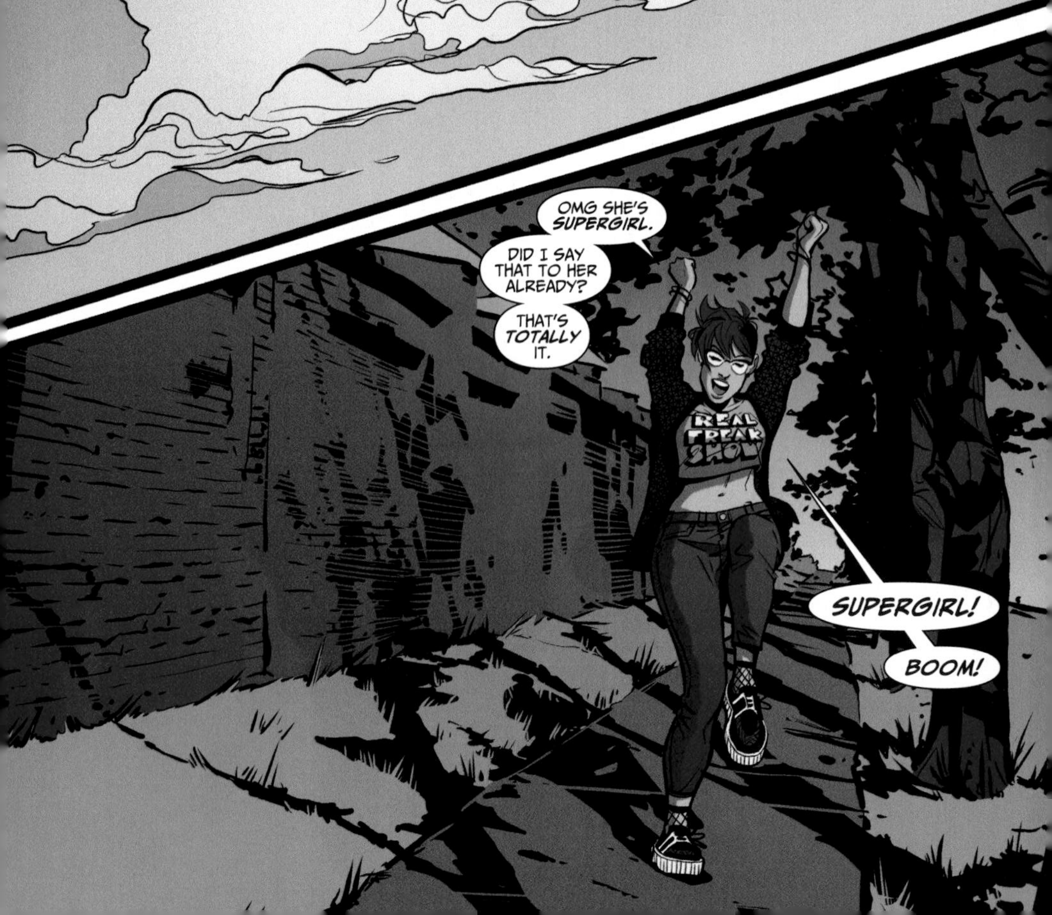
OMG SHE'S SUPERGIRL.
DID I SAY THAT TO HER ALREADY?
THAT'S TOTALLY IT.
SUPERGIRL!
BOOM!

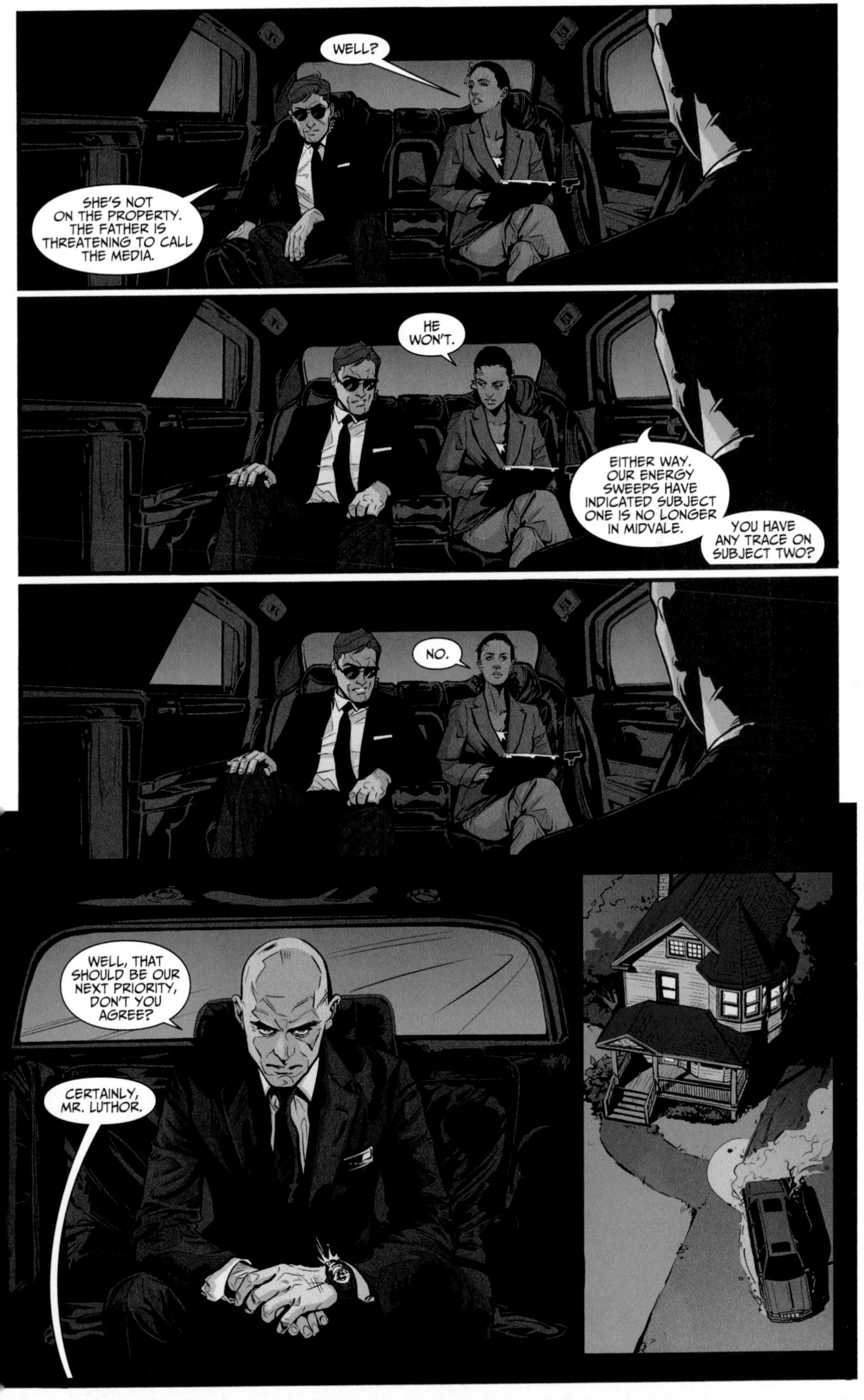

WELL?
SHE'S NOT ON THE PROPERTY. THE FATHER IS THREATENING TO CALL THE MEDIA.
HE WON'T.
EITHER WAY. OUR ENERGY SWEEPS HAVE INDICATED SUBJECT ONE IS NO LONGER IN MIDVALE.
YOU HAVE ANY TRACE ON SUBJECT TWO?
NO.
WELL, THAT SHOULD BE OUR NEXT PRIORITY, DON'T YOU AGREE?
CERTAINLY, MR. LUTHOR.

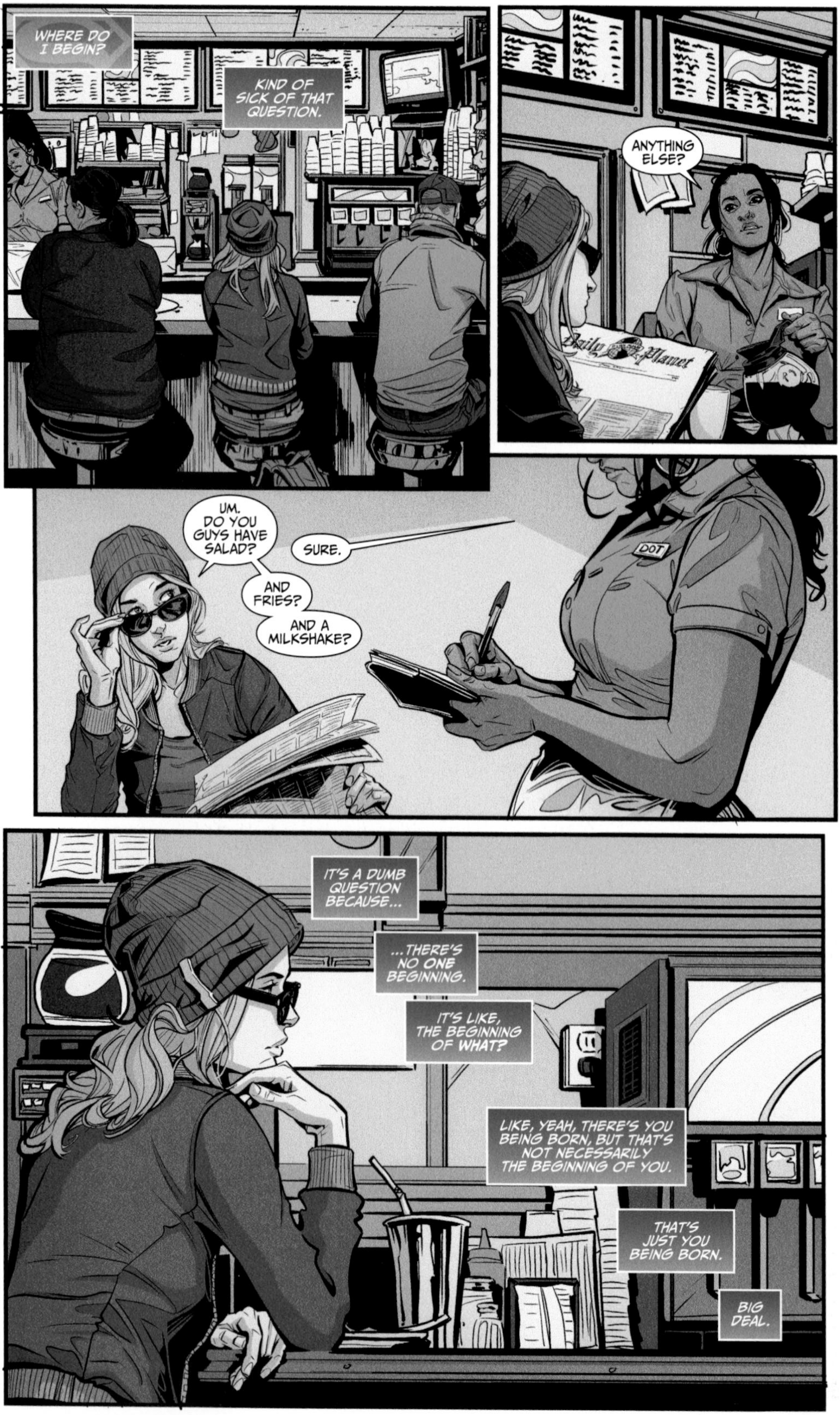
WHERE DO I BEGIN?
KIND OF SICK OF THAT QUESTION.
ANYTHING ELSE?
Daily Planet
UM. DO YOU GUYS HAVE SALAD?
SURE.
AND FRIES?
AND A MILKSHAKE?
DOT
IT'S A DUMB QUESTION BECAUSE...
...THERE'S NO ONE BEGINNING.
IT'S LIKE, THE BEGINNING OF WHAT?
LIKE, YEAH, THERE'S YOU BEING BORN, BUT THAT'S NOT NECESSARILY THE BEGINNING OF YOU.
THAT'S JUST YOU BEING BORN.
BIG DEAL.

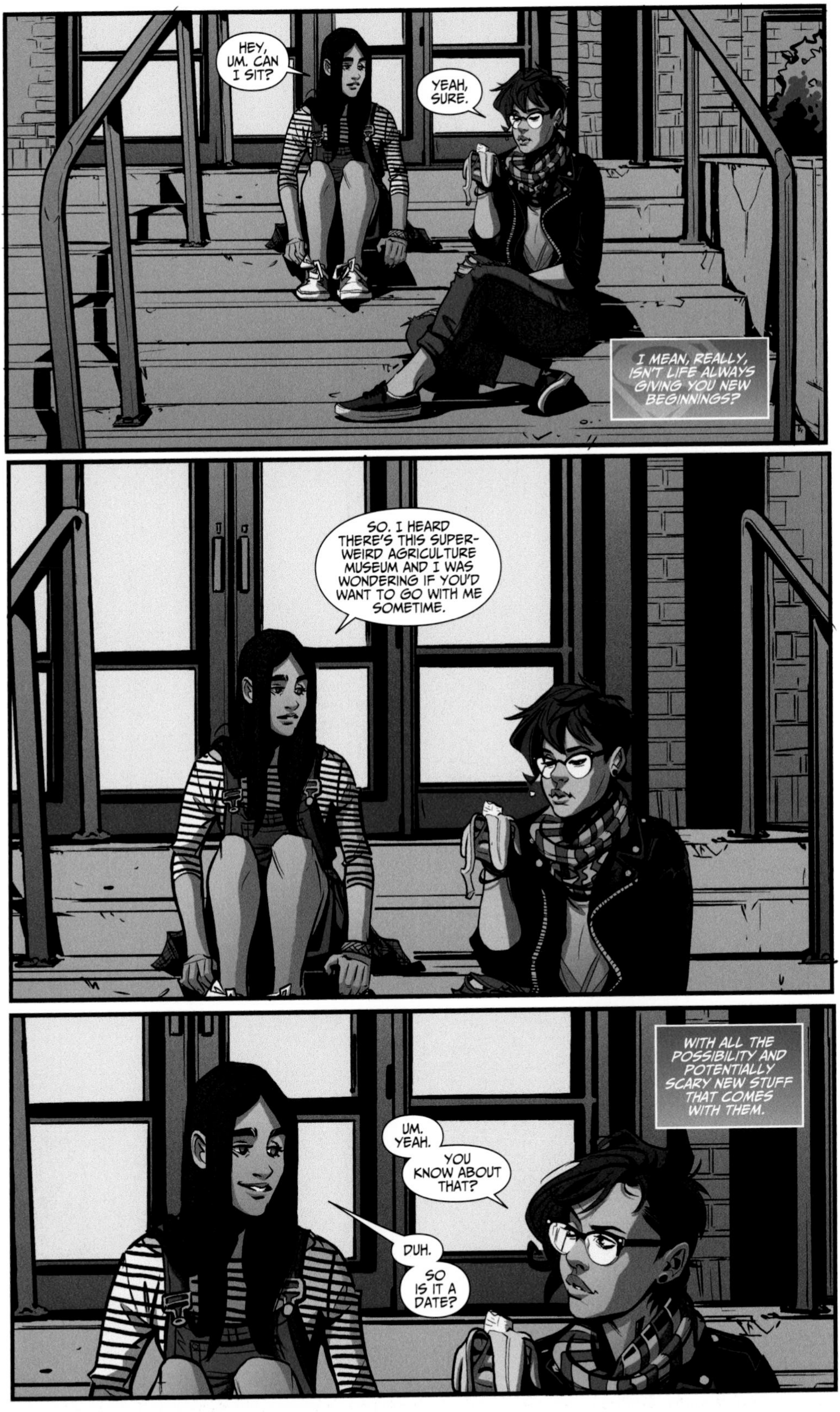
HEY, UM. CAN I SIT?
YEAH, SURE.
I MEAN, REALLY, ISN'T LIFE ALWAYS GIVING YOU NEW BEGINNINGS?
SO. I HEARD THERE'S THIS SUPER-WEIRD AGRICULTURE MUSEUM AND I WAS WONDERING IF YOU'D WANT TO GO WITH ME SOMETIME.
WITH ALL THE POSSIBILITY AND POTENTIALLY SCARY NEW STUFF THAT COMES WITH THEM.
UM. YEAH.
YOU KNOW ABOUT THAT?
DUH.
SO IS IT A DATE?

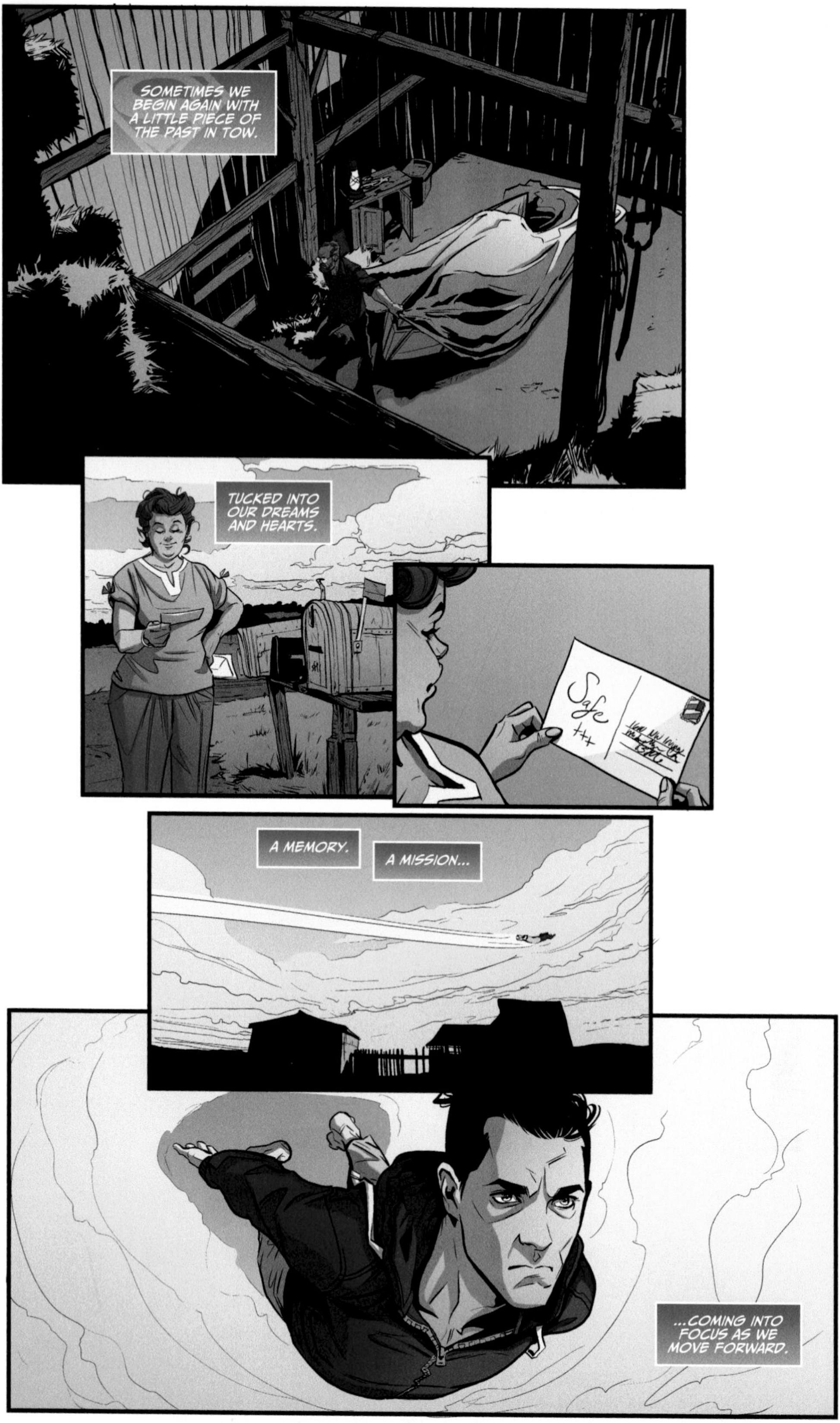
SOMETIMES WE BEGIN AGAIN WITH A LITTLE PIECE OF THE PAST IN TOW.
TUCKED INTO OUR DREAMS AND HEARTS.
Safe
A MEMORY.
A MISSION...
...COMING INTO FOCUS AS WE MOVE FORWARD.

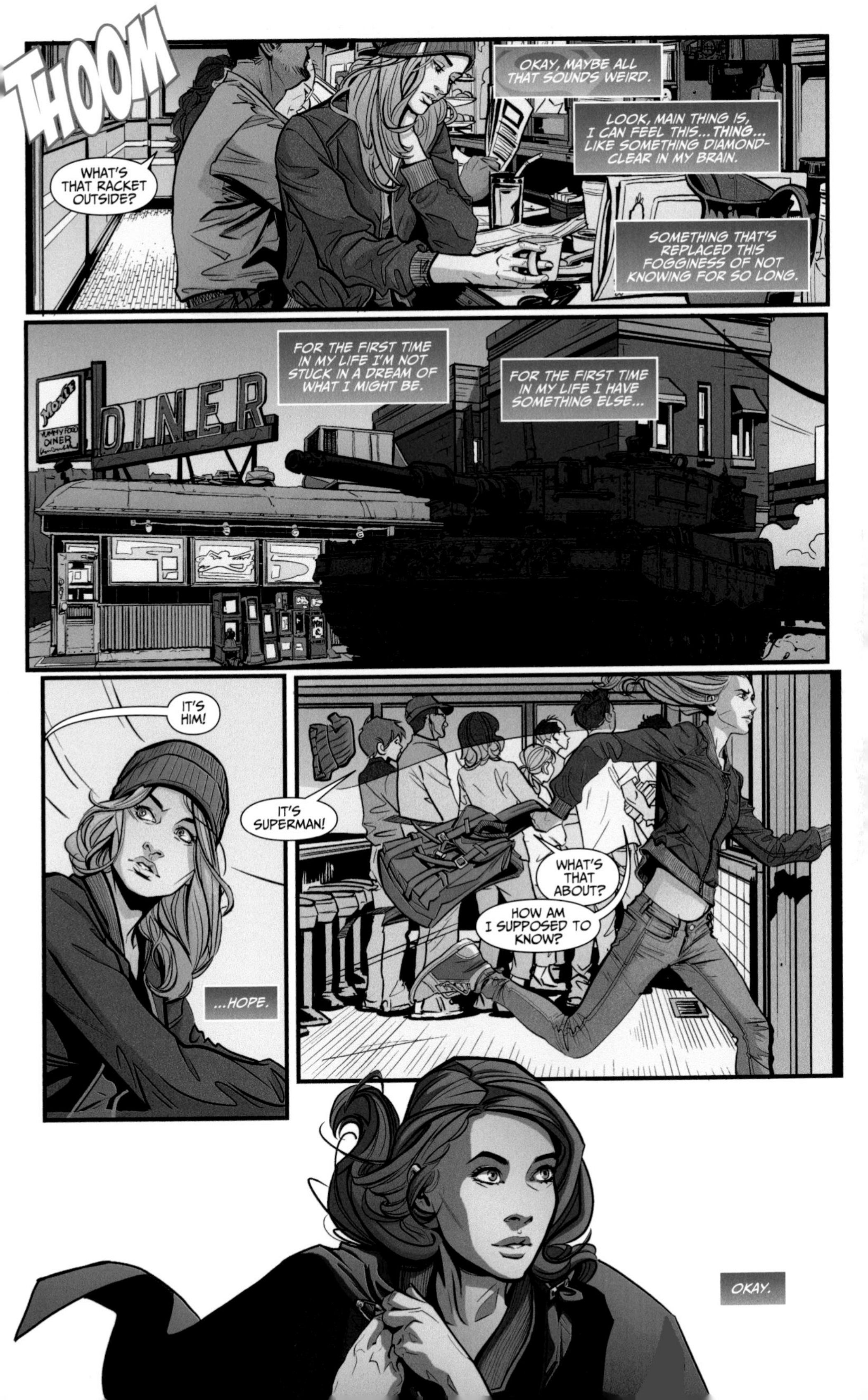
THOOM
WHAT'S THAT RACKET OUTSIDE?
OKAY, MAYBE ALL THAT SOUNDS WEIRD.
LOOK, MAIN THING IS, I CAN FEEL THIS...THING... LIKE SOMETHING DIAMOND-CLEAR IN MY BRAIN.
SOMETHING THAT'S REPLACED THIS FOGGINESS OF NOT KNOWING FOR SO LONG.
FOR THE FIRST TIME IN MY LIFE I'M NOT STUCK IN A DREAM OF WHAT I MIGHT BE.
FOR THE FIRST TIME IN MY LIFE I HAVE SOMETHING ELSE...
DINER
YUMMY FOOD DINER
IT'S HIM!
IT'S SUPERMAN!
...HOPE.
WHAT'S THAT ABOUT?
HOW AM I SUPPOSED TO KNOW?
OKAY.

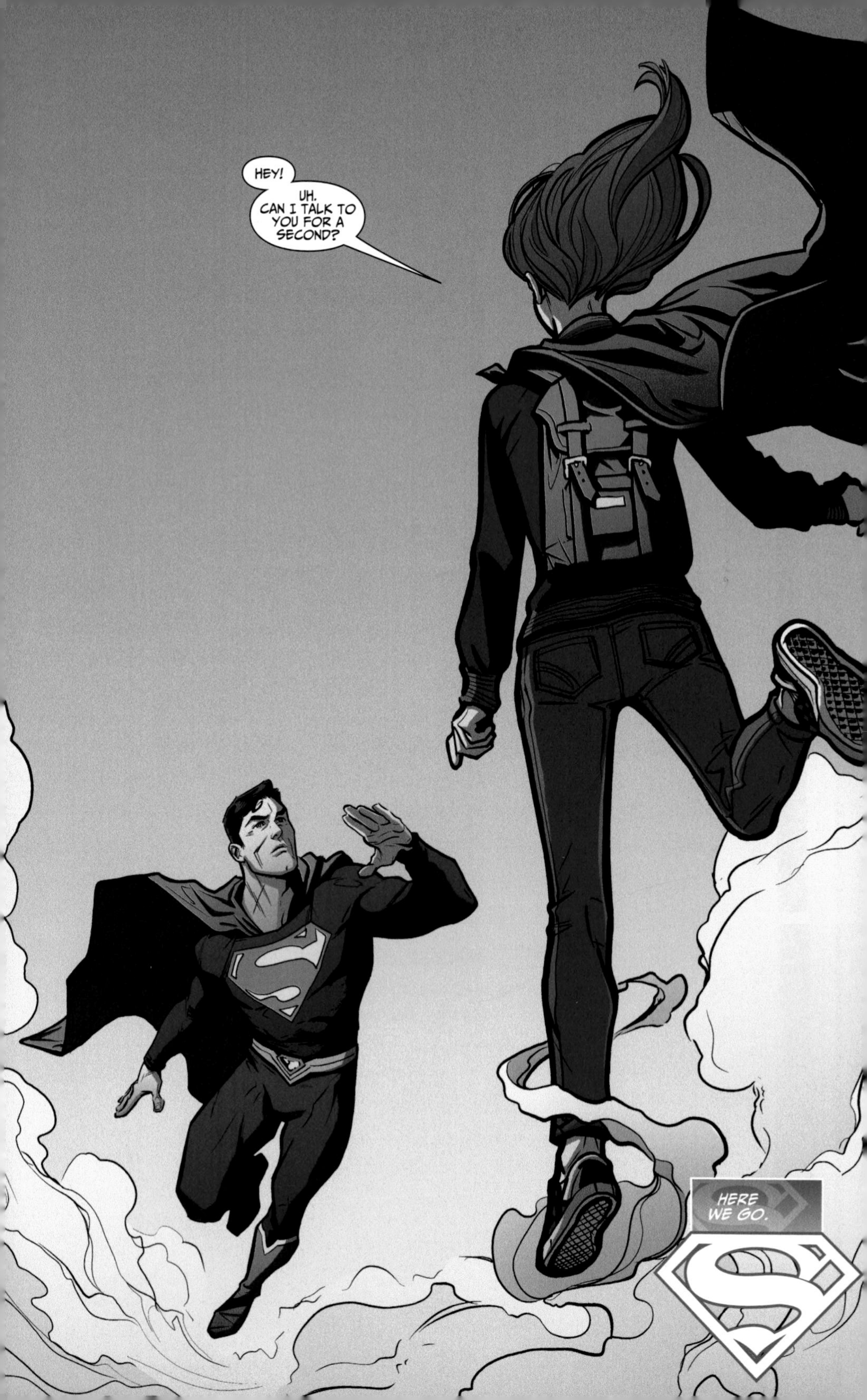
HEY!
UH. CAN I TALK TO YOU FOR A SECOND?
HERE WE GO.

MARIKO TAMAKI is an award-winning Canadian writer living in Oakland, California. She is the co-creator, with Jillian Tamaki, of *This One Summer*, which received the prestigious Eisner and Ignatz awards as well as Caldecott and Printz honors, and *Laura Dean Keeps Breaking Up with Me*, with Rosemary Valero-O'Connell. Her growing slate of critically acclaimed comics includes *Tomb Raider*, *Adventure Time*, *She-Hulk*, *Lumberjanes*, *X-23*, and *Harley Quinn: Breaking Glass*.

MARIKO TAMAKI

JOËLLE JONES is an Eisner Award-nominated artist currently living and working in Los Angeles, California. Since attending PNCA in Portland, Oregon, she has contributed to a wide range of projects including art duties on *Batman*, as well as writing and art for *Catwoman* at DC and *Lady Killer* at Dark Horse. Jones has also provided art for fashion designer Prada, as well as various projects for Marvel, BOOM!, Vertigo, Oni Press, and the *New York Times*.

JOËLLE JONES

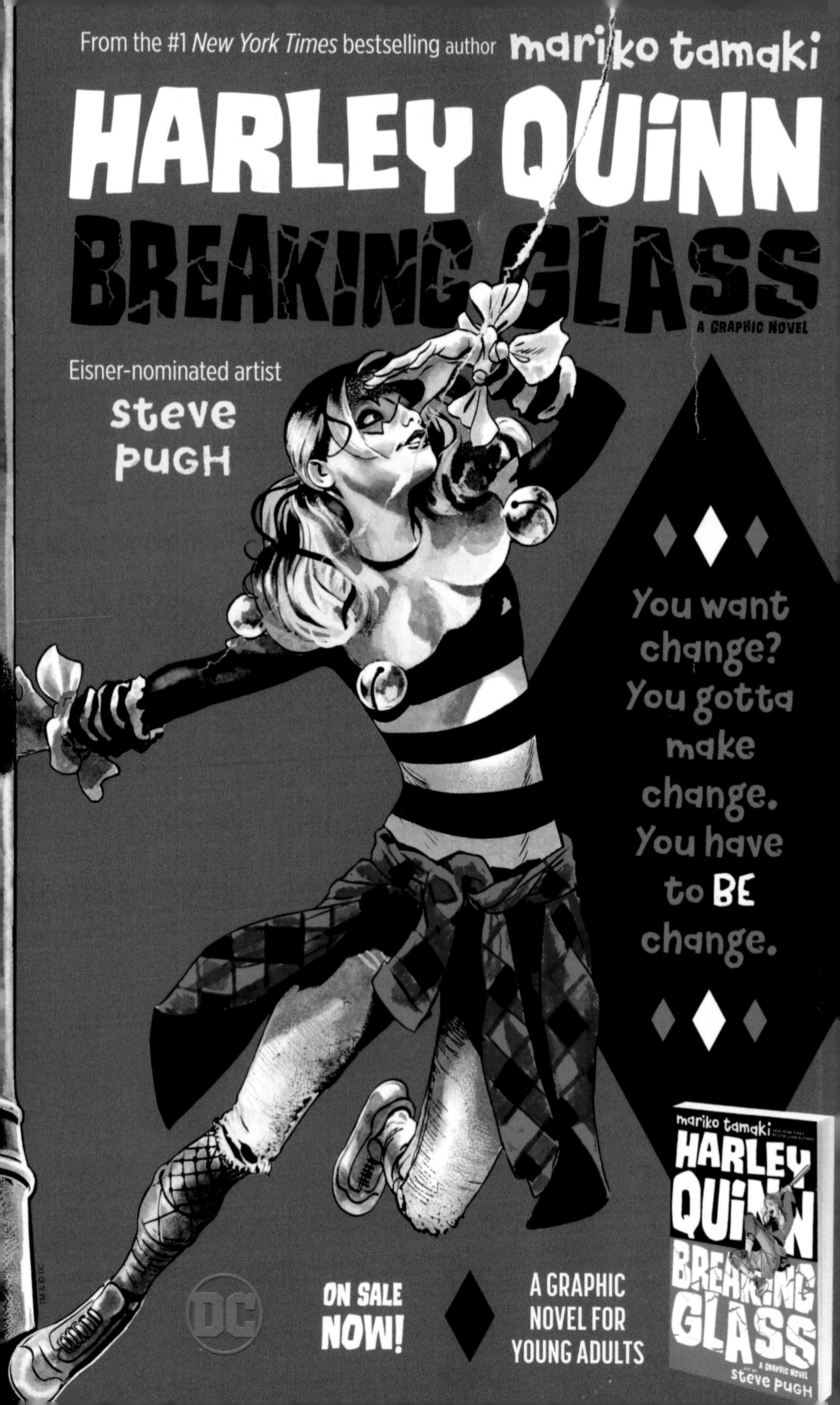
From the #1 New York Times bestselling author mariko tamaki
HARLEY QUINN
BREAKING GLASS
A GRAPHIC NOVEL
Eisner-nominated artist
steve
pugh
You want change? You gotta make change. You have to BE change.
TM & © DC
DC
ON SALE NOW!
A GRAPHIC NOVEL FOR YOUNG ADULTS
mariko tamaki
HARLEY QUINN
BREAKING GLASS
A GRAPHIC NOVEL
steve pugh